EMBRACING
THE DAWN

Visit us at www.boldstrokesbooks.com

By the Author

Threads of the Heart

Embracing the Dawn

EMBRACING THE DAWN

by

Jeannie Levig

2016

EMBRACING THE DAWN

ISBN 13: 978-1-62639-576-3

This Trade Paperback Original Is Published By
Bold Strokes Books, Inc.
P.O. Box 249
Valley Falls, NY 12185

First Edition: June 2016

Credits

Editors: Victoria Villasenor and Cindy Cresap
Production Design: Susan Ramundo
Cover Design By Melody Pond
Cover Photo By Erik Levig

Acknowledgments

My deepest love and gratitude to my wonderful family, friends, and spiritual circle for your unwavering love and support.

Enormous thanks to Jamie Patterson, my Ideal Reader, for reading every word I write—sometimes repeatedly—and for your honest and trustworthy feedback and to Laurie Slate for your insights into the psychological and emotional makeup of my characters.

Immeasurable appreciation and admiration for the amazing team at Bold Strokes Books. To Radclyffe for creating and tirelessly leading this publishing house that is so dedicated to making sure every book is of the highest quality and all of its authors are fully supported in their growth and development as writers. To Sandy Lowe for knowing pretty much everything about everything, and when you don't have the exact answer, for gently and patiently pointing me to the person who does. To my editors, Victoria Villasenor and Cindy Cresap. Vic, thank you for always being there for me, for your dedication to every draft, every chapter, every line of my work, for the depth of heart you put into your editing, and most of all, for making it such a positive and fun experience. Cindy, I am so grateful for your impeccable copy editing and everything else you do in the production of my books. And a huge thank you to all the behind the scenes people at BSB committed to excellence in publishing.

Finally, a heartfelt thank you to all the readers who buy my books and to those who take the time to send me an email or contact me on Facebook to let me know how you liked them. Thank you for sharing this amazing experience with me.

Dedication

To Jax,
Wherever you are.

Knowing you are well.

Chapter One

E. J. Bastien set one steaming mug of coffee on the nightstand and gripped the handle of the other as she stared down at the woman asleep in her bed. *What have I done?* She never—okay, she rarely—took a woman to bed on their first meeting, and she truly never had let one stay the whole night. She was here for her son's wedding, for God's sake, and while she had secretly come to town a day early for a little R&R before facing the entire family and new in-laws, she had really only intended to enjoy maybe a glass of wine and a little dancing. *Now, I've got some woman named Jinx in my bed, and I'm bringing her coffee. Perfect.*

Jinx's eyelids fluttered open, and she offered a slow smile. "Oh my God," she said, the words running together. "A beautiful woman in a slinky robe...*with* coffee? I must've died last night and gone to heaven."

And there, E. J. knew, was the reason she'd let Jinx stay—those laughing blue eyes, that Elizabeth Ashley voice, that flirty, slightly cheesy charm. She smiled at the memory of dancing in Jinx's arms. "Good morning," she said.

Jinx grinned. She rose onto an elbow, the sheet shifting to reveal the swell of a breast. "Morning."

Suddenly shy, E. J. felt her cheeks flush. This was ridiculous. In her early fifties, she'd had at least an adequate amount of experience in this area. Maybe it was the face-to-face in the morning light that was throwing her. She handed Jinx the cup.

Jinx took a deep swallow, looking at E. J. over the rim.

E. J. took in the collar-length, dark chestnut hair that had felt so sensuous between her fingers, the slender, yet strong hands that had touched her so intimately, those full lips that—

"Mmm, very good," Jinx murmured.

"What?" E. J.'s face grew hotter.

"The coffee." Jinx raised the cup a bit. "It's very good."

"Oh," E. J. said. "Yes. Well…room service." She waved her hand, indicating the bedroom of her hotel suite.

Jinx took another sip and studied her. "Are you uncomfortable? Do you want me to leave?"

E. J. considered the question. Yes, she was uncomfortable, but no, for some reason, she didn't want Jinx to leave. *Odd.* Normally, avoidance was her customary response to any kind of uneasiness. She cleared her throat. "No," she said, briefly averting her gaze. "I'm just not sure of the appropriate thing to say."

Jinx's mouth curved into that slow smile again.

E. J. remembered the feel of those lips, their softness on her skin. What was wrong with her? Was this what waking up with a woman felt like? No, she'd awakened with Rhonda plenty of times, and it wasn't like this. *Maybe this is what waking up with a stranger feels like.*

"Is that all?" Jinx held the mug in one hand while she lifted the sheet in invitation with the other. "C'mere, then. I'll walk you through it."

E. J. smiled. *Yup, cheesy.* She eased onto the mattress and into the crook of Jinx's arm. She felt the warmth of Jinx's skin through the oh-so-thin silk robe and down the length of her bare thigh. Playing along, she looked at Jinx as coyly as she could manage without breaking into laughter. "Now what?"

"Now," Jinx said, drawing out the word. She dropped the sheet and tucked it around E. J. "We get nice and comfy." She carefully switched the mug into her free hand. "We share a little coffee." She swallowed a mouthful and held the cup to E. J.'s lips.

E. J. did the same, all the while watching Jinx.

Jinx reached across and set the mug on the nightstand beside the other one and settled back against the pillows. "And then," she said, holding E. J. closely, "you tell me how amazing I was last night."

E. J. burst out laughing. "Oh, really?"

"Uh-huh. Now, c'mon. You admitted you didn't know how this went." Jinx pulled her in more tightly. "You have to trust me."

E. J. stifled a giggle. "Okay, then what?"

"Well, after you tell me how amazing I was, you tell me how I made you feel like no one ever has before, and how I touched you in places you never knew existed."

E. J. shook her head. "I see. And then you tell me all the same things?"

"No, that's not how it goes." Jinx grinned at her. "C'mon. Do you want to learn this, or not?"

"Okay." E. J. attempted a serious expression and turned in Jinx's arms to face her. "How does it go again?"

Jinx rolled her eyes and sighed. "Amazing…made you feel like no one ever has…touched you in places…"

"Okay, okay. I think I have it."

"All right." Jinx looked into her eyes. "Go ahead."

E. J. took a deep breath and tried to keep from laughing. "You… were so…What was it again?"

Jinx stared at her. "You are so bad at this."

E. J. laughed again and tucked her head beneath Jinx's chin.

"All right, never mind," Jinx said, stroking E. J.'s hair. "How about we just go out for breakfast?"

Still smiling, E. J. lifted her face to Jinx's. "How about if we just have breakfast here?"

Jinx remained silent, a half smile playing on her lips.

E. J. felt her body begin to respond to Jinx's bare flesh, her closeness, her warmth. She quelled her desire to move against her thigh.

"That sounds," Jinx whispered, "delicious."

E. J. blushed. "You don't even know what's on the menu."

"Mmm." Jinx kissed her lightly on the lips. "I know what I'd like to be on the menu, but I have to get to work." She sighed.

E. J. squeezed her eyes shut. "Ooooh." The word came out on a disappointed moan. "I forgot it's not the weekend." She eased away from Jinx. "In that case, I need some distance from you." She glanced at Jinx's toned body. "And I need you to put some clothes on." Wistfully, she ran two fingertips along Jinx's jaw and down to the hollow of her throat.

"I'm sorry," Jinx said. The words vibrated against the pads of E. J.'s fingers.

E. J. moved farther away. "You said we could go out to eat?"

"I was just thinking we could grab a bite and I'd still have time to run home, get a shower, and make it to work." Jinx pulled the sheet up a bit. "But if I start nibbling on you for breakfast, I know it'll turn into brunch. And then lunch...and then I'd lose my job and you'd have to support the family and the kids would go without shoes and milk money and I wouldn't have any pretty dresses anymore and I'd get all needy and you'd get resentful and I'd call you mean and you'd call me ungrateful and we'd fight and scream and both end up devastated. And all because we didn't go to breakfast."

E. J. enjoyed how easily this woman made her smile. "If I promise not to offer myself up as a croissant and cause all that, would you like to shower here and share some actual food with me here in the room? They make great eggs Benedict." She rose and straightened her robe. "Since I kept you up most of the night, the least I can do is send you off with a full stomach."

Jinx's gaze glided over E. J.'s body. "You're going to have to put something else on, too. That robe is a joke as clothing."

"It's a deal," E. J. said, picking up a coffee mug and handing it once more to Jinx. "You get in the shower, and I'll call room service. Then I'll put on some serious clothes."

When E. J. finished placing the order, she returned to the bedroom and dressed in a pair of designer jeans and a forest green silk blouse she knew set off her blond hair and emerald eyes. She had no intention of seeing Jinx again and liked the idea of leaving her with a good impression. She was just threading the French hooks of gold earrings through her lobes when she heard the shower turn off. She stepped back and studied herself in the floor-length mirror. She had planned to spend the day in her sweats, reading on the sofa until it was time to meet the family for drinks before the rehearsal, and that was still her plan. She would change again after Jinx left. For now, she wanted to evoke that slow smile a couple more times before they parted ways. More accurately, she wanted to feel the low simmer it evoked deep within her a couple more times. It was that smile that had drawn E. J. in the night before.

The bathroom door opened, and Jinx, fully clothed except for her bare feet, emerged, tousling her hair dry with a hand towel. Her gaze landed on E. J., and she whistled.

"Thank you," E. J. said. She knew she looked good. Her physical appearance had never given her any doubt. Her mother had seen to that. She had fancied E. J. up, as E. J.'s grandmother had called it, and stood by beaming whenever anyone commented on how pretty she was. She even rewarded E. J. with extra TV time if she stayed pretty all day. E. J.'s mother had married into wealth and had *caught* E. J.'s father with her beauty and rehearsed style. E. J. knew it was how her mother measured a woman's worth. As a result, however, E. J. spent much of her adulthood, particularly after her divorce, proving to herself her intelligence and her ability to succeed, rather than just be a pretty face. So much so she had worked right up to the day prior to her son's wedding instead of arriving early to connect with the rest of the family. Her ex-husband's new wife had made all the arrangements for the rehearsal dinner and everything else the groom's side traditionally handled. E. J. wasn't even sure what all that entailed.

"I should've known just covering you up wouldn't make it any easier to get out of here." Jinx closed the distance between them and dropped the towel onto the end of the bed. She slid her arms around E. J.'s waist. "You really are beautiful."

E. J. smiled and finger-combed Jinx's still damp hair into place. "Aren't you sweet." Reluctantly, she let her hands slip down to straighten Jinx's collar. "But look at you." She perused Jinx's soft contours beneath snug black jeans and the royal blue oxford shirt that deepened the color of her eyes, the open buttons at the neck revealing that delicate hollow of her throat. "You look just as sexy as when you walked into the bar last night. I never had a chance."

"Did you want one?" Jinx tightened her arms around E. J.

"Maybe not." She really hadn't. The moment she had seen Jinx, she had wanted to know who she was, know more about her, know *her*. In truth, though, as strong as her attraction had been, the real draw hadn't been physical. It had been a pull, almost like gravity, a sharp tug somewhere in the recesses of her mind. Something easy, familiar, however airy-fairy that sounded, and yet, E. J. knew they had never met. She knew it was why everything felt so effortless between them, and it was the reason she couldn't say those things, even in jest—especially in jest—that Jinx had teased her about.

Jinx *had* been amazing, but not just in her technique. She had known exactly what E. J. wanted, what she had needed. She *had* made E. J. feel like no one ever had, but not merely physically. She had made her feel seen, understood. Could she be more hokey? And she *had* touched her in places E. J. didn't know existed. How could that be? In the nine years since her marriage to Marcus had ended, she had been with a reasonable number of women. She knew herself pretty damned well. After only a couple of hours of dancing and a few more of incredible sex, it was ridiculous to feel any of this, and yet there it was. *Crazy.*

She couldn't say any of those things, though, not without sounding like a nutball—and not to this woman who she would never see again after a plate of eggs Benedict. E. J. felt a twinge of regret at that last thought, but she couldn't say that either.

A knock sounded on the door of the suite. "Room service," a male voice called.

Thankful to be saved from having to say anything at all, E. J. kissed Jinx on the cheek and stepped back. "Breakfast," she said lightly as she turned to leave.

While she waited for the meal to be laid out, then signed for it, and tipped the attendant, E. J. kept an eye on Jinx.

She walked around the room, exploring the décor, testing the softness of the couch, brushing her fingertips over the crystal base of the lamp. It appeared as though she had never been in an upscale hotel before, and maybe she hadn't. E. J. knew that not everyone lived as she did.

Jinx picked up the multi-function remote and closed, then opened, the vertical blinds that covered the picture window overlooking the large swimming pool five floors below. She turned the TV on and off and jumped up when the chair cushion she sat on began to vibrate.

E. J. suppressed a smile as she closed the door. "If you press the stereo button, we'll have some music to eat by," she said, walking to the table.

Jinx looked down at the remote and did as instructed. Chopin's "Raindrop Prelude" began to play. "That's nice."

Still watching her, E. J. smiled. "Ready to eat?"

"Very," Jinx said, settling into the chair across from E. J. She lifted the silver cover from her plate and inhaled the steam that rose from the dish. "Ooooh, that smells so good. I'm starving."

"They have great food here." E. J. dropped a napkin onto her lap.

"Do you stay here often?"

"I use the chain quite a bit for work."

Jinx slid the ham off her eggs Benedict and set it to the side of her plate.

"Do you not eat meat?" E. J. asked.

Jinx looked up. "Oh. No, sorry. But the rest will be good."

"I'm sorry. I didn't even ask. We could have ordered something else."

"Really, it's fine."

"So, you're a vegetarian," E. J. said, surprised at her interest in learning more about this woman who ultimately was nothing more than yet another one-night stand.

"Technically, I'm a pescatarian. I do eat fish." Jinx reached for a croissant and split it open with her knife. She slathered it with whipped butter, then added blackberry jam from the silver serving bowl between them. Without another word, she held it out to E. J.

"Oh," E. J. said, surprised. Her eyes met Jinx's as their fingers brushed. "Thank you."

"Thank *you*," Jinx said. "For last night. *You* were amazing." A tender smile touched her lips.

E. J. flushed with heat. How did Jinx do that? How, with one look, did she reduce E. J. to a puddle of need? She wished more and more they were still in bed. She shifted the thought. "Ah, so that's how it's done."

"Exactly." Jinx sat back in her chair. "Was that so hard?"

E. J. laughed. "Maybe I just needed it illustrated." She took a bite of the croissant. "I take it you do this often."

Jinx cut off a piece of egg and English muffin. "Every morning." She took a bite. "This is delicious."

Every morning? E. J. watched her. "I don't mean eat breakfast," she said with a smirk, suddenly understanding.

Jinx chewed and raised a questioning eyebrow.

"I mean go home with women from bars." E. J. tried to sound casual. She slipped a forkful of her own meal into her mouth.

"No. Hardly ever. In fact, this is only the second time. And the other one wasn't from a bar. It was from Tutti Frutti's."

"Oh, really?" E. J. chuckled. "Then how do you know all the rules?"

"I watch romantic comedies." Jinx grinned.

E. J. eyed her. She didn't know whether to believe her or not, but she supposed it didn't matter. She would never see her again. She didn't even know why she had asked. Now seemed a good time for a subject change to one with less potential for embarrassment. "So, what do you do that you're off to this morning?"

"I'm a dog washer," Jinx said, scooping up more eggs Benedict.

E. J. had never heard of such a thing. "You mean a dog groomer?"

"No," Jinx said. She rested her arm on the edge of the table. "A dog washer. I wash the dogs, then turn them over to the groomers."

"Oh. I've always thought the groomers did it all." E. J. sipped her coffee. "Do you like it?"

"I do," Jinx said, returning her attention to her food. "I love dogs, and it's more like just playing in the water with them than a job. But then, miraculously, I get handed a paycheck every two weeks."

E. J. chuckled. "You know what they say. Do what you love and the money will follow."

Jinx nodded. "I've heard that." She studied E. J. briefly, as though considering her next words. She glanced around the room. "You must love what you do a lot to live like this and not have to go to work on a Friday."

E. J. thought for a moment. She didn't exactly love what she did; she was simply good at it. "I don't actually live this way." She mimicked Jinx's eye movement. "This is how I travel because my company makes my arrangements." She did live well, but saw no reason to share that, and yet, she heard the words, "I live pretty nicely, just not quite like this," come out of her mouth.

"What do you do?"

"I'm a regional director for a major retail chain."

Jinx blinked. "So, what do you do?"

E. J. laughed. "I oversee our stores in northern and central California," she said.

"Really? What stores?"

"I work for Bad Dog Athletic Apparel."

Jinx's eyes widened. "I love Bad Dog," she said, her voice rising in excitement. "Although…" She became serious. "You know there's no such thing. Right?"

"No such thing?"

"As a bad dog."

"Ah, of course not." E. J. laughed. Jinx's lack of pretense was such a refreshing change from what she customarily encountered.

Jinx leaned forward in her chair. "I saw this shirt in a catalog once. I wish I had it," she said, her features animated. "There was one of the bad dogs, of course—the German shepherd—sitting with a half-eaten package of steak on the floor in front of him and a woman standing over him with her hands on her hips. And underneath it said, 'If only she'd gotten stuck in traffic.'" Jinx laughed, her eyes bright with amusement.

E. J. smiled. "I've always liked that one, too." Mostly what she liked right now was the joy in Jinx's face. "You didn't buy it?"

"No. I wasn't in a place where I could." A shadow at the back of Jinx's eyes rippled and shifted, then settled again. "I didn't know there was a Bad Dog store here."

E. J. wondered at the subtle diversion but followed it. "There isn't. I'm here for a family matter." She lifted her coffee cup to her lips.

"Your family's here?" Jinx set her fork on her empty plate.

E. J. hesitated. "My son." She held her mug in front of her. A drop of hollandaise sauce at the corner of Jinx's mouth drew her attention. She waited for Jinx's tongue to slip out and swipe it away. When it didn't, she reached across the table and touched it.

As if in reward, Jinx offered her that slow smile, then sucked E. J.'s fingertip between her lips and grazed it with her teeth.

Arousal flooded E. J. She tightened her thighs. "You have to stop that," she whispered.

"You started it." Jinx's tone was low.

E. J. pulled her hand back and laughed. "You're right. I'm sorry. Talk about something to take my mind off…you."

A wicked glint flashed in Jinx's eyes. "Your son."

The image of Jacob filled E. J.'s mind. She straightened. "Okay, that did it."

Jinx cleared her throat. "You're here to see him?"

E. J. took a deep breath and collected her remaining thoughts. "Yes. He's getting married tomorrow."

"Really? My niece is getting married tomorrow."

E. J. tensed. No. It wasn't possible. Was it? What were the chances?

"Wouldn't that be cosmic if they were marrying each other?"

Cosmic wasn't the word E. J. would use. Karmic, maybe—ending up sharing a family with one of her one-night stands. Traumatic, certainly, since no one in her family knew she was gay. She had always been afraid of upsetting Jacob, and there had never been anyone special in her life for it to matter—except maybe Rhonda. But that was over. As much as she was afraid to, she had to ask. "What's your niece's name?"

"Tiffany Stanton."

E. J. blanched and hoped her breakfast wouldn't come back up.

CHAPTER TWO

The room was silent for a long moment. Voices in the hall approached, then faded away.

At the sight of E. J.'s pallor, Jinx reached across the table and squeezed her fingers. "Hey, are you all right?"

E. J. withdrew and rose. "Yes," she said. "I mean...I don't know." She walked to the window and stared outside.

Jinx waited. She considered their conversation. What was the big deal? Why would it matter if E. J.'s son was marrying Andrea's daughter? Was it what Jinx had said about being a dog washer? *Does she not want her family to know she was slumming it?* "Hey, it's okay," she said, twisting in her seat toward E. J. "My family's not like me. I mean, they have money and know all the right people and... you know."

"What?" E. J. turned to face her.

"Tiffany's family. They're like you." Jinx gave an inward shudder. After what she'd experienced of E. J., she couldn't imagine how she could be anything at all like Jinx's sister Andrea, but E. J. seemed to live in a similar style, with her big, high-powered job.

E. J. grew still. Those gently sculpted features that'd held invitation in every expression, that soft gaze that'd caressed Jinx's skin, hardened. "I know your family has money, but even if they didn't...I'm not a snob."

Jinx fell silent. It was too soon for a reaction like this. The very few women she'd spent time with over the past three years hadn't gotten this mad until they'd found out the truth about her. "I'm sorry. I just thought..." Well, no need to repeat it. What she'd thought was already out, lumbering around the expensive suite, about to take a dump on the luxuriant carpet. "I'm sorry. My mistake."

E. J.'s demeanor eased ever so slightly.

"What *are* you upset about?"

E. J. hesitated. She turned back to the window. "I've never told my son I'm gay. No one in my family knows."

Jinx waited for some further explanation. None came.

E. J. stared out into the morning sky.

"I don't understand," Jinx said finally. "What does that have to do with anything?"

E. J. swung around, her arms folded across her middle, her shoulders drawn up tight. Incredulity flashed in her eyes. "I spent the night with you last night."

"Yeah," Jinx said cautiously. "I remember."

"And now we're going to be at the same wedding, in the same extended family."

"And you're afraid they'll know?"

E. J. gave an almost imperceptible single nod, seemingly satisfied Jinx had finally caught up with her.

"Oh, I get it," Jinx said. "Well, I *was* planning to wear my I-slept-with-the-mother-of-the-groom T-shirt, but I'm sure I can find something else in my closet."

E. J. stiffened. "You think this is funny?"

"I think it's a little ridiculous. How would anyone know?" Jinx shifted in her seat. "It's not like we're going to walk in together arm-in-arm. We don't have to interact at all. I won't even look at you if you don't want me to."

"You don't understand, and I don't expect you to," E. J. said, her voice hard. "I have a lot to lose."

E. J. was wrong. Jinx did understand. She understood all too well being rejected for things she'd done, for who she was. Not in the same way, perhaps, but she understood completely. "I get it," she said softly. She walked over to E. J. "Look, we may not even cross paths tomorrow. There are going to be a billion people there, I'm sure." She took E. J.'s hands in hers. "If we see each other, we'll pretend we've never met and just be two of the billion. Don't worry. I won't cause you any trouble."

E. J. lifted her eyes to meet Jinx's. Her expression held confusion, gratitude, longing, regret. "Thank you," she whispered.

Jinx offered her a smile she didn't mean, then kissed her forehead. "I need to find my shoes and socks and get going," she said quietly. "Thank you again for last night."

E. J. nodded, her conflict still apparent.

In the bedroom, Jinx sat in the armchair and finished tying a shoe. She knew not to take this personally. E. J. wasn't rejecting *her*. It was more complicated than that, and the issue was E. J.'s. They'd had a good time, briefly filled a void for one another, and now it was over. Jinx hadn't let herself entertain any other ideas. She'd had no thought of dating this dream of a woman so far out of her league, no delusion of happily ever after, not even a hope of ever seeing her again. Jinx wasn't looking for anything like that, regardless of how amazing E. J. might be. She had her hands full piecing a life together and learning how to live on her own. Besides, she had no interest in being someone's shameful little secret. She'd had enough of that growing up. If all that was true, though, why did she feel such a heavy weight of disappointment settling in her stomach like an anchor at the bottom of the ocean?

"Jinx," E. J. said softly from the doorway.

Jinx looked up.

"I'm sorry for my reaction. And I'm so sorry if I hurt your feelings."

Jinx lifted one shoulder. "You didn't," she said without another thought. "It's okay."

"No, it isn't. I don't want to leave things like this." E. J. crossed the room and knelt in front of her. "You are...Last night was..." E. J. searched Jinx's eyes as though expecting to find the ends of her sentences there. She sighed. "I'll never forget you."

Jinx slipped her fingers into E. J.'s hair and let herself feel the sincerity of the words. She smiled. "Hey, there might be hope for you yet."

E. J. laughed and pressed her cheek into Jinx's palm. "Will you be at the rehearsal dinner tonight?"

Jinx brushed E. J.'s temple with her thumb. "Oh, no. I'm shocked I was even invited to the wedding." The words were out before she could stop them.

E. J. looked up in evident surprise. "Why is that?"

Jinx paused. She really didn't want to tell her the truth—at least not all of it—but she didn't want to lie to her either. With E. J.'s son marrying into the Stanton family, Jinx figured she'd hear about all the bodies buried in the backyard before too long anyway, at least whatever version of the story Jinx's sister chose to share. "Let's just say I'm sort of the black sheep of the family. I don't get to come to everything." She didn't bother to say that other than Andrea slamming the door in her face three years earlier, she hadn't seen any of the family in over twenty-five years. She'd never even met Tiffany and had no idea why she'd been invited to the wedding. When she'd sent her RSVP and hadn't received a phone call saying it'd been a mistake, she'd hoped it was an olive branch of sorts. *I'll know tomorrow.*

E. J. rubbed her palm over Jinx's thigh. "I can see that. You don't seem anything like them."

Jinx leaned down and kissed E. J. on the lips. "Thank you. I take that as such a compliment."

"I understand. Andrea's a little scary, isn't she?"

"You have no idea. If I didn't actually know where she came from, I'd swear she burst out of someone's chest." Andrea hadn't always been that way, though.

E. J. smiled. "That's why you weren't at the engagement party," she said, her tone thoughtful. "And why I've never met you before?"

Jinx nodded. "That's why," she said. "Baaaaaa."

The spark returned to E. J.'s eyes as she laughed.

At least now Jinx felt like she could leave without having ruined everything, though leaving was the last thing she wanted to do. "I really do need to go, baby," she said gently.

In the space of a flinch, E. J.'s gaze went soft, then just as quickly, returned to normal. "I know," she whispered.

At the front door of the suite, E. J. caught Jinx's hand as she reached for the knob.

Jinx turned to her.

E. J. gave her a long look as though memorizing her. Then she kissed her.

As their lips moved against one another's, Jinx listened to the soft music playing in the background. She wanted to remember it. "What's the name of this song?" she asked when E. J. eased back.

E. J. tilted her head and listened. "'Clair de lune.'"

Jinx nodded.

"One more kiss?" E. J. said, gazing up at her. "Like the one you gave me right here last night?"

Jinx grinned, remembering when she'd knocked on the door and waited for E. J. to answer. Her heart had been pounding. She couldn't believe she'd accepted E. J.'s invitation to join her back at her hotel. She hadn't been with a woman in a long time, not since Val. She hadn't wanted to be, but somewhere between that first look in the bar and E. J.'s whispered enticement several hours later, she'd decided maybe it was time.

She took E. J. in her arms, just like the night before, and covered her mouth with her own. The smoldering embers of the morning ignited instantly.

E. J.'s lips parted, and she took Jinx in, fully and completely, just like the night before.

They kissed long and slow and deliberately—just like the night before—but this time, Jinx knew she had to leave. This time, she knew what they'd shared was over rather than just beginning. Suddenly, she felt a deep ache of loneliness she hadn't known since Val's death. This time, though, she knew it wasn't from the loss of Val. It was from the loss of something—someone—she'd never even had.

CHAPTER THREE

Jinx stood in the long column of wedding guests waiting patiently to move through the receiving line. The ceremony had been beautiful, the bride radiant, the mother of the groom irresistible—but Jinx had kept her promise. She'd even averted her eyes when E. J. was escorted down the aisle on the arm of an usher to her seat in the front row. Another woman and a second usher had gone next, closely followed by a man Jinx presumed was the father of the groom—E. J.'s ex-husband—and then came Andrea. Jinx had turned completely away as Andrea had passed, afraid that her mere acknowledgement of her sister might summon the hungry harpy within.

Nerves battled emotions, and Jinx felt faint at the invasion of both. Her invitation didn't make sense. In fact, it'd made so little sense she'd almost decided not to attend. Andrea had shown absolutely no interest in having anything to do with her since she'd been home—none, zip, zilch, *nada*—and Tiffany didn't even know her. *Someone* had invited her, though, and it was a foot in the door. She just hoped that door didn't slam, leaving her maimed.

As the wedding day had approached, in addition to her usual nightmares, Jinx had several new ones in which Andrea flew at her, screaming and demanding her off the premises. She knew it was crazy. That would never happen, at least not in front of all the guests, because Andrea would never make such a public scene. Her mother, Jinx's stepmother, and the queen of the high-society circle in her day, Nora Tanner, taught her daughter well in all matters of etiquette.

Jinx, on the other hand, had failed etiquette, along with so many other things, but she knew it was her mere existence that Nora found the most offensive. She felt a little queasy at the thought of Nora and wondered if *she* was the real cause of her nerves. Although no longer alive, her presence still lingered around the house and grounds where she'd reigned for so many years. Jinx could feel her—like the crackle in the air after a lightning storm.

Before Jinx had returned to town, she'd checked to see what she'd be up against in her attempt to mend her relationship with Andrea, and was relieved to find she wouldn't have to deal with her stepmother. Nora had terrified her from the first day Jinx had set foot on this property at the age of five. Sure, she was now forty-five and had survived worse, including a shooting and a stabbing, but she'd still breathed an enormous sigh of relief when she'd learned she'd never again have to face the formidable Nora Tanner. Did that make her a coward? Maybe. Maybe not. Maybe it was just the part of her that still felt like the little girl who'd been forced to come live with a father who was a stranger and a stepmother who hated her. The memories weren't all bad, though. There were some good ones of her father when Nora wasn't around and, of course, those of Andrea when she had still been Jinx's best friend.

The line began to move, and Jinx looked to its head. Across the vast expanse of lush lawn, the bride and groom, their respective parents, and the best man and maid of honor stood beneath a white canopy, greeting their guests.

Jinx steadied herself. *This is it.*

As she made slow progress along the lavender velvet ropes designating the path, she studied Andrea.

In appearance, she hadn't changed much in the last twenty-five years. She was still slender, her movements those of a toned, fit physique, not simply of one thin from a strict diet. Her dark brown hair, like their father's, held no gray, and her smile, though appropriately bright for the festivities of the day, was the practiced presentation she'd perfected so many years earlier. Her brown eyes had stopped smiling in her teens.

Jinx never knew why.

Tiffany looked remarkably like her mother, which wasn't surprising. Everything about Andrea smooshed out any evidence of her husband's input, whether in their child or in their life. After all, now that Nora was gone, they lived in Andrea's family estate, her husband now held her father's position as senior partner in her family's law firm, and their daughter didn't display a physical trace of his participation in her creation. Jinx remembered the ache of being so tangibly visible yet, at the same time, seemingly nonexistent. She looked at Andrea's husband. With his own pasted-on smile and robotic gestures, he showed no signs of minding.

Tiffany's smile was genuine, though. It not only touched her eyes, it lit her entire being. She greeted every single guest with authentic warmth, not the reserve with which her mother shook hands and kissed cheeks. Tiffany displayed the exuberance of the young Andrea, the eight-year-old Andrea, the ten-year-old, the twelve-year-old. *What changed?*

The line continued its slow pace forward, and Jinx took in the groom, Jacob. Now, there was a composite child, one who brought forth both parents. He had his father's height and athletic build, but E. J.'s coloring and finer features. She wondered if his eyes were the same captivating emerald green as his mother's. She remembered E. J.'s darkening a shade or two with arousal. She shook her head. *Knock it off.* It wasn't E. J. she was looking at. That was the problem, though. It was E. J. she *wanted* to be looking at. She could see her in her peripheral vision, standing right beside her son, and it was too tempting. She shifted her gaze away before coming back to Jacob. The setting sun glinted off gold streaks in his dark blond hair, and Jinx wondered if E. J. had the same highlights. She'd only seen her in the dimly lit bar and the darkened bedroom. Even the morning sunshine had been muted by the partially closed blinds. She had to know. She glanced at E. J., then did a double take.

E. J. stared straight at her.

Jinx tensed. She'd been caught. *But wait a minute.* E. J. was looking at *her*, too. *Don't the rules apply both ways?*

E. J. broke the connection and turned her attention to the next guest.

Jinx looked back to Andrea. As the line continued to move and the moment of truth grew closer, her stomach churned. Was this a good idea, confronting Andrea in public? She wouldn't see Jinx any other way, so it served her right. Jinx didn't think Andrea was really the one she was afraid for, though. The public part was what would keep things from getting out of hand, she reminded herself. She stepped in front of Andrea's husband.

He shook her hand. "Thank you for coming."

She just smiled. Then she looked to Andrea.

Andrea was turned away, easing back from a loose embrace with the woman beside Jinx. Her focus still on the last remnants of the exchange, she reached in Jinx's direction.

Jinx moved that last pace and took Andrea's hand. It was warm and soft. Her heart beat frantically, and she trembled slightly.

Andrea's gaze fell on her. "Thank you for—" Surprise flashed in her eyes—along with something else—before her expression closed and hardened.

"Hello, Andrea," Jinx said.

Andrea's manner frosted, and she looked at Jinx with a coldness Jinx had never experienced—and she'd experienced a lot. She cleared her throat. "Thank you for coming," she said coolly, her mask back in place, her eyes sharp and brittle. Her message was clear. Jinx was anything but welcome.

"Aunt Michelle." A tender voice broke through the tension, and a gentle hand pulled Jinx's from Andrea's. "I'm so glad you could come." Tiffany drew Jinx the short distance to stand in front of her. "It's so wonderful to finally meet you."

Jinx felt the warmth of Tiffany's embrace envelop her, but her attention remained on Andrea.

Andrea turned away, already focused on the next guest, as though nothing out of the ordinary had taken place.

Jinx inhaled deeply and regrouped. She gave Tiffany a squeeze before easing back. "It's nice to meet you, too," she said quietly. "You're a beautiful bride." She'd heard that in a movie once and had practiced it for today.

Tiffany smiled. "Thank you. I'd like to introduce you to my *husband...*" Her smile widened. "Jacob."

Jacob eyed Tiffany questioningly but shook Jinx's hand. It was obvious he'd picked up on something, but he evidently knew not to make a scene as well. He simply repeated the standard, "It's nice to meet you. Thank you for coming."

And then, there was E. J. right in front of her, stunning in her deep purple gown with its tasteful, mother-of-the-groom neckline. Her short blond hair—yes, streaked with golden highlights—stirred in the gentle breeze, a few wispy tendrils framing her face. "Thank you for coming today." She squeezed Jinx's fingers, a tender gesture. "It's nice to meet you...Michelle." Her lips quirked ever so slightly, and a teasing glint flashed in her eyes.

Her touch, her playfulness, maybe her mere presence, eased the tightness in Jinx's shoulders. She relaxed. "Thank you," she said, holding E. J.'s hand a second longer. "It's my pleasure." With reluctance, she released her grasp and made her way along the remainder of the receiving line.

As she emerged from underneath the canopy into the grassy area peppered with large round tables covered in lavender linen, she realized she'd broken out in a sweat. Droplets trickled down her spine and waves of heat wafted up her neck from beneath her collar. She slipped out of her blazer and let the early evening breeze cool her. The increasing distance from the receiving line slowed her heartbeat. *So much for the olive branch.* She approached the bar set up on the patio and ordered a Sprite.

She should leave. She knew that. With Andrea's reaction being what it was—what, in reality, she'd expected—no good could come of any further interaction. Not here. Not on Tiffany's special day. *What about Tiffany, though?* She'd known who Jinx was. She hadn't seemed surprised by her presence. The name had thrown Jinx a little. No one had called her Michelle in...She didn't even know the last time. Had Tiffany been the one to invite her? Why would she?

Jinx made her way along the landscaped divider that separated the yard from the pool decking, then stepped back beneath a large tree, letting its shadows from the setting sun veil her. She gulped down half her soda. Was she crazy to have come? What could she do, now?

There were a few people she recognized, more distant family members, but she didn't dare walk up to them and say hello, especially now, knowing for certain how Andrea felt about her presence. She could maybe sit with some strangers and strike up a conversation, but she didn't want to have to explain—or try not to explain—who she was in relation to the happy couple. Besides, that would most likely infuriate Andrea even more, because God knows who she could end up talking to. Another rush of anxiety hit her. *Nope. Time to go.*

She took a last survey of the backyard and fence line, and the arbored gate that led to the gardens—that magical place that'd transformed into so many fantasylands for her and Andrea, where they'd escaped for hours and could be anything and anyone they wanted—caught her attention. She felt its pull and had to see if they were the same. As she stepped into the gardens, the fragrance from the flowers around the archway filled her senses and fanned the embers of long-ago memories into a warm flame. She closed her eyes and inhaled deeply, basking in the same quiet relief that retreat into this space had always provided. The rest of the world fell away.

When she opened her eyes, though, she realized everything was different. The cement path that used to stretch out in both directions was gone, and instead, a brick walkway extended straight ahead, directly into the middle of the gardens. Bushes with large brilliant red, hot pink, and white blossoms lined both sides. Trees with bright pink blooms filled in the space behind. She followed the new path, taking in the beauty, breathing in the fragrance, reveling in the peace. She came to a fork and went left. She knew what she was looking for but doubted she could find it—if it was even still there. When she came to a second fork, she stopped and tried to get her bearings. Nothing looked the same.

"Can I help you?" a low voice asked from behind her.

Startled, she spun around.

A man leaned against a big tree trunk, his features veiled in the darkness behind the electric torch at the edge of the path.

Jinx's heart beat hard. "I was just—"

"Miss Michelle?"

This time when he spoke, she recognized the voice. *It can't be.* "Luke?"

He stepped out onto the bricks, a broad grin dominating his face. The same twinkle Jinx had always remembered flashed in his eyes, and his once coppery red hair, now mostly gray, was still thick and full.

Before Jinx knew it, she was in his arms, her happy tears soaking into his shirt.

He hugged her tightly for a long moment, then held her away from him. "Look at you. All grown up and gorgeous. Last time I saw you, you were a gangly teenager."

Jinx laughed through her tears. She wiped at her eyes. "God, I'm sorry. How embarrassing."

Luke chuckled. "Oh, never you mind. If I wasn't such a crusty old guy now, I'd be crying with you. It's great to see you."

Jinx got control of herself. She hadn't even imagined Luke was still there after all this time, but then, of course, he could be. He'd started working on the grounds crew for her father and Nora when he was only eighteen and the girls were seven. His main responsibility had always been the gardens, so she and Andrea had become quite close to him. "Is Emmy still here, too?"

"Yup. She's head of the house staff, now. And I'm head groundskeeper. We live in the main back house." He motioned in the direction of the outer wall. Jinx's father had built a caretaker's residence on the property along with a couple other homes for the longer-standing employees on staff. "Your family's been real good to us," he said with a fond smile.

Jinx grinned at him, unable to stop. "That's great."

"You're here for the wedding, I'd guess?"

"Yes," Jinx said.

"Miss Tiffany's a beauty, isn't she? And the sweetest little girl, just like you and your sister when you were young."

Jinx smiled.

"I sometimes see the two of you running through here, playing like the rest of the world didn't exist." He looked around the gardens.

Jinx followed his gaze. "It's sure different. I can't even find my way now."

"Yeah, your sister had me and my crew redo the whole thing when Mrs. Tanner passed. Said it was her way of making it her own."

Jinx wondered if it was actually Andrea's way of wiping out their childhood completely. Nora never spent any time in the gardens. It wasn't like they were ever really hers. She nodded, sadness creeping through her.

"What *you're* looking for is still here, though." Luke winked at her.

Her heart leapt. "It is?" Of course he knew why she was there.

"Come on, I'll show you." He led her along the path she'd been on, made another left, then a right, and turned onto a much smaller, less obvious walkway. He turned one last corner and stopped.

Jinx stepped up beside him and stared up into the large elm tree in front of them. And there it was—their tree house. She grinned. "Oh, my God, it's exactly the same."

"I keep it up," Luke said softly. "Put some fresh paint on every few years, replace any weak boards…"

Music started up from the direction of the main house but barely registered in Jinx's awareness. She stared in wonder at the one thing of joy left from her past.

"She still comes out here sometimes, you know?" he said.

"Who?" Jinx studied him.

"Little Andi." He turned to her.

Jinx laughed. "Do you still call her that?"

"Not to her face." Luke chuckled. "I'm close to retiring in a few years. Want to keep my job. Nope, I call her Mrs. Stanton, just like everybody else. But in my heart, she'll always be little Andi." He slipped his arm around Jinx's shoulders. "And you'll always be little Chelle."

Jinx encircled his waist, and they stood side-by-side, gazing up at the tree house. Emotion welled in her. "I can't believe you kept it." She choked a little on the words.

"Not me," Luke said. "Your sister ordered me to keep it. Had us keep all the big trees, add some smaller ones, then fill in the rest with new bushes and flowers. But she told me privately she wanted the tree house to stay, and she comes out here periodically and goes inside for a while. But don't you dare tell her I told you that." He gave Jinx a warning glance.

Jinx laughed. "Your secret's safe with me. She doesn't want to hear *anything* from me."

"Yeah," he said on a sigh. "She's had a mad on for you for a long time. But you're here tonight."

"Yes, I am, but I don't have any idea how or why."

He squeezed her. "Aw, where's that little girl who believes in magic?"

She looked up at him thoughtfully and smiled. *Yeah, magic. That must be it.*

"Want to go up?" Luke nodded toward the tree house.

She grinned. "I do."

As she pushed up through the trap door in the floor, she switched on the pocket flashlight Luke had given her and swept the beam slowly over the small area. In her memory, it was so much bigger. The checkerboard was gone—Luke had painted one on an old stump and hoisted it up there for them—but the bean bag chairs were still there. Granted, they were newer and bigger, but they looked like the ones from their childhood. A book lay opened and facedown on the upended crate acting as a table between them. She climbed the rest of the way in and stood. The smell was the same, the scent of wood mingling with the overall fragrance of the gardens below. She breathed deeply and went back in time to all the hours she and Andi had spent there, the games of Tarzan and Swiss Family Robinson, then the transformation of the tree house into a submarine or an outlaw gang's hideout.

She took a step and slammed her forehead into a branch she didn't remember being there. *Ow.* She grimaced and rubbed the spot, feeling a lump beginning to rise already. *Damn, that's going to leave a mark.*

She ducked and crossed to the window that faced the main house. She opened it and looked across the gardens, between the other trees to the lights of the wedding reception. Music floated across on the evening breeze that ruffled her hair. She could feel Andi here with her, but no…There was no Andi anymore. There was only Andrea, Mrs. Stanton, mother of the bride, queen of the upper-class social circle, like her mother. Jinx turned around. Who ordered Luke to keep the tree house, then, and who still came up here sometimes? And why?

Jinx picked up the book and glanced at the cover. A recent Jodi Picoult novel. She remembered coming up here by herself during the years after Andrea had changed. She'd spent time reading, doing her homework, sometimes just thinking and dreaming—anything to escape the loneliness of the house. At least here she'd had the memories of her best friend.

From the corner of her eye, she noticed something poking out from the side of the crate. She squatted and picked up a stack of books. *Treasure Island* was on top. She opened the cracked and weathered front. Michelle Tanner was scrawled in her own child's handwriting at the top of the inside cover. She went to the next one—*The Three Musketeers*, hers, also. *Anne of Green Gables, Jane Eyre, The Hobbit* along with a couple of titles from a mystery series she'd read in her teens. The last was *Fried Green Tomatoes at the Whistle Stop Café*, the book she'd been reading when she'd run away. She'd finished it years later. These books were all well used and tattered. She found a few more current bestsellers in the crate, but none showed the same wear and tear.

Jinx heard cheers and applause from the wedding guests and wondered how long she'd been away. She didn't really feel any need to get back—it wasn't like anyone would miss her—but she was afraid she was getting too drawn into the past. It was time to leave. She considered taking her books, but wondered if that would leave Luke in a difficult situation with Andrea. She returned them to the crate.

On the ground again, she slipped into her jacket she'd left draped over a bush, then turned and looked up to the still open window. In its frame, she saw Andi, aged eight, smiling and waving. "See you later, alligator," she called.

From beside Jinx, her own eight-year-old image waved back. "After while, crocodile." It was their customary farewell to one another, one adopted from their father when Nora wasn't around. They'd shortened it to "Later, gator," and "While, dile," when they'd become more cool. Jinx smiled.

As she made her way along the side of the house to leave, she felt herself drawn to the servants' entrance that led down a hallway to the kitchen and the back stairs. She inhaled the delectable smell of the meal being served to the wedding guests, reminiscent of those prepared by the Tanner family's private chef years earlier, and she let the sounds of a busy staff comfort her. These were the people she'd always felt more connected to, more at ease with. In her younger years, this was the way she'd usually entered and left the house because it allowed her to go straight up to her and Andrea's floor without having to walk through the ground level, where Nora was more likely to notice her. Later, after her father died and she'd been relegated to the small room behind the kitchen, this was the most logical way in and out.

She looked up the stairs, wondering how different the second floor was. Everyone was outside. *I'll just take a peek.* At the top, she cracked open the door and peered down the long hallway. The past rushed in on her.

The color scheme was different. Newer carpet, some new chandeliers, but still, it was all the same. The floor she'd shared with Andi had a bedroom and bath for each of them, a play room, a library/homework/music room, and an entertainment room, with a big screen TV and sound system. Their father and Nora's private quarters occupied the third floor.

She moved along the corridor, peeking into the different rooms. Some had obviously been used for the bridesmaids to get ready for the ceremony. *And maybe the bride? Of course.* This floor would have been Tiffany's once Andrea's family had moved to the estate. Her heart started to pound. She heard muffled voices. She pivoted toward the servants' door.

"Aunt Michelle?"

Jinx froze, then turned slowly.

Tiffany rushed toward her from the doorway of Andrea's old room. "I can't believe I'm finally meeting you. I'm so glad you came." She held the train of her wedding dress in a bundle in her arms. "I looked for you once the reception got going, but I couldn't find you. Then I had to pee," she said in a whisper and giggled. "So I came up here, and here you are. Oh my, I'm babbling. I'm so sorry." She had stopped directly in front of Jinx and now stared at her expectantly.

Jinx had no idea what to say. "I…" Should she tell her she'd been in the tree house? *No.* "It's…" She'd already told her it was nice to meet her in the receiving line. Hadn't she? "How long have you known about—"

"Forever." Tiffany seemed to vibrate with excitement. "Luke used to tell me about you and Mom when you were little. He had some old pictures. He always made you both sound like so much fun. You know, before you ran away and Mom...Well, I don't know *what* happened to Mom. I love her dearly, but she gets a little crazy sometimes."

Jinx chuckled. *Well said.* Before Tiffany could grab another breath and take off again, Jinx held up a hand. "You're the one who invited me?"

Tiffany looked surprised. "Of course. It's my wedding."

"What the hell are you doing up here?" Andrea's voice pierced the quiet of the hallway. "What the hell are you doing here at all?"

Jinx cringed. Andrea sounded so much like Nora. Loathing and contempt were an ugly mixture in her tone. Jinx hated it. She started to speak, but Tiffany's hand on her arm stopped her. It was a good thing, since she didn't have a clue what would come out of her mouth. *She* didn't know what the hell she was doing there.

"I invited her, Mom. It's my wedding. She's my guest."

Andrea's burning gaze turned to ice, and she shifted it from Jinx to Tiffany. "It might be *your* wedding, young lady, but it's *my* home, and *she's* not welcome in it."

Andrea was gone. All Jinx could see was Nora.

"I've wanted to meet my aunt for a long time." Tiffany's voice rose. "I told you that three years ago."

Jinx had to hand it to Tiffany. The girl had guts. Jinx had never been able to stand up to Nora, nor had the younger Andrea, for that matter.

"And I told *you*..." Andrea stabbed a finger at Tiffany. "You don't have an aunt."

"I *do* have an aunt, and she's right here, and you can't—"

"You're right," Jinx yelled over the argument. She had to stop this. She was ruining this special day for both Tiffany and Andrea. She'd never wanted to do that. "I never should have come. I'm sorry," she said to Andrea.

"No, you shouldn't have. And *you*..." Andrea was back on Tiffany, "never should have invited—"

Jinx stepped between them. "Andi, I'll go."

Andrea went rigid. Her eyes flamed. Her jaw tightened. "Don't you *dare* call me that."

She hadn't meant to—too much reminiscing, too many emotions. "Andrea. I'm sorry."

"Get out. Get the hell out of my house." Her voice rose again. "My mother was right about you. You're nothing but trash that came from trash."

The words cut Jinx as deeply and as painfully as a steel blade. One of Nora's favorite phrases, now coming from Andrea, sliced her open, and all the memories of Nora berating her, telling her she'd never be good enough to be a Tanner, calling her whore's trash, came tumbling out from that dark place she'd imprisoned them for so long. She couldn't breathe.

"Get out!" Andrea screamed.

Jinx fled. As she rounded the corner at the top of the main staircase, she came face-to-face with E. J.

E. J. stared at her, wide-eyed, for the briefest instant before Jinx ran down the stairs and out the front door.

Chapter Four

E. J. pulled her Lexus into the dirt parking area outside Bella's Bar and eased it to a stop beside a tricked-out Chevy truck. The lot was much fuller than it had been two weeks earlier, on the night she had met Jinx, but that had been a Thursday. This was a Friday, and although it was still early, the place seemed to be heading into full swing. E. J. had found it on Yelp, and it was the kind of small dive she liked going to occasionally. While the bigger, glitzier gay bars had their appeal, she enjoyed a more casual atmosphere if she just wanted to unwind. Places like this reminded E. J. of the bar and grill her grandparents owned when she was growing up—minus the gays and lesbians, of course—where she had spent many summer days and after school hours rolling coins and playing pool. When she had first walked into Bella's, she hadn't expected to meet anyone, but tonight, she was specifically looking for Jinx.

Since the wedding, she hadn't been able to get her out of her mind, hadn't been able to shake those horrible things she had heard Andrea yelling at her, or let go of the pain in Jinx's eyes as she had passed her at the top of the stairs. She wanted to make sure Jinx was all right. And then there were the memories of the night they had spent together she couldn't shake either. So, when she had finished her workweek two weeks later already two hours from home, she'd convinced herself the additional two-and-a-half-hour drive in the opposite direction from her condo in Sacramento made perfect sense. She had already been on the road for three days, what was one more night? Besides, the traffic would be lighter in the morning. With that, it had been decided. She would see if she could find Jinx again, and Bella's was the only place she knew to look.

She turned off the engine and watched two women, one in heels and a tight, short dress, the other in biker boots and black leather, walk arm-in-arm toward the entrance. She scanned the parking lot, trying to remember what kind of car Jinx had been driving, but she hadn't paid much attention when they had left. She'd had other things on her mind.

When she stepped into the bar, she paid her cover charge and surveyed the mixed crowd. The beat of Joan Jett's "Bad Reputation" pounded in the air. There was no sign of Jinx. E. J. wondered if she would recognize anyone Jinx had been with that night. She took a quick second appraisal of the room but saw no one who looked remotely familiar. Even the bartender was different. She sighed. *Pointless. I'll just grab a drink and then turn in.*

Two hours later, after declining a number of invitations to dance and one offer to *rock her world*, she noticed a couple making their way between the tables toward the back corner, where a group of friends had been playing pool and partying all evening. A thin bottle blonde hung on a larger woman in jeans and a denim jacket, her arm around her thick waist and her hand shoved into her back pocket. The group in the corner applauded as the couple approached.

E. J. studied the bigger woman. She thought she recognized her. *Damn.* She wished she had paid more attention, but she hadn't noticed anyone other than Jinx that night. She ordered a club soda and continued to study the big woman as she grabbed a pool cue and began to play. Finally, something clicked. E. J. didn't know what—the flash of a grin, the brush of a hand over her short cropped hair, maybe just the tilt of her head—but something. Was she the one Jinx had stopped and spoken to on the way out? After another twenty minutes or so of dividing her attention between the woman and the door, E. J. made her way across the bar. *What do I have to lose?* At worst, she might look like a fool to someone she would never see again, but at best, she might get some information about Jinx. Just as she reached the pool table, the bottle blonde stepped in front of her.

Her eyes were as hard as her stance. "Hold on there, sweet cheeks. This mama's taken." She wrapped an arm possessively around the larger woman's waist.

E. J. stopped short. "Excuse me?" She wasn't sure she had heard correctly over the Bonnie Raitt song playing on the jukebox.

"You've been checking out my woman all night. I've been watching you." She pressed a hip into her date's. "Back off."

Suddenly understanding the misunderstanding, E. J. flushed. "Oh. No. It's not what you think."

The other woman turned and arched an eyebrow at E. J., then grinned. She leaned on her pool cue and gave bottle blonde a tender smile. "Easy, sweet pea." She returned her attention to E. J. "This pretty lady isn't here for me. She's here for Jinx."

"Jinx?" Bottle-blonde-sweet-pea eyed E. J. suspiciously. "What do you want with our Jinxie?"

This wasn't going at all the way E. J. had hoped. Who was this woman? "I just want to talk to her. Do you know where she lives?"

"Yeah," bottle blonde said with a scoff. "She lives on Nofriggin Way."

The big woman chuckled. "I'm Reggie," she said in a friendly tone. She extended her hand.

E. J. exhaled in relief and shook it. "My name's E. J.—"

"I know who you are," Reggie said. She turned to bottle blonde. "Sweet pea, this is the lady Jinx left with a couple weeks ago, that night you went to your sister's."

"Really?" She looked E. J. over again, this time with curiosity.

"This is my wife, Sparkle," Reggie said.

Sparkle? Who names their baby Sparkle? "It's nice to meet you," E. J. said, wanting to get past all this so she could find out about Jinx.

"What do you want to talk to her about?" Sparkle asked. Her manner lightened, but she remained an obvious force to be reckoned with.

"I'm sure that's private," Reggie said before E. J. had to come up with an answer.

It gave her the opportunity to change the subject. "Do you know if she's coming in tonight? I came here looking for her in hopes that maybe she hangs out here."

"Hangs out *here*? Jinxie?" Sparkle snorted. "Honey, you might've gone home with her, but you didn't learn squat about her, did you?"

E. J. glanced at Sparkle but kept her attention on Reggie. She was obviously the better bet. "Do you know how I can reach her?"

Reggie studied her for a long moment, then pulled a cell phone from the breast pocket of her jeans jacket. She tapped the screen. Several seconds later, she moved away and spoke into the phone. The music drowned out her words.

E. J. turned to find Sparkle staring at her with an inquisitive expression.

"You look a little fancy for a place like this," Sparkle said, sounding not quite conversational. "In fact, you look a little fancy for this end of town at all."

E. J. remembered her tan linen slacks and black, short-sleeved shell she had put on that morning. The outfit was enhanced by a necklace of three graduated length strands of two-toned gold, decorated with clear crystals. Matching studs adorned her ears. She hadn't considered a need to blend in, and suddenly wished she'd stopped to change. "I came straight from work," she said. She glanced at Reggie's back.

"What brought you here? Slumming it tonight?" Sparkle asked. "Had a good roll with Jinxie a couple weeks ago and thought you'd come back for more?"

E. J.'s temper flared. Who did this woman think she was? "Look, you don't know me. You have no—"

Reggie stepped up beside Sparkle and eased an arm around her shoulders. "I apologize for my wife," she said.

Sparkle slapped her hand. "I don't need apologizing for."

Reggie smiled at her. "Sometimes you do, sweet pea." She kissed Sparkle's forehead. "E. J.'s a friend of Jinx's." She looked into Sparkle's eyes. The sentence was simple, but a deeper communication seemed to pass between them.

Sparkle turned back to E. J. "I'm sorry if I was rude." Her tone lacked sincerity.

"She's protective of Jinx," Reggie said with a gentle smile. "We both are." Her gaze was soft, but it still held the slightest hint of a warning.

E. J. nodded. *Understood.* She was glad Jinx had these two in her life, especially after seeing the way Andrea had treated her.

"She'll be here in about fifteen minutes."

E. J. smiled. "Thank you." Relief ran through her, and she relaxed slightly. She had found her. *And she wants to see me.* The thought awakened butterflies in her stomach.

"You want to join us while you wait?" Reggie asked.

E. J. looked at the group who had been watching the entire exchange. *Are they all Jinx's friends?* She turned back to Reggie. "I haven't played pool in a while," she said with a bit of a challenge. "Care to wager?"

Reggie grinned. "Rack 'em," she called out. "The lady wants to play."

When E. J. lined up her final shot and banked the eight ball into the corner pocket, a cheer went up.

Reggie laughed. "I think I got hustled," she said as she handed E. J. the two twenties from the side of the table.

"What's that they say?" E. J. teased her. "If you can't find the one being hustled in the pool room, it's you." She fanned herself with the bills and batted her eyes.

"I demand a rematch," Reggie said. "Soon."

E. J. laughed and turned to find Jinx watching her from where she leaned against the wall, thumbs hooked in the front pockets of her blue jeans, a tight black T-shirt giving her a bit of a bad-girl look. A rush of desire flooded E. J. How long had Jinx been there?

Jinx winked and pushed away from the wall. "You'd better watch out," she said as she approached. "You'll end up a regular here if you're not careful."

E. J. tucked her money into the pocket of her slacks. "How are you?" she asked over the opening bars of a country song. She wanted to slip her arms around Jinx's neck but stopped herself.

A tall butch slapped Jinx on the back as she passed and murmured something in her ear.

Jinx blushed and ignored her. "Can I buy you a drink?"

E. J. became aware of the number of women monitoring them. Her cheeks warmed under the scrutiny. "You know what? I've been here quite a while and don't think I need any more to drink, but I'm hungry. Have you eaten? Would you like to get some dinner?"

Jinx hesitated.

In the brief interval, E. J. lost herself in those vibrant blue eyes she had seen every time she had closed her own for the past couple of weeks. She struggled to keep from kissing her.

Finally, Jinx nodded.

As they started toward the door, hoots and woo-hoos went up from the group behind them. Jinx laughed and threw a wave in their direction. When they stepped out into the evening air, her face shone an even brighter red than before. "Sorry about that," she said with a shy smile.

"Do you know everybody in there?"

"No, I've met a lot of them through Reggie and Sparkle, but I don't really know many." Jinx paused. "What sounds good to eat?"

E. J.'s mind went blank. "I don't know." She hadn't thought past finding Jinx, but she couldn't say that.

"Are you in the same hotel? We can get something nearby."

"No," E. J. said. She had forgotten she hadn't found a room yet. Her assistant always handled that in advance, but this had been so spur of the moment.

"Are you staying with your son?"

"No." She hadn't thought about Jacob either. "He doesn't know I'm—" She cut herself off. God, what had she been about to say? Had she really been about to admit she had come only to see if, by chance, she could run into Jinx again? She would have to admit that eventually, though, wouldn't she? Unless…Maybe they could just grab something to eat, E. J. could casually bring up the scene at the wedding in conversation, and then they would go their separate ways. That wasn't what E. J. wanted, though. Yes, she wanted to make sure Jinx was okay, but she also wanted to spend time with her, to touch her, to share another night like the one they'd had before.

Jinx waited expectantly.

"I—" Then something came to her. *Thank God.* The silence was awkward. "Jacob and Tiffany are still on their honeymoon." The words came out too quickly.

Jinx didn't seem to notice. "Where are you staying, then?"

"I haven't gotten a room, yet. I'll find one after dinner. I'm starving."

Jinx frowned. "I don't know that you'll find one," she said as she took E. J.'s hand and eased her away from the doorway to let a couple enter the bar. "There's a car show and big race out at the track this weekend. The news said everything's booked." She still held E. J.'s fingers.

Shit. This was exactly why spontaneity was overrated. "Well, there has to be someplace that has one room left." E. J. warmed at the caress of Jinx's thumb over the back of her knuckles.

Jinx shrugged. "Probably, but finding it might take all night."

They stood staring at one another, each waiting. E. J. saw her own thoughts, her own desire, reflected back to her. They both seemed to be thinking the same thing—at least, E. J. hoped they were—but who was going to say it?

Jinx looked away. "You could stay with me." Her voice was uncertain. "You know...if you want." She gave E. J. a sidelong glance.

A wave of relief washed over E. J., and she realized how much she had been wanting to see Jinx again, how much she had wanted Jinx to want to see *her* again. She felt a little silly, a little *adolescenty*, but she didn't care. She didn't have to admit it to anyone. She had come looking for Jinx and had found her. And Jinx *did* want to see her, too. That was all that mattered. She squeezed Jinx's fingers and smiled. "I'd like that. Thank you."

Jinx's face lit up with a grin. Her eyes twinkled.

And as easy as that, the awkwardness was gone.

"Great," Jinx said, grasping E. J.'s other hand. "I can make you dinner, too. I was just about to throw some salmon and asparagus on the grill when Reggie called. The salmon's marinating. Do you like salmon and asparagus? Oh, and I've got strawberries from a guy with a roadside stand near my house. They're *so* sweet. You'll love them. If you like strawberries, I mean."

E. J. laughed at the excitement in Jinx's voice. "You cook, too?"

"Too?"

"Mm-hm." This time E. J. didn't hold back. She threaded her arms around Jinx's neck and pressed lightly against her. "Last time I discovered some of your other hidden talents, and now I find out you can cook. You'd better be careful. Before long, I'll know all your secrets."

That shadow that lay quietly behind Jinx's eyes rose, then settled again in a fluid motion, but her smile never wavered. "Where's your car? You can follow me home."

E. J. wondered about the tiny glimpses of—what was it? Self doubt, maybe? She had caught it a few times in Jinx's expression, but when she considered the conversation at the wedding, she figured it was likely old family wounds. *Everyone has them.* If Jinx wanted to talk about it, she would.

The drive from Bella's to Jinx's led through darkened, curbless streets lined with small houses. The occasional streetlight illuminated older model pickups and cars, similar to Jinx's faded and dented Corolla, parked in rutted driveways. When Jinx ushered E. J. up three steps onto the front porch of a tiny clapboard house, E. J. could almost smell her grandmother's fresh-baked bread. E. J.'s mother had hated her roots, but her grandparents' home had been one of E. J.'s favorite places in the world.

Under the lit porch light, Jinx unlocked the front door and motioned E. J. inside. She stepped in behind her and switched on the light to reveal one large room with a kitchen sink, counter, and appliances along the wall to the left and a small table with two wooden chairs in the back corner. The right side held a living room setup with an area rug in warm earth tones partially covering the marred but clean linoleum floor, a shelving unit holding a television and some books, and a double bed evidently serving as a couch. Two doors opened off the main room, one clearly another outside exit. The whole place was tidy, the bed made, the kitchen spotless. The atmosphere was homey and inviting, just like Jinx. "This is nice," E. J. said, moving farther into the room.

"I know it's not what you're used to, but considering you might have ended up sleeping in your car, it could meet your needs."

E. J. took in the words and the sexy rasp of Jinx's voice. She let her gaze roam over Jinx's body, her hands, her lips, and felt the stirrings of arousal at the memory of their feel and their touch. She could smell some delicious combination of herbs and spices that made her mouth water and her stomach grumble. She sighed. "Somehow, I think every need I have tonight could be met right here in this room."

Jinx offered her that slow, easy smile that undid E. J. every time, and crossed to where she stood. She set E. J.'s suitcase on the bed. "We can make sure of that," she said as she fingered one of E. J.'s stud earrings, caressing the lobe in the process.

E. J. closed her eyes and inhaled deeply.

Jinx kissed her lightly on the lips. "If you want to freshen up, the bathroom's through there."

E. J. opened her eyes and followed Jinx's gesture toward the inside door.

"I'll start dinner," Jinx said.

E. J. found the bathroom off what was obviously designed to be a bedroom. It held a dresser, a desk, some weights, a bicycle, and a small pile of shoes and boots in the corner. When she had washed up and brushed her teeth, she stared at her reflection in the mirror.

She relaxed, shedding the tension of the evening and the worry she might not be able to find Jinx. She breathed in the mingling aromas of citrus and something sweetly spicy that heightened her desire when combined with Jinx's natural scent, but here, on their own, they soothed her. She ran her hand over a soft, plush bath towel that seemed at once out of place, yet perfectly Jinx.

She felt comfortable here, maybe because it reminded her of her grandparents' home. Not the floor plan or décor, but the energy, the atmosphere. Who would have guessed someone she picked up in a bar would live in a place so similar to her childhood safe place, where she had felt free and accepted, where she had been truly happy? *She* would never have guessed it.

Here she was, though, in Jinx's bathroom, in her quaint little home. Some people, maybe many, might call it run down or shabby, and had E. J. not spent so many hours, days, occasionally weeks with her grandparents, she might, too. After all, in comparison to the condo she had spent a small fortune purchasing and furnishing, this place wasn't much, but E. J. already felt more at ease here than she ever did at home. The condo had always been just a place to sleep, much like the hotels where she stayed on the road. Tonight would be a nice escape from the world, a visit to the solace of her past. *With some fringe benefits.* She smiled.

As E. J. re-emerged into the main room, Jinx was coming in the back door. "Dinner's on the grill. It'll just be a few more minutes." She opened the refrigerator. "Do you want…" She ran her fingers through her hair. "Oh, wow. I don't really have much to offer. Apple juice? Milk? Water?" She looked at E. J. with a rueful smile. "I'm sorry. I didn't know I was having company."

"Apple juice sounds great." She sat at the table and watched Jinx. "How long have you lived here?"

"Two and a half years." Jinx set a glass in front of E. J. and another across the table.

"So, a bed instead of a couch? Is that to save time?" E. J. teased her.

Jinx laughed. "No, it's just because I like stretching out and watching movies. And no one ever comes over, so it doesn't really matter."

"You never have guests?" E. J. asked, surprised. How could that be? Jinx was so open and friendly and attractive, and so…well, good in bed.

"Reggie and Sparkle have been over a few times, but mostly I go to their house. So, no. No one else has been here. Until now." Jinx grinned. "Be right back." She headed outside.

When she returned, three plates held salmon and asparagus. She added rice, then covered one with plastic wrap and grabbed a thermos from the back of the counter. She set both items outside the front door. "It's for a friend," she said in answer to E. J.'s questioning look, but offered no further explanation. She put a plate in front of E. J.

"This looks delicious and smells even better," E. J. said. She tasted the salmon and moaned. "Oh, my God. *This* is wonderful."

"Thanks," Jinx said, sitting across the table. "That'll be one need taken care of, then." Her tone was playful.

E. J. couldn't even speak until she had devoured almost the entire meal. When she was able to slow down and focus on something other than the flavor exploding in her mouth and the satisfaction in her stomach, she sighed. She leaned back in her chair and found Jinx studying her. "Is something wrong?"

Jinx hesitated. "I'm just wondering what you're doing here."

"What do you mean?"

"You said Jacob and Tiffany are still on their honeymoon, and there aren't any Bad Dog stores here, so why are you here?"

Here it was, the moment she had to admit she had overheard Andrea, that she had been concerned about Jinx, that she couldn't stop thinking about her. "I was a little...I heard..."

Jinx waited. "So, this whole inability of yours to finish sentences, is it a chronic thing?" Jinx's lips quirked.

E. J. laughed. "So it would seem." She took a deep breath and steadied herself. "I know it's none of my business, but I heard all the things Andrea said to you after the wedding, and when I saw you on the stairs, you looked so upset. I was worried about you. I wanted to make sure you're okay."

Jinx stared at her.

"I'm sorry if I've overstepped a boundary," she added quickly. "I know it's none of my business."

"You came back to town just to see if *I'm* okay?" Something flickered in Jinx's expression.

Oh God, have I offended her? How would E. J. feel if someone had listened to a private conversation *she* was having and then brought it up to her? Why hadn't she thought of the possibility before now? "I'm sorry."

"I don't know what to say." Jinx's tone was soft. She sounded bewildered.

"I just...You looked so hurt." Jinx's image flashed in E. J.'s mind, and the pain in Jinx's eyes made her heart ache.

Jinx averted her gaze. "I'm fine, really. I should have just left. I never should have gone in the house." She sighed. "I shouldn't have been there at all."

"But those things she said. They were awful."

Jinx stiffened. When she turned back to E. J., a veil had fallen over her eyes. "It's fine, really. *I'm* fine." She looked at E. J.'s hand resting on the table. "I just can't believe that's why you came back. You're so sweet."

Sweet? E. J. couldn't remember ever being called *sweet. Ever.* It wasn't a word people associated with her, wasn't a word *she* associated with her. Efficient? In all areas. Respectful? For the most part. Professional? Absolutely. Sweet? She wasn't even entirely sure what that involved. She'd have to look it up.

Jinx took E. J.'s hand. "Thank you."

E. J. cleared her throat. "You're welcome." She laced her fingers through Jinx's. "You're sure you're all right?"

"Let's change the subject," Jinx said. "Do you still have those other needs you mentioned?"

There was that slow smile again, and her eyes darkened. E. J.'s earlier desire reignited. Her pulse quickened. She had forgotten just how intense her response to Jinx was. "Definitely," she whispered.

"C'mere, then." Jinx coaxed her to her feet with a gentle tug and scooted away from the table. She gazed up into E. J.'s face as E. J. straddled her lap.

E. J. pressed herself into Jinx and moaned.

Jinx slipped her hand around the back of E. J.'s neck and urged her down until their lips met. She held E. J. still. Her grasp was soft, her breath warm.

The pressure against E. J.'s mouth and sex built until she had to have more. She could feel the hard fly of Jinx's jeans through the thin barrier of her own slacks and panties. She tightened her thighs.

Jinx began to kiss her, slow and long and deep.

E. J. groaned and twined her arms around Jinx's neck, returning the kiss. She explored Jinx's mouth, let Jinx have hers. She went deeper, drew it out longer.

But Jinx kept the pace measured, making E. J. hunger even as she feasted.

She wanted it faster. She wanted it harder. She wanted more—more contact, more movement, more Jinx. She tore her mouth free. "Touch me," she whispered. "I need to feel your skin."

Jinx tugged the hem of E. J.'s shirt from her waistband and slipped her hands beneath it. When her warm fingers caressed the small of E. J.'s back, E. J. gasped and arched upward. Her clitoris pressed firmly against Jinx, and she cried out in pleasure. She moaned under the feel of Jinx's hands moving up her spine, caressing and massaging. She tightened her arms around Jinx's neck as those tantalizing fingers loosened her bra, then made their way beneath it to fondle the sides of her breasts. The lace teased her swollen nipples. She clenched her eyes shut and thrust her hips.

"Stay with me, baby."

Jinx's low murmur barely penetrated E. J.'s lust, but the word baby—Jinx calling her *baby*—melted her.

"Don't go over, yet."

E. J. groaned. She wanted to. She wanted to right then, but she also wanted more. She eased back, hoping Jinx would find her aching nipples.

Instead, Jinx's hands slid out from under E. J.'s shirt and up to her nape. Unhurriedly, she unfastened her necklace, let it slip down her torso, and placed it on the table. Then she raised the hem of E. J.'s top, urging her arms above her head, and eased the garment upward for E. J. to slip out of it. Finally, with excruciating slowness, she inched E. J.'s bra down the length of her arms and off. She set it beside the necklace. She sat back and admired E. J.'s bare breasts. "You are so beautiful," she whispered.

E. J. waited, the heat of Jinx's gaze burning into her flesh. Surely, she'd touch her. With the need evident in her expression, she had to be as aroused as E. J.

Jinx didn't move. She just stared, her breath quickening.

E. J. pushed her fingers into Jinx's hair and cupped the back of her head. She brought Jinx's mouth to a taut and aching nipple. "Suck me," she said urgently. When Jinx's mouth closed over it, she threw back her head and groaned.

Jinx sucked softly, closing her fingertips around the other nipple. Her tenderness drove E. J. mad with need. Jinx's feather-like caress, her gentle suckling, made her feel so cherished, almost worshiped, while at the same time, it tortured and tormented her to the height of desperation.

She gasped as Jinx's arms encircled her waist and she stood, lifting E. J. with her. She clenched her legs around Jinx's hips, her arms around her neck, and lost herself in the sensations of Jinx's lips sucking her nipple deeper into her mouth. She closed her eyes and cried out. The next thing she knew, she was lying on the bed, Jinx's teeth gently grazing her other nipple, as she opened E. J.'s slacks. She lifted her hips and let Jinx slide the pants down her legs. When she looked up, Jinx stood over her, staring down at her naked body with an almost reverent expression.

"You are *so* beautiful," Jinx murmured. Her eyes shone with what could have been wonder. "I didn't think I'd ever see you again."

E. J.'s desire raged under Jinx's adoration, and she *needed* more. "Jinx, please." She barely recognized her own voice. "I need to feel you. I need you on top of me, against me, *inside* me." Her plea seemed to work.

Jinx's eyes snapped up to hers. She yanked her T-shirt over her head and scrambled out of her jeans. When her undergarments joined the pile of clothing on the floor, she eased the full weight of her body onto E. J.'s.

E. J. gasped, and she thrust up into Jinx. It felt so good. She had missed her so much. Feeling Jinx against her again was like coming home.

Jinx sucked on E. J.'s neck, on her shoulder, not gently now but hungrily. She bit down as she nestled her hips between E. J.'s thighs and surged against her.

E. J. opened wider for her, rubbing against her.

Jinx groaned and found E. J.'s nipple again. She sucked it fully into her hot mouth, hard and fast. She dragged her own breasts across E. J.'s abdomen.

Yes, this was what E. J. wanted, what she needed. She *wanted* it hot. She *wanted* it hard. There would be time for gentleness, later. They had all night together before she went back to her real life.

❖

Eyes closed, E. J. nuzzled her face against Jinx's abdomen, the soft triangle of curls tickling her cheek. She played her fingertips through Jinx's wet, silken folds and enjoyed the jerk of her body with each residual spasm of release. The taste of her arousal and climax still lingered on E. J.'s lips and tongue.

They had been in bed for hours, and E. J. still hadn't gotten enough. Would she ever? Something about Jinx kept her wanting more, no matter how intense her orgasms, no matter how many she had. Tonight *had* to be enough, though. She couldn't keep coming back for sex to the city where her son and daughter-in-law lived. It was too risky. Granted, it was far from likely she would run into either of them, or Andrea, in this part of town, but there was no need to take the chance. E. J. never had difficulty when she wanted a woman in her bed, and though she didn't need one often, there were plenty of other women and plenty of other cities.

E. J. sighed at the feel of Jinx's fingers combing through her hair.

"C'mere," Jinx murmured.

E. J. cuddled against her side.

Jinx held her close.

"Thank you again for letting me stay the night." E. J. ran a fingertip between Jinx's breasts.

"My pleasure." She caressed E. J.'s back. "It's been a really long time since I had a slumber party."

E. J. laughed softly. She wondered *how* long, then wondered why it mattered.

"But don't get too comfortable. We still have to watch a horror movie and call someone and ask if their refrigerator's running. And it's only a *real* slumber party when everyone's dancing around in their panties, screaming." Jinx's tone was playful.

E. J. liked that about her. She *was* an adult and definitely had the sexual allure of the attractive, experienced woman she seemed to be, and yet there was an innocence to her as well, a naiveté. E. J. thought back to earlier that night when she had first seen Jinx, leaning against the wall in the bar. Jinx had looked so sexy, so dangerous, but then when that woman had whispered something to her, she had blushed like a schoolgirl. Suddenly, E. J. was curious. "What did that woman say to you tonight?" She traced circles over Jinx's bare stomach.

"Mmm. What woman?" Jinx's eyes were closed.

"The one in the bar. The butch that whispered something in your ear right before we left."

Jinx smiled lazily. "Nothing."

"She said *something*. And it made you blush. What was it?"

"Nothing appropriate for you to hear."

"Oh, please. What am I? A virgin?"

Jinx turned onto her side and slipped her arm over E. J.'s waist. "You're an angel." She draped a leg over E. J.'s thighs.

E. J. laughed. "I don't think some of the things I did tonight were angelic."

"Doesn't matter. It's my house." Jinx pressed her lips to E. J.'s neck. "My house. My rules. And I say you're an angel. Besides, everything you've done tonight felt pretty heavenly to me."

"That's bad," E. J. said with a giggle. But she liked it. *God help me, I like it.*

"You're *my* angel." Jinx snuggled closer. "My princess." She nuzzled her ear. "My little kumquat," she murmured, a smile in her voice. Her breath tickled E. J.'s skin.

E. J. laughed and pushed her away. "You're not going to tell me, are you?"

"Nope." Jinx rolled onto her back again then off the bed. "I *will* bring you strawberries, though. And I promise, they'll be way better than a bunch of words." She crossed to the fridge and retrieved a large bowl.

E. J. rested her head on an arm and admired the strong lines of Jinx's naked body, the firm muscle beneath smooth skin. This everything-in-one-room design had its benefits. She focused on a long scar that ran half the width of Jinx's lower back. She had felt it under her fingers and palms when she had run her hands down the length of Jinx's spine or gripped her waist to pull her harder against her center. She had pressed her lips to it, run her tongue over it on her way to lower places. She hadn't been about to stop what she was doing at the time to ask about it. Could she now? She remembered the other scar, the round one along her side.

Jinx grinned at her on her way back to the bed.

There was no point in asking, no reason. E. J. would leave in the morning and, this time, she'd *really* never see Jinx again. She now knew Jinx was fine. She had seen for herself the state of Jinx's and Andrea's relationship and knew the chance of running into Jinx at family gatherings was nil. And there was no need for them to know anything personal about one another. This was the way E. J. managed her private life. No strings, no entanglements. Just a good time and then it was over. She wasn't looking for anything more.

Jinx plucked a strawberry from the bowl and pressed it oh-so-lightly to E. J.'s lips.

E. J. took it and just the tips of Jinx's finger and thumb into her mouth. She sucked gently. Sweetness coated her tongue, and her eyes went wide. "Mmmmm." She took the berry fully and bit into it. "Oh, my God," she murmured as the flavor flooded her senses. "That is so good."

"I told you."

"I've never had a strawberry *that* good."

Jinx chuckled. "That's because you probably buy them in a store." She fed E. J. another one, then ate one herself.

"Why does that matter?" E. J. closed her eyes and savored the taste.

"Sparkle says the ones in the stores are grown for shipping."

At the mention of the hostile little woman's name, E. J. flinched inwardly. She would never see *her* again either. *Not a bad thing.*

"Their skins are a lot tougher and they're picked too early. They never get fully ripe." Jinx lay beside E. J., and they snuggled against each other again. She placed another berry on E. J.'s tongue.

I could get used to this. But she wouldn't.

"Sparkle told me to only buy berries from the local growers because those are grown for eating. They have tender skin and are perfectly ripe right when they're picked." Jinx put one in her mouth then kissed E. J.

They shared the sweetness along with the heat that still simmered between them, and E. J. no longer cared about tomorrow or Sparkle or where to buy strawberries. All she cared about was the sound of Jinx's moans, the taste of her kiss, and the feel of her touch.

Chapter Five

Jinx stood in line, staring at the menu above the counter. She'd never been in a Starbucks before, never had any reason to be. She didn't drink much coffee, and when she did, she was happy with a basic cup from Mike's Donuts near her house, or from whatever restaurant she happened to be eating in at the time. The best cup she'd ever had, though, was the one she'd shared with E. J., and that was because she'd gotten to look at E. J. in that thin robe while she'd taken her first swallow. Bacon fat would have tasted good in that moment. This morning, the coffee wasn't even for her. She'd wanted to pick up a cup for E. J. since she didn't have any in the house, and she knew Starbucks was supposed to be the be-all end-all.

She searched the menu. Bakery. Starbucks Petites. Bistro Boxes. Hot Breakfasts. Starbucks Refreshers. Everything but...*Ah, there it is.* Freshly Brewed Coffee. *Oh, wait...*Blonde Roast? Caffè Misto? Clover Brewed Coffee? *What the heck is clover brewed?*

"May I take your order?" the girl at the register asked the businessman two people in front of Jinx.

She needed to make up her mind. Iced coffee? *No.* That just seemed wrong. Chocolate Beverages? *Oooooh.* Peppermint Hot Chocolate. That sounded good. Or Salted Caramel Hot Chocolate. *Even better.* She remembered the salted caramel milk chocolate bar Sparkle had put in her Christmas stocking last year, and her mouth watered.

Oh, wait. No, E. J. Coffee. Her brain wasn't quite functioning yet. She and E. J. had fallen asleep only an hour before Jinx had to get up for her morning ritual and then get ready for work. She was here to get coffee for E. J. A column entitled Espresso caught her attention. That was coffee, too, wasn't it? What was the difference? She looked down the list. Twenty-nine? There were *twenty-nine* different kinds of espresso? How was she supposed to decide?

"I'll have a cinnamon dolce latte half-soy nonfat decaf," the woman in front of her said to the clerk. "Oh, and extra hot."

Twenty minutes later, Jinx walked out of Mike's Donuts with a large Styrofoam cup of coffee and three containers of vanilla creamer. She balanced it all in one hand while she drove with the other, since the cup holder in her fifteen-year-old Toyota was broken, and thanked the coffee gods she hadn't scalded herself as she pulled up to her house. When she'd stepped outside earlier, she'd been happy to see E. J.'s Lexus hadn't been stolen or stripped during the night, and knew she had Pablo, the kid next door, and the gang he ran with, to thank for keeping an eye on her place. Now, she was just glad to see it because it meant E. J. hadn't left. Her adventure into the land of the magic beans felt like it'd taken a decade. She glanced at her watch. She needed to get a move on.

As she closed the front door behind her, she took in the twisted sheet and blanket on the empty bed, remnants of another night of… Jinx wasn't sure what to call it. It didn't feel like just sex—it felt like way more than that—but at the same time, it *was* damned good sex. It couldn't be making love because Jinx didn't really know what that was. Besides, how could they be doing anything that could be called *making* love when they'd only just met? It certainly wasn't anything like what she'd had with Val, except for maybe the feeling of connection, but it was a different kind of connection—way different. And it was absolutely nothing like the other homeless girls and addicts she'd hooked up with on the streets when she was much younger. She didn't have any frame of reference for anything like what she felt with E. J.

She heard the clank of pipes that accompanied the water turning off in the bathroom. The door was closed.

"Knock knock." She leaned against the jamb.

"Who's there?" E. J. said after a pause. Her voice was lower than usual, her morning voice Jinx remembered from the hotel.

She smiled to herself. "Al."

Another pause. "Al who?"

"Al give you coffee if you open up."

The door opened immediately, and E. J. stood with one of the two towels Jinx owned wrapped around her middle. It covered just enough, but still not very much. She had dark smudges under her eyes. "Coffee?"

Jinx held up the cup.

"Oh God, you're a saint." E. J. took it.

"That *is* what they call me," Jinx said, handing her the creamers. "Jinx of the caffeine, patron saint of the sleepless."

"I looked for a coffeemaker," E. J. said while emptying the cream into her cup. "But you don't have one." She took a deep swallow.

"I know. That's why I went and got you that."

E. J. released a half-sigh, half-moan, then focused on Jinx. "I thought you left."

"I did. I went to get you that."

E. J. laughed and took another drink. She stroked Jinx's cheek. "Thank you."

The jasmine scent of E. J.'s shampoo or body wash or perfume or whatever it was, made it difficult for Jinx to think. The softness of E. J.'s touch and the warmth in her gaze stirred Jinx's desire. She stuffed her fingertips into her jeans pockets to keep from running her hands over the soft skin of E. J.'s bare shoulders. She had to go to work.

E. J. smiled and stepped past her. "I meant, I thought I wouldn't see you before I needed to leave."

"You heading out?" Disappointment rippled through Jinx, but she had known that. Of course E. J. would leave. She'd said she'd only come because she was concerned about her, and Jinx had told her she was fine. She didn't want E. J. to know just how wrecked she'd been following the scene with Andrea. She didn't want her to know it'd taken her several days to remind herself that Andrea's reaction was what she'd expected—before she'd gotten caught up in all the memories and learned that Andrea had wanted to keep the tree house. She didn't want E. J. to have seen her so upset and running out of the house. In fact, if she'd thought about it when Reggie called, she probably would have been too humiliated even to go to Bella's the previous night. She was glad she didn't think of it.

"I have to get home." E. J. settled onto the bed and pulled the sheet over her legs. The towel still covered her torso, its corner crimped at E. J.'s breast.

Jinx wanted to ask where home was, but the less she knew about E. J., the easier it might be to just tuck her away as a fond memory. She nodded and turned toward the kitchen counter. "I'm making a sandwich for lunch. You want a PB&J so you don't have to stop on the road?" She opened the fridge and retrieved the blackberry jam. When E. J. didn't answer, she glanced over her shoulder.

E. J. sat smiling at her, holding her coffee in her lap. "I think I do." She sounded surprised. "I haven't had a PB&J in eons."

Jinx grinned. "Then I'll make sure it's the best PB&J ever. I'll add my secret ingredient."

"What's that?"

Jinx rolled her eyes. "If I told you, it wouldn't be a secret."

"Oh, of course. My apologies." E. J. giggled.

Jinx found the peanut butter and bread in the cupboard, grateful for something to focus on besides E. J.'s smooth skin. As she worked, she heard movement in the room—a squeak from a shift on the mattress, the rustle of bedding, bare feet on linoleum. It felt oddly natural, relaxed, to be doing something as mundane as fixing lunch with E. J. there in her house. This was normally her space alone, but she liked having E. J. there.

"*Turner and Hooch?* I love this movie," E. J. said, breaking the comfortable silence that had settled into the room. She held up a DVD from Jinx's entertainment unit.

Jinx smiled. "Me, too. It's the best romantic comedy ever. A romance *and* a dog. Doesn't get much better than that."

"And *Hotel for Dogs?*" E. J. flipped another case and began reading the back. "This sounds cute."

Jinx felt herself blush at E. J.'s discovery of the kids' movie, but she loved that one, too. "No romance, but lots of dogs." She shrugged. Jinx went back to the sandwiches. "So, what does E. J. stand for?" she asked without thinking. *Dang it! What happened to it being easier if I don't know anything more?*

"What?" E. J. sounded distracted.

Jinx turned to look at her. She couldn't back pedal now without it seeming awkward. "Your initials," she said. "What do they stand for?"

Still in the towel, E. J. tapped on the screen of her phone. Without looking up, she laughed. "Oh, no. You have your secret ingredient. I have *my* mysteries."

Jinx grinned. E. J. was fun. Along with the other obvious things she liked about her, she was fun. "That's not the same thing."

E. J. finished her message and dropped her phone into her purse. "A mystery is a mystery." She picked up her suitcase and opened it on the bed.

"No, no." Jinx played along. "My secret ingredient is like a family heirloom. I have an obligation to keep its identity safe. A name's just a name."

"What if my name has been passed down for generations, and it's only known to our royal lineage?" E. J. began folding the shell she'd worn the previous night. "I don't think we know each other well enough for me to divulge such a secret."

Jinx waited, but E. J. offered nothing more. "Really?" She chuckled. "I can run my hands and mouth all over your body, give you screaming orgasms, cook for you, bring you coffee, make you a sandwich *with* my secret ingredient, but I can't know your *name*?" She shot E. J. a glance.

E. J. only smiled and put her folded slacks into her suitcase.

Jinx eyed her. *She has to be joking.* Was she really not going to tell her? "Elizabeth." She took a stab at it. "Elizabeth Jane."

"No," E. J. said.

"Is either one of them right?" She wrapped up the PB&Js and collected several apples and some carrot sticks from the crisper drawer of the refrigerator.

"No." E. J. pulled some clean clothes from her bag.

"Eleanor Joyce." Jinx leaned against the counter and folded her arms.

"No."

"Will you tell me if I guess?"

"Sure," E. J. said. Her tone was smug. She ran a brush through her hair.

"You don't think I can do it." Jinx felt herself rise to the challenge.

"No." E. J. fluttered her lashes at her.

Jinx closed her eyes meditatively. "Edwina," she said as the name came to her. "Edwina Josephina."

E. J. laughed. "No." She pulled out a jewelry case and opened it.

Jinx began bagging both lunches. "You have to tell me if I get either one."

"Okay." E. J. slipped a small gold hoop through an earlobe.

Her superior air was starting to bug Jinx. "Ethel June. Ethel Julia. Ethel Judith."

E. J. dropped the towel and planted a fist on one hip. "Do I look like an Ethel anything?"

Jinx took in E. J.'s tantalizingly naked body and thought of Ethel from *I Love Lucy*. "Not at all."

"All right, then."

"This isn't fair," Jinx said, trying to ignore the low burn between her thighs. "You know *my* real name."

"I do," E. J. said, sounding self-satisfied. "But *you* didn't tell me."

Jinx wavered between irritation and amusement. She decided to try a new tactic. "Eliza Jewel. *That's* a pretty name."

"Aww, it is a pretty name, but it's not mine." E. J. stepped into a pair of blue lace panties, then put on a matching bra.

Jinx couldn't take her eyes off her. "Earl Jarvis," she said.

E. J. laughed as she pulled a snug-fitting, pink shirt with the Bad Dog poodle on the front over her head. "Yes, that's it. You've been sleeping with someone named Earl Jarvis."

Jinx paused, trying to think of another plan.

"Why do your friends call you Jinx?" E. J. asked. She shimmied into a pair of dark blue jeans and buttoned the waistband.

Jinx laughed in amazement. "Why would I tell you that?"

"Well, since your secret ingredient is so guarded, *maybe* I'll trade my name for why you go by Jinx. A name for a name."

Jinx studied her. Suddenly, she seemed more serious. "Some friends in high school started it." It was only a partial lie. They were friends at the age she should have been in her senior year. "They thought I was like the superhero Jinx, so they started calling me that. It just stuck."

E. J. stopped and tilted her head. "A superhero?" She was clearly intrigued. "What are your super powers? Other than the ones I already know," she said suggestively.

Jinx smiled, feeling a little self-conscious. "*Jinx's* super powers are being able to conjure earth tremors, create blasts of wind, dissolve solid matter, and summon emerald flames." She rattled off the list, feeling seventeen again. She'd liked taking on the name.

"Really?"

"Mm-hm. She's an elemental sorceress. She also has precognitive powers and can detect danger before it happens."

"Aren't sorceresses usually evil?"

Jinx shrugged. "She *is* a villain."

"Ah, a bad girl." E. J. gave her a sultry grin. Enjoyment danced in her eyes. "What about you reminded your friends of her?"

Jinx shifted nervously. She didn't want to go too far. She wanted E. J. to think of her as she was now. "They said I had precognitive powers, because I never got caught doing things." She remembered the night she'd backed out of hot-wiring a Mercedes because she felt something wasn't right. She'd awakened the next morning to learn two of her friends had been arrested. She wasn't going to share that, though.

E. J. closed her suitcase, then crossed to where Jinx stood. She slipped her arms around Jinx's waist and leaned into her, her expression searching.

"What?" Jinx asked, hoping her uneasiness didn't show.

"I'm just trying to figure you out." E. J. ran her hands up Jinx's back. "Your friends name you after a villain, but there doesn't seem to be anything villainous about you."

"Well, that was a long time ago." Jinx tried to make light of it.

"You obviously don't drink coffee, but you had some with me at the hotel."

Jinx enjoyed the play of E. J.'s caress. She rested her hands on E. J.'s hips. "I don't drink it very often." She refrained from adding that she didn't do anything very often that was potentially addictive.

"And I've been in a bar with you twice, but haven't seen you drink." E. J. retraced her path down Jinx's spine to her back pockets. "So, I assume you don't."

Their thighs touched.

Jinx shook her head.

"You're a fabulous cook and know all the ways to touch a woman to drive her insane, but you never have anyone over."

Jinx averted her gaze, embarrassed by the compliments and wary of the scrutiny.

E. J. slipped her fingers under the hem of Jinx's T-shirt, beneath the waistband of her jeans, along the thick ridge of raised skin across the small of her back. "Can I ask you something?"

Jinx tensed. She didn't want to explain the scars, neither of them. There was no reason to. E. J. was leaving. She'd never see her again. She didn't have time this morning to tell the whole story—even if E. J. would listen—and she didn't want to leave things on that note. E. J.'s eyes, though, her closeness, her touch, penetrated Jinx's usually sound defenses, and she felt herself nod.

"Since you love dogs so much, why don't you have one?"

Jinx flinched. Not the question she'd expected.

E. J.'s expression was serious.

Jinx almost would have preferred to talk about her scars. But no, she could talk about Rex. "I did," she said. "For a while. But he died."

E. J.'s features softened. "I'm sorry."

"Thanks, it's all right. He was old, and he died quietly." Jinx remembered the night she'd spent on the kitchen floor with Rex in her arms. "He knew he was loved in the end."

"How long did you have him?"

"Not very. About six months."

E. J. tilted her head, inviting the story.

"I found him. Someone dumped him on the side of the road outside the kennels."

"The kennels?"

"Reggie and Sparkle's place. Where I work," Jinx said. "It's a kennel, a grooming salon, and an obedience school all together."

E. J. arched an eyebrow in obvious surprise. "Really?"

"It's called Canine Complete." Jinx swallowed, the memory raising old emotions. "I saw him one day when I was leaving work and tried to get him to come to me, but he wouldn't. He wouldn't go to anyone. He just hung out there, right where he'd been left, for several days, like he was waiting for whoever left him to come back. But no one ever did."

E. J. listened intently, her fingers maintaining their gentle caress of Jinx's back.

It felt good to talk about Rex, like the release of a long-held breath. Reggie and Sparkle were always reluctant to bring up the subject in fear of upsetting Jinx, but this seemed to be what she needed. "Finally, after about a week, he got hungry enough to accept some food, and he was weak enough that I could grab him and keep hold of him to get him into my car. From that point on, he stayed right with me until the night he died. His name was Rex."

E. J. cupped the back of Jinx's head and coaxed her down to E. J.'s shoulder. She held her close.

Jinx tightened her arms around E. J.'s waist and buried her face in her neck. She inhaled the sweet scent of jasmine, the slightest hint of vanilla, and the salty smell of her own tears. *No. Don't.* She tried to jerk away, but E. J. held her snugly.

"It's okay," E. J. whispered, her breath warm on Jinx's ear. "I've got you."

Jinx gave in. She squeezed her eyes shut and crushed E. J. to her. The tears flowed freely, but they weren't for Rex—not really. Jinx knew Rex was safe, renewed, maybe even reincarnated as a brand new puppy or a little boy like in *The Art of Racing in the Rain*. These tears were for her, for how good it felt to be held in someone's arms, someone who seemed to care about her for no apparent reason. These tears were for the fact that she couldn't even remember the last time anyone had held her this way. Val had held her sometimes, but not like this, not so tenderly, so protectively. That wasn't Val. Sure, Jinx had felt—she'd *been*—safe with Val, but, in an entirely different way. Val protected Jinx the way she'd needed at the time, protected her from being jumped in the yard, raped in the shower, shanked on the way to mess. And they'd shared more, but not like this.

As the intensity of her emotions ebbed, Jinx became aware of E. J.'s body pressed firmly against her own, E. J.'s thigh nestled between Jinx's. She moved her mouth against E. J.'s neck and bit softly.

E. J. moaned and turned her head, giving Jinx better access. Her fingers tightened in Jinx's hair.

Maybe she could be a little late for work. Reggie would understand. She'd nodded toward E. J. and given Jinx a thumbs-up while E. J. had been mopping up the floor with her at the pool table. Jinx had meant to ask E. J. where she'd learned to play, but—so many questions, so little point. Sparkle would give her hell, though, if she came in late. Sparkle had that redneck-mama thing going where Jinx was concerned, even though they were pretty much the same age, but Jinx didn't mind. She knew it was Sparkle's way of showing her love. Even so, she didn't like making her mad. It was unpleasant. Besides, it'd been hard enough saying good-bye to E. J. the last time, and she knew it would be even more difficult after the previous night. If they ended up in bed again, especially after what'd just happened, the emotions that'd overtaken Jinx, she'd be a mess for God knew how long. No, this was it. It had to be. E. J. was leaving and, this time, not coming back.

Jinx lifted her head and loosened her hold. "I can't be late for work. And if we...you know..." she said softly.

E. J. nodded.

Jinx thought of the cinnamon loaf she'd splurged on earlier in the week. "How about some French toast? With a little surprise," she said in an attempt to lighten the mood.

E. J.'s eyes snapped open. "Surprise." She blinked. "I can't believe I forgot. I have a surprise for you." She pulled away, grabbed her keys from her purse, and raced out the front door.

Stunned, Jinx stood motionless. *What the heck?*

E. J. was back in under a minute. She held something behind her back and gave Jinx a wide grin. She sidled toward her. "Take off your shirt."

"What?" Jinx laughed. "Baby, really. I need to eat some breakfast and go to work."

"No, it's not that," E. J. said, mischief flashing in her eyes. "I promise I won't molest you...much. Trust me."

Jinx eyed her, a little suspicious, but did as E. J. asked.

When Jinx stood in just her jeans and sports bra, E. J. whipped something from behind her back with a flourish and held it up for Jinx to see. "Ta-da."

Jinx took in the light blue T-shirt, with the German shepherd on the front, the woman, the half-eaten package of steak. Excitement flooded her, and she felt her eyes go wide. She pointed. It was the shirt she'd told E. J. about, the one she'd wanted from the catalog years ago. "It's...I can't...How'd you..."

E. J. laughed. "Now who can't finish a sentence?" She reached up and pulled the shirt over Jinx's head. "Let's see how it looks."

Jinx pushed her arms into the sleeves and pulled it down over her torso. "I can't believe this." She smoothed her hands over the picture on the front.

With a huge smile, E. J. ran her gaze over Jinx's chest, then up to her face. She stilled, and her expression changed. "It looks great on you."

Jinx couldn't stop grinning and rubbing her palms over her middle. "Where'd you get this?"

E. J. chuckled. "I work for Bad Dog," she said. Her tone said, *duh*. "It's a popular shirt, so it's usually in stock in some of our stores. When I saw it yesterday, I had to get it. I took it as a sign that I should follow my instincts and come try to find you."

Jinx couldn't stop feeling the fabric and staring down at the decal. "Thank you." She wanted to say more, something that would convey what she was feeling. There was gratitude, but there was more than that, too. No one had ever done anything like this for her, at least not in a *very* long time. Her father would occasionally bring her a special gift from a business trip to an unusual place, and Andrea had given her a music box once that played "Teddy Bear Picnic"—Jinx's favorite song at the time. They were ten. And Reggie and Sparkle had given her gifts, and she'd loved them and been thankful, but that made more sense. They were her best friends. They knew her and cared about her. E. J. was almost a stranger—though Jinx had to admit, she didn't feel like one. "How did you know what size to get?" was all she could think of to say.

E. J. smirked. "I do have a little knowledge of your body."

Jinx laughed and pulled her close. She held her and rubbed her cheek over E. J.'s hair. "Thank you."

E. J. embraced Jinx, and they stood in each other's arms for a long moment.

Jinx remembered their good-bye kiss at the door of E. J.'s hotel suite, and the ache of loneliness that'd chilled her. She felt it creeping close. She couldn't do that again. She cleared her throat and eased E. J. away. "How about breakfast?" she said softly.

They ate and cleaned up, touching occasionally, but Jinx was careful to keep a thin barrier between them. If she didn't, she'd likely make a fool of herself. She didn't want to ruin what they'd shared. E. J. seemed a little distracted, probably eager to get on the road, to get to whatever waited for her at home.

They shared one last kiss, then E. J. pressed against her. "Echo Jenay," she whispered.

Jinx willed herself quiet at the caress of E. J.'s breath across her ear. "What?"

"E. J. stands for Echo Jenay." E. J. stepped back and smiled.

A beautiful name for a beautiful woman, was what Jinx wanted to say. "Much better than Earl Jarvis," was what she said.

E. J. gave one last wave as she backed out of Jinx's driveway and headed down the street.

As Jinx watched the Lexus turn the corner, she took a deep breath and shifted her thoughts to the day ahead. She had responsibilities. *Dirty dogs need me.*

She stepped into the business office of Canine Complete, where the employees signed in, to find Sparkle, rather than the actual secretary, at the desk.

"I expected you to be late this morning," Sparkle said, scrolling through something on the computer screen.

Jinx checked the wall clock. Two minutes to spare. "Nope. Why would I be late?"

Sparkle narrowed her eyes. "Did your friend spend the night?"

Jinx shifted uncomfortably. Where was Reggie? She'd save her from this inquiry if she was here. Jinx knew, though, that Sparkle was only asking because she cared. "Yes. She did."

"Ha!" Sparkle slapped the desk. "I knew it. Reggie said, *Sweet Pea, Jinx is a grown woman and her private life is none of our business*, but I knew it the second you walked into that bar. You were on her like a rat on a Cheeto. I *knew* you took her home with you."

Jinx laughed. "Well, she would have had a hard time finding a room this weekend."

"Uh-huh, I'm sure that's the reason." Sparkle clicked the mouse and the printer whirred into action. She leaned back in her chair. "What's she like?"

What's she like? Jinx let the question roll around in her mind. *Sweet. Amazing. Beautiful. Classy. Sexy. Kind. Soft.* E. J. was all those things. *And gone.* E. J. was gone, and the worst thing Jinx could do was to dwell on everything else E. J. was or how she made Jinx feel. "It doesn't really matter," she said. "We won't be seeing each other again."

"Why not? Isn't she the mom of the guy who married your niece?"

"Yeah, but it's not like I'll run into her there."

"Not with that bitch sister of yours," Sparkle muttered. "But she'll be back in town sometimes to visit them, won't she?"

"Yes," Jinx said, checking the clock again. She wanted to get to work. She wanted to be done talking about E. J. "But she'll be visiting *them.*"

"Is that what she's doing here this weekend?" Sparkle asked as though she already knew the answer. She always sounded that way. It was that mom thing she did. Jinx had heard her do it with her kids.

"No."

"Why *was* she here?"

Jinx hesitated. Then in a rush, she said, "She came to see if I was okay after the blowup with Andrea."

Sparkle arched an eyebrow. "That's the *only* reason?"

Jinx nodded. "Seems so." She hadn't really wanted to have this conversation, but now that it was taking place, she was curious what Sparkle's take on that would be. Jinx hadn't been able to figure it out.

Sparkle gave her a measuring look. "Oh, Jinxie. If she hurts you, I'll have to hunt her down and kick her ass." She pulled the pages from the printer tray and handed them to Jinx.

Jinx felt that deep loneliness again, and this time it was on her before she could stop it. She had to get a grip and get E. J. out of her mind. The problem was, she didn't want to.

"Whose ass are you kicking so early this morning?" Reggie asked as she came through the back door. She was a welcome interruption. Reggie's presence always gave Jinx a sense of belonging.

Sparkle smiled sweetly. "That little—"

"No one," Jinx said quickly. "We were just chatting."

"Good, 'cause I don't want to have to bail my wife out of jail." Reggie grinned. "You have a nice night?" she asked, draping an arm over Jinx's shoulders.

"I did. A very nice night." Jinx's cheeks heated.

"Good." Reggie gave her a squeeze.

"And now I'm off to earn my keep." Jinx held up the schedule Sparkle had given her and headed to the grooming salon.

By six o'clock, she was finishing up the Slater schnauzers, Punch and Judy, who would only agree to baths if they could take them together. Jinx indulged them and always ended up almost as wet as they did. She finished drying them and handed them off to the part-time groomer, who filled in on Saturdays. On the way home, she picked up a garden special pizza and a salad—her monthly treat—and was more than ready to settle in for the evening with a Netflix movie by the time she pulled into her driveway. As she climbed out of her car, she waved to Kenny, who was sitting on the steps of the empty house across the street. "Be right back," she called.

On her way in, she picked up his dishes from the night before. She'd met Kenny shortly after she'd moved in and established some rapport with him over the course of a few months. She didn't know much about him, but she did know he lived on the streets of the neighborhood, moving around throughout the days so as not to get run off. Jinx had started sharing her dinners with him one day when she'd found him collapsed alongside her driveway. He'd refused anything more. She liked cooking for him. It gave her a sense of connection, kind of like having a family to look out for.

She divided up the food and took his portion to him, then said good night.

He left happy, off to wherever he planned to sleep.

She knew the challenge of finding someplace new often enough so as not to draw attention, yet safe enough to know it was okay to close your eyes. She'd offered Kenny the bedroom she didn't use, or even a spot on her back porch, with no strings attached, but he'd declined. She could empathize. It was hard to trust anyone when you lived on the streets.

With her own dinner, she settled on the bed and reached for the TV remote. E. J.'s scent drifted up from the bedding. Jinx inhaled, then lifted the pillow and buried her face in it, breathing in deeply. She was instantly aroused, and a sweet ache swelled in her chest.

No, she didn't want to forget E. J. yet. She wanted to hold on to her just a little longer. She picked up the small CD player from the end table, pressed the buds into her ears, and punched the play button. Claude Debussy's "Clair de lune" began, and she remembered kissing E. J. good-bye in the hotel. She lay back on the bed they'd shared and let herself remember more.

She'd start forgetting tomorrow.

CHAPTER SIX

E. J. sat at her desk and approved the drafts her administrative assistant placed in front of her. She had started out listening to each explanation Gwen gave—this is the authorization for the hiring of additional staff in Palo Alto, the request to HQ for the acquisition of the adjacent storefront in San Jose, the letter to Brian in Frisco about…Somewhere along the line, though, she had stopped, distracted as she had been for the past week and a half.

She had really believed seeing Jinx again and knowing she had recovered from the confrontation with Andrea would be all she needed to put the whole experience out of her mind—and it *had* put *that* out of her mind. She was no longer concerned about her. Now, however, in addition to the memories of that first night they had shared, she also kept reliving Jinx's excruciating tenderness. It had threatened to break E. J. apart—both physically and emotionally—and then, later, the strength of her thrusts inside E. J., the care and nurturing with which she fed her those delicious berries, that look with which she had taken her in, and her vulnerability talking about Rex. E. J. had never felt anything like it. Days later, she still couldn't let it go.

She shoved her fingers into her hair. *What is it about that woman?* What did she do to E. J. that made her break all her own rules, forget everything else? She never should have let Jinx stay the night in the hotel room. That had started everything. When she had awakened after their first round, she should have roused Jinx and politely told her it was time for her to leave, that E. J. needed to be up early in the morning. That always worked. Instead, she had eased on top of her and kissed her awake. Effective, but with an entirely different result.

Then, when she *had* gotten away, she had *gone back*. Something else she never did. There had been women she had seen more than once, but when she truly decided something was over, it was over. This time, not only had she returned, but she had been so tempted to stay, to wait for Jinx to get off work and spend another night with her—and she knew it wasn't just for the sex. They'd had enough sex, enough bone-melting sex, throughout the night to last E. J. for weeks. The normal E. J. The sane E. J. No, it was the dinner Jinx had cooked for her, the easy way she made her laugh, the fact that she had gotten up in the morning and come back with coffee just for her, the look in her eyes—oh God, those eyes—when E. J. had given her the shirt. And that PB&J. What the hell had been in it? Jinx had said she had a secret ingredient, but that truly was the best PB&J ever made. She'd had the fleeting thought of turning around and going back after that. Thank God she had been almost home.

She straightened and shook her head. She had to stop this. She *had* made it home, and now she needed to be in the moment. Not so preoccupied with all these thoughts and memories that she might as well still be in Jinx's comfortable little house, in her bed, in her arms. *Not helping.*

She walked to the window and stared out over the Sacramento River. She forced her mind to the plethora of details and decisions she *should* be thinking about. She had a pile of work on her desk, as well as three stores she needed to visit over the next two days. She focused. The expansion in San Jose and that damned sexual harassment threat in Fresno. She had met Frank twenty years ago at the kids' Little League tryouts and had written a letter of recommendation for him when he applied at Bad Dog. She was friends with him and his wife. There had to be an explanation. And...*Penguins? Did Gwen say something about penguins?* Baffled, she leafed through the papers Gwen had left. She stopped at a special request purchase order. *Seventeen penguins, one with a red ski mask, and a polar bear.* She strode out to Gwen's desk, paper in hand.

"Fifteen minutes," Taylor said, perched on the corner of Gwen's desk. The gray pencil skirt of her business suit and her white button-up blouse indicated she had been conducting interviews all day. The missing jacket and rolled-up sleeves suggested she was done for the afternoon. She grinned at Gwen. "I win."

"Fine." Gwen handed her a five-dollar bill.

Confused, E. J. held out the purchase order. "What is this?"

"It's an are-you-anywhere-on-the-planet test," Gwen said, taking the sheet. "You failed." Her pixie haircut complemented her delicate features. If her ears had been pointed, she would look like an elf, in all the cute ways.

"But you won me five bucks." Taylor snapped the bill. "We had a bet on how long it would take you to notice that."

E. J. frowned. "Don't you have work to do?"

"You're not my boss." Taylor tucked her winnings into her cleavage.

"Who is these days? Someone should be keeping tabs on you." Taylor and E. J. had started at Bad Dog at the same time and gone through their training together. They had been best friends ever since. Taylor's career choices had taken her into personnel.

"That's not the question. The question is what's had you so completely gone you don't respond to a request for penguins. Which we don't sell, if you were wondering."

E. J. sighed. Had it been that obvious? Apparently so, at least to the two people closest to her. "I'm sorry. I just…I don't know." She rubbed her forehead in an attempt to ward off a budding headache.

Without being asked, Gwen fished a small bottle of Tylenol out of her desk drawer and offered a couple to E. J. "Do you want to talk about it? We could go for ice cream."

"I have a date," Taylor said.

Gwen glared at her. "We could *all* go to Gunther's for ice cream." She returned her attention to E. J. "If you want to talk about it."

E. J. took the pills and downed them with a swallow from the partial bottle of water Gwen handed her. "I met this woman."

Gwen's eyes rounded and her lips formed a perfect o in her "Oh no, Mr. Bill" imitation from old *Saturday Night Live* reruns. "A woman?" Her voice squeaked. She turned to Taylor. "You say it. She can't fire you."

Taylor's expression held astonishment. "The ice queen met a woman with the power to melt her to distraction? Hold the presses."

"Stop it." E. J. checked to make sure no one was waiting at the bank of elevators. "I don't want to talk about it here. I don't know if I want to at all. There really isn't anything to talk about. I'm not seeing her again."

"Oh, there's something to talk about," Taylor said incredulously. "I've *never* known you to lose focus over a woman."

"You have a date," E. J. said, dismissing her.

"Forget my date. I just met her. This is too good." Taylor smiled wickedly. "Besides, I'm only killing time dating. One of these days, Gwen's going to dump that uptight boyfriend of hers and run away with me."

"She's too young for you," E. J. said.

"I don't discriminate."

"I'm too *good* for you," Gwen said in her own defense.

❖

E. J. sat at a table in Gunther's Ice Cream Shop, their standard location for serious talks, and waited for Taylor, who paced the sidewalk outside on the phone. Gwen had made a stop to pick up her dry cleaning. E. J. was a little uncomfortable at the assumption that this was *a serious talk*. It wasn't, really. She had seen Jinx twice. Both times had been a pleasurable escape from her daily life. That's all. There wouldn't be another time. She just had to get her head back in the game.

E. J. watched as Gwen rounded the corner, grabbed Taylor's phone from her hand, and walked inside.

Taylor—as planned, no doubt—hurried after her. "Hey, I wasn't done." Her long dark hair, clipped at her nape, flowed over one shoulder.

"You are, now. We're here for E. J." Gwen smiled pleasantly as she sat down across the table. She handed the phone back to Taylor, the call obviously disconnected.

E. J. smiled.

Gwen had been her admin assistant at Bad Dog since E. J. had *had* an admin assistant, and had moved up with her through her promotions. They worked well together, Gwen often knowing E. J.'s thoughts before E. J. did, and somewhere along the line, they had become friends. Gwen and Taylor together helped keep her on track. With one another, however, they picked and bickered and teased and sometimes downright pissed each other off. E. J. often thought they maybe should just sleep together and see if that alleviated some of the electricity between them.

"Hi, Dennis," Taylor said to the waiter as he set down three water glasses. "I'll have my usual."

"Me, too," E. J. said.

"I'm here to serve." Dennis grinned.

Gwen paused. "Could I see a menu, please?"

"Oh, come on." Taylor took Gwen's purse as she handed it to her and hung it on the back of Gwen's chair. "You know everything they have. Just order something so we can get to the good stuff. We're here for E. J., remember?" She fluttered her lashes and mimicked Gwen's higher tone.

"Okay. I'll have a hot fudge brownie."

"All right. So?" Taylor said to E. J. as Dennis moved away from the table.

E. J. hesitated. She met Taylor's eager gaze, then Gwen's concerned one. She knew they would want to hear different things. Taylor would want to hear where and how she met Jinx and how hot the sex was. Gwen would want to know how E. J. felt and what it was about Jinx that was so different it distracted her all day long. She was more comfortable with Taylor's interests. She took a deep breath. "I met this woman the weekend of Jacob's wedding."

Taylor blinked. "The wedding? And we're just now hearing about it?"

"Hush. Let her talk." Gwen played with the single pearl at her throat. "We can get after her for that later."

What next? E. J. folded the corner of her napkin. "Her name's Jinx."

"Like the cat?" Taylor asked.

"Or the superhero." Gwen's offer seemed more a suggestion than a statement.

"The superhero," E. J. said. She softened at the memory of their banter over the names.

Gwen and Taylor exchanged glances.

"Her real name's Michelle, but I heard only her family call her that." E. J. thought of Tiffany and the warm greeting she had given Jinx. "She introduced herself to me as Jinx. And that's what her friends call her."

Taylor's brow furrowed. "You've already met her family and friends?" she asked, the implication evident.

"Not the way you mean," E. J. said. Why was this so hard? These were her besties. "She's Tiffany's aunt. So she's actually part of the family...sort of."

"Sort of?" Gwen sipped her water.

"I don't know all the details," E. J. said, "but something happened, and she isn't welcome in the family anymore. Apparently, her sister, Tiffany's mother, hates her. Tiffany invited her to the wedding without telling her mom."

"Okay, that sucks for them, but what does it have to do with you?" Taylor's cut-to-the-chase approach sometimes irritated E. J., but this time she appreciated the help staying on point.

"I met Jinx two days before the wedding in a bar, and we spent the night together."

Gwen's mouth dropped open. "The *whole* night?"

"I know," E. J. said. "And no, I can't tell you why I let her stay. Other than I just..." She gave a small shrug. How could she say it? It seemed so simple, and yet, it made no sense. "It just feels good to be with her."

Taylor fell back in her chair and stared at E. J. "Man, that must have been one hell of a night."

"It was, actually." E. J. felt herself blush. "And so was the second one." There. How was that for cutting to the chase?

Now, both her friends were staring at her.

"And I can't get her out of my head. I can't stop wondering what she's doing. There are questions I wanted to ask her but didn't, and now I wish I had."

Taylor and Gwen continued to stare.

E. J. waited. "Say something," she said finally.

Taylor narrowed her eyes. "Who are you, and where's E. J.'s body?"

E. J. propped her elbows on the table and buried her face in her hands. "I know. That's exactly how *I* feel." She pressed her fingertips to her forehead, wondering if she had actually taken the Tylenol Gwen had given her.

"Are you going to see her again?" Gwen asked.

"No," E. J. said firmly. She sounded confident, even to herself.

"Why not?" Gwen's voice was softer.

E. J. sat back as Dennis set her black and tan in front of her. "Thank you." She smiled up at him and waited for him to finish serving the others. It gave her a moment to process the question. *Because I'm not looking for anything other than casual. Because I don't have time for a relationship.* Those were the reasons she used most. More specific to this case? *Because my kids don't know I'm gay, and Jinx is way too close to the situation. Because I need to be careful with Jacob due to what happened to him.* She sighed and picked up her spoon. "Because it's too complicated," she said. "And I don't do complicated."

Gwen pushed her hot fudge brownie to the center of the table, and E. J. scooped the cherry off the top and ate it with a spoonful of her own whipped cream.

"It sounds like she's different," Gwen said, her tone conversational. "And like you felt a connection with her. It might be worth it."

"She is different," E. J. said, although she couldn't figure out how the words made it out of her mouth.

"How?" Taylor still studied her.

E. J. pondered the question. She remembered that innocence she had seen in Jinx, how she had blushed in the bar, the shy way she had invited E. J. to stay at her house, how she had cried over Rex in E. J.'s arms. *Have I ever cried in someone's arms?* She recalled the sparkle in Jinx's eyes and her excitement when she had told E. J. about the shirt she liked. Her pure joy when E. J. had given it to her was like a child's at Christmas. Then there was the heat, that slow smile that lit

E. J.'s desire, the dark blue of her eyes that pulled E. J. in close, her touch, her kiss. And what about that shadow that revealed itself at certain times, the pain evident at the mention of Andrea, those scars? She was very different, different in ways that made E. J. want to know more about her.

"I don't know." E. J. trailed her spoon through her ice cream as she tried to formulate an answer. "I feel different when I'm with her." She lifted her gaze to Taylor and suddenly felt foolish at what she was about to say. She shifted to Gwen. "I feel...safe...when I'm with her. But not safe from being mugged or murdered or things like that. Safe like..."

Gwen watched her with an expectant expression.

Taylor's spoon had stopped halfway to her mouth.

"Safe like what?" Gwen's voice was barely above a whisper.

"Never mind," E. J. said. "Maybe it was just the wedding. My son got married, for God's sake. And you know how weddings are. They turn the most reasonable people into blubbering romantics. And then there was her house. It reminded me of my grandparents' house, and I got all nostalgic about that. Maybe I'm just emotional about Jacob getting married. And did I tell you Mandy's getting more serious with Russ?"

"Is she?" Gwen asked.

"And they were at the wedding, of course."

Gwen nodded. "So, you think you might be emotional because your kids are all grown up?"

"Wait a minute," Taylor said. "Her house reminded you of your grandparents' house?"

"Yes."

"Your grandparents were broke."

"They were not," E. J. said defensively. "They owned their own business. It didn't do great, but it supported their family. And they loved it."

"You said they didn't live in a very good part of town."

E. J. pursed her lips. "I don't want to get mad at you, so get to the point."

"I was just thinking. Is this woman after your money?"

The thought alone made E. J. burst out laughing. "No," she said after regaining control.

"How do you know?" Taylor asked.

"Let's see. First of all, she hasn't asked me for a thing. Second, she fed me the whole time I was there last weekend. And third, she has never once mentioned us seeing each other again or asked anything about how to stay in touch with me. *I'm* the one who went back looking for *her*. And I'm not doing that again, so you can save your gold digger worries for *your* next girlfriend."

"It was just a thought," Taylor said, sounding a little embarrassed. "You do make a lot of money." She took a bite of her banana split. "She must have been truly outstanding in bed, to cause all this ruckus."

Gwen shook her head. "It always comes back to that with you, doesn't it?"

"Not always." Taylor's tone held a note of defiance. She turned back to E. J. "Was she?"

E. J. arched an eyebrow but didn't answer. "I'm done with this conversation," she said. And she was—done with it with Taylor and Gwen, and with herself. She could control her thoughts, get refocused, and forget all about Jinx. "Thank you, both, for helping me figure out that I went a little crazy over the wedding and my kids both settling down. Now, we have all this ice cream to get through, so what's going on in your lives?"

Chapter Seven

Jinx set the reusable bag filled with groceries on the backseat of her car and climbed in behind the wheel. It'd been a good day. She'd begun early with her frequent practice of watching the sunrise, then taken a long bike ride. The schedule at work had been full, the way she liked it, and she was looking forward to vegetable stir-fry and rice for dinner. The only moment that'd given her pause had been the conversation with Reggie about starting to train as a groomer.

That's what Reggie and Sparkle had wanted from the beginning when they'd hired her, but Jinx had felt overwhelmed when she'd gotten out. So many things were different. The world had changed so much in the years she'd been away. There was so much to learn, so much to get used to. That'd been three years ago, though, and she *had* learned a lot. She was managing. Maybe it was time. If not for herself, maybe for Reggie and Sparkle.

Jinx was aware they'd created the job they'd given her just for her—there were no other *dog washers* in the shop—and even if there had been, Jinx knew what she got paid was well above what a position like that would warrant. She was by no means wealthy—far from it. She lived in a low-income neighborhood, but she was able to live on her own and do it comfortably on what Reggie and Sparkle paid her, as long as she was careful and stuck to her budget. She didn't need much. She was grateful for what they'd given her, and for their offer. Maybe it was time to step it up, start training as a groomer, and pull more of her weight in exchange for everything her friends had done for her.

As she turned onto her street, she saw a car in her driveway. She stared in surprise. Not just a car, a Lexus. Not just *a* Lexus, *E. J.'s* Lexus. Her heartbeat quickened at the same time her stomach knotted. It'd taken a lot longer to stop thinking about E. J. the second time than it had the first. In all honesty, she hadn't completely stopped thinking about her at all, but it'd taken longer to douse that ache of loneliness that gripped her each time they'd said good-bye. And it'd been harder. She didn't know how many more times she could do it, and yet, she wanted nothing more in that moment than to see her again.

She pulled in behind E. J.'s car and turned off the engine.

E. J. sat on the front steps in black slacks and a silvery top, her arms folded over her drawn-up knees.

Jinx retrieved her groceries and looked at E. J. across the roof of the Corolla. E. J.'s expression was uncertain, but more than that, unhappy. Jinx made herself grin. "You know, the longer I live here, the packages the mailman leaves me just get better and better."

E. J. smiled that full, bright smile that lit her face, but it didn't quite reach her eyes today. "He just leaves you things you didn't order?"

Jinx crossed the small yard. "Yup, he's great like that. Kind of like Santa Claus." But if thinking about someone every other waking minute counted, E. J. was exactly what she'd ordered. She set down the bag and eased onto the top step beside E. J. She took in the sadness still evident in her features, then leaned in and pressed her lips lightly to E. J.'s. She held the kiss for a long, luxurious moment.

When they parted, E. J. sighed, her face close to Jinx's. "You feel so good," she whispered. She motioned to the bag. "Look at you, so environmentally conscious."

Jinx continued watching her. "Sparkle gave it to me. She told me to use it."

Something flickered in E. J.'s expression, but she remained silent.

Jinx kissed her again, just a touch of lips, just another little taste. "What are you doing here?" she asked gently.

E. J. hesitated. "I had a horrible, horrible day," she said. She rested her head in the nest of her arms. "And this was the only place I wanted to be."

Jinx drew up her knees and mimicked E. J.'s position. "What happened?"

E. J.'s eyes misted with a veneer of tears. She blinked rapidly. "I had to fire a friend and file charges against him for sexually harassing a sixteen-year-old employee." Her voice broke slightly, but she maintained control. She stared at Jinx as though waiting for something.

Jinx sighed. "What can I do?"

E. J. gazed at her. "Make me laugh." Her voice was barely audible.

Jinx sat up and thought for a moment. "Okay. A priest, a minister, and a rabbi want to see who's best at their job. They each go into the woods, find a bear, and try to convert it. Later, they get together to compare notes. The priest goes first. 'When I found the bear,' he says, 'I read to him from the Catechism and sprinkled him with holy water. Next week is his First Communion.' The minister goes next. 'I found a bear by the stream and preached God's holy word. The bear was so mesmerized, he let me baptize him.' Then they both look down at the rabbi, who's lying on a gurney in a body cast. 'Looking back,' says the rabbi, 'maybe I shouldn't have started with the circumcision.'"

E. J. burst out laughing. Her eyes were still moist, but a new light sparked in them. "That's kind of appropriate for the situation, isn't it?"

Jinx chuckled. "I thought so."

E. J. sat up, giggling. "Do you know another one?"

"Do I know another one?" Jinx asked incredulously. E. J. had no idea how many hours of Jinx's life had been whiled away with shared joke books. "When a zoo's gorilla dies, the zookeeper hires an actor to put on a costume and act like an ape until the zoo can get another one. In the cage, the actor makes faces, swings around, and draws a big crowd. He then crawls across a partition and onto the top of the lion's cage, infuriating the lion. But the actor stays in character—until he loses his grip and falls in. Terrified, he screams, 'Help me! Help me!' But it's too late. The lion pounces, opens its massive jaws, and whispers, 'Shut up! Do you want to get us both fired?'"

E. J. laughed again. "Okay, more. This is working."

"What did the bartender say when Charles Dickens ordered a martini?"

"I don't know."

"Olive or twist?"

E. J. laughed harder.

"Why shouldn't a lawyer play hide-and-seek?"

E. J. shook her head.

"Because no one will look for him."

E. J. snorted.

"What do you call a potato that's gone over to the Dark Side? A Vader Tott."

E. J. chortled and kicked her feet.

Jinx laughed, enjoying her responses. "Why can't you hear a psychiatrist using the bathroom? Because the P is silent."

E. J. threw her head back and cackled. She clutched her sides. "Oh God, stop. I need air."

Jinx laughed and waited for her to get control.

As E. J. calmed, chuckling now and then, she took Jinx's hand. "Thank you. You always make me laugh."

"You're welcome." Jinx smiled. "Is that really the reason you're here?"

E. J. made a noncommittal noise. "One of them." She glanced down to their intertwined fingers. "Is it okay? That I'm here?"

Despite the fact E. J. hadn't actually answered the question—or maybe she'd asked the wrong one—it was *so* okay E. J. was there. Jinx grinned and nodded.

E. J.'s manner eased, and she squeezed Jinx's hand before eyeing the bag. "What's in there?"

"Ah. Hungry?" Jinx caught sight of Kenny shuffling down the sidewalk in front of the house. She waved.

"Do you know him?" E. J. asked, leaning a little closer to Jinx.

"His name's Kenny."

"He was sitting across the street watching me earlier. It made me nervous."

Jinx rested her arm around E. J.'s shoulders and stroked her neck with her thumb. "You don't need to worry about Kenny. He was just making sure you didn't break in and steal my good silver."

E. J. smiled. "So, he's security?"

"Well, you know." Jinx shrugged. "I don't have a guard dog." She tightened her hold and pulled E. J. closer, inhaling the light scent of jasmine left from a long, busy day. "You want some dinner?"

"Mmm." E. J. brushed her lips across Jinx's. "I'd love some dinner."

As Jinx unpacked the groceries, laying the fresh vegetables out on the counter beside the cans of baby corn and water chestnuts, E. J. surveyed the scene. "What can I do to help?"

"Nothing," Jinx said, folding up the bag and sliding it into a drawer. "You had a bad day. You get to be pampered and taken care of. Isn't that the way it works?"

In truth, Jinx didn't have a clue how it worked. She'd never been in a relationship in the real world. *Oh God!* Is that what this was—a relationship? It felt like it. It felt like E. J. had been in her life forever at moments like these. But no, this wasn't a relationship. It couldn't be. She was still trying to piece together a life on the outside, as well as make peace with Andrea. She had her hands full. And E. J.? She didn't want a relationship. She didn't want anything that might reveal the lie she was living, and Jinx was done lying. Besides, E. J. didn't even know her, and as soon as she did, whatever this was would probably be over.

E. J. stepped into Jinx's arms and sighed. "Where have you been all my life?"

Jinx shifted nervously. *If you only knew.* She'd have to tell her, though. This was the third time they'd seen each other, their third date in their own odd little way. And yes, each time, Jinx had truly believed they'd never see one another again, but E. J. kept coming back. If Jinx let it go on much longer without coming clean, it would turn into an actual deception, and Jinx had promised herself, this time around, to live authentically. No more lies or dishonesty. No more breaking laws. No more hurting people. She had to tell her the truth about her past, about her time in prison and the reason for it—but first, food. Jinx smiled. "You just relax. Freshen up, if you want. Dinner will be ready in about a half hour."

As Jinx started the rice and began chopping vegetables, E. J. retrieved her suitcase from her car and disappeared into the bathroom. Jinx heard the shower turn on and paused to listen. She remembered how natural it'd felt the morning E. J. had been there drinking her coffee as Jinx had made sandwiches. Jinx had been so comfortable. Now, she closed her eyes and allowed herself to feel E. J.'s presence, the sense of companionship, of connection, and not only was E. J. there again now, but Jinx had more than an inkling that somehow, even though it'd been unspoken, they'd already agreed she would be staying the night once more. Jinx smiled to herself, but the knowledge of all she had to reveal to E. J. settled like a stone in the pit of her stomach.

What if E. J. bolted? What if her reaction was to put as much distance between them as she could, as fast as possible? Could Jinx blame her? That might actually be for the best, for E. J.'s sake as well as her own. E. J. was already worried about her son finding out she dated women. What would his response be to her sleeping with a felon? And Jinx's feelings for E. J. grew stronger every time they saw one another, every time they touched. If her past was going to be a deal breaker, which it had been with the two other women she briefly dated since returning home, wouldn't it be less painful for things to end sooner rather than later? Torn between not wanting to take the risk and knowing she must, she returned her attention to the meal.

When E. J. emerged from the bathroom, Jinx was scooping the stir-fry over two plates of rice. She'd bought enough for three servings, but they'd been for her and Kenny's dinner and leftovers for her lunch the next day. The same had happened the last time E. J. had shown up unexpectedly, but Jinx didn't care. She'd loved her PB&J the next day, given it reminded her that E. J. had come back and she'd gotten to spend another night with her. Tomorrow's PB&J would be just as delicious for the same reason. She'd gladly eat PB&Js every day until her next paycheck for more time with E. J. She glanced over her shoulder to ask if E. J. had found everything she needed, but the words never made it out.

E. J. stood there, hair damp, eyes bright, wearing tan, loose-fitting athletic shorts and a yellow tank top with, clearly, no bra.

Jinx's breath caught. She'd seen E. J. in her work clothes, classy, professional, head-turning. She'd seen her, and felt her, completely naked, the curves of her hips and breasts and the slight roundness of her belly, her skin warm and soft to the touch. In either circumstance,

Jinx could barely take her eyes off her, but this—the sight of E. J. so casual, so at ease, the expanse of bare flesh that teased the memory of the rest concealed beneath the light fabric—was far more than simply beauty or sexiness. *This*, Jinx was sure, was a side of E. J. very few people got to see, and her body responded to the realization that she was one of those few. Some of E. J.'s guard appeared to be down—not all, Jinx could tell, but some—and a different E. J. peeked out.

"What's the matter?" E. J.'s smile faded. She looked down at herself. "I'm sorry. You said to relax. Is this too—"

"Uh...no." Jinx cleared her throat. "Not at all. You look...very... relaxed." She turned back to the plates to quell the desire pulsing through her. She tore off a piece of plastic wrap from the roll and started covering Kenny's dinner.

E. J.'s arms snaked around Jinx's waist and the full length of her body pressed against her backside.

Jinx stilled, a quiet moan escaping her throat.

E. J. rose onto her toes and lifted the hair off the back of Jinx's neck. She kissed the bare skin. "Dinner smells good," she whispered.

Jinx turned in her embrace, Kenny's meal in one hand. "It'll be just a sec." She looked down into E. J.'s eyes, their green darker with arousal.

E. J. glanced at the covered plate and stepped back. "Okay, you have to tell me what that's about."

Jinx chuckled at the abrupt shift in focus, but she was grateful for the reprieve. "It's for Kenny."

E. J. looked up. "Kenny? The guy outside?"

Jinx nodded.

E. J. blinked, looking confused.

"He's homeless," Jinx said. "He doesn't have anything."

"So, you feed him?"

Jinx shifted, uncertain of E. J.'s questions. "Just dinner." E. J. couldn't be one of those people who wouldn't give a homeless person money because *they'll just spend it on booze* or wouldn't give them food because *it'll just encourage them to hang around*. Could she? If she was, Jinx was fairly sure an ex-con wouldn't be in the picture long. Again, better to know now. She waited.

E. J. hesitated. "Every night?"

Jinx nodded again. She looked away, then back to E. J.'s bemused expression. "He won't take anything else. But he doesn't have any food. And he—"

E. J. pressed her fingertips to Jinx's lips, silencing her. Then she replaced them with her mouth in a deep, fervent kiss.

Jinx struggled to hold on to the plate. She gripped E. J. around the hips with her free arm and pulled her against her. When E. J. finally drew away, they were both panting.

E. J. stared into Jinx's eyes. "Every time I see you, you amaze me in a new way."

"What do you mean?" Jinx wasn't even sure she'd heard correctly. All she knew was one more kiss like that and she'd have E. J. down on the kitchen floor.

"That's so kind." E. J.'s breath was still uneven. She traced Jinx's jaw, then slipped her fingers into Jinx's hair. She started to lean in again.

"No, no." Jinx caught her by the waist and eased her away. "Let me take this to Kenny."

"Of course." E. J. smiled a little sheepishly. "I'm sorry."

Jinx waved to Kenny from the doorway, then set the plate and thermos on the porch as she did every night. They rarely spoke, but every once in a while, she'd find a small bundle of wildflowers beside his empty dishes the next day. When she stepped back inside and closed the door, E. J. still watched her.

"Okay." Jinx felt herself blush a little. E. J.'s attention, what she thought of her, the intensity of her desire, was so incredibly unbelievable, sometimes it overwhelmed her—and, already, the potential loss of it terrified her. "Okay, now, what would make you happy? Food or…"

"Both," E. J. said without hesitation. She shot Jinx a burning gaze. "In that order and very close together."

Jinx grinned. "I have the perfect plan, then." She retrieved a pair of chopsticks she'd saved from takeout and grabbed the remaining plate. This had actually been her plan all along. She took a bottle of water from her fridge and held it out to E. J. "White wine?"

E. J. laughed and took it. "Mmmm," she said, studying the label. "A very good year."

"Follow me." Jinx led her to the bed, propped a pillow against the headboard, and settled into it. She opened her arms, the plate in one hand, and patted the hollow of her shoulder. As E. J. snuggled in against her, Jinx's arousal simmered, but she could get through dinner—she hoped. "I'm sorry if I smell like wet dog. I could go take a quick shower while you eat, if you want."

E. J. snaked an arm over Jinx's stomach and a leg across her thighs. "You're not going anywhere." She tilted her head up and inhaled deeply. "At least you smell like *clean* wet dog." She giggled. She buried her nose in Jinx's neck. "Actually, you know what you smell like?" She whispered. Her warm breath feathered across the sensitive spot behind Jinx's earlobe.

Jinx's pulse jumped. "What?"

E. J. nuzzled closer. "You smell like a well taken care of, clean, wet dog." She inhaled again. "You smell like the delicious stir-fry you so sweetly made for Kenny and me. You smell like laughter. And kindness. And comfort." She looked up into Jinx's face. "And the best damned sex I've ever had."

A flurry of desire caused a tremor in Jinx's abdomen. Arousal pooled between her thighs, but she managed a grin. She picked up a mushroom with the chopsticks and held it to E. J.'s lips.

With a smile, E. J. took it. "You certainly know how to pamper," she murmured as she chewed.

Jinx took her own bite.

They ate quietly for a while, the only sound in the room an occasional contented sigh from E. J. as she closed her mouth around a clump of sauce-soaked rice or baby corn, or a low moan from Jinx at E. J.'s hand caressing her stomach beneath her T-shirt.

"Do you always eat in bed?" E. J. asked finally as she tightened her leg over Jinx's hips and sat up, straddling her.

"Only when I'm feeding a beautiful woman." Jinx smiled up at her and gave her some bok choy.

"I hear that's never," E. J. said with a teasing glint in her eyes. She rotated her hips ever so slightly. "I heard no one ever comes over."

Jinx jerked as a jolt of arousal shot through her. "That seems to be changing." She nudged up into E. J. "Just a couple weeks ago this gorgeous blonde called me from a bar, and when I went to get her, she came home with me and we ate strawberries right here in this very bed."

"Hmmm," E. J. said, accepting the last bite of stir-fry. "She sounds like a floozy."

Jinx laughed. "Maybe, but a very sexy one."

E. J. gasped and swatted Jinx's side. "You were supposed to defend my honor."

"It's a little hard when you're sitting on top of me looking like that."

"Looking like what?" E. J.'s tone was seductive. She took the plate and leaned over to set it on the nightstand. Her breasts hung loose in the confines of the tank top, and the stiff points that'd been taunting Jinx since E. J. came out of the bathroom moved closer to Jinx's face.

Jinx cradled a breast in each hand, their weight playing against her palms. She thumbed the nipples.

E. J. moaned and tightened her thighs around Jinx's hips.

"Like that," Jinx whispered, wanting to keep E. J. right where she was. Jinx was learning when E. J. wanted to wait and when she couldn't, when she needed release before anything else. Jinx could always wait, and right now she wanted nothing more than to take her time pleasuring E. J. for as long as E. J. could stand it.

❖

As E. J. began to calm from an all-consuming orgasm, Jinx covered her lips with her own.

E. J. moaned softly into Jinx's mouth as Jinx let her fingers linger with two final strokes, then slipped out. E. J. collapsed onto her, and Jinx took her into a gentle embrace.

E. J. lay quietly for a long time, her breathing slow, her body relaxed. Just when Jinx thought she might have fallen asleep, she spoke. It was almost a whisper. "As I said, you certainly know how to pamper."

Jinx laughed softly. "I'm not done." She kissed the top of E. J.'s head. "There's a lot more pampering to be done."

E. J. smiled up at her. "Well, there are some things I'd like to do to you, too. Do you think there's time?" She eased her hand beneath Jinx's shirt.

Jinx fought to stay focused as E. J.'s nails grazed her bare skin. "I don't know. How long can you stay?" She'd meant it as a joke, but E. J. sobered.

A light blush colored her cheeks. Her fingers slowed. "Would you mind very much if I stayed the weekend? If you don't have other plans, that is. If you do, I—"

"No." The question took Jinx by surprise. "I...That's..." A dozen thoughts raced through her head at once. "I'd love that," was the winner, and she couldn't help but grin when she said it. "Oh, I have to work tomorrow."

"That's fine. I have work I can do to keep me busy. And I want to make you dinner, so I'll need to do some shopping."

Jinx chuckled. "You've thought this all out." But Jinx hadn't. She tensed. If E. J. stayed that long, she'd *have* to tell her about her past.

E. J.'s eyes darkened. "I have. But—"

"Yes," Jinx said, resolved.

E. J. smiled and kissed her tenderly. "Now, about those things *I* want to do." She sat up and moved her other hand under Jinx's shirt. She pushed the fabric up Jinx's torso. "You're way overdressed for them."

Anxiety rolled through Jinx. It was time, especially now that this wasn't going to be another one-nighter. She couldn't let things go any further. As much as she wanted out of her clothes, as much as she wanted to feel E. J. naked against her, she didn't want a lie between them, didn't want *anything* between them. If E. J. knowing the truth was going to ruin everything, better to know, now.

Jinx caught E. J.'s hands and stilled them. "Baby," she said, hoping it wouldn't be the last time she could call her that. "I need to tell you something."

Chapter Eight

E. J. sensed a shift in Jinx, and a weight settled into the room. She looked down from where she sat astride Jinx's thighs to find her watching her, and that shadow that normally lurked in the depths of her blue eyes was now veiling them. *What happened?* "That's a line rarely followed by anything good." She tried to alleviate the strain. "Don't tell me you're a Buddhist nun and you've broken your vows of celibacy for me." She attempted a grin but knew it fell flat.

Jinx smiled hesitantly. "No. No vows of celibacy here." She swallowed. "But you *are* the first woman I've slept with in over ten years." She eased her shirt down. "Can we get up? Maybe sit at the table?"

E. J. tried once more to lighten the mood, pushing away the anxiety building inside. She ran her fingertip down Jinx's fly. "You're sure you don't want to finish first?"

Jinx caught her hand. "Baby, please. I want to get this over with."

All signs of Jinx's playful nature—the laughter in her eyes, that slow smile, the crinkle of her tiny laugh lines—were gone, and that shadow seemed to have shaded her entire face.

"All right," E. J. said, easing off the bed. "It sounds important."

"It is."

They settled at the table.

Jinx looked at the refrigerator, the front door, the end table... anywhere but at E. J. "Now I don't know where to start." Her lips trembled slightly.

E. J. took her hand. She had never seen Jinx like this. Granted, this was only the third time she had been with Jinx at all—if you didn't count the wedding...*The wedding.* She *had* seen Jinx like this, at the top of the stairs after Andrea had said those horrible things. Was she about to learn what all that was about? She leaned across the table. "Just start anywhere, sweetie. It's okay."

An uneasy moment passed. "Okay," Jinx said finally. "I'm going to say the worst first."

E. J. nodded.

"I spent twenty years in a federal prison for bank robbery," she blurted. "I've only been out for three years."

E. J. froze. Not in surprise. Surprise was what you felt when people jumped out from behind the couch on your birthday. Shock? No, that was still too mild. E. J. was stunned. In fact, she couldn't have been more stunned if Jinx had told her she was a man. This just didn't fit. Everything she knew about Jinx, everything she felt when she was with her, didn't fit with being told she was a bank robber. She felt her face go pale, then instantly saw tears well in Jinx's eyes.

Jinx looked away. "You can go if you want. It's okay."

A part of her did want to leave—a part of her wanted to bolt without looking back. That's what she always did at the first sign of conflict or drama. She had seen that same deep pain in Jinx's face at the wedding, though. She couldn't bear to be the cause of it. But what was she supposed to say? Her mind was just as frozen as her body, but she had to say something. What if Jinx *had* told her she was a man? She would have questions, right? Surely, there were questions to be asked here as well. *So ask something.* "Bank robbery?" was all she could manage, but it bought a little time.

Jinx nodded. A few tears escaped and fell from her chin.

E. J. cleared her throat. "That doesn't make any sense. How could someone like you rob banks?"

"Bank." Jinx turned to her with a hopeful expression.

"What?"

"Just one," Jinx said.

Okay, that was something. *Just one.* At least she wasn't Bonnie or Ma Barker. *One bank. But why?*

Jinx took a deep breath. "I was twenty-one. I was an addict and living on the streets. We started stealing to buy drugs. Small stuff, at first, and it just kept getting bigger and bigger."

"We?" It wasn't the most important thing to focus on, but it was something—something to keep E. J. in her seat. *Breathe.*

"Me and some friends." Jinx looked down at her hands.

E. J. watched her. She thought of Andrea, what she had heard about Tiffany's grandparents, Andrea's—and Jinx's—parents, the huge estate. "Why were you living on the streets?"

"I ran away after my father died. Nora...his wife, my stepmother...was going to ship me off to some boarding school so her friends wouldn't know when she cut me out of everything. I decided if I was going to be on my own, I'd rather it be someplace I knew. Either way, I'd be living on the streets. Doing it here seemed like a better option. So I left."

E. J. looked into Jinx's eyes. They were still wet, but they were clearer. The more Jinx shared, the steadier she seemed. That made sense. Someone like Jinx would hate keeping a secret like this. Still, a part of E. J. wished she had. This changed everything, didn't it? She rose and paced the kitchen, feeling Jinx's gaze on her each time she changed direction. It still didn't make sense. The Jinx she knew— even though she had known her for such a short time—wouldn't do something like rob a bank. And something else wasn't right. What was it? E. J. slowed. "Twenty years?"

Jinx nodded.

"That's your entire adult life."

Another nod.

E. J. paused. She didn't want her next statement to sound like an accusation, but she didn't know a way around it—and she had to know if there was more. "Isn't that a long time for just one robbery?"

"I only got twelve for the robbery." Jinx rested her elbow on the table and rubbed her forehead. "When I'd been in for ten, there was a turf war between two gangs. Some people died. Everyone involved got time added to her sentence."

E. J.'s heartbeat quickened. "People died?"

"Yes. But I didn't kill anyone, E. J., I swear," Jinx said in a rush. "It all happened so fast. Val got jumped, and I went for her...

Then everybody was in it. And nobody could get out." Her eyes went unfocused as though she had gone back in time, seeing it, reliving it.

E. J. waited. She wanted to go to her, but she couldn't make herself move.

When Jinx shook her head and returned her attention to E. J., they stared at one another.

With a jolt, E. J. remembered. "Is that where you got those scars?"

"One of them. The one on my back. I got shanked." Jinx looked away. "The one on my side is from a gunshot during the robbery." Her voice broke.

E. J. swayed. Suddenly, there wasn't enough air in the room. Jinx had been cut with a knife *and* shot. She could have died twice. E. J. had no frame of reference for any of this. These kinds of things—stabbings, shootings, bank robberies, fights between prison gangs—didn't happen to people she knew. She only read about them in newspapers, books, or saw them in movies. She gripped the edge of the counter for balance.

Jinx was at her side, slipping an arm around her waist. "C'mon, baby. Come sit down." She led her back toward the bed.

E. J. clutched at Jinx's shirt. She couldn't shake the realization of what Jinx had just said. She *should* be grappling with the fact that she had been sleeping with an ex-convict, a felon. Instead, she was fighting back panic from the thought of Jinx possibly dying before E. J. had found her. Tears burned her eyes.

Jinx eased her onto the mattress and sat beside her.

"You could have died." Terror gripped E. J., and she began to tremble. She gasped and pulled Jinx close. She held on tight. "I can't lose you."

Jinx wrapped her arms around E. J. and cradled her. "Baby, I'm okay. It was a long time ago." She stroked E. J.'s back. "I'm right here."

E. J. felt Jinx's warm breath on her face, her heartbeat beneath her hand. She began to calm. Embarrassment flooded her. She had to get control of herself, gain some composure—or at least fake it. She didn't fall apart in front of lovers. She never gave up her edge. She took a deep breath and cleared her throat. "I'm sorry," she said, easing out of Jinx's embrace.

Jinx studied her, eyes wide. "Do you want some water…or something?"

Wine. No, something stronger. Whiskey. But she knew Jinx had neither. She shook her head. "I'm fine." She had to focus on something else. What had Jinx said? *Bank robbery.* Yes, but she couldn't go there, yet. *Living on the streets? Father's wife? Nora?* She forced herself to focus. "Nora Tanner wasn't your mother?"

Jinx blinked. "Uh, no."

E. J. knew what she must be thinking: *Out of everything I said, that's what you heard?* Truthfully, though, out of everything Jinx had said, *that* was about all she could grasp at the moment. She forced herself to let go of Jinx completely and scooted farther onto the bed. She leaned back against the pillow and headboard. "Tell me about that. How you ended up living there. What happened to your mother?"

Jinx's posture relaxed, but her expression remained wary. "Okay." She moved up beside E. J. "I don't remember much about her. Just what my father told me. He said he and my mother were high school sweethearts, but his parents didn't approve. She wasn't good enough for him."

E. J. stared straight ahead and let Jinx's voice soothe her as it always did.

"They told him he had to break up with her, but he kept seeing her behind their backs. Finally, when he graduated, he had to go away to college. He said he intended to come back and marry her, but once he moved away and started hanging out in the circles his parents wanted him in, it got easier to just go along with what they wanted. He met Nora, and their parents agreed it was a perfect match, so they got engaged."

E. J. let herself sink into the story. She could do this one. The rest? She had no idea what to do with the rest. She should be leaving—packing her things and marching straight out the door. She had left women, affairs, flings, for far less than anything like a criminal record and a prison sentence. In fact, *every* time she had left, it was for far less, because *this* kind of thing just didn't happen. She had ended her involvement with Rhonda, the only woman she had ever considered herself even remotely serious with, because Rhonda wanted her to meet her sister when she had come to town, and *that*, E. J. felt, had held too much potential for drama. Yet—she had already overlooked the fact that Jinx's niece was married to Jacob and had repeatedly come to the same city in which they lived, for the sole purpose of seeing Jinx. And here she was, listening to Jinx's childhood story, *knowing* there were still the explanations of living on the streets, drug addiction, bank robbery, and twenty years of prison to come. *And who the hell is Val?*

"He never stopped loving my mother, though," Jinx said, her tone even. "He felt guilty for not going back and taking a stand for her. A week before the wedding, he went to see her to say how sorry he was, but seeing her again brought up all his feelings and they ended up in bed. That's when she got pregnant. He went forward with the wedding, and she never told him. He didn't know anything about me until my mother was killed in a car accident when I was five, and a social worker contacted him."

E. J. glanced at Jinx. While her voice held no emotion, her eyes were hard with what looked like a mixture of anger and sorrow.

"He had to explain the whole thing to Nora, and they took me in, but she made sure we both paid for my existence until the day he died and the day I left."

E. J. remembered Andrea's words. *My mother was right about you. You're nothing but trash that came from trash.* Who would say that about a child? Who would even think it? E. J.'s heart ached for the little girl Jinx had been. "I'm so sorry." She slipped her hand over Jinx's.

Jinx flinched, then softened when her gaze met E. J.'s.

"Do you remember anything about your mother?"

Jinx's eyes clouded faintly and grew distant as though searching the past. "Not a lot. A bright red shirt with a big smiley face on it. And the smell of maple syrup. I think we ate French toast a lot. And part of a song—something about a sheep and a lion." The very corners of her mouth tipped upward, and she shook her head slightly. "I don't know."

E. J. listened, hoping for more, for Jinx's sake. She couldn't imagine not remembering her mother. She had been no picnic in the park, but at least E. J. had childhood memories of her, even some nice ones.

"I remember her lips on my forehead," Jinx said, a hint of excitement in her tone. "That's how she kissed me good night." She turned to E. J. "I've never remembered that before."

E. J. squeezed Jinx's hand. "Do you look like her?" She would be fine as long as she stayed on this topic.

Jinx shrugged. "I don't look much like my father. Andrea takes after him. So, maybe."

E. J. took in her features—those deep blue eyes that always pulled her in, that easy, warm smile, the dark chestnut hair. This was Jinx, the Jinx E. J. had come to know and trust, the Jinx that made her feel so intensely. She wasn't that other person who robbed banks. She caught herself—bank. Who took drugs. Who spent much of her life in prison. A convict. A felon. No, *this* was Jinx—E. J.'s Jinx.

"E. J.—"

"Shh." E. J. pressed her fingertips to Jinx's lips. "I can't...Just let me..." Let her what? Let her think? Process? She focused on the young Jinx, the young Michelle, who at five was taken to live with strangers, with a woman who hated her very existence. And what about Andrea? That was a question she could ask. "Has Andrea always felt about you the way she does, now?"

"No." Jinx's eyes saddened. "We used to be best friends. We're only three months apart in age, and when we first met, we were instantly inseparable. Our dad had the nanny clear out one of the rooms on Andrea's floor for me, and that's where we lived together for eleven years—until Nora moved me into a room behind the kitchen after my father died. We did *everything* together, when we were little." Jinx seemed far away as she relayed her past.

E. J. listened, eager for every detail.

"Andi loved to sing, and when I first got there, she decided we'd start a singing group. She taught me her favorite songs, and we pretended the coffee table in the TV room was a stage, and we'd put on concerts for Stephanie, our nanny." Jinx laughed softly. "And for me, we'd dress up like pirates and search for buried treasure. I got to be the captain, and Andrea was always the wench."

E. J. smiled, losing herself for a moment in the vision of the two little girls.

"And then, Luke came," Jinx said. Her eyes sparkled, and she grinned. "He worked on the grounds crew and helped take care of the gardens. He played hide-and-seek with us on his breaks, and he built us a tree house." She turned to E. J., her features animated. "It's still there. I saw it at the wedding. We used to play in it for hours. It's where we went to hide from Nora." She chuckled. "God, we had fun."

"What happened?" E. J. asked softly, but she instantly regretted the question.

The light in Jinx's eyes went out, and she shook her head. "I don't know. All of a sudden, when we were about twelve, Andi started changing. She stopped wanting to do anything together at home, and at school—we went to this fancy private academy—she made new friends. I never really fit in there, so I just hung out in the library and studied. As we got into our teens, I tried to talk to her about it, find out what I'd done, but it just made her mad. Finally, she told me she didn't want anything to do with me and to leave her alone. So, I did. After that, I just hung out with Luke or Emmy, his wife—she worked on the house staff—and spent a lot of time in the tree house."

E. J. caressed Jinx's hand.

Jinx gripped her fingers tightly.

"When did your father die?"

Jinx looked down. "When I was sixteen. He had a heart attack. I think he just couldn't take his life anymore. He told me a few months earlier he was sorry he couldn't be stronger for me. Looking back, it was like he was making his amends before leaving me."

E. J.'s temper flared at Jinx's father leaving her so alone in the world at such a young age. *What a coward.* She knew they were getting close to the part she wasn't ready to deal with, but she had to know the rest of the story with Andrea and Nora. "What happened next?"

Jinx sighed. "That's when Nora moved me into a room behind the kitchen so Andrea would have more space to entertain her social circle and *appropriate suitors.* I lost touch with her completely at that point. A little later, I overheard a conversation between Nora and her attorney about sending me to a boarding school in Boston where no one would know when she cut me off at eighteen. So, I saved her the trouble. That's when I ran away."

Jinx paused and looked at E. J., evidently knowing they had reached a crucial moment in the conversation. Maybe Jinx felt the same way. Maybe it was easier to talk about a heartbreaking childhood than a life of drug addiction and crime.

"Jinx, I..." E. J. shifted on the bed. "Can we talk about the rest another time?"

The shadow returned to Jinx's eyes. She nodded.

"Maybe tomorrow," E. J. said quickly. She didn't want Jinx to think she was shutting her down, that she was just planning her escape—and she hoped she wasn't. E. J. just wanted to hold her and sleep. She had no idea how—or even if—she would be able to deal with *the rest* ever, never mind the very next day, but she knew she couldn't right this second. "This is just a lot. Maybe we could both use some sleep."

Jinx looked hopeful. "You'll be here tomorrow?"

"You said I could stay the night." *She said I could stay the weekend.*

"Yeah," Jinx said. "Of course."

As they readied for bed, Jinx watched E. J. as if for cues.

E. J. slipped out of her shorts and tank top. "I want to feel your skin. I want to be close to you."

Without a word, Jinx shed her clothes and crawled under the covers.

E. J. snuggled against her. She needed to feel her warmth, her strength. She needed to feel the Jinx she knew, the one who took care of old dogs and fed homeless people, the one who was so tender and kind and funny. Not a bank robber. Not a convict. She felt Jinx sigh and tighten her arms around her. She let herself sink into the sanctuary of Jinx's little house and her embrace.

Grateful for the respite, she let herself escape into sleep.

CHAPTER NINE

E. J. woke in the early hours of the morning, her naked body tangled in the soft sheets. Surprisingly, she had slept peacefully and as always with Jinx, awakened with that slow simmer of desire. She was curious that hadn't changed with everything she had learned. Still, there was that voice in the back of her mind saying, *Get out. Move on. This is too complicated.* But that voice was always there, no matter who she was seeing. It might be a tad louder now, but it wasn't nearly as deafening as she would have expected. She reached behind her but found only an empty spot where Jinx had fallen asleep earlier, her arms snugly around E. J.

She rolled onto her back and squinted into the darkness of the living room. She glanced toward the bedroom doorway to see if any light from the bathroom threw shadows along the floor. Only the night met her. Her eyelids fell closed, then opened. She wanted more sleep, but she also wanted to know where the heck Jinx was. She sat up and rubbed her face. Where was her phone?

She remembered Taylor texting before dinner, asking if she wanted to hit a club. When she had answered that she wasn't in town, the questions had come in rapid fire. Where was she? Was she with the hot babe from the wedding? When was she coming home? Was she being careful? E. J. had answered the first and the last, then switched off her phone to return her attention to Jinx. *Then what did I do with it?* Her purse?

She climbed out of bed and stumbled toward her little pile of belongings in the corner. She stopped herself. What was she thinking?

She still didn't even have Jinx's number. She would have to remember to get it this time. Even with everything Jinx had told her, she doubted she would be able to stop thinking about her. Maybe even more so, now. *There's still twenty years of prison to get through, though. What am I going to do with that?* She still wanted her number. For now, though, she had no way of contacting her to find out where she had gone in the wee hours of the morning.

She crossed to the window above the sink and peered out into the darkness to see if Jinx's car was in the driveway. All she could see was her own. She moved down the counter and craned her neck, closer to the glass. She still couldn't see. Then, from the corner of her eye, she caught a glimpse of something out the back window of the house. Or someone? A shrouded figure sat on the steps of the back porch. E. J. crept closer. Was it Jinx? She strained to see. It had to be. Who else would it be? She thought of Kenny, then wondered if anyone else hung around Jinx's house for kindness or care. Even if that was so, at this time of night, it really had to be Jinx. She cautiously turned the doorknob and peeked out the crack. "Jinx?" she whispered. Her heart pounded.

The figure turned. "Hey." Jinx's voice was quiet. "What are you doing up?"

E. J. sighed in relief. "I think I woke because you were gone." She eased the door open a little further. The chill of the night air tightened her nipples and raised goose bumps along her bare flesh. "Are you okay? What are you doing out there?"

Jinx hesitated, then opened the blanket wrapped around her in invitation. "C'mere. I'll show you."

"I don't have anything on."

"It's okay. Nobody's out here, and none of the windows from the other houses face this way." Jinx beckoned her with the open blanket. "C'mon. I'll keep you warm."

With a glance around, E. J. scurried across the small porch and beneath Jinx's extended arm. She settled on the lower step between Jinx's legs, the wood cold against her butt and thighs.

Jinx enveloped her in the warmth of the blanket and her body, wrapping her arms tightly around her.

E. J. snuggled in close, relishing the heat on her bare skin and the safety she always felt in Jinx's embrace. She drew up her knees and tucked her feet into the cocoon.

"How are you feeling?" Jinx asked.

"I'm okay," E. J. said, still a little surprised that it was true.

Jinx kissed her temple.

E. J. pressed back into Jinx's small, firm breasts. "What are we doing out here?"

"Wait," Jinx whispered. She closed her lips on E. J.'s earlobe and suckled. Her teeth gently tugged the diamond stud. "Is this all right?"

"Oh, yes." E. J. tilted her head back into the hollow of Jinx's shoulder. "This can't be why you're out here, though," she murmured. "You had no way of knowing I'd come out."

"Shhh." Jinx dipped her head and ran the tip of her tongue down the side of E. J.'s neck. "Trust me."

E. J. did trust her—more and more. Strange that would be true with everything Jinx had shared. But that was just it. She had been so honest, so forthcoming. She arched, giving Jinx more access, and sighed. Her body heated.

Jinx kissed the sensitive spot where E. J.'s neck curved into her shoulder before biting softly.

E. J. released a quiet moan.

"Hold the blanket," Jinx whispered. She shifted and pressed the edge of the fabric into E. J.'s hands, then cupped E. J.'s breasts. She pressed a languid kiss to her neck, then another while she caressed E. J.'s nipples.

E. J. groaned and closed her eyes. Her simmering desire began to boil. Somewhere in the back of her mind, she was vaguely aware they were outside with houses in either direction, but what had Jinx said—something about nobody...no windows? To trust her. Again, E. J. did. She let herself go, let herself feel her nipples swell, let the sensation move lower to find its home between her legs. She tightened her thighs in exquisite response.

Jinx squeezed her nipples, then rolled them, as she sucked more fervently on E. J.'s neck, then her shoulder, then back to her neck.

E. J. felt the stiff points of Jinx's nipples and the heat from between her legs, on her bare back. Arousal flooded her. "Take me to bed." The words came out in a hoarse whisper.

Jinx remained silent. Her hands kept moving. Her mouth continued teasing. "Not yet."

E. J. moaned in frustration.

"Open your eyes," Jinx murmured.

E. J. did. A thin pink line crested the horizon. The soft hue against the gray sky mingled with the sensations in her body. Somehow, she could feel the color, cool and tantalizing. As the line widened, the pink lightening, then touching the bottom of the clouds that hung low in the dawn, E. J. felt Jinx trail a hand down her stomach and across her abdomen. She teased the edge of E. J.'s curls, then brushed her fingers through them. The light pressure shot through her sex.

Jinx ran the tip of her tongue around the outer edge of E. J.'s ear, beneath the lobe, and into the well, her hot breath heightening E. J.'s need, while her fingers seemed to make love to first one nipple, then the other. A band of rich purple blended into the sunrise as Jinx's other hand slipped between E. J.'s thighs, a finger dipping into her wetness.

E. J. bit back a cry of pleasure.

Jinx's fingers swirled through her folds, slipping inside her, traversing her swollen clitoris, easing into a pattern that matched the striations of blue mingling with the purples and pinks in the sky.

E. J. wanted to close her eyes, but she couldn't. The sensations, the need building in her body, the impending crescendo, all felt too intertwined with the colors in the sky. What if it all vanished when she closed her eyes?

She remained transfixed on the dawn, mesmerized by the tinge of yellowish gold following the cooler hues, heating the sky just as her body heated. She clenched the blanket and pressed back into Jinx as her climax grew closer. Her breath was ragged, her muscles tense. Just as the sun broke the horizon, she came.

Jinx stilled, her fingers pressed to E. J.'s clitoris and nipples, her lips against E. J.'s neck. As the orgasm eased, she began again, slowly and gently.

E. J. groaned with the waves of pleasure as she watched the sun rise fully. Finally, she slumped into Jinx's arms and did close her eyes. She moaned. "The things you do to me."

Jinx's lips curved in a smile against E. J.'s temple. "Now, I'll take you back to bed."

❖

When E. J. woke again, sunlight peeked through the slit of the curtains on the front window. This time, she *was* alone. She could feel it. At the same time, though, she also could still feel Jinx—in the bed, in the room, in *her*.

She turned onto her back and gave herself over to a long, luxurious stretch. The thin fabric of the sheets caressed her skin. She felt rested, satisfied, well used, deliciously taken care of, and…happy. How could that be with everything she now knew? She should be feeling tense, apprehensive, even panicked. Shouldn't she? In spite of it all, it seemed only one thing was missing on this unusual morning.

She looked toward the kitchen, and there it was—a piece of paper stuck in the top of the microwave door with the word *coffee* scrawled across it. E. J. laughed out loud. Of course, something as crucial as coffee wouldn't be missing. Of course, Jinx would have made sure of that.

E. J. crossed to the kitchen and peered into the microwave to find a large, bright yellow Winnie the Pooh and Piglet mug. The brew that filled it was cool. She checked the digital clock and was surprised to see it was already ten forty-five. She realized she hadn't slept this late since before her kids were born and wondered what time Jinx had left. She set the coffee to heat and headed for the bathroom. On her return, she noticed a note and a key on the dining room table.

Good morning. You're beautiful when you sleep. I left you a couple of blueberry muffins in the fridge, and help yourself to anything else you want. You said something about going to the store, so I left the key. It's the only one I have, so it'd be good if you were home when I get there. If you've changed your mind about staying, I understand. Just leave the key under the mat.
I get off at six.
Enjoy your day—and thanks for staying last night.

It was signed with a smiley face.

E. J. pondered Jinx's thank you. Of course Jinx knew E. J. had wanted to run. Her own sister wouldn't even accept her. How many other people had turned away from her when they had heard her story? E. J. was glad Jinx had Reggie and Sparkle. She wondered how they had met.

She went back to the word *home*. She glanced around the small house. It did feel like home. She felt as though she was in some kind of time warp or alternate universe when she was here—like she was back with her grandparents and, somehow at the same time, fifty-two years old with all of her life experience intact. Her gaze landed on Jinx's bed in the middle of the living room, the CD player on the nightstand, the lesbian romance Jinx had said she was currently reading atop a copy of *Go Set a Watchman*. The weights and bicycle were visible through the bedroom doorway. No trace of her grandparents there. *This* home was decidedly Jinx's, and yet, it still felt a little like hers as well. Maybe that was the reason she was still there, why she hadn't bolted out the door the previous night. Maybe it was because when she was here with Jinx, it seemed like nothing else mattered, nothing else existed—not her kids' unawareness of her sexuality, not who Jinx's family was, not the past or even any thought of the future. It was just Jinx and her, together, in this safe little hideaway in the vastness of the universe.

There they were again, those foreign thoughts she always had any time she was around Jinx, or thinking about Jinx, or trying not to think about Jinx, or trying to convince herself she would never see Jinx again. Today, though, she was staying. She had to hear the rest of Jinx's story, at the very least. She wanted to give her that. Her stomach churned with apprehension at the thought of what twenty years in prison might hold...and the bank robbery. Did she want to hear about that? She touched the smiley face on the note. She had to. She had to reconcile the things Jinx had done with who E. J. knew her to be, now. Otherwise, she would never be able to trust her instincts again.

Settled back in bed, her coffee on the nightstand and her computer in her lap, she started with her habitual check of her work email, then pulled up the financial report she was putting together. Her mind wandered a couple of times to her incredible experience of the dawn that morning. Where did Jinx come up with stuff like that? Had she done it with other women? A twinge of something she hadn't felt since high school when her best friend, Sandra, fell in love tightened in her chest. *Jealousy.* She had decided at the time it was a ridiculous emotion. She could never be with a girl the way Sandra was with Tim, not and still fulfill her mother's expectations. She had determined she just wouldn't feel anything where Sandra was concerned, and later, where any woman was concerned. And feelings had never been an issue with men. Even when she had known Marcus was having an affair, she hadn't felt jealous. She had actually been relieved he was no longer turning to her for his needs.

The next time E. J. looked up from her work and checked the clock, it read a little after four. Where had the day gone? Jinx said she got off at six, and E. J. wanted to have dinner ready when she got home. She still had to go shopping, and she hadn't even taken a shower yet. *Damn it!* She raced into the bathroom and turned on the water. Thirty minutes later, she closed the front door behind her and hurried down the steps of the porch. As she started toward her car, she rummaged through her purse for her keys.

"*Ay, mami,*" a male voice said.

E. J. startled, coming to an immediate halt. She looked up.

On the other side of the driveway, a young man in his late teens sat on the porch railing of the house next door. One leg dangled off the edge, the other was bent at the knee, his thigh supporting a sketch pad. He held a pencil to the page. Both arms were fully tattooed, and a black teardrop leaked from the corner of one eye.

E. J. tensed. Despite a flutter of apprehension, she was a little offended. "I'm sorry. Did you just call me mommy?"

The boy grinned. "Naw, it means sexy. You know, like, oh, girl, you so sexy." He winked. "Jinx got herself a hot one."

E. J. felt herself blush. She *was* easily old enough to be his mother. She took in his black fedora, baggy white T-shirt, and khaki pants. He had gangster written all over him, but his gaze was soft and playful. She relaxed. "You know Jinx?"

"*Sí.* She's my neighbor." He pointed at her house with his pencil. "She helps my little sister with her homework."

Of course she does. E. J. smiled.

"Nice ride." He motioned to E. J.'s car.

"Thank you," she said.

"Be sure and keep it in the driveway."

"I beg your pardon?"

"You know, don't park it on the street," he said. "My boys know not to mess with anything at Jinx's place, and we'll track down anyone who does. But if it's across the street, I can't guarantee anything."

E. J. paused and let his meaning sink in. "You watch out for Jinx?"

He pursed his lips and gave a slow nod. "*Sí*. She helps my *hermanita*, and she takes my mom to work if it's real cold or hot or in the middle of the night. I pay her back."

E. J.'s heart went out to the boy. She was touched by the people who looked after Jinx, but more than that, how many lives Jinx impacted with her kindness. "Thank you."

He nodded again.

When she pressed the lock release on the fob and rounded the end of her car, he jumped down from the railing and quickly opened her door.

He tipped his hat, revealing a shaved head. "Your chariot," he said, a bright smile lighting his face.

E. J. paused and studied him. She had read somewhere that a teardrop tattoo meant he had either spent time in prison or killed someone. She couldn't imagine either. "Thank you—" She faltered. "I'm E. J." She extended her hand.

He shook it after shifting his sketch pad under his arm. "Diablo."

E. J. smirked. "Is that what your mother calls you?"

He gave her a sheepish grin. "Pablo."

She arched an eyebrow. "Like Picasso?" She gestured to the pad. "May I see?"

Pablo hesitated but handed it over.

E. J. stared in wonder at the intricately detailed sketch of the Lexus. Pablo had captured every curve and angle of the body, every delineation of shade, even the shadow cast by the door handle and the tiny knick where someone had bumped it in a parking lot. She thought of the artists for Bad Dog. Pablo had potential. "This is amazing."

Now, *he* blushed and shrugged.

"I'm serious. You're quite good." She returned it to him. "It was nice meeting you, Pablo." She slipped in behind the wheel. "And thank you for making sure nothing happens to my car...or to Jinx."

He smiled. "Maybe I'll see you around."

E. J. considered him briefly. "Maybe you will," she said thoughtfully.

❖

At six fifteen, E. J. heard a car pull into the driveway. She switched on the broiler and ignited the burner beneath the water for the pasta. All the prep work was finished. All that remained was the actual cooking. E. J. never spent a lot of time in the kitchen, but she always made sure it was time well spent if she did.

"Hi," Jinx said as she came in. Her expression was difficult to read. It seemed to hold a mixture of pleasure and anxiety, along with maybe a little gratitude.

E. J. smiled. "Hi. How was your day?"

Jinx glanced at the counter. "I thought you'd be gone," she said, ignoring E. J.'s question.

E. J. considered making a joke, but at the thought of the number of people who *had* left Jinx, decided against it. "I want to finish our conversation," she said, hoping to reassure her. "Besides, you said I could stay the weekend." She dropped some butter into a frying pan on the stove. "Hungry?"

Jinx grinned. "Starving. And something smells great. I'll get cleaned up." As she headed to the bathroom, she slowed. "What's that?" She walked to the dinette and picked up the sheet from Pablo's sketch pad E. J. had found propped against the front door when she had returned from the store.

It was a fully detailed sketch of E. J. leaning on the open door of her car, gazing up at the artist. When she had seen it, she had tried to remember if she had actually been in that position during their conversation. There was a split second just before she climbed behind the wheel, and Pablo had captured it perfectly, even a little flatteringly, E. J. thought. "I met your neighbor," E. J. said, dumping the minced garlic into the melted butter.

"So it seems." Jinx studied the picture. "You must have made a good impression."

"Always," E. J. said teasingly.

Jinx laughed. "No doubt."

"He has a lot of talent. Does he paint, too?"

"When he has paints. They don't have a lot of money." Jinx laid the sketch on the table. "And when he does get money from…you know…he usually gives it to his mom."

"Ah, yes," E. J. said. "I did learn he's your *real* security, and the reason my car hasn't been stolen."

Jinx chuckled. "No doubt about that either."

"He also said you help his little sister with her homework?"

"They're good kids, and their mother works hard. Pablo's just a little misdirected."

E. J.'s attention was on stirring the garlic to keep it from burning, but she remembered the teardrop tattoo. "Has he been in prison?"

"Not yet." Jinx's tone was resigned.

E. J. tensed. "Has he killed someone? I read once that a teardrop means one of those two things."

"It can also mean some other things," Jinx said. "Pablo got his to honor his best friend, who was killed in a street fight."

E. J. sighed in relief. "I'm sorry he lost his friend, but I'm so glad he didn't kill anyone. He seems like a nice kid."

"I'll get cleaned up," Jinx said again. Then she was gone.

What was that? Had E. J. said something wrong? All she had said was…*Did Jinx kill someone?* She said she hadn't in that…what had she called it? A turf war? But maybe…E. J.'s hand shook. *No.* She wasn't going there. She was going to assume the best about Jinx unless and until Jinx told her differently. Wasn't that the very reason she *had* stayed—to hear the rest of the story?

By the time Jinx returned, E. J. was draining the cooked pasta, and the lobster tails were under the broiler. The table was set.

Jinx opened the refrigerator as E. J. poured the tomato, garlic, and basil mixture over the noodles and tossed it together for capellini pomodoro. "Will you grab the salads while you're in there?" E. J. asked, opening the oven door. "And there's a bottle of Caesar dressing on the top shelf."

"Sure. I need to make something for Kenny real quick," she said, studying the contents.

"Already done. And I took it over to him. He was at that house across the street."

Jinx looked at her. "Oh. Thanks. That was nice of you. What did you make him?"

"A lobster tail, capellini pomodoro, and a Caesar salad," E. J. said, dishing up the seafood and pasta. "Same as us. I just did his earlier since he seemed to be waiting."

Jinx blinked. "You made Kenny lobster?"

"Mm-hm."

Jinx laughed. "He was probably as excited as I am. I can't remember the last time I had lobster."

"That's what *he* said. The two of you need to get out more." E. J. set the two plates on the table. "The salads?"

"He talked to you?" Jinx brought the bowls and the dressing and sat down, looking confused.

"He said thank you and that he hadn't had a meal like this in a very long time." E. J. set an open bottle of sparkling cider and two glasses of ice on the table and lowered herself into the chair across from Jinx. "Why?"

Jinx paused. "He doesn't usually talk." She stared at E. J. "How'd you get him to talk?"

"I just talked to him. I introduced myself and told him you weren't home yet but that I'd made his dinner." E. J. filled Jinx's glass, then her own. "He did look a little scared at first, but then he thanked me and said he hadn't had lobster in a long time. He seemed excited."

"Huh. That's more than he's said to me in all the time I've known him."

E. J. smiled. "Don't take it personally. Maybe I just caught him on a good day."

"He must like you better."

E. J. laughed gently. "You feed him every night. *I* just showed up today. I doubt he's thrown you over."

Jinx smiled, but her expression was distracted.

They ate quietly for a few minutes, then Jinx commented on how good dinner was. A longer stretch of silence followed.

E. J. watched her. "Are you nervous about the rest of our conversation?"

"Yes," Jinx said matter-of-factly.

"Me, too." E. J. hoped confessing her own apprehension wouldn't make it harder for Jinx. "Should we just dive in?"

Jinx considered her. "Will you do something for me first?"

E. J. saw the vulnerability in Jinx's eyes, the reluctance in her expression. "What do you need, sweetie?"

Jinx swallowed. "Will you tell me some things about you? About your life? Your childhood?"

For the first time, E. J. realized how one-sided things had become in the last couple of days, how much Jinx had put herself out there while E. J. had risked nothing. The dynamic wasn't unusual for E. J. She rarely risked anything with the women she saw. Jinx was obviously different, though, and she finally had to fully admit that—at least, to herself. "What do you want to know?"

Jinx shrugged. "Anything. Tell me about your mother. I'm curious about a woman who would name her baby Echo."

"Ah, my mother." E. J. laughed softly. "What can I say about her?" She hadn't thought about her mother in quite a while. She hadn't actually spoken about her in much longer, and that had only been in therapy. A wave of inadequacy washed through her. *And there's why.* "My mother was terrified of being ordinary, which included being terrified of having an ordinary child."

"So, she named you after a mythological Nymph?"

E. J. smiled. "She thought it was exotic."

"How did it get changed to E. J.?" Jinx took a bite of pasta.

"My grandfather *didn't* think it was exotic," E. J. said, remembering him warmly. "He said it was pretentious and always called me E. J. I spent a lot of time with my grandparents, so by the time I started school, I was more used to E. J. than Echo."

"Your mom didn't mind?"

"As long as I was what she wanted me to be when I was around her, she didn't care. When I was with her, in her world, I was always Echo or Echo Jenay. And I was dressed up, and I behaved appropriately, and I didn't cause her embarrassment or scandal. As long as I remembered that, we got along fine."

"And your dad?"

"My dad wasn't around," E. J. said, leaning back in her chair. "He didn't care about any of it." She studied Jinx and thought about the similarities in their stories. Neither of them were accepted for who they were, not by their parents, although E. J., at least, had her grandparents. Jinx had Andrea when she was young, and maybe that guy Luke. That was as far as it went, though. E. J. knew nothing she shared about her childhood could compare to what Jinx had been through. "My mother married my father for his money and the lifestyle he could provide. My father liked having a wife whose priority it was to maintain the family image of respectability while looking the other way while he had all the affairs he wanted. It was a match made in heaven. It wasn't love, but as long as we all played our parts, everyone got along."

"Are they still alive?" Jinx ate some lobster.

"My father is," E. J. said, noting the enjoyment on Jinx's face. "But I haven't seen him in years. My mother died ten years ago."

"You don't miss them?"

E. J. had never really thought about it. "To be honest, there really wasn't that much to miss," she said. "I miss my grandparents, though. They were the ones I really knew loved me." She looked around the room. "This place reminds me a lot of their house. I spent a lot of time there."

Jinx arched an eyebrow. "Really? I pictured your childhood in a big mansion like Andrea's."

"Well, that's officially where I lived. But my grandparents owned a small bar and grill, lived in a little place like this one, and that's where I felt at home. Where I felt loved."

Jinx finished the last of her salad and cleared her dishes. "Thank you," she said, returning for E. J.'s. "For telling me all that."

It had been the most E. J. had ever shared in one sitting, except maybe with her therapist, or Gwen and Taylor. She felt exposed, but she couldn't say that to Jinx, not with everything Jinx was revealing. She just smiled. "You're welcome."

An awkward moment stretched between them.

"So, I guess it's my turn," Jinx said, taking her seat again. "Is there anything in particular you want to know? Anything you thought of from last night?"

Here it was, the moment she could ask her earlier question. But she didn't. "Just start where we left off, I suppose."

"Okay." Jinx took a deep breath. "When I ran away, I didn't have a clue where to go, or what to do. I had some money, but it ran out pretty fast. After a while, I found a group of kids, other runaways, and hooked up with them. I was hurting so badly. I missed Andi so much. I'd missed her before, when I was still at the house, but I hadn't realized how much just being there around her, having the memories, and having Luke helped. I couldn't stand it. One day, Paul, one of the kids on the street, offered me something. Drugs. I don't even remember what kind. Maybe I never knew. I took it, and for the first time in a long time, I wasn't in pain." Jinx gave E. J. a questioning look as if asking if she understood.

E. J. nodded.

"When it wore off, the pain came back, so I took more. And that's how it all started. You can get food from church food banks or Dumpsters behind restaurants, but drugs...to get those, you need money. A constant stream of it. And every time I emptied from the drugs, the pain filled that space up again, so I made sure I was never empty. Paul and Rainbow and Dirk and I, we just stayed high. We did whatever we needed to do for our next fix. We started out stealing from unlocked cars or open garages, taking anything we could sell. After a while, we started breaking into houses. Then one day, Dirk got the idea of robbing a liquor store, and Paul convinced us we'd get more from a bank." Jinx laughed humorlessly. "God, drugs make you stupid." She leaned forward and rested her elbows on her knees. "By that time, I was strung out on heroin and crack, and I would have done anything."

E. J. was speechless. She couldn't imagine any of the things Jinx was telling her. She couldn't imagine Jinx doing any of them, not the Jinx of today, not her Jinx. She didn't have to say anything, though. Jinx seemed to have gone someplace far away.

"We picked a bank near a freeway on-ramp for our big escape, and we went in right after it opened, so there'd be fewer people. When we walked in, I could smell the floor polish, feel the chill coming off the granite counters and all the steel and glass. I could see people's lips moving, but all I could hear was the pounding of my heart and the rush of blood in my ears. I was so scared. I could feel the weight of the pistol in my jacket pocket." Jinx paused, inhaling deeply. She trembled slightly. "Paul started yelling at everyone to get down on the floor. I pulled out my gun and started doing the same, but when I spun around, there was this old lady. She was terrified. I was standing there with my pistol pointed right in her face. Then she grabbed at her chest and cried out. She started to fall. I dropped my gun and tried to catch her. And then there was a shot, and I went down. "

Every muscle in E. J.'s body was taut. She stared at Jinx. "Your other scar."

Jinx nodded, still distant.

"Who shot you?"

Jinx ran her hand over her face. "The commotion with the old lady distracted Paul, and the security guard jumped him. Paul's gun went off in the struggle. He punched out the guard, and he and Dirk and Rainbow ran, but I couldn't get up."

E. J. had to ask. "Did the woman die?"

"No." Jinx swallowed. "She had a heart attack, but they got her to the hospital in time."

"Because you tried to help her, and it stopped the robbery."

Jinx held her head in her hands. She scoffed. "Don't try to make me a hero, E. J. It was my fault she had the heart attack to begin with."

But she *had* tried to help her. Would a real criminal have done that? E. J. combed her fingers through Jinx's hair. "What happened to your friends?"

Jinx shrugged. "I never saw them again."

"You didn't turn them in? They weren't tried with you?"

Jinx shook her head. "They were my family," she said quietly. "The only family I had."

"But they left you." E. J. knew she was talking about something she had no concept of, but she was trying to understand. "You might have gotten less of a sentence if you'd turned them in."

"They were my family," Jinx said flatly, the subject obviously closed.

"And Nora and Andrea never came looking for you in all that time?"

"No. I don't blame them, though. I was so messed up by then," Jinx said, straightening in her chair. "Andrea came to my trial one day. I saw her in the back when they brought me into the courtroom. I think she was crying later in the day, but I'm not sure. She never came back."

E. J. searched Jinx's face. She saw fatigue, worry, regret, and fear. But mostly, she still saw the Jinx she knew, not the child who had lost her mother and been unprotected by her father, not a runaway, or a drug addict, or a criminal. She saw Jinx Tanner, whose beautiful blue eyes had met E. J.'s that first night and held her captive, who touched her so tenderly and deeply, who made her laugh and feel safe and happy just by being who she was. How could she reconcile what *she* knew of Jinx with everything she had been told in the last two days? Did she have to? After all, wasn't the important thing who a person is now?

She couldn't think anymore, and yet later, she couldn't stop. They had left the heavy stuff for a while, talking about lighter, surface things before going to bed. She lay with Jinx in her arms, Jinx's gentle breathing calming her and, at the same time, raising new questions with each inhalation. She dozed in and out of restless dreams. She woke each time Jinx's body jerked. She soothed her back to sleep from obvious nightmares. Finally, in the gray light of dawn, E. J. woke with a jolt, Jacob's image still in her mind.

The dream had been short but startling.

"I don't even know you. How can you be my mother?" His face loomed in the darkness, angry and contorted. "It's bad enough you're a dyke, but then you come home with a criminal as well. And the one hated member of my wife's family."

E. J.'s biggest fear had always been that he would find out she was gay and despise her for it, but now…This was all so much worse—or would be, if he really did learn about her relationship with Jinx. And how could he not…eventually? *What was I thinking? That I could just sneak into town whenever I want, see Jinx, and sneak out again?* Had she thought if she only saw Jinx in the insulated little world they had created, if she kept it compartmentalized and separate from the rest of her life, it could go on indefinitely? Sooner or later, she was bound to be found out, and now that she knew *why* Jinx was really the black sheep of her family…She was sure by this time Jacob knew all about Tiffany's mystery aunt. Tiffany would have told him about her blowup with her mother and how she had invited Jinx to the wedding over Andrea's objections. Then, on top of that, if—or when—he found out his own mother was *sleeping* with her...E. J.'s stomach soured with anxiety.

Jinx shifted beside her. "Baby, you awake?" she whispered.

The endearment threatened to choke E. J. She remained still. She closed her eyes and fought to keep her breathing even. Her heart beat so hard from her dream, she couldn't imagine how Jinx couldn't feel it or hear it.

Jinx eased out of bed.

E. J. listened to the sound of Jinx's bare feet on the linoleum, then heard the bathroom door close before she opened her eyes. She couldn't shake the dream's words, her own fears. Tension twisted her stomach. She felt nauseous. She had always known the risk of acting on her attraction to women. For years, she had sworn she would never do it, at first because her mother would never accept it, then later, even more strongly, because of Jacob's ordeal at age ten, when he was molested by a man from down the street. She had felt so guilty. She had been so wrapped up in her work and social events as Marcus's wife. She had hired people to watch the kids, but when everything came to light, as ridiculous as it was, she told herself if *she* had been there, it wouldn't have happened. Then there was the day in family therapy when Jacob was fourteen that he denounced all gays as deviants and perverts. *I fucking hate them all*, he had screamed. E. J. had known there was no correlation between a pedophile and being gay, but Jacob hadn't. Both she and his therapist had tried to explain it, but Jacob refused, or was unable, to hear it.

From that moment, E. J. had known for certain the part of her that wanted to be with a woman could *never* see the light of day. She wouldn't lose her son, not for anyone. And yet, years later when her marriage to Marcus ended, she still decided to explore the possibility, despite her fears and the potential repercussions—regardless of the wounds it could rip open in her son. *How selfish can I be?* And now, for him to find out she was sleeping with an ex-con *and a woman?* And, as Jacob's dream image had said, *the hated member of his wife's family?* She buried her face in her arms. Could she have screwed this up any worse?

The pipes clanked as the shower turned on.

To complicate matters even more, she had to admit she had let herself become emotionally involved with Jinx, no matter how much she had lied to herself before now and denied it. The depth to which she had felt Jinx's pain and sadness, the degree to which she had wanted to protect her, the strength of her anger at Nora Tanner, Jinx's father, and even Andrea, made her feelings impossible to refute any longer. What was she supposed to do with that, though? It was her and Jinx, or Jacob. She couldn't hurt him again. She couldn't lose him. He was her son.

She had to let go of Jinx.

How could she face her, though? She knew she couldn't, not and see that look in her eyes, that same look she had seen at the top of the stairs, the same look she had seen when talking about the loss of her mother, of her father, of Andi. E. J. would be just one more person who had cared about Jinx and abandoned her. No, E. J. couldn't face her.

She listened to the running water.

She scrambled out of bed and started pulling her things together, hoping to be gone before Jinx got out of the shower. *You're a coward.* She swallowed back the tears and kept moving, running—the way she always had.

CHAPTER TEN

Jinx turned off the water and toweled herself dry. She was amazed E. J. was still there. She'd sensed several times—more like every other minute—E. J.'s desire to flee. Jinx had seen her go pale at the initial confession and had been certain it was all over in that instant, but E. J. had stayed. Again, at the explanation of the length of her sentence and the brawl in which Val had been killed, she was sure E. J. would bolt, but she'd rallied. Throughout that first night, she'd become aware E. J. had kept the focus on Jinx's childhood, Jinx as the innocent instead of the criminal, but when they'd finally gotten to her life on the streets and the bank robbery, E. J. hadn't shied away. She'd said she would stay, and she had. And with all those memories stirred up, when Jinx had woken from an old nightmare of kneeling beside Val, covered in her blood, to E. J.'s comforting touch and this morning to the feel of E. J. beside her, she hadn't been able to believe it.

She knew better, though, than to think the discussion was over. E. J. could still walk out of her life. After all, they hadn't even touched on who Val was, or anything that'd happened in prison, but if E. J. was still here, Jinx still had a chance. In the years since Val's death, she'd learned to believe in hope, in possibilities, in letting go of *how* something could happen and just hold on to the knowledge that it could. Without that, she probably never would have gotten out of prison, never would have returned to try to heal her relationship with Andrea, and certainly never would have met E. J. Sure, there'd been times when hope had all but deserted her—when Andrea had slammed the door in her face, when one of the women she'd briefly dated excused herself to use the restroom after hearing Jinx's much-abbreviated version of her past and had never returned to the table. When Jinx was working up the nerve to tell E. J., that damned voice in her head kept saying, *you're an idiot if you think she's going to want anything to do with you.* But E. J. was still here, and Jinx *did* have hope. She was different from who she'd once been, and that had to count for something.

She wiped the steam from the mirror and stared at her reflection. She *had* changed. She didn't look all that much different—healthier certainly, older, but other than that, pretty much the same. She was a different person, though, from the one who'd walked into that bank so long ago, from the one who'd stolen and lied when she lived on the streets.

During her time in prison, she'd seen a lot of things, met so many people, heard all their stories, and through it all, she'd learned a lot about herself. She'd figured out her life was her own responsibility and was built on her own choices, even if they were hard ones. She'd realized the importance of family, of connection and relationships, and though she'd found she *could* make it on her own, she preferred to be involved with people she cared about and who cared about her. She liked to help people, to be useful, to share what she had with those who could benefit from it, and she'd learned the meaning of the adage, *giving and receiving are one and the same.* Then, when she'd been released, Reggie and Sparkle had opened their hearts and home to her, given her a job, and been there for her on every step of her return to the outside world, all due to their gratitude for what Jinx had done for Sparkle's little sister, Trisha, on the inside.

And *now*, she'd met E. J., a woman so different from anyone she'd ever been with, who kept coming back so unexpectedly, who was more than a one-night stand, more than a fling, as Jinx had thought. Now, she'd stayed after hearing everything—well, almost everything—unlike the others with whom Jinx had tested the waters of truth. Jinx knew the day ahead wouldn't be easy. Some more tough stuff remained to be discussed and explained, but a day of that *with* E. J. would certainly be easier than a day alone, facing the realization that no matter how much she'd changed, the fact of who she'd been might always make her unacceptable to anyone she cared about. She drew in a steadying breath and left the bathroom.

She pulled on a pair of jeans and her new Bad Dog T-shirt from the dresser, then slipped into a pair of flip-flops before grabbing her keys to head out for E. J.'s coffee. In the doorway, she halted at the scene.

E. J. leaned over her open suitcase on the bed, rummaging through its contents. Her laptop, returned to its case, lay beside it.

All optimism faded, and Jinx felt sick to her stomach. "What are you doing?" she asked reluctantly. But she knew.

E. J.'s movements stilled, the mere length of a flinch, before she continued her frenzied search for whatever the lost item was. "I can't find my phone," she said, her tone sharp.

Jinx couldn't speak. She had to say something to keep E. J. from leaving, but she couldn't think of anything.

E. J. straightened and turned to face her. She wore gray slacks and a fuchsia blouse, the attire of someone going out into the world, nothing like what she'd worn for just hanging around Jinx's house. "Do you know where it is?"

Her expression was one of fear, conflict, and regret, much like that first morning at the hotel when it turned out they'd be at the same wedding. But now, she looked resolved, too. *That can't be good.*

"E. J., please don't leave." Jinx's voice came out barely above a whisper. "I'm not that person anymore. Let me explain."

E. J. squeezed her eyes shut. When she opened them, she turned and looked out the window. "I know you're not. I can feel that."

Optimism sparked. "Then please stay. Hear me out."

E. J. hesitated. Her lips trembled, then firmed. "I can't," she said, turning back to Jinx. "I can't do this. I'm not made for drama, for complications. This is too…I can't do this. I can't do this to Jacob."

"To Jacob? What does any of this have to do with him?"

"I can't hurt him again. I was careless with him when he was young. I should have been there. And then, I was selfish. I ignored my vow never to act on my attraction to women because I thought I could keep it away from him, but now, here I am with you, a member of his new family—the member who's been banished. And in addition to being a woman, you're a…"

"Say it." The hope Jinx had held for the day gave way to resignation. At least she'd know. She'd hear it from E. J.'s own lips and wouldn't have to guess.

"Okay." E. J.'s voice rose. "You're a criminal. You've been in prison. And not just for a little while...for *twenty* years. Jacob's a lawyer. He's married into a family of lawyers—*your* family of lawyers—so even if I wanted to tell him I'm gay, which I don't, there's now all the rest of this to deal with. I won't lose my son."

Maybe E. J. was right, but Jinx wasn't willing to let her go without a fight. "This isn't about Jacob. This is about you and me... about us."

E. J. studied her, then inhaled deeply. She straightened her back and her face went calm. "There is no you and me. This was fun, but that's all." It sounded rehearsed, a practiced response used many times. E. J.'s guard was up, and it was like they'd never met.

Jinx's temper flared at not being allowed to talk to the woman *she* knew. "I don't believe that's what you think. Or what you feel. I've been with you. I've *felt* you open up to me, to *us*. I've felt you feel us."

E. J. averted her gaze but remained rigid. "You don't understand, and I don't expect you to."

There was that same line from that first morning, too. *Is that her standard brush-off?* Surely, they'd shared more than that. She couldn't be *that* wrong about what she felt. "Then, damn it, E. J., explain it to me." Now, Jinx's voice rose. "I opened my soul to you this weekend. I told you things I've never shared with *anyone*. I talked about my mother to you. I've cried in your arms, and all I get from you is, *you don't understand and I don't expect you to?* What the hell is that?"

"It's all I have," E. J. yelled. "I don't do..." She waved her hand in the air. "...*this*. It's too complicated. It's too risky. I can't love..." She turned back to the bed and yanked open her purse. "It's too *much*."

Jinx froze. What had E. J. almost said? That she couldn't love Jinx? *Does she?* "E. J.?"

"No," E. J. said firmly. She tore through the contents of her suitcase again. "God damn it, where is my fucking phone?"

Jinx watched her grow more frantic. She could feel her anxiety continue to rise. E. J. was done talking. That was clear. What had her own thought been Friday night? *If her past was going to be a deal breaker, better to know now than later when it would be more painful.* She couldn't imagine the ache in her heart at the mere thought of watching E. J. walk out the door being any worse, though, and yet, she knew it would be. She sighed and looked at the floor. "It's on the counter next to the microwave."

E. J. glanced at the kitchen, then zipped her suitcase closed and grabbed her purse and laptop. She crossed the room and snatched up her phone. She paused.

Jinx kept her eyes down and inwardly begged E. J. not to say anything else. *If you're going, just go.*

"Jinx, I'm sorry."

The sound of her name on E. J.'s lips forced her to blink back tears. All the other times, she'd loved hearing it, whether E. J. was just talking to her, being playful, or whispering in her ear in bed, but this time, it felt like a knife in her chest. She clenched her teeth. The silence grew awkward, but Jinx wasn't going to tell her it was okay, or she understood, because it wasn't and she didn't. She wasn't about to make this easier for her. She turned away and listened to E. J.'s footsteps as she walked to the front door.

When E. J. stepped outside, there was another pause. She released a long sigh. "Could you move your car? I can't get out."

Jesus H. Christ! Could this exit drag out any longer? Keys in hand, Jinx stalked past E. J. and down the porch steps. As she backed into the street, she looked at the Lexus and remembered how excited she'd been to see it in her driveway just two days earlier, how good it'd felt to be the one E. J. wanted to be with after a bad day, how unbelievable it'd been that E. J. had asked to spend the whole weekend. Now, such a short time later, she watched as E. J. drove off down the block.

Jinx glanced at her house. Her throat closed and her chest constricted at the thought of going back inside, seeing the dishes from the wonderful dinner E. J. had made and the rumpled blankets on the bed they'd shared. She tightened her grip on the steering wheel until her anger resurfaced and overrode her pain. She climbed from her car, returned to lock her front door, then headed off for Canine Complete. There was always work to be done there. She could keep herself distracted all day.

❖

Jinx stepped through the side gate into the kennels. She knew at this time on a Sunday morning she'd find Reggie feeding and chatting with the boarded dogs before letting them out for exercise and socializing. During the first six months Jinx was home, when she'd lived with Reggie and Sparkle, she'd helped Reggie on Sunday mornings since most of the rest of the staff shared that day off, but once Jinx had moved into her own place, Reggie had insisted she take that day to relax as well.

Jinx watched her through the long row of windows that ran the length of the kennel. Reggie offered soft greetings to reassure any dog new to the experience of being boarded or a boisterous good morning to those who were regulars and familiar with her and the daily routine. She always knew exactly what someone needed, whether canine or human. Between salutations, she seemed to have a perpetual smile. The comfort it gave Jinx made her smile as well.

When Jinx entered the kennels, Reggie looked up and flashed a wide grin, but it quickly vanished. "What are you doing here?" she asked, but the concern in her eyes said she already knew. Jinx had told her and Sparkle the day before that E. J. had returned to town and was spending the weekend. She'd also said they were in the middle of a discussion about her past.

Jinx's throat closed on any response. She couldn't say the words, but she didn't have to. She shrugged. "Can I help?" She gestured to the food bucket.

Reggie watched her for a moment, then closed the distance between them and took her into a hard hug. "I'm sorry, Jinx."

Jinx wrapped her arms around Reggie's broad middle and held on tight. "Thanks," she said just loud enough to be heard over the din of barking dogs.

"You want to finish feeding?"

Jinx nodded, knowing if she tried to say anything else, she'd end up a blubbering fool. She'd been enough of a fool where E. J. was concerned. It was time to pull up her big girl panties and move on. She took the scoop from Reggie.

"Okay," Reggie said, stepping back and giving Jinx an affectionate slap on the shoulder. "I've got a couple of training sessions. When you're done here, head on up to the house. Sparkle's making peach pie to go with dinner. The kids are coming over, and Trisha will be here. You'll spend the day with us." She turned and walked outside, the matter settled.

Gratitude flooded Jinx. She'd known this was where she'd spend the day, but Reggie's immediate and unsolicited confirmation reminded her there was one place in the world she was always welcome, no matter what. It didn't alleviate the pain of E. J.'s rejection, but it gave her somewhere to be, people to be with, a place she could feel she belonged.

Jinx picked up where Reggie had left off and fed and watered the next three dogs, taking time to love on them a little and assure them they'd be running free in the yard soon. When she opened the next gate, a huge Rottweiler bounded toward her. Her mood instantly lifted. "Hey, Dylan. I didn't know you were here." She dropped to her knees and looped her arms around his thick neck.

His owner, Ms. Meyers, a quirky English teacher and poet, brought him in religiously once a month, and Jinx always looked forward to her time with him. His full name was Dylan Thomas, after the poet. He snuggled up to her, his stub of a tail wagging excitedly, and bathed her face with a huge, sloppy, wet kiss as was his customary greeting. He always made her laugh, and thankfully, today was no exception.

She scrubbed her hands over his back, causing him to wiggle his whole rear end frantically. "I didn't know you were staying with us. Where's your mama?"

He licked her again.

She chuckled. "Okay, that's enough." She wiped her face on the sleeve of her T-shirt. "Let's see what wisdom you have for me today."

In addition to her affection for him, Jinx enjoyed the custom tags Ms. Meyers made for him—a new one every time Jinx saw him—

each of which held the inscription of a different quote from one of her poems. She joked that it was the only way to ensure some of her work would be published. The quotes always somehow seemed to fit whatever Jinx was going through at any given time, which made her think of a friend she'd made in prison, a yoga-practicing, meditating guru of the cellblock who'd been dubbed Namastacey. Her real name was Stacey Evans, and she was serving life for drug trafficking and assaulting a federal agent, but she'd found a new path in prison and, thus, a new way of being. Namastacey always said that you already know everything you need to know, and as a reminder, it showed up all around you if you just paid attention.

Jinx scratched Dylan's chest with one hand while she found the tags dangling from his collar with the other. Today's quote read, *Lovers grow cold, attention fades; But love only sleeps, always to bloom again.* "Huh," Jinx said and rubbed the dog's huge head. "Once again, sage advice." Following her confrontation with Andrea at the wedding, and three days of wallowing in self-pity, Dylan had come into the shop with a tag that read, *To mope is for fools, for fools have lost hope.* Today's quote was an equally strong eye-opener.

Jinx knew it was the truth. E. J. leaving her life didn't mean she wasn't loved, or that she'd never have romantic love. She hadn't been looking for that when she'd met E. J. She was still trying to get her life together, to learn how to live on her own, and to figure out how on God's green earth to get her sister to talk to her. Those were her priorities. If all that was true, though, why did watching E. J. walk out this morning hurt so badly? Why did she now feel so empty? Was it just her ego? She never would have believed someone as classy and successful as E. J. would find her attractive, and with her past being what it was…E. J. could have anyone she wanted. Why would she choose an ex-con whose own family even had no interest in her?

She loved looking at E. J. She loved touching her. She loved her softness, her scent, her taste. She loved talking with her, telling her jokes, her laugh. She loved…Did she love *her*? She thought about E. J.'s aborted statement earlier. *I can't love…*Did E. J. love her? That was ridiculous. Whatever they felt for one another or were to each other, it couldn't be love. They'd been together only three times, had just met—what was it—a month ago? Could that be right? Jinx felt good with E. J. She felt special. Every time E. J. showed up again, Jinx felt like a brand new sun had risen to shine only on her. Yup, she decided, that definitely had to be ego. Who *wouldn't* feel good with someone like E. J. beside her? Who *wouldn't* feel special?

There were some things, though, about E. J. that would get annoying very quickly. That whole obsessive thing she had around her son and her fear of him finding out who she really was. How long could that go on without causing issues? *Apparently, one month.* That *was* how long they'd known each other, only one month. All of this was ridiculous.

Jinx's inner voice—or perhaps, Namastacey's—spoke up. *How is that any different from your fear about people knowing you're an ex-con or a drug addict? How is her irrational focus on Jacob different from your insistence that Andrea talk to you?*

None of it mattered anyway. E. J. was gone. She undoubtedly wouldn't be back this time. She'd made her feelings crystal clear. What they'd shared until that morning had been awesome, at least for Jinx, and *that's* what she would hold on to. That's what she wanted to remember, if she could do it without it hurting. If she couldn't, well, the whole thing would have to go. She'd made enough of an idiot of herself over E. J. It was time to move on.

Jinx fed Dylan his special food and gave him one of the new toys Ms. Meyers customarily left with him, then finished with the rest of the dogs in the kennels. She basked in the warmth of the sunshine on her face while she supervised the dogs' playtime in the community yard, before heading up to the house to watch Sparkle make homemade peach pie.

In the kitchen, Jinx found her putting the pies into the oven. She'd missed the part she liked best, seeing the dough for the crust being made and spread out in the tins. Watching Sparkle make pies and do certain other tasks around the house made Jinx feel at home, even more so than how she always felt being there. She never knew why. Maybe it was because she'd never been in what she would actually consider a home with the people who made it such, at least, not that she remembered. Or maybe it was some old, forgotten memory of what it'd been like with her mother.

"Hey," Jinx said, sliding onto a stool at the bar.

Sparkle glanced over her shoulder as she closed the oven door. She straightened and scowled. "That bitch. Who does she think she is, judging you?"

How did Sparkle know? Jinx frowned. Of course, she knew the same way Reggie had. Jinx wouldn't be here if everything had gone well the night before. "She didn't exactly judge me. It was more about her being afraid her son would find out she's gay." She shrugged. "And dating me," she admitted.

"What'd she say?"

"Nothing that wasn't true. That I'm a criminal and her son's a lawyer and I'm the banished member of his new wife's family. That it was all too complicated."

Sparkle wiped her hands on a dish towel and crossed to the bar. "You *were* a criminal. You're not anymore. You served your time— and then some. You have a job. You help people and animals. You're a good person. And I, for one, am glad you were in prison. You saved Trisha's life, helped her pass her GED, and now my baby sister's out and has a new life. You deserve the same."

These were words Sparkle had said many times before, and sometimes Jinx could feel them. Sometimes not. This morning, she was trying, but the cool, removed look on E. J.'s face once she'd obviously made up her mind hovered in front of her like a barrier. She knew there was truth in Sparkle's words, but would she ever fully be able to leave the past behind? She looked down at her hands. "It's okay."

"It is certainly *not* okay." Sparkle slapped the towel against the counter. "She's got no right judging you. I'm sure *she's* got a few things in *her* past she'd like to do over, too. We all do."

Jinx thought back to E. J.'s allusion to being careless with Jacob, not being there, what she'd said about being selfish. Those had to be things she wished she could do over. Jinx wondered what'd happened, then remembered she'd never know. Hell, the only things she knew even now were those she'd specifically asked about. E. J. had never actually volunteered a single thing about herself.

"I told you," Sparkle said, jabbing a finger at Jinx. "If she hurt you, I'd hunt her down and kick her ass, and I meant it."

Jinx adored Sparkle. She was such a champion for the people she loved. Jinx smiled. "I appreciate that, but you'll have a hard time doing it. I don't even know what city she lives in."

Sparkle considered her for a long moment, her demeanor softening. "Jinxie, how'd you go so ga-ga over a woman you don't even know?"

Jinx shrugged. "I don't know." And she really didn't. She just knew she had. The door she'd begun to close on those feelings started to creep open again. She tried to slam it shut. "I was a moron, but I'll be fine."

Sparkle continued to watch her. "I've never seen you like this, all mushy over someone. Even when I was writing to you in prison and you talked about Val—and I *know* you loved her—you weren't like you are with this one. What is it, Jinxie?"

Jinx shook her head. "I don't know. It's just...I feel good when I'm with her. I feel like I used to, a long time ago. You know, before everything. When she looks at me, it's like she's only seeing the good in me...until this morning, that is. But even last night, after she knew all the worst, she still seemed to see something else." *So, what happened this morning?*

Sparkle cocked her head and raised an eyebrow.

"I know. It's nuts. I'm nuts."

"No," Sparkle said quietly. "It isn't. It's what I feel with Reggie. When she looks at me that way, it makes me want to be everything she believes I am. Makes me want to be a better person. I had no idea that's what this was. I guess I was too hell-bent on trying to protect you to see it. But no one can protect you from your heart, and from that person who makes you feel like being more."

"What?" Jinx was lost.

"Yup. You're going to have to see this thing through." Sparkle's tone was suddenly matter-of-fact.

"See what through? It's over. She's gone."

Sparkle slipped onto the bar stool beside Jinx. "If that's true, then you'll always have that special way she made you feel. If it isn't, if she comes back again—"

"She won't." Jinx remembered the conviction in E. J.'s expression when she'd told Jinx she *couldn't do this*, that she *couldn't love*…What the hell had she almost said? Whatever it was, she'd been certain of it. Jinx could feel the pain of E. J.'s exit eking into her heart again, the pain she'd felt each time E. J. had left. She couldn't do it anymore, especially now that she'd revealed so much. She was too vulnerable, too raw.

"If she does, you're going to want to see her again. To give her another chance."

Jinx blinked in disbelief. "What happened to kicking her ass?"

"I still might do that. It depends. But *you* have something with her."

Jinx sighed. "I can't, Sparkle."

"Trust me."

"She's not coming back."

"Just…if she does…trust me."

"I'll think about it."

The afternoon was relaxing. She watched a movie and prepared dinner with Reggie and Sparkle, and spent the evening playing Liverpool Rummy with all the kids and Trisha. More than anything, though, Jinx was grateful to be distracted from thoughts of E. J. Later, as she turned onto her street, as much as she fought it, she felt a tiny twinge of hope that E. J.'s car would be in her driveway, announcing some miraculous change of E. J.'s heart, but the driveway was empty.

Jinx knew what awaited her inside and steeled herself for it. She walked into the house after leaving the plate Sparkle had made for Kenny on the front porch—still a little disgruntled that he'd so easily talked to E. J. when he still so rarely spoke to her—and froze at the sight of the dishes, the bedding, the CD player. Reminders of the past two nights. All the feelings of rejection, loss, and loneliness flooded back in. She had to get her place back if she was going to have any chance of moving through this.

She quickly did the dishes and put them away, then stripped the bedding from the mattress. She'd never be able to sleep enveloped in E. J.'s scent. She grabbed the bath towel still redolent of jasmine before stuffing everything into a pillowcase. She caught a glimpse of herself in the bathroom mirror and stared at her cherished Bad Dog

T-shirt. It had to go as well. With resolve, she yanked it off, strode to the kitchen, and grabbed a pair of scissors from a drawer. Before she could change her mind, she cut the fabric into strips and dropped it into the trash. Next, she took the Debussy CD from the player and broke it in half. After pulling on another shirt, with trash bag in one hand and laundry in the other, she headed out the door. When she returned, her house and her life would be hers again.

But what about my heart?

Chapter Eleven

I can't do dinner. I have too much work." E. J. indicated the files and papers covering her desk and the computer screen lit up with a financial report. It wasn't a complete lie. She did have a lot of work, but much of it was the same work she'd had ever since she had gotten home after her cowardly retreat from the weekend with Jinx. Her customary withdrawal into the many responsibilities of overseeing ten stores following any kind of drama had failed her. She couldn't concentrate. So, she had just spent hour after hour, day after day, staring at words and numbers, pretending to be all-consumed. "We'll do it soon, though. I promise."

Mandy planted her fists on her hips. "Come on, Mom. There's always work. It'll still be here tomorrow. We haven't talked since the wedding."

That was no accident. E. J. had been putting Mandy off ever since she had met Jinx and gotten so loopy over her, because Mandy could read E. J. too well. They were very much alike, so it would take only ten minutes face-to-face, and Mandy, even if she didn't know what, would know something was wrong. "I'm sorry, sweetie, I just...I can't."

"I'm heading home," Gwen said from the doorway.

Mandy shot her a pleading look.

Gwen hesitated. "E. J., why don't you take your daughter up on dinner? I'll bet she'll even treat. That's the advantage of raising successful children." She leveled her gaze at Mandy. "Are you still seeing Russ?" She arched an eyebrow.

Mandy squinted slightly, then said, "Oh. Yes." She turned back to E. J. "And I need your advice on something."

E. J. rolled her eyes. "Really? You think I'm oblivious to your schemes? Besides, you're way better at intimate relationships than I am. *I* should be asking *you* for advice." She hoped it sounded light despite the truth of the statement. She briefly wondered what wisdom Mandy might have for her about Jinx, if she could talk to her about it. She had considered coming out to Mandy over the years. She was fairly certain Mandy would be fine with it, but as close as she and Jacob were, it wouldn't be fair to ask her to keep such a secret from him.

"We could do that, too." Mandy smiled. "Russ has an uncle—"

"Oh, God, no." E. J. shoved her fingers into her ears. "I'm sorry I said anything."

Gwen laughed. "How about this? E. J., you agree to a dinner within the next week, and, Mandy, I will personally add it to her calendar and make sure she shows. She wouldn't be any fun tonight anyway. She's been a grouch all week."

Mandy eyed E. J. "Mom?"

"Yes, that sounds like a good plan. How's next Monday?"

When Mandy had gone, Gwen lingered in the doorway.

E. J. pushed back in her chair. "Okay, let's have it. What do you have to say?"

Gwen glanced at her watch. "Since it's after hours and nobody's here, I'm going to be blunt."

"For a change?"

"I'm wondering," Gwen said as though E. J. hadn't spoken, "when you're going to actually talk about whatever happened the last time you saw Jinx, instead of walking around sulking, avoiding the people who care about you, and biting off everyone's head."

"I'm not sulking." E. J. flicked a pen on her desk.

"You are." Gwen straightened the papers in front of E. J. before stacking them on some file folders.

"Hey, I'm working on that."

"No, you aren't. You're staring at it. You haven't done any work for weeks." Gwen shut down E. J.'s computer. "Come on. We're leaving. Let's go to your place."

E. J. looked up at her, equally annoyed and grateful. She needed to talk and never would have initiated it on her own. She was too angry, too humiliated, too conflicted. "What would I do without you?"

"I shudder to think."

❖

E. J. changed into lounge wear, gave Gwen some designer sweats, and stood in her kitchen, staring at the wine rack. As much as she wanted something to bolster her strength for the ensuing conversation, as much as she wanted to go numb, nothing looked good.

"Taylor's bringing Chinese," Gwen said as she strode into the room. "So pick something that goes."

E. J. shot her a questioning look.

"I called her on the way over. She deserves to hear this, too. You've yelled at her three times that I know of. Besides, she has more of an understanding of your weirdo desire to stay independent."

E. J. wanted to be irked, but instead, all she said was, "Will you call her and tell her to pick up some apple juice?" That was all she seemed to want to drink these days.

Gwen lifted one eyebrow in evident surprise. "Sure."

E. J. ignored it. "You and Taylor can pick a wine."

When Gwen returned her cell phone to her purse, she flopped beside E. J. into the plush cushions of the large sectional. She let out a long sigh. "I love this couch." She stretched, then moaned. "Since you're so much older than me, will you leave it to me in your will?"

E. J. gave a small smile and tilted her head back to stare at the high ceiling, a position she had spent a lot of time in lately.

"Oh, wow." Gwen's voice held concern. "This must be worse than I thought. That line normally would have been worth at least ten minutes of banter."

E. J. pursed her lips and closed her eyes. Gwen was right. It was worse than she could possibly know. It was worse than even E. J. had suspected, and *she* knew the entire story. She had never in her life gone through anything that couldn't be blocked out by submersion in work. Even immediately following the discovery of Jacob's molestation and the subsequent counseling, she had been able to hide her emotions in her job and commitments, at least for short periods. This thing with Jinx, though, seemed inescapable. Everything was a reminder. Even things that didn't have anything to do with Jinx somehow brought E. J. back around to her.

Just that morning, she had been sitting at a stop light and saw a man who looked a lot like a guy who had dated her college roommate. It made her wonder where her roommate was living now and what she was doing. Last they'd spoken, she was working in hotel management and was married to a stockbroker, but then E. J. remembered she had heard from a mutual friend that she had gotten a divorce and was now married to a psychiatrist. *That* reminded her of Jinx's joke about why you can't hear a psychiatrist using the bathroom, and there she was, back to seeing that spark of laughter in Jinx's eyes.

"E. J.?" Gwen's tone was tentative. "Are you okay? You're shaking."

E. J. turned to her. "I don't know. There's so much about this I don't understand. So much I've never felt before." She looked again to the ceiling and blinked back the beginning of tears. "I hate feeling so out of control. I'm afraid I'm going crazy."

Gwen took her into a tight hug. "You're not. I promise. We'll work it all out." She eased back and locked eyes with E. J. "There's never been anything the three of us couldn't handle in any of our lives. Has there? Even my mother moving in with me for six months. Remember that one?"

E. J. managed a soft laugh. She nodded.

"Okay then. Taylor and food will be here shortly, and we'll take this thing apart."

"Chinese delivery." Taylor's voice rang through the condo, followed by the slam of the front door.

"Speak of the devil," Gwen said just loud enough for Taylor to hear.

"Devil, you say?" Taylor sauntered into the living room, wearing designer jeans and a maroon blouse. She kissed the top of E. J.'s head in greeting. "You ain't seen nothin' yet, baby."

E. J. winced at the endearment. From now on, it would always make her think of Jinx and the soft way she said it, never mind E. J.'s reaction to it. She had always hated when anyone else called her baby, but every time Jinx did, it melted her.

Taylor bent close to Gwen. "Give me a chance and I'll show you devil—in a good way." She leaned in and brushed her lips across Gwen's cheek.

"Food," Gwen said. "I'm starving."

E. J. got plates and glasses, while Taylor and Gwen spread out the takeout containers on the coffee table and squabbled over which wine would go best. Her apple juice tasted delicious and, of course, brought Jinx to mind—as if Jinx wasn't already consuming her every thought. Within minutes, they were dishing up their meals.

"Okay," Taylor said. "Why are we here? I hope we get to find out why you've been Queen Bitch since your last little tryst with your mysterious stranger." She glanced at E. J. "Otherwise, we're going to have to kill you."

"I know." E. J. sighed. "I'm sorry. Let me just start with that."

"Yeah, yeah," Taylor said, holding a piece of walnut shrimp to Gwen's lips with a pair of chopsticks.

E. J. looked away, forcing aside the unwanted memory of Jinx doing the same for her.

"We've all been through enough together not to have to commence with apologies." Taylor scooped a serving of the seafood dish onto her plate, then reached for the pot stickers. "Just get to the juicy stuff. What the hell happened?"

Where to begin? E. J. suddenly understood Jinx's dilemma the night she had started telling her story. She couldn't think of an opening sentence that wouldn't immediately launch a barrage of questions, many of which she might not be able to answer. She needed to control this. "Okay, I'm going to tell you everything, but it's a long story. So you have to promise not to say a word until I'm finished."

"We can do that," Gwen said, sounding confident.

E. J. wasn't so sure. She eyed Taylor. "I mean it. No questions, none of your snarky remarks, until I've said everything. And even then, I could do without the snarky remarks."

Taylor's eyes widened, and she looked mildly offended.

Gwen slapped her thigh.

"All right, I promise," Taylor said. She glanced at Gwen. "This is going to be good. I can tell."

"Okay." E. J. thought for a minute. "Remember I told you something had happened between Jinx and Tiffany's mother, and Jinx was no longer welcome in the family? Well, it goes back further than just Andrea." E. J. continued with the story of Jinx's childhood, up through her father's death, and to the part about her running away. It felt more natural than simply blurting out the worst as Jinx had done, and E. J. found herself wishing *she* had heard it all this way. The moment of truth was inevitable, though, and soon, she heard herself saying, "She robbed a bank and was in prison for most of her adult life. She just got out three years ago."

Gwen dropped a glob of rice down the front of her shirt.

Taylor, who had stopped eating at the drug addiction, stared at E. J., her mouth agape. "Holy shit! Are you—"

E. J. held up a hand. "Not a word. You promised."

Taylor let out a frustrated garble, then turned to Gwen in an obvious plea for support.

Gwen gave a warning shake of her head as she cleaned up her mess.

The hardest part over, E. J. finished with the rest, including her failed attempt at a spineless getaway. When she was done, she stared at her friends, waiting.

Both had stopped eating, and E. J. realized she herself hadn't taken more than a bite or two. She picked up her plate and ate some cold shrimp. She felt oddly calm, calmer than she had felt in weeks, but then she hadn't yet addressed what *really* had made her bolt from Jinx's. "Now, you can say something," she said finally.

Gwen and Taylor looked at one another.

"Man, I thought our last conversation about this Jinx chick was astonishing," Taylor said, sinking into the couch cushions. "What is it with her? You hate drama. You *never* deal with family. And you hardly ever sleep with anyone more than once. Everything about this woman is over the top, and yet, you're still all wigged out over her."

"I'm not wigged out," E. J. said, trying not to sound defensive.

"E. J.," Gwen said softly. "You haven't been yourself since the day you met her. You've broken all your own dating rules, which I'm not saying is a bad thing, but still...You're barely present at work, which is *so* unlike you. You've avoided Mandy since the wedding, and I'd bet you haven't even spoken to Jacob, with Jinx being related to Tiffany and all. And even with us, you've been distant."

E. J. met Gwen's gentle gaze. She couldn't deny any of it. "I know. I'm sorry. I just…" She went to the long panel window beside her fireplace and stared out at the setting sun. She folded her arms across her middle in an attempt to quell the flutter of desire stirred by the swirls of pinks, purples, and oranges. She would never be able to watch a sunset or sunrise again without wanting to relive that morning with Jinx. She turned her back on the sight. "I've never felt like this before. I don't know what to do with it."

"How do you feel, exactly?" Gwen asked.

E. J. shook her head. "I'm confused. I feel too much. It's all too much." She tightened her arms and drew up her shoulders in hopes of warding off her growing anxiety.

Gwen held up her hand. "Take it one thing at a time. How do you feel about being involved with someone with that kind of past?"

E. J. thought back through Jinx's story, to her reaction. Yes, she had been shocked. No, she hadn't known what to say, but she had stayed. She had listened. A part of her had wanted to run right away, but she hadn't. Why not? Because she had wanted to know Jinx. But what she had wanted to know was about Jinx as a child, not Jinx as a drug addict, a thief, a bank robber, or a—she could barely form the word in her mind—a convict. She couldn't say she had wanted to know *that*. In fact, a part of her wished she still didn't. "I don't know if I can be okay with it. No matter what my feelings for her are. I think it's better if I just leave it alone and get over her."

"That hasn't really worked so far," Gwen said with no trace of sarcasm.

E. J. said nothing.

"E. J.," Taylor said, still watching her from the sofa. "I've known you a long time. I knew you when you were married to Marcus. I was there when you went through the divorce. I was right by your side the first time you picked up a woman, and I heard all about it the next day and was there to hear about many more. I was even there when you actually considered something more serious with Rhonda, until you blew her off, and through it all, I've never seen you like this."

E. J. bit her lip and closed her eyes again. Her friends were right. She *did* have feelings for Jinx. She was *already* involved. And not just a little. She was already deeply, emotionally involved.

"Are you in love with her, E. J.?"

Gwen's voice touched E. J.'s consciousness with the lightness of a feather. E. J. opened her eyes, and her exquisitely decorated and expensively furnished living room snapped her back to reality. "I can't be," she said, tightening her hold around her torso. "How can I be in love with a convict...a felon? How do I know she isn't *still* a criminal? I have no frame of reference for anything like this. I've never even known one."

Gwen glanced at Taylor, then down at the table.

Taylor was silent for a long moment. "Yes, you have," she said finally.

"What are you talking about?" E. J. asked.

Taylor hesitated. "I have a felony on my record."

E. J. blinked in amazement, then began to laugh. "You do not."

"Yes. I do."

Gwen ran a hand down Taylor's arm.

"It was a long time ago, just like Jinx. I got involved with drugs and did a lot of stupid things. When I was twenty-one, I did the ultimate stupid thing. I tried to smuggle drugs across the Mexican border for my boyfriend. Fortunately, I got arrested on the U. S. side. Otherwise I'd have had the *Brokedown Palace* experience in a foreign prison and might still be there. As it was, I served four years. By the time I got out, I'd learned a *whole* lot about what I didn't want my life to be and straightened up."

E. J. couldn't speak. She couldn't move. "How...What...Why did you never tell me?"

Taylor shrugged. "When we first met in training, that sweet, old Mr. Harvey had just hired us, and even knowing my past, he'd given me a second chance. Before getting that entry level job at Bad Dog, the best I'd been able to do since getting out had been to wait tables. I didn't want to jinx it—no pun intended." Taylor laughed. "Later, when we'd become good friends, it just seemed so long ago, it felt like that time in my life belonged to someone else."

E. J. didn't know what to say.

"I guess that's my point. People can change, E. J. And we can all do crazy things. Everyone can make bad decisions. We all just do what we do, or what we think we have to. It doesn't make us bad people."

"How do I know?" E. J. asked. "I mean, *you* changed, but I know you. How do I know if Jinx really changed?"

"You're smart, E. J. You're great at your job because you're good with people, a good judge of character. Go with that. Besides, she can't still be robbing banks or she'd live in a better neighborhood." Taylor gave her a little smile. "Better yet, trust your heart."

E. J. felt her eyebrows shoot up into her hairline.

Gwen chuckled.

"I know, Taylor Matthews, playgirl, terminally single, talking about the heart. Hardy-har. But really, I've never seen you this strongly affected by anyone, not even your husband of however many years. Give her a chance."

E. J. considered Taylor's advice, as shocking as it was. Could she do it? Could she set everything aside and give Jinx a chance, give *them* a chance? She felt like she did know Jinx, despite having met her such a short time ago, despite having learned things about her E. J. had no experience with. She knew Jinx was no longer the person who had walked into that bank.

"You're right. It isn't who she is today. At least, it doesn't seem to be," E. J. said, relaxing slightly. "In fact, I was amazed at who she is before I even knew about her past, but now, I can't believe how kind and gentle and sweet she is with everything she's been through. I mean, she feeds this homeless guy named Kenny every night, even though she doesn't have a lot herself. She helps the family of a gang kid next door for no reason other than it's just who she is. She took in an old, abandoned dog and loved him until he died."

"All right, all right," Taylor said, holding up her hands. "But before we canonize her, what made you run? Was it just her past?"

It was, but it wasn't. In her heart, E. J. knew that, but she didn't really want to admit the rest. Reluctantly, she shook her head.

"What then?" Taylor asked.

E. J. averted her gaze. "Jacob."

Taylor sighed. "Oh, E. J., when are you going to stop living your life based on guilt and fear over Jacob? He's a grown man. He's married. He's happy. He's successful. He's—"

Anger ignited in E. J. "My kids are my family."

"I know that, and you want them to be happy," Taylor said, crossing to E. J. "And you're their family. Don't you think they'd want you to be happy, too?"

"What do you know about family? You don't even have one."

Taylor arched an eyebrow. "*That* was mean. If I were the type to be hurt, that would have really hurt. But I'm not. And you're not going to distract me." She threaded an arm around E. J. "We're going to talk about Jacob…finally."

E. J. tried to pull away, but Taylor held her close in a firm yet gentle grasp.

"I've never said this before because you weren't ready, but it's time to say it. You've made up this whole big thing around Jacob and what happened to him and how you can never come out to him, even if it means you could be happy, so you'd have what you think is a legitimate and noble excuse to never let a woman *in*."

"I have not." E. J. pushed harder against her.

"Yes, you have, and somewhere, deep inside, you know it. You know it. I know it. Gwen knows it. And probably every woman with whom you've used it as a reason to break up knows it. And I've never said anything before now—we've never said anything—" Taylor glanced over her shoulder at Gwen. "Because, until now, there's never been anyone you showed the slightest interest in actually being intimate with. Besides, you were my buddy who always just wanted to talk about sex. I'll miss that." She squeezed E. J.'s shoulders.

Gwen cleared her throat.

"Right," Taylor said, obviously regaining focus. "But this woman? She's got your attention. She's somehow opened you up and reached inside."

If Taylor only knew the extent of the truth of that statement. E. J. rested her head on Taylor's shoulder. "How do you know about all this heart and openness stuff? You're always just in it for the sex."

"My heart's had its openings." Taylor laughed softly against E. J.'s hair. "Take it from me. You want to be a willing participant, otherwise it feels like someone's taken a can opener to it."

That was exactly how she'd felt for the past month and a half. E. J. raised her head and looked up at her. "Really? And why don't I know about this either?"

Taylor lifted a shoulder. "Maybe it's time for us to let each other in a little more, too."

"Oh my. I am so proud," Gwen said, stepping up beside E. J. "I think my babies are growing up." She slid her arm around E. J., beneath Taylor's. "I'm feeling a flutter of hope." She patted her chest.

"I hate it when she gets all high and mighty," Taylor whispered.

"Mm," E. J. murmured her agreement and put her head back to Taylor's shoulder. Her thoughts drifted again to Jinx. "Why does this have to be so close to Jacob and Tiffany, though?" E. J. asked no one in particular.

Gwen jostled her. "You *have* had other opportunities, you know. You just didn't take them. That's how the Universe works. We create easier opportunities to do something, and if we don't do it, we keep creating more complex ones that touch our lives in ways more and more important to us, until finally, we *can't* ignore it anymore. We have to do something different."

"I hate it when she talks about the Universe, too," Taylor whispered again. "It makes me feel like I'm being watched. It's creepy."

E. J. smiled, but she couldn't stop worrying about Jacob. "What if I lose my son?"

"You won't," Gwen said. "You raised him better than that. Even if he struggles a little, you'll be able to work this out. You've just never been willing to try before."

"Well, maybe she was just waiting for Jinx," Taylor said with a note of defiance. "Maybe we're all just waiting for that right person to confront the hard stuff for."

Gwen smiled at Taylor and tilted her head, a spark of affection in her eyes. "Maybe," she said quietly. "And," she said to E. J., "you'll know if Jinx is that person, but only if you go back to see her."

The thought of facing Jinx after the things she had said and the way she had left brought a flush to E. J.'s cheeks. How could she ever go back? Yet, she knew Gwen was right. Gwen was always right. *Damn it!*

Chapter Twelve

Jinx sat at her dining table, checking over a sheet of math problems for her young neighbor. She'd been grateful Angelita's seventh grade accelerated math class had begun a unit on geometry. It gave her something to keep her mind off E. J.

A quick rap sounded at the front door, followed by Pablo sticking his head into the room. As usual, he wore his cherished fedora. "Hey, *mija*. Mama says dinner's ready. You guys about done?"

"Just finishing up," Jinx said as she handed the paper back to Angelita. "You'll want to look at number twelve again. Other than that, I think you've got it."

"Thank you, Jinx." Angelita smiled and closed her binder.

"*Nice!*" Pablo whistled.

Jinx glanced up to find him looking over his shoulder toward the street.

"Your *chica* get a new car?"

Jinx's stomach clenched. E. J.? She didn't want to see her. Who was she kidding? Of course, she wanted to see her, but she didn't want to see her. "What are you talking about?"

"Oh, no. This is a new *chica*. But she looks too young for you. I could take her off your hands."

Jinx stood, knocking over her chair. "*What* are you talking about?"

Pablo laughed. "Relax. I won't steal her."

"Excuse me?" The female voice was clear and slightly familiar. "Does Michelle Tanner live here?"

Pablo flashed Jinx a broad grin. "Michelle?"

Jinx righted the chair and crossed to the door.

"Don't be a jerk, Pablo," Angelita said as she clutched her books to her chest and followed.

Jinx halted. "Tiffany?"

Tiffany smiled. "Hi."

Pablo leaned in close. "She's hot, but I like E. J. better," he said under his breath. "E. J.'s got that older woman, classy thing goin' on."

Jinx shot him a glare. "This is my *niece*, Tiffany. Tiffany, this is Angelita and Pablo, my neighbors," she said more pleasantly. "They were just leaving." She gave Pablo a gentle shove.

He grinned and tipped his fedora. "Nice to meet you." He placed the hat on Angelita's head, then wrapped an arm around her shoulders and guided her off the porch.

"It's nice to meet you," Tiffany echoed as they made their way across the lawn and driveway.

Jinx stared at her. "What are you doing here?"

"I'm sorry. I didn't mean to run off your company."

"You didn't. It's okay. They had to go home for dinner." Jinx hesitated. "What are you doing here?" she asked again.

"I probably should have called first, but I don't have your number."

Jinx couldn't take her eyes off her. She was sure there was something she should be saying, but only one question filled her mind. "What are you doing here?" she asked yet one more time. Then Andrea flashed in her mind. She tensed. Her heartbeat quickened. "Did something happen to Andrea?"

Tiffany gasped. "Oh! No, no. Mom's fine." She shifted her weight. "I'm sorry. I didn't mean to scare you. I just wanted to see you."

Jinx blinked in astonishment. "See me?" She was blowing this. A member of her family wanted to see her—had actually gone out of her way to see her. It wasn't Andrea, the one she'd always hoped it would be, but Tiffany *was* family. And Jinx was just standing there like a bumbling idiot. "Uh…you want to come in?" She managed a gesture toward the open doorway behind her.

Tiffany smiled. "Yes, thank you." Inside, she glanced around, her gaze landing on first the kitchen area, then the dinette, then the bed.

For the first time, Jinx regretted having no couch, no place for company to sit and be comfortable. Until now, her only visitors had either been fine just flopping onto the bed or being invited into it. "I—I'm sorry there's no place…We can sit over here." Jinx motioned Tiffany to the dinette. "It's not—"

"It's fine," Tiffany said as she crossed the room and sat.

"Do you want anything to…" Jinx faltered. "Do you want some water?" *Damn this whole drop-in company thing.* How was anyone ever prepared for it? Since it was becoming more common, she should ask Sparkle.

Tiffany smiled again. "No, thank you. I'm fine."

They stared at one another.

Jinx was astounded at how much Tiffany resembled Andrea. She'd noticed it at the wedding—the same dark brown hair and eyes, the same slightly turned up nose—but here, now, with Tiffany in navy slacks, a cream-colored blouse, and low heels rather than a designer wedding dress, the likeness was uncanny. Though older than Andrea had been when Jinx left home, Tiffany could have been her twin.

"You still look a lot like your pictures," Tiffany said, evidently conducting her own perusal.

"Pictures?" Jinx sat across from her.

"Luke has some. He gave me a few." Tiffany retrieved an envelope from her purse and handed it to Jinx. "I made copies for you. I thought you might like to have them, if you don't already." Her cheeks turned pink.

Jinx sifted through the photos. She slowed at several snapshots of her and Andrea that she actually remembered Luke taking—he'd always made a point of taking a picture of the two of them on each of their birthdays every year—then stopped at a small, formal portrait from her last year at the private high school they'd attended. It was taken shortly before her father died.

"I think you still look most like that one," Tiffany said, her words sounding a little rushed. "But this is my favorite." She pulled out a snapshot of Jinx, at ten, halfway up the ladder to the tree house, looking back over her shoulder at the camera. "I like it because your smile's so big and you look happy, but there's also fight in your eyes. I've always wondered what Luke said right before he took it."

Jinx remembered, but it hadn't been Luke. She shifted her gaze to Tiffany. How much should she tell her without knowing why she was here? She *was* here, though. Wasn't that more important than why? "It wasn't Luke," Jinx said, her tone low. "It was your mom. And she'd just told me that something your grandmother had said to me that morning wasn't true and when we got older, we'd…get even with her." Andrea's wording had been far more colorful, but Jinx didn't think she needed to share the details with Tiffany. She smiled at the memory of Andrea's chivalry on her behalf.

Tiffany's expression softened. "My grandmother was terrible to you," she said flatly.

Jinx wanted to agree. That part of her that could still feel the pain of all the cutting words and rejection, the part that had wanted revenge someday, that little girl that felt robbed of something so basic as a family, wanted to say, *yes, she was horrible.* Nora was Tiffany's grandmother, though, and although Tiffany clearly knew some things—had Luke told her? Surely, it hadn't been Andrea—Jinx wouldn't add to it from her own baggage. "It was a difficult situation for everyone," she said finally.

Tiffany's lips curved into a gentle smile, but her eyes held sadness. "You're very generous."

Jinx didn't want to go down this road with Tiffany. She didn't want to dredge up old hurts and resentments. She wanted to take advantage of the moment and be fully present in it, maybe learn a few things about her niece. "What are you doing here, Tiffany?" She straightened the pictures in her hands. "Don't get me wrong. I'm glad you're here. In fact, I can't believe it, but I'm wondering why. Your mother was very clear at the wedding that she didn't want you having anything to do with me."

Tiffany leaned forward in her chair. "I want to get to know you. I always have, ever since I first heard about you."

"When was that?" Jinx couldn't imagine Andrea had voluntarily told her daughter anything about her convict aunt.

"When I was nine, I was playing in my mom's jewelry box, and I found a picture of you."

"*Your mom* had a picture of *me*?" Jinx needed verification she'd heard correctly.

Tiffany nodded. "And she was really upset that I took it and made me give it back, even though she said it was nothing important. Have you ever seen or met someone you want to get to know, and you just can't let it go?"

E. J.'s image filled Jinx's mind. She pushed it aside. *You don't get to be here. You didn't want to be.* "Yes," she said. She, at least, couldn't deny the truth of that.

"That's how I felt when I saw your picture. I used to sneak back into my parents' room and look at it, making up stories about who you might be. Then one day, Luke mentioned a Chelle when he was talking about my mother as a child, and I asked him who that was. He didn't want to tell me at first. He said it would upset my mother, but when I showed him the picture, he did. When I asked him why I'd never met you, he said you left home way before I was born. He told me a lot of stories about you and Mom after that." Tiffany smiled. "He loves you both so much."

Jinx warmed at the memory of Luke's welcoming grin and the feel of his arms around her in the gardens the night of the wedding. "He's a great guy," she said around a swell of emotion. "I saw him the night you got married. He's pretty taken with you, too."

Tiffany blushed. "He's always been my confidant."

Jinx chuckled, remembering all the secrets Luke had been privy to, from the names of imaginary unicorns to the hidden location of buried treasure, from Andi's fears of always falling short in her mother's eyes to Jinx's inner struggle to hold on to the knowledge that she wasn't what Nora Tanner said she was. "He was always that for your mom and me, too."

"I think he still is, for Mom, I mean. I used to see them talking every once in a while. And once, after Grandmother died and we'd moved to the estate, I went out to the tree house, and I heard my mom crying and Luke talking to her."

Andrea crying in the tree house? Keeping a picture of Jinx in her jewelry box? Jinx would never have imagined either of those occurrences, based on Andrea's reaction to her both times she'd seen her. She had no reason to doubt Tiffany, though. She was relieved to discover Andrea wasn't as hardened and calloused toward her and their childhood as she seemed. Maybe Andrea was just pissed, and pissed was far more manageable.

"I'm sorry. Maybe I shouldn't be telling you all this," Tiffany said in a rush. "I have a tendency to run off at the mouth when I'm nervous."

"Why are you nervous?"

"I was afraid you wouldn't want to see me, wouldn't want to talk. It took me a long time to work up the nerve to try to get in touch with you. That's why I invited you to the wedding. I thought if you had no interest in any contact, like Mom said, you wouldn't come, and if you did come, it meant you might be open to more. I'm so sorry about what she said to you, though. I never meant for anything like that to happen."

Jinx shook her head. "None of this is your fault. The thing between me and your mom is our stuff, not yours. It goes back a long time. I'm glad you invited me."

"You are?" Tiffany looked relieved.

"I am." The last thing Jinx wanted was for Tiffany to feel bad about anything. "I got to see Luke. I got to go up in the tree house again. And I got to meet you, all things I never thought would happen. I admit, my reunion with my sister wasn't everything I dreamed it would be," she said with a smile, hoping to lighten the mood.

Tiffany laughed. "Things with Mom rarely are. But she's not a bad person, Aunt Michelle. She's just...I don't know. She's just always seemed so sad, but she won't admit it."

Sad. Jinx supposed that could be what lay beneath Andrea's hard and angry exterior. She'd never thought of it that way. "Sad about what?"

Tiffany was quiet for a moment. "I'm not sure. You, maybe."

Jinx blinked. "Me?"

Tiffany nodded. Her expression grew serious. "Sometimes when we've talked about you...Well, to be honest, most of the time we've fought about you, but once in a while, she gets this look in her eyes. I think she misses you."

A short laugh escaped before Jinx could catch it. "Tiffany, I don't think that's what your mom feels about me. I've tried to see her, to talk to her, twice since I've been home. The first time she wouldn't even let me in the house, and you saw what happened the second."

"You tried once before?"

"When I first got home."

Tiffany hesitated. "She said you didn't want to see us. That you'd made your choices and didn't want anything to do with us."

Jinx's throat tightened. "No, that isn't..." She didn't want to call Andrea a liar, but she couldn't let Tiffany think that. "That isn't the case. I wanted to see her, and meet you, very much. I even wrote to her a few times over the years, but she never answered." Suddenly, Jinx wondered how much Tiffany really knew. "Do you know where I was all those years?" Here it was, that moment when everything could change in a heartbeat, when someone interested in her could instantly transform into a person who never wanted to see her again. She braced herself.

"You were in prison," Tiffany said matter-of-factly. "You robbed a bank and were sent to prison."

Jinx relaxed a little, grateful she wouldn't have to tell the story so soon after doing so with E. J. "And before that, I was a drug addict, and I stole and lied. I think those are the reasons your mom's mad at me and doesn't want you to have anything to do with me."

"Are you still?" Tiffany asked.

"What?"

"Do you still take drugs? Are you a thief and a liar? Do you still rob banks or anything like that?"

"No," Jinx said, confident in the truth.

"Okay then," Tiffany said.

Jinx couldn't help but laugh. She found Tiffany refreshingly direct. "Okay then?"

"Okay, then I'd like to get to know you." Tiffany's features settled into a determined expression. "Aunt Michelle, I'm an only child. I don't have any other aunts or uncles or any cousins on Mom's side, and on my dad's, there's only my cousin Harold. The last time I saw him, we were eight and he was eating paste. So I want to get to know you. And once we know each other, if we decide we don't like one another, then okay, but I'd at least like the chance to decide. This isn't my mother's decision."

Jinx smiled, relieved to have that settled. "Sounds like a plan. You can go first, since you're company."

Tiffany grinned. "Goodie." She rubbed her hands together playfully, then thought for a few seconds. "What do you like to do for fun?"

Jinx enjoyed Tiffany's enthusiasm and was encouraged by her openness. "I like to read and watch movies," she said, relaxing into the ordinariness of the conversation. "I love dogs and to get up early and watch the sunrise." She once again pushed E. J. from her mind. "And take long bike rides. What about you?"

"I love to cook. I like creating new dishes or putting my own spin on recipes I find." A spark flashed in Tiffany's eyes, those rich brown eyes so much like Andrea's.

Jinx remembered that same spark any time Andrea talked about painting. She wondered if she'd kept up with her art.

"And I love to swim," Tiffany continued. "I love the feel of water on my skin. And I like to read, too. Maybe we can talk about books sometime. If we like the same kind, that is."

That last comment seemed to suggest this wasn't a one-time visit, that Tiffany wanted more. Excitement and hope stirred in Jinx like a bird opening its wings, but the memory of E. J.'s departure squelched it. Tiffany knew about Jinx's past, had known about it before she ever made contact, but people changed their minds so quickly. And one never knew at what point someone might reach their limit. Jinx was reluctant to let herself get too optimistic about anything in the future. It was better to simply focus on now, and now, she was happy Tiffany was there. "That'd be nice. We'll have to compare reading lists." She offered a reserved smile.

Jinx recognized her own distraction in Tiffany's expression. They'd been talking, but it seemed each was preoccupied with her own thoughts. "Are you sure you want to do this, Tiffany? It's all right if you've changed your mind." She almost choked on her own disappointment and doubt.

"I'm sure," Tiffany said. "I just wish I didn't have to hide it from Mom. I really thought if she saw you were open to contact, she might be more willing to…I don't know. It just didn't work out the way I wanted."

"I understand." Jinx covered Tiffany's hand with her own. "I've hoped that, too. I really think if I could get her to stay in the same room with me long enough to have a conversation, we could work things out. I mean, we used to be so close. If I could just explain things to her."

Tiffany's eyes widened slightly. "You mean, you haven't given up?"

"I kind of had, until today." Jinx squeezed Tiffany's fingers. "Until you showed up. If you think there's still a possibility, I'm willing to keep trying. I'll just have to figure out a new approach." In the back of her mind, she saw E. J.'s face frozen in a silent scream at the prospect of Jinx getting closer to the family Jacob married into. But what did it matter what E. J. thought? She was gone. Jinx knew, though, she would keep E. J.'s secret.

"We'll work on it together." Tiffany smiled. "Let's see, what else am I dying to know about you?" She tilted her head. "Is there a special man in your life?"

"No." Jinx watched her. "No man. I'm a lesbian."

"A special woman, then?" Tiffany asked without hesitation.

Jinx pondered the question, or more accurately, the answer. The truth was that there *was* a special woman. She just wasn't *in* Jinx's life anymore. She was still in Jinx's heart, however. *Damn it!* But that wasn't what Tiffany had asked. And what would be the point of telling her about this wonderful woman she'd met and spent time with only to then have to say she wasn't around any longer? "No," Jinx said, glancing away. That was the truth. "What about you and your new husband? How do you like being married?" *Nice segue to a new subject.*

A huge smile brightened Tiffany's face. "I love it. Although, I have to admit, so far it's consisted of traveling through Europe, staying at five-star hotels, and having romantic dinners and lots of sex. Who wouldn't love that?" She laughed. "But seriously, I love Jacob so much."

Tiffany's happiness was infectious. Jinx couldn't help smiling as well. "I'm glad." It felt odd talking about Jacob with someone other than E. J. Granted, she and E. J. hadn't spoken about him a lot, but he was E. J.'s son, and Jinx knew how scared she was of him being anywhere near Jinx—even in this six-degrees-of-separation kind of way.

Tiffany's glow faded slightly. "That's something I'm going to have to do, though."

Jinx arched an eyebrow in question.

"Tell Jacob I came to see you."

"He doesn't know?"

Tiffany shook her head. "I wanted to find out if you and I had a chance at a relationship before I told him. He was a little upset with me for inviting you to the wedding without my mother's knowledge."

"Oh. So he knows the whole story?"

"He doesn't care about that. He thinks I shouldn't have done that to Mom. He says I blindsided her, and I suppose I did," Tiffany brushed her bangs from her eyes. "He says he'd never do that to his mother." She frowned.

Jinx shifted uncomfortably. Maybe E. J. was right. Maybe all of this was too close. She felt like she was sitting between two thin veils, with E. J. behind one and Jacob the other, so close, they were all breathing the same air. And yet, she was intrigued. This was a chance to hear about E. J.'s relationship with her son from a different perspective, perhaps from one that wasn't skewed by fear and defenses. "Are he and his mother close?" she asked, trying to sound casual.

"Not now," Tiffany said. "She isn't around much. Jacob says when she and his dad got divorced, she became much more career oriented, and that's where she puts most of her time and energy. Even for our wedding, she couldn't be here until the night before."

Jinx felt a twinge of guilt. Would E. J. have spent more time with Jacob and her family had she not met Jinx in the bar that night? "Does that upset him?"

"He misses her, but he says he understands." Tiffany looked at Jinx as if evaluating her. "She helped him through a really hard time when he was young. He says he wouldn't have made it through without her. But then, when she and his dad got a divorce, she just sort of disappeared. I mean, they still text and talk, and sometimes she visits, but he says it's not the same, that something is different."

Jinx listened, pondering E. J.'s fear of Jacob discovering her sexuality. *Is that when it happened—when E. J. got a divorce? Is that when she started seeing women?*

"Mandy, Jacob's sister, sees her a little more, but they still live in the same town."

Jacob's sister? E. J. has a daughter? She'd never even mentioned a daughter. Now that Jinx thought about it, she never mentioned her son either, unless it was to freak out. Was E. J. that compartmentalized? Jinx had thought she was getting to know her, but now she wondered if she'd known her at all.

"Oh, I'm so sorry." Tiffany sighed. "I shouldn't be boring you with all this. Why would you care about Jacob's mother? It's just, you're really easy to talk to."

Jinx knew she shouldn't still care about E. J., but she did. She wanted to ask more. She wanted to figure out why E. J. was so afraid of Jacob's rejection, why she thought he *would* reject her. Tiffany hadn't even flinched when Jinx told her she was gay, and clearly had no problem with Jinx's past. Would someone so open-minded and accepting fall in love with a narrow-minded bigot?

Jinx also wanted to learn more about E. J. via her relationship with Tiffany and Jacob, but she couldn't press without it seeming odd. Besides, she already had a lot to process from the conversation—and E. J. was no longer her concern.

CHAPTER THIRTEEN

The fluttering in E. J.'s stomach increased with each turn that took her closer to Jinx's house. After her conversation with Gwen and Taylor, she had planned to return to see Jinx the following weekend, but she had chickened out. Now, a full week later—an entire month since her craven retreat—she still wanted to run the other way. How could she face Jinx? And yet, she had to—if for no other reason than to apologize and thank her for the time they had shared.

She hoped for more, though. She didn't know how, exactly, to fit Jinx into her life, but she had come to realize she needed to try. She had made her decision. The remaining question was for Jinx. Would she let E. J. back in, or was that door already closed?

E. J. glanced at her peace offering nestled in the passenger's seat. She felt a little guilty, as though she was taking unfair advantage. Perhaps she was, but she had been afraid to show up empty-handed, afraid to come alone. Had she always been such a coward? Maybe so. She had run from anyone who had ever felt anything for her, and she was terrified to let her kids know her fully. Didn't that make her a coward? Her butterflies now felt like they had wings of iron as she made the final turn onto Jinx's street.

Jinx's car sat in the driveway. The porch was dark, but a light shone through the window from inside the house.

E. J. turned off the engine. Had Jinx heard it? She stared at the front door, waiting for it to open. When it didn't, she scooped up the sleeping gold and brown puppy beside her, bed and all, and climbed out of the car.

The puppy stirred and blinked up at E. J. blearily. He had begun the trip standing on his hind legs, front paws on the armrest, tail wagging, and smearing his wet nose all over the window. As the hour grew late, though, he had wiggled into E. J.'s lap and fallen asleep under her stroking fingers. At the last rest stop, she had pulled his new bed from the trunk and settled him into it for the remainder of the drive. "It's time to wake up," she whispered. "But we have to be quiet. You're a surprise."

He flipped onto his tummy and stretched up to lick her chin.

She laughed and tiptoed up the porch steps. When she set the bed in front of the door, the puppy stood and shook himself.

"No, no," E. J. whispered. "You have to stay there. Sit." She pressed her hand to his rump and coaxed him to his haunches.

He gazed at her adoringly and cocked his head as if to say, "Like this?"

"Good boy." E. J. rubbed him under his chin. "Now, stay." She didn't have a clue as to whether he understood anything she was saying. She had gotten him from a Labrador rescue facility. Originally, when the idea of getting Jinx a dog had come to her, she had looked at breeders, but then she realized Jinx would want a shelter dog. And she had almost gotten an older one, since the woman she had dealt with told her that puppies always found homes, but when she thought of Rex, she had decided to give Jinx as much time with her new friend as possible. The woman had said he was a lab mix, about eight weeks old, and the runt of a litter of nine, but very smart and irresistibly sweet. "Ready?"

The puppy whined softly.

E. J. took a deep breath and rapped on the door, then stepped into the shadows. She heard footsteps, then the door open. A pause.

"Hey there," Jinx said in evident surprise. "How'd you knock?"

E. J. saw Jinx's knees as she squatted and her hands as she reached for the puppy. As soon as she got to his level, he leapt on her, bathing her face in kisses. Jinx laughed and tipped over backward onto the floor.

The puppy climbed onto her chest and began to bark.

"Okay, you guys," Jinx called out. "If you're trying to cheer me up, it's working."

E. J. summoned her courage and stepped around the corner.

Jinx, still laughing, did a double take, confusion and conflict in her eyes.

The puppy scrambled over her, licking and nipping, while she struggled to get a hold on him.

E. J. couldn't help but smile.

Jinx's gaze returned to her again and again until, finally, she held the puppy to her chest and managed to get to her feet. She stared at E. J., her expression clouded. "What do you want?"

The sharpness of the question bit into E. J., but she knew she deserved it. She cleared her throat. "I wanted to see you. To tell you I'm sorry."

"You already said that. On your way out. Don't you remember? I do." Jinx set the wiggling puppy on the floor and knelt beside him, petting him until he calmed.

E. J. watched her stroke the puppy. She wasn't sure what to say. She had practiced several speeches on the drive down, but now, all escaped her. It was just as well. She realized a rehearsed discourse wouldn't do it here. She needed to speak from her heart. She had to be honest. She had to be vulnerable. "I got scared, Jinx. It was all so much, so fast. And then I had a dream...where Jacob...I got scared. And when I get scared, I run. I'm sorry."

Jinx looked up at her. "You don't think I was scared?" Her voice hardened. "Of your reaction being exactly what it was? You deciding I'm not good enough for you? That I'm not worth it?"

E. J. swallowed. "I know that's how it must have felt—"

"It wasn't a feeling, E. J. It's exactly what happened. If that wasn't what you thought, you would have stayed. We would have talked more. You would have let me try to explain." Jinx's eyes darkened with obvious anger, but her fingers that combed through the puppy's fur and scratched behind his ear remained gentle.

E. J. was glad Jinx was angry. She could handle anger. She could stand up to a fight. It was the softer emotions that terrified her. If she had looked into Jinx's face and seen the hurt she knew Jinx must be feeling—the hurt *she* would be feeling if the tables were turned—she would have needed to nail her feet to the floor, but this? This she could do. "I don't think any of those things," she said firmly. "And

I wasn't thinking them then. I just…got scared. And I'm still scared, but I'm here."

Jinx returned her attention to the puppy. "A *month* later. What have you been doing all this time if not deciding my worthiness?" Sarcasm dripped from her words.

Honesty. E. J. had to be honest. Jinx had bared her soul. E. J. had to do the same. "I was trying to forget you," she said quietly. "Well, the first two and a half weeks, I was trying to forget you. The last week and a half, I was trying to work up the courage to face you again. But that isn't particularly because of what you told me about your past."

Jinx looked up at her but said nothing.

At least she was listening. E. J. took it as an invitation to continue. "Jinx, I don't know what to do with you. Since that very first night, every time I've left, I've tried to forget you, tried to file you away as just another woman I met on the road, because that's what I do. That's what I've always done since I started seeing women. But you…" She waved a hand at Jinx and let out a short laugh. "I can't get you out of my mind. No matter where I am or what I'm doing, you're there with me. Your smile. Your laugh. Your jokes. Your touch." E. J. hesitated. How far should she go? "Your tenderness." She shook her head. "I can't…Do you want to know what I really think of you?"

Jinx's eyes narrowed slightly. "No."

Surprised, E. J. inhaled to stop her next words. The question had been rhetorical, but now that Jinx had answered it, she had to honor the answer. Or did she? "You're the bravest person I know. The most honest. Even before you told me you've been in prison, I admired how direct and unpretentious you are. That takes courage."

Jinx continued to stroke the dog.

"You are who you are, comfortable with your job and where you live, and the fact that your relationship with your family is strained."

Jinx snorted.

"I'm not saying you don't want some things to be different," E. J. said, opening her arms. "You're so honest about it all. And everything you told me about your childhood and being on drugs and in prison…I can't even imagine how hard that was for you to share, but you did it so I would know the truth. So, if I wanted to, I *could* go, even though you didn't want me to. I didn't know what to do with that kind of honesty. It scared me because I lie every day about who I am. So, I ran." Her eyes welled with tears. "Jinx, I'm so sorry. If you want me to go now, I will."

Jinx stared at the floor.

The puppy looked past her, then dashed into the house and leapt onto the bed. He snatched a sandwich off a plate on the nightstand and chewed frantically.

"Hey!" Jinx said as she sprang to her feet. "That's my dinner." She crossed the room in even strides. "You little thief." She grabbed a glass of milk a split second before the puppy's nose dipped into it.

E. J. laughed despite the serious conversation.

"Look what your dog did." Jinx shook the empty plate at E. J.

"I guess he's hungry," E. J. said. "We didn't stop to eat on the way down. I have some dog food in the car." She retrieved a bag of puppy kibble, along with the food and water bowls she had bought, from her trunk and returned to the porch. Once again in the doorway, she watched Jinx roll around on the bed with the puppy. She let herself enjoy Jinx's laughter mingling with his playful growls and yips. She was glad to be back. It had been such a long month, and she knew they still had a lot to work out, but it was a start. She just hoped Jinx would let her stay.

Jinx grabbed the puppy and held him tightly. "Now, I've got you." She grinned and looked up. Her gaze met E. J.'s. She arched a brow.

"May I come in?" E. J. asked tentatively.

Jinx rolled her eyes. "Yes, you can come in. You have to feed your dog, don't you?" She rubbed noses with the puppy. "It's not his fault his mama's a big fat chicken."

E. J. smiled as she set the bag of food on the bed. She pulled the string to open it.

"What's his name?" Jinx asked, dropping to her knees on the floor in front of him. He began licking her again.

"He doesn't have one yet."

"What? How can he not have a name? Everyone has a name. You just have to find it," Jinx said. "How long have you had him?"

"Since this morning." E. J. scooped kibble into the bowl.

"You have a name, don't you?" Jinx turned her head and let him lick her ear. "Tell me." She scrunched up her face and giggled. "Pete," she said finally. "His name is Pete."

E. J. laughed. "He told you that, did he?"

"He did." Jinx took the bowl and set it on the floor, then put the puppy in front of it. "But you know, he's your dog. It's up to you."

"Actually," E. J. said hesitantly. "He's yours. I got him for you."

Jinx stared at her. "Oooooh, that's just…" She shook her head. "That's so wrong." She looked down at Pete.

"I know." E. J. sat on the edge of the bed.

Jinx looked up at her. "You really *are* a chicken."

"I am." E. J. searched Jinx's face. "I was afraid you wouldn't see me if I just showed up."

Jinx stroked Pete's back. "That's so manipulative."

E. J. nodded. "It is."

"And just…*wrong*." Laughter flashed in Jinx's eyes. "I mean, you used this poor, innocent little puppy in your scheme."

"I did." E. J. began to relax for the first time in weeks. "I don't know that he suffered much, though. Let's see, he got rescued from a shelter, had a nice bath that he enjoyed very much, saw miles of countryside and got to bark at cows, was loved on while he slept in a snuggly lap, and is wolfing down a bowl of food almost as big as he is. And he gets to live with a beautiful, sweet woman who's the biggest dog lover on the face of the planet. I think he made out pretty well in the exchange." E. J. could feel the warmth of Jinx's body along the length of her leg and fought her desire to touch her. "I just hope I'll get to see him…a lot."

Jinx gave her a measuring look. Uncertainty and hope mingled in the depths of her blue eyes, but the shadow that had lingered there was gone. "I'm still mad at you," she said softly.

"I know."

"And Pete ate my sandwich when I still thought he was yours, so you owe me dinner."

E. J. smiled. She brushed her fingers across Jinx's cheek. "Pizza?"

❖

E. J. wiped the corner of her mouth with a napkin, then crumpled it and tossed it onto her plate. "That was so good."

"You're leaving the best part," Jinx said, picking up the crust E. J. had left. She took a bite before tearing off a tiny piece and feeding it to Pete.

"No." E. J. rested her elbow on the table and cradled her chin in her hand. "The cheese is the best part."

Jinx let a small smile touch her lips. "At least we won't fight over pizza."

The conversation over dinner had been light, E. J. talking about the entire re-staffing that needed to be done at one of her stores—Jinx had missed which one, distracted by the memory of E. J.'s mouth on hers—and Jinx sharing her adventures of learning the various types of poodle cuts. Jinx was glad E. J. was there, but at the same time, she didn't want to be. She wanted to stay mad, to be getting over E. J. She didn't want to hurt anymore. She cleared the dishes from the table and set them in the sink, then turned and leaned against the counter.

E. J. sat at the dinette, watching her. "Well," she said, drawing out the word. "I should get going. I need to get a room."

Jinx's stomach clenched. She didn't want E. J. to leave. *Damn it*. She thought she'd been so careful. She looked down at Pete sitting at E. J.'s feet.

He wagged his tail. He wasn't going to help her.

Jinx pursed her lips and folded her arms. "I think Pete wants you to stay. You can, if you want."

E. J. tilted her head and studied her. "Are you sure?"

Jinx wasn't at all sure. She thought of the times E. J. had left before, all the moments, the days, the nights Jinx had wished she was there. Then she remembered the last time, the way she'd shut Jinx out, how cold she'd seemed. Jinx didn't like that E. J. "I'm sure I don't want you to leave," she said cautiously. "I'm *not* sure I want you to stay."

E. J. gave her a sad smile. "Oddly enough, I understand that." She waited, her gaze direct, until Jinx looked away. "I'd like to stay, but I'll do whatever you want."

Jinx remembered what Sparkle had said. *You have something with her. If she does come back, you're going to want to see her again.*

To give her another chance. Even without that, though, she knew which part of her would win. She sighed. "If you give me your keys, I'll get your stuff."

When she returned with E. J.'s suitcase and a PetSmart bag containing a leash, a stuffed squeaky rabbit, a package of small bones, and a puppy-sized Kong, she found E. J. drying their plates and glasses and putting them in the cupboard. She looked so at home in Jinx's kitchen.

"If you have some foil, I'll put away the leftovers," E. J. said, glancing over her shoulder.

Jinx stepped up beside her and opened a drawer. "I have plastic wrap." She handed her the roll. "Sparkle says it's better for the environment. Aluminum has a heavier manufacturing footprint." She repeated the words verbatim, though she wasn't completely sure what they meant.

E. J. stiffened almost imperceptibly. She stared at the plastic wrap. "Do you do everything Sparkle says?" There was the slightest edge to her voice.

Jinx had noticed E. J.'s reaction to Sparkle's name every time it'd come up, and then there was Sparkle's attitude toward E. J. She wondered what'd taken place between them the night they'd met in the bar. "Sparkle says I should give you another chance."

E. J. grinned. "Sparkle is *so* smart." She tore off a piece of plastic wrap. "Have I ever told you how smart I think she is?"

Jinx laughed. She was having trouble holding on to the anger she'd cultivated over the past weeks and the flare-up at seeing E. J. in her doorway this evening. She wasn't sure she wanted to be mad anymore, but it'd protected her. What if she let go of it now and E. J. left again? She wanted to talk, needed to know what E. J. was thinking, and she needed to be out of the house, away from the bed, before she let her guard down fully. Otherwise, she knew where they'd end up. Maybe she shouldn't have invited E. J. to spend the night, but she was afraid to let her go. "You want to go get some frozen yogurt?"

E. J. smiled and nodded.

As Jinx gave E. J. directions, she held Pete in her lap and enjoyed his antics of sticking his head out the window and occasionally barking at someone in another car, or walking down the sidewalk. It seemed he was wary of people in hats.

The evening was ideal, the heat of the day giving way to a cool, light breeze. It reminded Jinx of the wedding reception and the feel of the air on her face as she'd stared across the lawn at E. J. in her deep purple gown. E. J. was saying something, telling her about something to do with her work. Jinx knew it was more chitchat and hated it. There was so much for them to talk about, so many things to be cleared up, but she had no one to blame but herself. E. J. was taking her cues from her, waiting for Jinx to open the door. It was up to her to start any meaningful conversation.

"Right there," Jinx said, pointing to the yogurt shop.

E. J. maneuvered into the parking lot and angled into a spot. "Tutti Frutti's?"

"Yup," Jinx said, climbing from the passenger's seat and setting Pete on the ground. "The best salted caramel frozen yogurt ever."

As they headed toward the storefront, E. J. took Pete's leash. "That's what I'll have, then. We'll wait out here." She led the puppy toward the outdoor seating.

"Don't go anywhere," Jinx said in an attempt at levity. "Especially not with my dog."

E. J. smiled. "You'd better hurry back, then."

Jinx grinned. Okay. This was more like it, more their usual interaction. She just had to let it be all right.

Inside, Jinx filled two cups with frozen yogurt, one salted caramel, the other peanut butter—her favorite flavors—then busied herself at the topping bar.

"Jinx!" The sound was more a squeal than a word.

Jinx knew it was Wendy. She turned to see the petite girl coming out of the back room, towel in hand.

Wendy ran over and hugged her. "I have something to tell you."

"Not until your break," the manager said from behind the register. Wendy grimaced.

"It's okay," Jinx said. "I'll be right out there." She gestured toward the front window. "No rush." After paying, she made her way back to E. J. and Pete.

E. J. studied her as she took a cup, clearly wanting to say something.

"What?" Jinx asked warily.

"Is that her?" E. J. asked. "The other woman?"

Jinx drew a blank. "What other woman?"

"The morning in my hotel suite, when I asked you if you went home often with women from bars, you said that was only your second time and the first wasn't from a bar but from Tutti Frutti's. Is that the other one?"

"Oh, yeah." Jinx chuckled, remembering the conversation. It seemed so long ago. "That's Wendy."

E. J. paused. "Jinx, she's a *child*." Her tone was incredulous.

Jinx looked at her in surprise, then glanced through the window of the yogurt shop. "I guess technically she is. She's seventeen."

E. J. stared at her. "You slept with a seventeen-year-old?"

"Whoa! What?" Jinx flinched and almost dropped her yogurt. A dollop slid off her spoon and plopped onto the toe of her shoe.

Pete quickly lapped it up.

"Jinx?" Wendy called, hurrying to their table. "I've been waiting for you to come in. Where have you been?"

Jinx stood. "Wendy, this is—"

"I passed." Wendy threw her arms around Jinx's neck and jumped up and down. "I passed."

Jinx broke into a grin and hugged her. "That's great. I knew you could do it."

"And," Wendy said breathlessly, "I have an appointment with an advisor at the JC to schedule classes for the fall." She beamed at Jinx, then looked at E. J. "I'm going to college."

"That's wonderful," E. J. said, her bewilderment evident.

Wendy dropped onto one of the seats at the table. "Jinx is so sweet. She went home with me one night after work and spent the whole night teaching me how to write an essay so I could pass that stupid proficiency test. I'd flunked it twice." She rolled her eyes.

Jinx smiled. "You just needed a little direction."

Realization settled in E. J.'s expression, and it softened. She looked at Jinx affectionately. "Yes, she is very sweet," she said to Wendy.

The girl sat with them, sharing every detail of the essay she'd written, then excused herself to finish her shift.

Jinx watched her until she stepped back into the bright lights of the yogurt shop. "She's got a lot going for her," she said, remembering herself at that age. "I'm glad she's going to do something with it."

"Something about knowing you makes people want to do better." E. J. laced her fingers through Jinx's. "Makes *me* want to do better. I'm sorry I thought you'd slept with her. That you *would* sleep with her."

Jinx brought E. J.'s hand to her lips. She brushed a kiss across the palm. "Baby, the only person I want to sleep with is you."

E. J. squeezed her eyes shut, and moisture seeped from beneath her lids. "Don't call me baby unless you've forgiven me," she whispered. "Unless you're not going to send me away."

"I can't send you away." Jinx pulled E. J. to her and held her. "If I could, I would have done it when you first stepped into the doorway. That's when I was the maddest. And I couldn't do it even then. I'll be honest. Sometimes, I've wished I could. But I can't."

E. J. sat back. "Jinx, I'm trying very hard not to be afraid. I want so much not to be. But you're the first person who's ever mattered enough for me to even try. So, I don't really know how. I'm so afraid of losing Jacob's love."

"I understand that fear, baby. I have to stare it down every time I have to tell someone about my past. And most of the people I've told couldn't get away fast enough. But I have to believe that someday I'll find somebody it doesn't matter to, somebody who'll love me anyway. You already know Jacob loves you. Why don't you trust that?"

E. J. inhaled a deep breath. "No one has ever loved me just as I am. Well, except my grandparents. But they're gone." She tried to ease her hand from Jinx's, but Jinx held it firmly. "My mother expected specific things from me—good grades, acceptable behavior, a marriage that presented well. Then Marcus needed a wife beside him on his climb up the professional ladder. And my kids…Well, a mother is supposed to be certain things."

"It doesn't sound like you've ever given anyone the opportunity to love you as you are," Jinx said.

"What do you mean?"

Jinx shifted in her seat. She knew what she was about to say might make E. J. mad, might summon that cold, shut-down E. J. Jinx didn't like. It might make her run again, but it had to be said. "If all you ever show people is who you think they want you to be, how will you ever know if they'd love you for who you are? You have to stop pretending to be someone you're not, before anyone can love and accept *you*. It's up to you to make a different choice. You have to choose to let yourself be loved, without giving up who you are to be what someone else might need."

"It's not that simple," E. J. said, glancing down at Pete where he'd settled between them.

"It is that simple. It might be scary, but it's only hard if we make it hard." Jinx ran her thumb over the back of E. J.'s hand. "When I tell someone—"

"Jinx, Jacob hates gays and lesbians."

"What?" She remembered Tiffany's reaction—or rather, lack thereof—to Jinx's answer about whether or not there was a special man in her life. She still thought it unlikely that someone so accepting would be married to someone who went so far as to *hate* gay people.

"He was molested when he was young by a man in our neighborhood. The man wasn't gay, but when Jacob got older and learned what gay meant, he drew an incorrect conclusion. He was still struggling with what had happened, and it all got mixed in together. We all tried to explain it—me, Marcus, his therapist—but he was just so angry. His therapist said, for the time being, it was more important that Jacob feel heard."

Jinx waited for more, but nothing else came. "He said he hates gays?"

E. J.'s laugh was humorless. "He didn't say it. He screamed it. And I realized then I could never tell him about my attraction to women, until I knew if he'd come to terms with what happened to him and understood it had nothing to do with homosexuality. I started seeing women in secret when Marcus and I divorced, and I always thought there would be some magical right moment to check in with Jacob, but I never seemed to find it. I don't know what to do. But I know I want to do things differently with you, with us, but I'm scared. I can't hurt him again. I just can't have him hate me."

"You didn't hurt him. That guy did. Jacob knows that, I'm sure."

"But I didn't protect him." E. J. pulled free and buried her face in her hands. "A mother is supposed to protect her children."

"You feel guilty."

"Of course, I feel guilty." E. J.'s voice broke. "I didn't protect him."

"What did you do when you found out?"

"I had that son of a bitch arrested." She sniffed. "And I got Jacob into therapy. But I wasn't there to stop it from happening in the first place." She began to cry. "So, I've done everything I can, all my life, to make sure nothing I do ever hurts him again."

Jinx stroked E. J.'s hair, then pulled her into her arms. "But you stopped it once you found out. It wasn't your fault, baby. All kids have stuff to go through, some of us more than others. And the love and support of their parents makes them stronger. That's what you gave Jacob." Jinx wished she could tell E. J. what Tiffany had shared with her about Jacob feeling he never would have made it through the *hard time* Tiffany had alluded to, without his mother. She'd have to tell E. J. about the two visits she'd had with Tiffany and that they planned to continue getting together, but not now. Not in the midst of everything else going on this evening. "Have you been punishing yourself by not letting anyone love you?"

E. J. stiffened.

"Hear me out," Jinx said cautiously. "You won't let yourself actually be in a relationship with a woman because you're afraid of hurting Jacob. And you keep yourself distant from Jacob"—she wanted to mention E. J.'s daughter as well, but that was something else she couldn't admit knowing—"because you're afraid he'll find out you're gay. So, you don't get to be close to anyone. That's what happens with guilt, E. J. Guilt calls for punishment, so we punish ourselves."

"Taylor says I use my guilt about Jacob to push people away," E. J. said into the front of Jinx's shirt.

"I don't know who Taylor is, but she sounds like someone to listen to." Jinx rocked E. J. gently.

"She's one of my best friends." E. J. looked up into Jinx's face. "I'd like you to meet her sometime. And Gwen, too."

Jinx waited for a *but*, or some kind of qualifier.

None came.

"Really?" She felt the beginnings of a smile from deep within.

E. J. nodded and wiped her tears. "I'm still scared, and there's still so much I want to know about your time in prison and the drugs. I've never known anyone who's been through that. And I still don't know exactly how to have you in my life, but you're important to me. So I want to try. I know I'm going to have to face my fears about Jacob and, like you said, stare them down. And I think I can do that, because…I feel safer in your arms than I've ever felt in my life." She caressed Jinx's cheek, traced her lips with her fingertips. Her eyes pooled again. "Just, please…Please, don't give up on me."

CHAPTER FOURTEEN

E. J. scratched Pete's chest as he stood in her lap, his entire body wiggling at the scenes flowing past the passenger's window: pedestrians on the city sidewalks—one on roller blades that warranted a brave bark—a cement truck and a man in a hard hat, and now, some workers in a field all seemed brand new through his eyes. Or maybe E. J. was simply trying to distract herself to calm her nerves.

Jinx turned her Toyota off the main road, and passed beneath a tall, wooden arch that reminded E. J. of those in old westerns that said things like the Triple Bar Ranch or Thistleweed Acres. This one read Canine Complete in bold black lettering against a whitewashed background. The knot in E. J.'s stomach tightened.

The previous night, when they had returned to Jinx's, E. J. had let Jinx set the tone and pace for anything that might happen. She wanted to be with Jinx, but she didn't want to push. She'd changed from slacks and blouse into something more casual and Jinx had remained in her jeans and T-shirt, but kicked off her shoes. They'd settled comfortably onto the bed and watched a Netflix movie. Jinx had slipped an arm around E. J. and cuddled her against her chest, while Pete made himself at home where their bodies met, but they hadn't talked further about anything serious, nor had they had sex or even kissed. It was different, definitely, but E. J. found it calming. She was grateful to be in Jinx's bed once again. She'd missed it, and she hadn't realized it wasn't only the sex she had missed until she felt herself sigh as she had lain against Jinx. They'd laughed through the movie and fallen asleep in each other's arms afterward, fully clothed.

When E. J. awakened, she was alone, but this time she knew exactly where to find Jinx. On the back porch, without a word, she nestled between Jinx's thighs on the step below her and sank into the warmth of Jinx's arms enfolding her in the blanket. Together, they greeted the dawn, sans the incredible orgasm, while Pete explored every inch of the backyard.

At breakfast, though, E. J.'s newfound serenity had been shaken.

"I'm off today, but I thought we could take Pete to meet Reggie and Sparkle," Jinx had said casually.

We, she had said, and now here *they* were, heading up the long driveway to the building and grounds that apparently comprised Canine Complete.

"This first building is the main shop and the grooming salon," Jinx said, a hint of pride in her voice. "Over there is the training facility." She gestured to a building and several rows of outdoor pens to the left. "And that empty field over there is where Reggie and Sparkle want to add an emergency vet clinic, someday. The kennels are in the back. You can't see them from here."

"It's lovely," E. J. said. And it was. Pristine white buildings and fences set against lush greenery reminded her of the beauty of *Anne of Green Gables*. She took in a deep breath and tried to dispel her nervousness, but she remained tense. She had wanted to beg off from accompanying Jinx this morning, but if she was going to make a go of being in Jinx's life, she needed to do it.

What was she anxious about? She had met Reggie and Sparkle before. Though, she hadn't known they were Jinx's best friends at the time, and *they* hadn't known much about her—hadn't known that every time she left Jinx she had no intention of returning, hadn't known she had run out on her when she had learned of her past. Now, they unquestionably knew all of that, and she was sure Sparkle had opinions about it. If someone had treated Gwen the same way, *she* would certainly have opinions, and she doubted she would tell Gwen to give him another chance.

Jinx continued around the side of the main building, past a sign that read Employees Only, and parked in a back lot with a couple of other cars. From there, a long building and large circular yard could be seen across an expanse of a lush, grassy field. Mature oak trees provided tranquility and shade.

The view stole E. J.'s breath. "This really is beautiful," she said, standing beside the car and taking it all in. She hated to admit her surprise even to herself. She hadn't been consciously aware of it, but she had created a picture of what this place might look like based on her judgment of Sparkle. She had to start fresh, treat this as a first meeting.

Pete pulled on his leash, trying to make a dash across the field, then sat and chewed on the leather strap.

Jinx took her hand and gave it a gentle squeeze. "Ready?" She hadn't said anything, but she seemed to sense E. J.'s unease.

E. J. gripped her fingers gratefully and nodded.

Jinx led her toward the back of a house that hadn't been visible from the front parking lot. It, too, was painted a gleaming white, and a veranda ran the full width and up the sides. Sparkle stood at the back door. "Well, look what the cat drug in," she said, looking directly at E. J. The words weren't particularly friendly, but she was grinning. It could have been a joke.

E. J. smiled. "Hello, Sparkle. It's nice to see you again."

Sparkle ignored the pleasantry. "Who's this cute little guy?" She knelt as Pete raced up the steps, Jinx scrambling behind to avoid choking him.

Jinx unclipped the leash. "Sparkle, meet Pete," Jinx said with a formal air. "Pete, this is your aunt Sparkle." She ruffled the fur on his head.

Sparkle laughed when he planted his front paws on her knees and tried to lick her face. "No, you don't." She caught him and eased him to the wooden deck. "Your aunt Reggie will break you of that before the day's out, I'm sure. Where'd you find him?"

"E. J. brought him," Jinx said, sounding like a little kid.

Sparkle shifted her gaze to E. J. still at the bottom of the steps. "Oh, you're good."

E. J.'s cheeks heated. She knew her ploy had been transparent, but it had gotten her in the door. And now, they had Pete. *They.*

"Hey, where's Reggie?" Jinx asked. "I want her to meet Pete."

"Out in the training field, working with a dog off leash," Sparkle said, continuing a playful jostling of the puppy who growled and batted at her. "Head on out there. Pete will be a good distraction for the training. I'll keep your girl company," she added, glancing at E. J.

"Oh. I can go with Jinx," E. J. said. "I don't want to keep you from whatever you were doing."

"You won't make it halfway in those shoes." Sparkle nodded at E. J.'s open-toed, backless sandals. "There's all sorts of stickers and burrs, and you'll get those polished toes all dirty."

E. J. couldn't tell if Sparkle was making fun of her or inviting her to stay for a conversation. She decided the latter was inevitable, regardless of shoes or timing. Sparkle was obviously the guardian at Jinx's gate.

Jinx looked at E. J., her expression hopeful.

"If you're sure," E. J. said to Sparkle.

Jinx grinned and jumped off the steps. She kissed E. J. firmly on the lips—their first kiss in over a month.

E. J.'s heart melted. *Damn!* She was such a sucker for this woman.

"We won't be long," Jinx called as she trotted off, Pete at her heels.

"No hurry," E. J. said. "I'll be fine." And she knew she would be. Now that she was face-to-face with Sparkle, she no longer felt intimidated. And Jinx looked so happy, running off with her new dog to show her best friend on this beautiful Sunday morning.

"Coffee?" Sparkle said, recapturing E. J.'s attention.

E. J. smiled. "That would be great. Thank you."

Sparkle motioned her to one of the Adirondack chairs in a grouping near the door. "Take a load off. I'll be right back."

E. J. sat and shifted her sunglasses to the top of her head. She leaned back, enjoying the shaded veranda, relaxing more than she would have thought.

Sparkle returned with a tray holding all the makings for the perfect cup of coffee along with some biscotti biscuits. "I knew you'd be back." She sat opposite E. J.

E. J. looked at her in surprise. So they were going to just dive right in? No testing the water. No wading. She was more accustomed to social politics and tiptoeing around a topic in polite, if obvious, evasion. Sparkle felt warmer this time, though, not the arctic ice floe she had seemed at their first meeting—not *warm*, but *warmer*. E. J. appreciated the effort. "You could have said something," she said with a chuckle. "It could have saved us a few weeks."

Sparkle filled two mugs from a large carafe and set one in front of E. J. "Where's the fun in that?" A hint of a smile touched her lips. "'Sides, nobody knew how to reach you. Including Jinxie. She says she doesn't even know what city you live in. Seems she isn't the only one with secrets."

E. J. felt herself blush. "Yes." She sighed. "We need to exchange phone numbers." It wasn't as though she hadn't thought about it, and even intended to, before. It was just so easy to get distracted when she was with Jinx. She didn't think Sparkle wanted, or needed, to hear that, though.

"That'd be a good start."

"And I live in Sacramento."

"I don't care where you live." Sparkle settled back into her chair. "But Jinxie does." She sipped her coffee.

A small laugh escaped E. J. She was going to end up liking Sparkle. She could tell. She studied her.

"Something on your mind?" Sparkle asked. Gold flecks softened the sharpness of her green eyes.

E. J. hesitated. She wanted to know more about Jinx, and she got the feeling Sparkle would be of help with that. She would have to let her guard down, though—something she didn't often do. Hadn't she been doing things she didn't often do since the moment she met Jinx, though? "I was wondering...Jinx said you told her to give me another chance."

Sparkle nodded.

"Why? I mean, I haven't gotten the impression you like me much."

Sparkle rested her elbows on the arms of the chair and held her coffee in front of her. "I told her to give you another chance because that's what she wanted to do—what her heart was aching to do. But she needed to be able to pretend, at least until you came back, that she didn't want it. She needed someone to tell her to so when it came time, she could do it without losing face, as they say."

"How did you know that?" E. J. was aware Sparkle had sidestepped addressing whether she did or didn't like her, but that was okay. They were talking. *It's a start.*

"A little bit because of the things she said about you, but mostly from the things she didn't, from the way she was any time she thought she'd never see you again."

"How was she?"

"Wounded." The word held a bite. "Every time you left, you cut out a little piece of her and left her bleeding. Then just about when she was starting to mend, you showed back up again."

That was the perfect description of how E. J. felt when she had left each time—and what had ultimately made her return. She sighed. "Me, too," she whispered.

"Oh, no," Sparkle said sharply. "You don't get to do that. You're the one who keeps leaving and coming back, then leaving again. Tough it up, and make it right if you're going to be with Jinxie. If not, leave her be. She's not a ride you come back to when you feel like it."

The short tirade hit its mark. Sparkle was right. E. J. had no business feeling sorry for herself or playing the *poor me* card. She had been the one to maintain the distance, both literally and emotionally, the one to keep control over how and when they saw each other. She had been coming and going as she pleased, with little thought for how it would feel on the other end. "You're right. I'm sorry," she heard herself saying, but her mind had moved on. "Would it be better if I left her alone?" The question was sincere. Maybe she wasn't good for Jinx. She searched Sparkle's face.

Sparkle rolled her eyes. "For God's sake, woman. No. It wouldn't be better if you left her alone. It'd be better if you stepped up and were actually *with* her. She needs you. And whether or not you know it, you need her, too."

The statement startled E. J. She blinked in surprise. "What does that mean?"

"When you first met Jinxie what did you feel?"

E. J. smiled at the memory. "I couldn't keep my eyes off her. I felt an immediate connection," she said cautiously. Had she just admitted that to a total stranger?

Sparkle nodded, clearly satisfied. "Reggie says that Jinxie was the same way. She walked into that bar to bring Reggie her phone, took one look at you, and forgot everything else."

E. J. warmed at the words.

"She's never done that before. Usually, she's focused on what she's doing. And for her to go home with you told me something really different was going on." Sparkle paused. "I'm sure Jinxie's told you it's been a really long time since she's been with a woman."

"She did." How long had Jinx said? *Ten years?* With everything else that had been said that night, she had forgotten.

"That's why I was a little concerned when you showed back up." Sparkle's expression was serious. "Chronologically, Jinxie's forty-five, but emotionally, and in dealing with life outside of prison, she can be a babe in the woods. She spent her entire adult life having someone else make all her decisions."

"I hadn't really thought of that," E. J. said.

"On top of that, there's something really special about Jinxie. She's got such a kind heart. She'll do anything for anyone. I think of her as kind of a hero. Both of them, actually." Sparkle looked across the field.

E. J. followed her gaze to where Jinx, Reggie, and Pete were entering one of the pens on the far side.

"They don't really know it. They don't think of themselves as heroes because they don't have big S's on their chests or wear superhero costumes, but they help people. They fight for people who can't fight for themselves. They save people." Sparkle kept her eyes on the trio, or maybe on Reggie. Her voice had softened in that way a woman's voice does when thinking of her lover.

"Did Reggie save you?" E. J. asked quietly.

Sparkle nodded. "She doesn't know it. Reggie just thinks she does what needs doing, that pulling me out of a car I'd deliberately driven off a pier is something anyone would do for a stranger on her way to see her mom. Or that training service dogs for free is how everyone spends her spare time. That tracking up into the mountains in the middle of winter with her rescue team to find a missing moron of a hiker who ignored the weather report, is the same as an afternoon walk." Sparkle picked up some biscotti and handed a piece to E. J.

"And Jinxie…" She shook her head. "That girl believes helping neighbor kids with their homework and watching over them when their mom's working nights, feeding a homeless guy, taking in some old dog and lying all night on the floor with him so he won't die alone, holding some junkie…" Sparkle wiped her eyes. "…through withdrawals, and then scaring the bejeezus out of her so she stays clean…she actually believes those things don't make a difference in the world, because that bitch of a sister of hers won't talk to her. They're both clueless, but they're both heroes."

E. J. remembered the origin of Jinx's name. She warmed inside. She had herself a real live superhero. As she processed Sparkle's words, she watched Reggie point at Pete, say something, coax him into a sitting position, and then repeat the whole routine. She knew most of what Sparkle had shared about Jinx. "Who's the junkie?" she asked gently.

"My baby sister, Trisha. They were in prison together for a while. Jinxie literally saved her life, then kept the idiot kid alive long enough for her to get out. She gave her back to me. That's how we met Jinxie."

Jinx was on the ground with Pete, lavishing him with obvious praise and love.

Admiration, respect, and deep affection swelled within E. J. The things Jinx and Reggie did weren't things done by anyone in the circles *she* had lived in all her life.

"The puppy was a great trick," Sparkle said.

E. J. glanced at her warily.

"Because, you know, who can say no to a puppy?" She smiled. "But that aside, Jinxie should have a dog."

E. J. watched as Jinx now went through the training routine with Pete. Suddenly, she wanted to know more. She was ready to hear more. "Do you know anything else about Jinx when she was in prison?"

"I know she worked in the education department and helped a lot of those girls get their GEDs, so they at least had a high school credential when they got out. She even taught some others to read. And she got herself stabbed trying to save someone in a fight. That's about what I know."

"Val?" E. J. couldn't help but ask.

Sparkle shook her head. "No, Val was already dead when Jinxie got injured." She paused. "Trisha said she heard Jinxie had actually gotten out of the fight, but then she saw this stupid-terrified new inmate get yanked into the brawl. Jinxie pulled her out but not before she got herself cut open."

E. J. trembled slightly as the image of Jinx falling to the floor flashed in her mind. Her stomach knotted, and she blanched.

"You okay?" Sparkle asked.

"I'm fine." E. J. tried to sound as though it was true, but the whisper of her answer gave her away. "Why would she do that? Why would she go back in?"

Sparkle was quiet for a moment. "Do you know anything about twelve-step programs?"

"Not a lot."

"One of the most important steps is making amends, which is when they apologize to anyone they hurt when they were using and ask for forgiveness." Sparkle leaned back in her chair. "But sometimes, it's not possible. Either people aren't around anymore or they just can't forgive. In those cases, there is something called living amends. They can't change what they've done, but they can change how they live and what they do from that point on. So, they do good deeds, help people. Try to make a difference."

"Jinx definitely makes a difference in a lot of people's lives." E. J. took another sip of coffee.

"And *you* can make a difference in hers."

"What could *I* do that could make the kind of difference Jinx does?"

"If you're going to be with her, then actually *be* with her. No more of this back and forth crap so she never knows if she can count on you. It's your job to love her, no matter what."

E. J. stilled.

"Oh, don't go getting all squirmy over the L-word. You already love her, whether you want to admit it or not. Just stay now and be here for her."

E. J. wanted to run, but she wouldn't. She took strength from Sparkle's steady gaze.

"She's here for you, too, if you'll let her be."

"She is?"

Sparkle laughed and patted E. J.'s knee. "Of course, she is. She'll help you through all that stuff with your son, if you'll let her."

"She told you about that?"

Sparkle smirked. "Didn't you tell your friends about her being in prison and the stuff with her family?"

E. J. flushed. "Yes."

"There you go," Sparkle said briskly. "And here come our heroes."

Jinx ran the last twenty yards or so, excitement lighting her face. "Watch what Pete can do," she said, skidding to a stop. She gave the puppy a series of commands, each one of which he followed perfectly.

E. J. and Sparkle laughed and applauded, while Reggie stood by with a wide smile. When the performance was complete, she stepped up onto the porch. "It's great to see you again, E. J." She gave her a wink.

E. J. felt her warmth. "Thank you," she said. "It's nice to see you again, too."

Reggie leaned down and kissed Sparkle. "What have you two been talking about? Or do I want to know?"

Sparkle took her hand. "You don't want to know."

"I didn't think so." Reggie looked at the two of them skeptically. "I don't think we should leave these two alone very often," she said to Jinx.

"I don't know," Jinx said, smiling at E. J. "The last time I left E. J. alone, I came home to a fantastic dinner."

"Well, if you're hungry now, you and Sparkle are going to have to whip something up," Reggie said, returning her attention to E. J. "This lady owes me a rematch."

"We're going to the bar?"

"Nope, there's a pool table right inside." Reggie took E. J.'s hand and coaxed her to her feet. "And this time, I'm on to you."

"Why, I don't know what you mean," E. J. said innocently.

❖

E. J. stepped out onto Jinx's back porch. She had enjoyed the afternoon with Reggie and Sparkle, had beaten Reggie at pool again, and had lost a hundred and sixty-nine tooth picks—a hundred of her own and sixty-nine she borrowed from Jinx—playing poker. She had also learned Reggie and Sparkle had been together for eighteen years. It was inspiring, and she even allowed herself a brief fantasy of her and Jinx growing old together. Perhaps a little ridiculous after knowing one another for only two months, one during which they hadn't even spoken. She stepped behind Jinx at the railing and barely kept from slipping her arms around Jinx's waist. Jinx still hadn't initiated any contact between them other than holding her the night before and the one kiss at the kennels.

Jinx turned to face her. "Your dog apparently can't find the perfect spot to go to the bathroom."

E. J. glanced out into the yard where Pete seemed to be wandering aimlessly. "*My* dog?" She inhaled the scent that was uniquely Jinx and felt her natural response. Arousal tightened in her abdomen. "I brought him for you." She wanted to touch her so badly.

Jinx smiled, but there was a sadness in her eyes. She took E. J.'s hand and ran two fingertips along the length of one finger.

E. J. looked down and watched the movement. The sight, the touch, the stroke was so sensual, so tender. She got lost for a moment.

"E. J., I have to tell you something," Jinx said softly.

Oh my God. More? E. J. looked up to see if it was a joke. It was too soon to be joking about it. They hadn't even fully discussed what she had already told E. J.

"I want to kiss you," Jinx said. "I mean, really kiss you, not like this morning. And I want to go to bed with you, have sex with you—"

"Oh, God, Jinx. I want that, too." E. J.'s desire flared hotter.

"But I can't until I tell you something that happened since the last time I saw you. It might make you change your mind, so you need to know first."

E. J. watched Jinx's lips, felt the warmth of her fingertips on her skin. What was she saying? What had she done? Had she slept with someone else? That would sting, but E. J. couldn't really blame her if she had. "It's okay. We didn't—"

"Baby, please, let me say this."

E. J. fell silent. Jinx was so serious. "Okay."

"Tiffany contacted me. She wanted us to get to know one another. I've seen her twice." The words spilled out in a steady stream, as though she was afraid if she paused, she wouldn't be able to finish.

E. J. went still, but her thoughts raced. *Tiffany's seeing Jinx, talking to her? God, what had they talked about? Did Jinx tell her...? No, Jinx wouldn't do that. Or if she had, she would have included that little tidbit.* E. J. felt her fear and anger rising. Why wasn't anything ever enough? She had gotten herself to come back, convinced herself to deal with whatever might come up for her about Jinx's past. She wanted to see how Jinx might affect her life and her relationship with Jacob, in the future. *In the future. Not now.* But here it was, already in her face. Tiffany in contact with Jinx...so close.

"E. J.?" Jinx said softly. "Are you okay?"

E. J. slipped her hand from Jinx's grasp. She wasn't okay, but could she be? She remembered Sparkle's words about being there, so Jinx knew she could count on her. The previous night she had cried in Jinx's arms and asked her not to give up on her. But if she was going to ask that of Jinx, *she* couldn't give up either. She moved beside Jinx and gripped the porch railing.

Jinx remained where she was. She stared at her feet.

"How did she contact you?" E. J. asked.

"The first time she came by because she didn't have my number. The second, she called, and I met her for something to eat." Jinx's voice sounded as hollow as E. J.'s.

E. J.'s anxiety heightened. "She knows where you live."

"Yes."

E. J. knew Jinx must be waiting—waiting for her to freak out, run into the house, pack her stuff, and vanish again. She had tried that, though. It didn't work. She couldn't forget Jinx. Besides, she didn't want to. She had spent the past week and a half deciding to face her fears, to give herself the chance to be happy like Taylor had said. And she still had time. Tiffany wasn't actually here. She simply wanted to get to know Jinx. "Does Jacob know?"

"No. Tiffany wants us to get to know each other before anyone else comes into it." Jinx's voice was stronger, but she still didn't look at E. J.

She was terrified to ask the next question, but she had to know. "Did you tell Tiffany about you and me?"

Jinx jerked her head up, her eyes wide with evident surprise. "Of course not. E. J., I wouldn't ever—"

"Shhhh." E. J. turned to her and brushed her fingers across her shoulders. She needed to touch Jinx, needed Jinx to touch her, needed to feel that safety she always felt in Jinx's arms. "Hold me?" she whispered.

Jinx stared at her. "You're not leaving?"

She wasn't. She couldn't. She wanted to stay. She wanted to *be with* Jinx, not just for the night, but the way Sparkle had said. And, at least for tonight, she could relax. She knew Jacob and Tiffany were in Napa for the weekend. She had time to figure out what was next. She could enjoy tonight with Jinx. She shook her head. "I'm staying. But I need you, Jinx. Take me to bed."

Jinx sighed and her eyes shone. She grabbed E. J., pulled her hard against her, and covered her mouth in a heated kiss. No lingering touches. No buildup. Just need.

E. J. molded against her in pure surrender.

They kissed long and hard and deep, Jinx's hands clutching at E. J.'s shirt, E. J.'s fingers twisting in Jinx's hair, until they felt little paws on their legs and heard a soft whine from Pete.

Jinx pulled away. "I guess we need to put the baby to bed first," she said, her breathing ragged.

E. J. laughed and groaned simultaneously. She rested her forehead on Jinx's shoulder. "Welcome to parenthood."

"I'll take care of Pete," Jinx said, caressing the small of E. J.'s back. "Meet me in bed?"

E. J. nodded.

She lay naked beneath the cool sheet, watching Jinx. She loved the way she moved, the gentleness of her hands as she settled Pete into his bed, her slow strokes as she petted him until his eyes drooped closed.

"He's had a big couple of days. He's sleepy," Jinx said, straightening. She looked down at E. J.

E. J. rolled to her back and pulled the sheet from her body. She met Jinx's darkening eyes. "Your turn," she said with a smile.

Jinx paused, raking her gaze down E. J.'s length. Finally, with unexpected slowness, she gripped the hem of her T-shirt and pulled it up and over her head.

E. J. took in the small, firm breasts, the rosy, stiffening nipples, the flat stomach and toned arms as Jinx stepped out of her jeans and left them on the floor. She reached for Jinx and wrapped her arms around her as Jinx eased herself onto her. Their bodies melded, flesh to flesh. E. J. gasped with pleasure. "You feel so good," she whispered.

Jinx moaned and lay still.

E. J. closed her eyes, intensely aware of their hearts beating against each other. If not for the aching need between her thighs, she could have lain there, contented forever.

At length, Jinx rose onto her elbows and framed E. J.'s face between her hands. She combed her fingers through E. J.'s hair as she stared down at her. "Thank you for staying," she murmured.

E. J. ran her palms up Jinx's spine to cup the back of her head. She thought of how frightened she had been on the drive down. Her eyes burned with tears. "Thank you for letting me." She pulled Jinx into a languid kiss.

Jinx's mouth was hot, and she slipped her tongue between E. J.'s lips at the same instant she slid her leg between E. J.'s thighs.

E. J. lifted her hips, moaning at the pressure against her center.

Jinx began moving against her, unhurriedly, deliberately. Her thighs parted around one of E. J.'s, and E. J. felt her hot, wet arousal.

E. J. groaned and probed Jinx's mouth deeper. She nipped, then sucked Jinx's lower lip.

Jinx jerked and ground against her.

Desire flooded E. J.'s body, the same desire she always felt with Jinx, but there was something more this time. Underneath the pure lust and need lay that connection, that oneness she had fought back at other times they had been together. It had scared her before, but this time, it felt inevitable. This time, E. J. knew it was right. She opened to Jinx completely, opened those places Jinx had joked about that first morning without knowing the truth of her words, those places no one had ever touched—before Jinx. And now, here was Jinx again, touching them so tenderly, so deeply, E. J. thought she might disintegrate into a million tiny pieces. To her horror, she felt the swell of emotion and the sting of tears. She bit them back. She opened her eyes to find Jinx watching her as they kissed, as their bodies caressed one another. She lost herself in the deep blue of Jinx's soul.

Jinx eased away, trailing kisses down E. J.'s neck, leaving a path of sensation as though dropping breadcrumbs to find her way back to E. J.'s mouth. She ran the tip of her tongue along E. J.'s collarbone, teasing the underside until she eased lower still to find an aching nipple. She kissed it lightly, tenderly.

E. J. gasped and arched into her.

Jinx sucked as she pressed harder into E. J.'s throbbing center, keeping a rhythm that brought E. J. to the precipice of orgasm again and again without taking her over the edge.

E. J. could feel Jinx's need was just as intense, as with each thrust, she rubbed herself against E. J.'s thigh. But she wasn't letting up, nor was she giving either of them any release. E. J.'s moans became one long groan.

Finally, Jinx shifted and sucked E. J.'s other nipple into her hot mouth at the same time she slid her hand between E. J.'s legs and entered her, slowly and deeply.

E. J. cried out in agonized pleasure. She needed release.

Jinx sucked hungrily as she found E. J.'s clitoris with her thumb, circling it with each excruciating thrust into her. Her hips still pumped against E. J. in tandem with her thrusts.

E. J. clawed at Jinx's back. "Oh, God, Jinx. Please." Each word rode a ragged breath.

Jinx shifted with a sudden movement and pressed her pelvis against her hand as she continued her long, even strokes into E. J.'s swollen center. She quickened her pace. "Come with me, baby."

E. J. gripped Jinx's hips and pulled her hard against her with each thrust, lifting her own to meet them. Her orgasm exploded from deep within her, heightened by Jinx's cries of pleasure and her grinding motion that pushed her fingers deeper into E. J. and tore every spasm of release from her.

They rocked against each other, slowing little by little, until every twinge, every pulse, subsided.

Jinx lowered herself onto E. J. and nuzzled her ear. "I missed you so much," she whispered.

E. J. felt a sob gather in her soul, then make its way up her throat and out between her lips. She heard it as though it came from someone else. Tears slid from the corners of her eyes. She gripped Jinx and crushed her to her. "I can't lose you," she said as she cried.

Jinx held her tightly. "I'm not going anywhere, baby. I'm right here."

Embarrassed, E. J. tried to collect herself. She had never cried after sex. She had been with women who had, but *she* had *never*. But then, this hadn't felt like sex. It had been something else, something she had never experienced before. She had caught wisps of it the other times she had been with Jinx, but she had always shut it down, closed the door. This time, though...This time, she had...With the realization, another sob wracked her body.

She had just made love...for the first time...ever.

She let herself cry in Jinx's arms.

CHAPTER FIFTEEN

Jinx lay with E. J. cradled in her arms, listening to her even breathing as she slept. The past two weeks had felt like a dream, beginning with the moment she'd realized E. J. really was staying with her after finding out about Tiffany's visits. It had continued through each nightly telephone conversation—no matter where E. J. was—and peaked the previous evening when Jinx was able to touch her again, make love to her through the night, and wake with her this morning. Today was a workday for Jinx, but she'd left at noon after calling in a few favors to cover her afternoon appointments. And now, here she was, back in bed with E. J., with no intention of anything else for the rest of the weekend. Except maybe food.

E. J. stirred slightly, and her fingers curled in a soft caress of Jinx's chest.

Jinx smiled. "Knock, knock," she said quietly.

She felt E. J.'s lips curve against the hollow of her shoulder. "Who's there?"

"Wanda." Jinx ran her hand down E. J.'s bare back.

E. J. shifted and looked up at Jinx. "Wanda, who?"

"Wanda call out for Chinese?"

E. J. laughed. "Why are all knock-knock jokes so bad?"

"It's their nature." Jinx trailed a fingertip down E. J.'s spine and was rewarded with a shiver and the sight of E. J.'s lithe body arching into a luxuriant stretch. "Their inherent badness is what makes you laugh." She sat up and pressed her lips to the back of E. J.'s neck.

E. J. sighed. "You know what I really want?"

"Hmm."

E. J. twined her arms around Jinx. "I want one of your PB&Js."

Jinx lifted her brows in surprise. "You do?"

"Mm-hm. I can get Chinese food anywhere, but that PB&J..."

Jinx eyed her. "You're just after my secret ingredient." She lay against the pillow and pulled E. J. on top of her.

E. J. grinned. "I am."

Pete whined from the side of the bed.

"C'mon." Jinx patted the mattress beside them.

He jumped up and nestled in the blanket.

"I think it's so amazing that you taught him to ask for permission."

Jinx kissed E. J. lightly on the lips. "I knew there'd be times I didn't want him in the middle of the bed." She stroked Pete's head. "And he's a good boy," she added to the dog.

"He's been very good this afternoon. He's been so patient with all this sex and mushy stuff." E. J. scratched behind his ear. "And he probably needs to go out."

"Tell you what. You handle that, and I'll make the sandwiches. That way you can't peek and discover my secret."

E. J. smiled and pinned Jinx with a sensuous kiss. "I'll get it out of you someday," she murmured.

It was a joke, but Jinx loved hearing E. J. refer to the future.

E. J. pulled on her jeans that'd been thrown on the floor the second Jinx had come through the door, then grabbed the T-shirt Jinx had been wearing and slipped it over her head. A bright smile lit her face. "You can put on the shirt I gave you. It brings out your eyes."

Jinx tensed. They'd talked about a lot of things in phone calls over the past couple of weeks—Jinx's drug habit and Narcotics Anonymous; parts of her time in prison; Trisha; E. J.'s marriage; Marcus's affair; her brief, uninteresting relationship with Rhonda; her grandparents; her friends Gwen and Taylor—but they hadn't talked about E. J.'s retreat or how Jinx had coped with her feelings about it. They'd discussed the feelings themselves, but not the fact that she'd destroyed everything that reminded her of E. J.

E. J.'s smile dimmed. "Oh." Comprehension dawned in her eyes. "I'm sorry—"

"It's okay. I'll get you another one. But this shirt…" She glanced down at the Canine Complete logo on her torso. "It's going with me. I need something that smells like you when I'm away. Something to wrap around myself." Her smile was back.

"Okay," Jinx said from the edge of the bed. "What do *I* get?"

E. J. straddled her lap and looped her arms around her neck. "I brought something extra special for you to keep."

"Really? That sounds like it could be dirty." Jinx grasped E. J.'s waist and pulled her tightly against her.

"It could be." E. J. rotated her hips. "Or it could just be something for you to snuggle with when you miss me."

Jinx nuzzled E. J.'s throat. "You have my attention."

"I know I do." E. J. arched away and got back to her feet. "But for now, Pete needs to go out, and you promised me a PB&J," she said as she danced out of Jinx's reach.

Jinx grinned as she watched her and Pete disappear out the back door.

Once dressed, she retrieved the sandwich makings and thought about her secret ingredient. If E. J. only knew. As she spread the peanut butter, she heard the muffled sound of raised voices from the house next door. Both windows were closed, so the disagreement had to be a heated one. Pablo and his mother had been arguing more lately. She was pushing for him to quit the gang and finish school. Out of respect for their privacy, Jinx busied her mind with thoughts of E. J.

A knock sounded at the front door.

Jinx strode to answer it. She froze at the sight of Tiffany, all flushed cheeks and sparkling eyes.

"Hi, Aunt Michelle. I'm sorry to barge in on you, but I dropped my cell in the toilet and lost all my contacts."

Jinx had seen Tiffany twice since she and Jacob had returned from Napa. Both times, they'd gone out to eat. Both times, Tiffany had called first to make arrangements. Neither time had she come to the house.

"I know what you're going to say. I should have used the backup function, and now I will. But I need your number again." She held up what was evidently a new phone and waved it in the air. "And I thought we could schedule our next lunch, while I'm here. I owe you Thai. I won't keep you. I can see you have company." She glanced toward the driveway and tilted her head. "It's so funny. That car looks a lot like my mother-in-law's."

As if summoned, E. J. stepped in the back door.

Pete dashed past her.

"E. J.!" Tiffany said with obvious pleasure. "When did you get into town? We didn't know you were coming. I was just telling Aunt Michelle..." She pointed to the car. She squinted slightly, then looked from E. J. to Jinx, then back again. "I'm sorry. I'm confused. I didn't know you knew each other."

Jinx looked at E. J., her anxiety through the roof. There was no way of knowing how E. J. would want to play this.

Her pallor was ashen. She pressed her hand to the doorjamb. "Tiffany," she said, perhaps only to buy another split second. "Yes, we met at the wedding."

Jinx had no idea what to do, didn't have a clue what E. J. was thinking. She wished she could stop time, or suspend it, so they could...What could they do? Tiffany was here.

"Of course you do." Tiffany laughed. "Otherwise, why would you be here?"

After making a full circle of the room, Pete skidded to a stop in front of Tiffany.

"What a cute puppy," she said, leaning down to pet him. "What's his name?"

"Uh, Pete," Jinx said, grateful, finally, for something to say.

"Hi, Pete," Tiffany said. She seemed to have forgotten about E. J. Or maybe the whole scene didn't seem all that odd to her. How could it not, though?

Pete bumped his nose against the keys in her hand, then grabbed them and ran off.

"Hey, you can't have those," Tiffany said, going after him. She'd gone several steps before seeming to catch herself.

Pete leapt into the center of the bed and burrowed into the blanket.

Tiffany laughed. "He's so cute. How long have you had him?"

"Just a couple of weeks," Jinx said. She passed a look to E. J. again. *What the hell is she thinking?*

Tiffany watched Pete roll around in the covers, shake her keys, then try to dig a hole to bury them. She giggled, a wide smile shaping her mouth. Suddenly, her expression changed to one of confusion as she looked at Jinx, then comprehension, as she took in E. J. A deep blush crept into her cheeks. "Oh." She put her hands to her face. "Oh, my gosh. I'm so sorry." She turned toward the front door, then pivoted back toward the bed. "My keys. I'm sorry. I need my keys."

"Tiffany, wait. Please." E. J. walked toward her. It was the other E. J.—the guarded E. J., the in-command E. J. "I met your aunt at the wedding, and we got to talking. She said she was interested in looking for a job with a company like mine, and I was in the area yesterday, so I brought her some information."

Tiffany studied E. J., then glanced at Jinx. "I thought you liked working at Canine Complete with your friends."

Jinx shifted her gaze to E. J. This was crazy. She knew how badly E. J. must be freaking out on the inside—even though she looked together on the outside, if a bit pale—to have said something so ridiculous, but she didn't know how to help her. She'd learned the truth usually trumped crazy, though. And she wasn't about to lie to her niece so E. J. could continue with her charade. "I do," she said.

E. J.'s eyes went cold.

Tiffany turned back to E. J., her attention first on Jinx's shirt, then on her bare feet. "E. J., it's okay. You don't have to pretend anything. If you and Aunt Michelle are happy together, I'm glad. It actually explains some things about you I've never understood."

E. J.'s breathing became shallow. She looked panicked. "No, it isn't what you—"

"E. J., stop," Jinx said gently.

E. J. swayed and stumbled toward the bed.

Both Jinx and Tiffany rushed to steady her.

"Oh, God. This can't be happening." E. J. rubbed her forehead as they eased her onto the mattress. She hugged herself and began to rock. "Oh, God." Tears rolled down her cheeks.

Eyes wide with evident concern, Tiffany looked at Jinx.

"She needs to hear it from you," Jinx whispered.

Tiffany swallowed. She squatted in front of E. J. and took her hand. "It's really okay. I know a lot of lesbians, and gay guys, too. It's not that big of a thing anymore."

"Jacob," E. J. said, obviously trying to catch her breath. "Jacob doesn't know."

"Well, *that's* true." Tiffany gave Jinx a sidelong glance. "He wants to fix you up with one of the senior partners at the firm," she said to E. J. "His wife died a couple of years ago, and Jacob thought…"

E. J. was staring at her.

"Yeah, that won't work." Tiffany squeezed her hand. "Jacob would want to know, though. He loves you."

"No. No, he can't…Please don't…" E. J.'s breathing quickened again.

"I won't tell him," Tiffany said softly. "I promise. That's between you and him."

With that, E. J. began to calm. She got control of her breathing and wiped the moisture from her cheeks. "Thank you."

Tiffany smiled and rose. "Well, I've caused enough drama for one afternoon, so I'm going to leave you two to your day." She still held E. J.'s hand. "And don't worry. I won't say anything, but please, think about telling him." She picked up her keys from where Pete had dropped them and now sat watching the scene.

E. J. gave a slight nod. "Thank you," she said again.

On the front steps, Jinx embraced Tiffany, partly as a good-bye, but mostly in gratitude.

"Is she going to be all right?" Tiffany asked.

"She'll be fine," Jinx said, but she wished she had more confidence. She stepped back inside and closed the door.

E. J. still sat on the edge of the bed, hugging herself and staring at nothing.

"E. J.?"

"I can't," E. J. said. "I can't do it. I'm not ready. But now, Tiffany knows."

Jinx remembered something Namastacey had told her when Val died. *We know we're ready for something because it happens.* It'd helped her, but something told her E. J. wasn't in the mood for jailhouse wisdom. It could wait until E. J. was calmer. "That's okay, baby. You don't need to be. She said she wouldn't say anything to Jacob."

"How long will that last? How long will it be before she realizes she's keeping a huge secret from him, keeping a lie between them, and feels the need to tell him?"

"I don't think Tiffany would do that. Not without talking to you first."

E. J. blew out a breath. "How do you know? You've known Tiffany for a minute and a half," E. J. said, her tone sharp.

Jinx closed her eyes. *E. J. is scared, and people say things when they're scared. It isn't about me.*

"I've seen them together. They're so close. She's not going to want this between them. And how's she then going to explain that she already knew, if and when he does find out? How's she going to explain why her loyalty was to me, and not him?"

"E. J., let's take it a step at a time. Right now, all that happened is your daughter-in-law now knows something important about you, and she's being supportive. She said it isn't a big thing. She's known I'm gay from our first conversation, and it hasn't mattered at all. And today, she said she's glad if we're happy together. This should be a good thing."

E. J. finally focused on Jinx, her eyes angry. "You think this should be a *good* thing? Even after I've told you what happened to Jacob and why I've never told him?"

Jinx hesitated. "I think you feel guilty about that, and your guilt is coloring your perspective. Tiffany said Jacob's grateful to you for helping him through that. He said he couldn't have made it through it without his mother."

E. J. stiffened. "You talked to Tiffany about me? About me and Jacob?" Her voice was glacial.

"*Tiffany* talked to *me* about you. I didn't bring it up."

"But you went with it? Why? Because you think it's going to get you something you want? You think if you can *figure* me out, it's going to get you a place at our Thanksgiving table? That you're going to be part of our big, happy family?" E. J. stood and began to pace.

"What?"

"We don't have a big, happy family, Jinx. So you're going to have to just make up with your own."

Jinx was dumbfounded. How did this get turned around on her? Her own temper flared. "Maybe *you're* the reason you don't, because you're too scared to let them know you. And we're not talking about *my* family. *My* family knows me, for better or for worse. Until now, I thought none of them wanted anything to do with me, but at least they've known the truth, both about what I've done *and* that I haven't given up on them. *I'm* still trying. You've given up on Jacob. You decided what he can and can't handle, and you've taken yourself from him, and he doesn't even know why. And what about your daughter? Mandy, is it? The daughter you've never even mentioned because you're so obsessed with Jacob? How long ago did you give up on her?"

E. J. stopped pacing and gave her a steely glare. It was that other E. J. again. Jinx had poked the dragon. "How dare you talk to me about this? It doesn't concern you."

"Somebody has to." Jinx shoved her hands into her jeans pockets. "You've shut everyone else out. You're so terrified to let anyone know you, to let anyone love you. This isn't about your kids, E. J. It's about you. What is so scary about letting someone love you?"

"What's scary about it?" E. J.'s tone was incredulous. "*This!*" She pointed at the floor. "*This*, right here, is what's scary about it. My life was fine—*I* was fine—before I met you. And then, I met you... and...and..." She pressed her fingertips to her temples. "I met you, and I couldn't think. And I couldn't stop. And all my rules went out the window. And now my daughter-in-law knows the one thing I've worked so hard to keep separate, to keep in its own little box for me to enjoy. Now I've lost control. It's no longer up to *me* who knows. If she decides in some *moment of intimacy*," she almost spat the words, "to tell my son, I can't do a damned thing about it. And all because I let someone in. I let *you* in"

Jinx couldn't hold back a scoff. "*This* is *in*? You haven't let me in. You've controlled every second of what we've shared. You've kept me at arm's length. You've come into my life if and when and how far you please, at any given moment, and pull completely out of it whenever you choose—whenever we start getting too close. Hell, I didn't even know what city you live in until a week ago."

"You never asked."

"Oh! Is that it? I just have to ask?" Jinx paused as if to think. "Okay. Let's see, then. What about your daughter? You know, the daughter you never mention. What's up with her? You have this whole little world you've built up around Jacob and why he can't know you. Why can't Mandy?"

E. J. glared at her.

Jinx shrugged. "I asked."

E. J.'s expression was hard, her eyes an iced green. "I'm not doing this. I can't." She left the room and returned with her things from the bathroom.

"What are you doing?" Jinx asked.

E. J. pulled her suitcase from the corner.

"Oh, yeah," Jinx said. "Here we go. Here's the E. J. *I* know, walking out the door." She waited for her stomach to knot, for that feeling of panic, that ache of loneliness. It didn't come. Instead, calm came over her. Was she done? No, not done. Just clear. She couldn't alleviate E. J.'s fear. That was up to E. J. She had to decide what it was worth to be loved. In that moment, she realized the conversation had stopped being about E. J.'s kids, and whether or not they could love her for who she was. She realized *she* loved E. J., had fallen in love with her—God help her—but she'd learned to love herself as well. And she couldn't do this anymore. She couldn't keep watching E. J. walk out the door in some bizarre *Groundhog's Day* loop. She wasn't ashamed of who she was, and she wasn't going to be treated like a dirty little secret.

"You know what? You're right." Jinx crossed to where E. J. was packing. "I can't do this anymore either. If you leave again, you can't come back."

E. J.'s response was barely a flinch, but it was something.

"Baby, I'm not pretending to have all the answers, and I'm not telling you how and when to come out to your kids. I'm just saying you can't dump me every time you get scared. If you care about us at all, you have to stay and trust we can work something out."

E. J. shoved a shoe into the back of her bag.

Jinx didn't want to watch. She retreated to the bathroom and shut the door. She sat cross-legged on the counter and leaned against the mirror. She waited, listening for the sound of E. J.'s heels on the linoleum, the opening of the door, the start of an engine. She closed her eyes and drew in a deep breath. She had no idea how long she'd been sitting there when she became aware of her surroundings again, but the house was quiet. She was sure E. J. was gone. Maybe she'd take Pete for a walk. When she rounded the corner into the living room, she halted. Her heart leapt.

E. J.'s bag still sat on the bed, and E. J. lay curled beside it. Her shoulders shook. Pete snuggled into the curve of her body.

Jinx stood over her, looking down.

E. J. petted Pete tenderly. She sniffed. "We scared him."

Jinx lowered herself onto the bed and spooned E. J. She slipped her arm over her waist and stroked Pete's muzzle. "We scared me, too," she whispered.

He licked her palm.

E. J. laced her fingers between Jinx's and tucked their hands beneath her chin. "I can't not come back," she said, her voice trembling. "So, I can't go. But I don't know what to do."

"I don't know either," Jinx said quietly. "Maybe the thing to do is to not do anything. You've been trying to keep every detail, every moment, every aspect of your life so controlled and separate. Maybe it's time to just let everything be what it is, let everyone be who they are, and see what happens."

E. J. took in a shuddering breath. "Oh God, Jinx, that terrifies me."

"I know, baby." She rubbed her cheek against E. J.'s hair.

"I do care about us," E. J. said. She kissed Jinx's knuckle. "Tell me we can work this out."

"We can." Jinx tightened her hold. "We have to. We've both been through too much to finally find each other, only to lose one another again."

"I'm so tired," E. J. whispered.

"Sleep, baby. I'll be right here." She'd get up later and make Kenny something to eat, but for now, holding E. J. was all she needed to do.

She lay pressed against her, listening to her breathe, to Pete's occasional doggie-dream woofs, to the quieting sounds of evening as darkness blanketed the room.

Then a gunshot, a scream, and the squeal of tires shattered the night.

Chapter Sixteen

E. J. bolted upright, her heart pounding. "What was that?" Pete leapt off the bed, barking.

Someone outside screamed.

"Sounded like a shot," Jinx said, halfway to the door. "Call 911." Before E. J. could respond, Jinx was gone.

E. J. grabbed her phone and made the call, then hurried outside.

A small crowd gathered in the yard next door, and there was a commotion on the front porch.

As E. J. crossed the driveway, she heard a woman sobbing and saw Jinx huddled at the top of the steps with a couple of other people.

Jinx ripped a strip of fabric from the hem of her shirt.

E. J. moved up behind her and looked down.

A little girl of about eleven or twelve lay on the cement deck, blood almost instantly soaking the makeshift bandage Jinx had applied to her head wound. The woman kneeling beside her continued to cry and cross herself, repeating something over and over in Spanish.

"Oh my God," E. J. whispered.

Jinx looked back at her. "Get me some shirts from the top drawer of my dresser. Hurry."

E. J. raced back to the house. She grabbed an armful of Jinx's T-shirts and dashed back. Her thoughts reeled. *Who would shoot a child?* She handed several to Jinx, then knelt beside the crying woman and encircled her trembling shoulders.

The woman slumped in her arms.

In the distance, sirens wailed in the night as Jinx folded one shirt over the wound and tied it into place with another.

"C'mon, Angelita, stay with us. Your mama needs you."

There was no response from the little girl.

When the police and the paramedics arrived, E. J. and Jinx held Angelita's mother between them and helped her to the bottom of the steps to give the emergency team room to work, and so an officer could take her statement. E. J. caught only bits and pieces between the noise of radios and the woman lapsing into Spanish frequently. Angelita's mother's name was Mercedes, and Angelita had been sitting on the porch swing, listening to a CD, when someone had fired from a passing car. The terms *gang* and *drive-by* drifted through the air.

Jinx stayed with Mercedes through it all, and when the paramedics lifted the gurney into the ambulance, she offered to follow and make sure Mercedes got to the hospital. They started toward Jinx's car.

With Mercedes settled in the front seat, Jinx turned to E. J. for the first time.

E. J. winced at the sight of Jinx's blood-streaked hands and the crimson stains on her jeans and torn T-shirt where she had wiped them. She had to look away.

"I don't know how long this is going to take," Jinx said. She glanced over her shoulder at the woman in the car. "We might be there all night and into tomorrow."

"I know," E. J. said. She focused on Jinx's eyes. She couldn't keep Sparkle's words out of her mind. *She's a hero.* E. J. could see that and yes, heroes help people and save people. They also die sometimes, though, and so much blood on Jinx disconcerted her. "Do you think Reggie and Sparkle would take Pete?"

Jinx tensed. "You're leaving?" Her tone was edged with resignation.

"No. I want to come to the hospital and be with you." E. J. caressed her arm. "But since we don't know how long it will be, I don't want to leave him alone. If they can take him, I'll grab you a change of clothes, drop off Pete, and meet you at the hospital."

A tender smile made its way across Jinx's lips. "Thank you," she said, already on her way around the car to the driver's side. "I'll let them know you're coming."

Forty-five minutes later, E. J. found Jinx and Mercedes in the ER waiting room. Pablo sat beside his mother. Jinx introduced her to Mercedes's two sisters and several other family members before moving to two seats where they could sit together. There was no word yet on Angelita's condition. Jinx had obviously taken the time to wash her hands, but her clothes were still stained and torn.

E. J. handed her the PetSmart bag she was carrying. "Here, why don't you go change? It will make you feel better while we wait. And it would probably be better for the family, too."

Jinx nodded and disappeared into a nearby restroom.

While E. J. waited, she watched Angelita's family, some crying, all wearing expressions strained by worry and dread. Pablo had greeted her when she first arrived but hadn't met her eyes. Now, he slumped forward, elbows on his knees, making a quick swipe of his hand over his face every few minutes.

"Any word?" Jinx asked, sitting beside E. J. again.

E. J. shook her head. "Where was Pablo tonight? I didn't see him earlier."

"I don't know. Probably out with *his boys*." Jinx's tone was tinged with disgust.

E. J. glanced at her. She had never heard Jinx express any kind of judgment, of anyone, even implied as it was here. "You mean his gang?"

Jinx nodded. She pinched the bridge of her nose.

E. J. looked back at the boy. He really did look like a boy tonight. "Well, it was a drive-by. He couldn't have done anything to stop it if he *had* been home."

"No, but it's the choices he's made that led up to tonight. The choices he makes every day that could get him killed. Mercedes has been trying to get him to get out of the gang."

"What about you?" E. J. asked, genuinely curious.

Jinx looked confused. "What about me?"

"Have you talked to him?"

"We've talked about him being in it, but not much about him getting out. If he won't listen to his mom, he's not going to listen to me."

"I would think you'd be the one he *might* listen to." E. J. covered Jinx's hand with her own.

"Why?"

"Because he respects you. I could tell that from the way he talked about you in the conversation we had. And because you spent twenty years in prison, which is where he could end up if he keeps doing what he's doing. You can tell him, firsthand, what it's like, where bad choices can land him. And because you know what it feels like to lose people you love because of those choices. Not in the same way as tonight, but lose them still."

Jinx had kept her gaze on their hands as E. J. spoke. She tightened her grasp on E. J.'s fingers. "You really think so?"

"I do."

Jinx looked at her thoughtfully, then turned in Pablo's direction.

The door beside them whirred open, and several guys in gang attire came in.

Pablo looked up, then said something to his mother and rose. "Hey," he said as he approached his friends. "'Sup?"

"Yeah, man, it's all over the street. They think they got you. She was wearin' your hat."

Pablo clenched his jaw. "Well, they didn't get me. Motherfuckers. They got my kid sister." His voice shook, whether with pain or rage, E. J. couldn't be sure.

"Ms. Mendoza?" a doctor called from the emergency room doorway.

Mercedes rose, and the doctor came to her. The rest of the family gathered around. E. J. and Jinx moved closer.

"The wound itself isn't that bad," the doctor said. She reminded E. J. of Mandy, with her direct approach and sincere eyes. "It's technically a graze, but it fractured your daughter's skull. We did a CT, and there's no sign of any other injury, but she hasn't woken up yet." Maybe she wasn't like Mandy at all. Maybe E. J. was thinking of her because someone's daughter was lying somewhere behind that door not waking up. She slipped her arm around Jinx's waist for comfort.

"Would you like to go sit with her?" the doctor asked Mercedes.

"Yes, please," Mercedes said weakly. She turned to Pablo. "Come with me?"

Pablo's expression was hard. "No, Mama. I got something to take care of."

Mercedes looked at his friends. "Pablo, no. Please, come sit with Angelita." She gripped his arm.

"You go. I'll be back." He eased from her grasp and walked toward the door.

E. J. had heard enough about gang retaliation, seen enough movies like *Boyz in the Hood*, to know what was most likely happening. "Pablo," she called, but Jinx was already going after him. She followed.

"Pablo, wait," Jinx said in the corridor.

He stopped. "It's okay, Jinx. I know what I gotta do."

"Don't be stupid."

Pablo looked to his friends. "Get the car. I'll be there in a sec."

One glared at Jinx, then led the others down the hall.

"They shot Angelita," Pablo said to Jinx. "I gotta take care of my family."

"This isn't the way. How are you going to take care of them if you're in prison? Or worse, dead."

"Stay out of it, Jinx." Pablo's eyes sparked. "I know what I'm doing."

"I don't think you do, because if you did, your little sister wouldn't be lying in there with her head bandaged."

Pablo's jaw clenched and his neck muscles tightened.

"If you knew what you were doing, she could sit on her front porch without your rival gang coming by gunning for *you*. If you knew what you were doing, your mother wouldn't be in there praying for the lives of both her children right now."

"Shut the fuck up," Pablo said, his voice rising. "My family's none of your business." He spun to leave.

Jinx jumped in front of him. "None of my business?" Her pitch matched his. "You don't have any problem with your family being my business when I drive your mom to work or the grocery store, or when I help Angelita. Or even when I give you money to buy your mom a birthday present. But now, all of a sudden, none of you are my business?"

"Get out of the way," Pablo said.

"No." Jinx squared off in front of him. "If you're going to go, you're going to have to go through me."

A small gasp escaped E. J.'s lips. Jinx was taller than Pablo, but Pablo was stockier and had at least twenty pounds on her.

"Get the fuck out of the way," Pablo said again, his tone menacing.

"No," Jinx said more firmly.

Pablo started to move past her, shoving her aside.

Jinx grabbed his shoulder and yanked him back.

He spun and took a swing at her.

In one smooth motion, she dodged the punch, then caught his wrist as he came around, twisted his arm behind his back, and shoved him forward into the wall. She pinned him with her body. "You're not going," she said through gritted teeth.

"Get off me, bitch," Pablo yelled.

"You want me off you? Then what? Then you go hunt down the shooter and kill him? Then his gang sends someone after you, and this time they do take you out? Or maybe this time, it's your mom they hit—because you bangers don't seem to be too smart. All it takes is a *hat* to confuse you."

Pablo jerked against Jinx's hold but couldn't move.

"Or, if you don't end up dead, you get sent away. You think *that's* easy? Who's going to take care of your family, then? Who's going to look out for Angelita while your mom works two jobs, or maybe even takes on a third one so she can put money on your books, because you know she will." Jinx pressed closer to Pablo's ear, and something in her demeanor seemed to shift. Her voice hardened. "And believe me, you're gonna want her to, even though it's gonna suck her dry, because let me tell you what it's like in there when you got nobody on the outside, when you got no money coming in."

He struggled against her.

She pushed him harder against the wall. "If you got nobody on the outside sending you money, sending you things you need, you got nothing to trade. Oh, wait. No, you do have something to trade. You got your body. And believe me, a little piece like you? You're gonna be in high demand. So you're gonna need to find someone to ride with. Some Big Daddy who can protect you. But he ain't gonna do it for free. No, there's a price, and it's a high one. It's your dignity. But you're gonna be willing to pay it, because the alternative is worse.

The alternative lands you in the ding wing on brake fluid or doing a dance on the blacktop."

E. J. had no idea what Jinx was talking about, but it hit home with Pablo.

He stilled.

"Meanwhile," Jinx said, adjusting her hold. "All you're gonna be able to do is *wonder* about your family. How's your mama holding up under the pain of losing her son to the streets? What's Angelita learning about life with the stellar example you've been? Is she still in her accelerated classes? Is she still working toward going to college? Or is she spreading her legs every Saturday night for one of your *homies*? And that's given she even wakes up tonight."

"Shut the fuck up," Pablo screamed.

"What's the matter, tough guy? If you can't even *hear* about it, how you gonna live it? Huh? How you gonna wake up every morning being a piece of meat with no family 'cept the one you pay such a high price for in there, 'cept the one that'll turn on you at the slightest misstep. While your real family, who you think *taking care of* tonight is going out and killing someone, forgets you, or doesn't want anything to do with you." Jinx's face contorted, and she squeezed her eyes shut, but her voice remained steady.

Pablo's chest heaved, and he began to cry.

"You're not that guy, Pablo," Jinx said quietly. "You're not this guy, tonight. You're the guy who lies on the floor with his little sister, helping her make friendship bracelets out of gum wrappers. You're the guy who still holds his mom's hand when she's worried or scared, the one who really wants to be in there with her, now. You're the guy whose favorite thing to do is sit in the park and sketch little kids on the swings or dogs chasing squirrels. Be *that* guy," she added softly.

Pablo slumped against the wall and cried quietly.

Jinx shifted from pinning him to embracing him.

E. J. exhaled the breath she'd been holding. She glanced down the hall and locked eyes with one of Pablo's friends.

His expression was unreadable. He turned and walked away.

"Let's go back inside. Let's go support your mama. That's taking care of family," Jinx murmured to Pablo. She released her hold and dropped an arm over his shoulders.

He wiped his face on his sleeve and nodded.

As Pablo talked to the nurse at the window and was ushered back to sit with his mother and sister, E. J. studied Jinx. She wondered what toll the visit to her past had taken on her. She looked a little shaken. E. J. slipped her arms around Jinx's neck and felt her trembling. "You did good," she whispered.

Jinx came to her easily and rested her head on E. J.'s shoulder.

It was almost dawn before Angelita woke, and word came out that she would be fine. She had a concussion and stitches and would need to be careful with the fracture, but all would heal quickly. The emotional trauma of being shot, however, would undoubtedly take longer.

On the way home, E. J. sat curled sideways in the passenger's seat of her car, watching Jinx. Jinx had loaned her Toyota to one of Mercedes's sisters, who had to leave before the rest of the family to get to work on time. E. J. liked watching Jinx drive. She liked the way one hand draped over the steering wheel while the other rested on E. J.'s thigh. She liked being able to examine Jinx's profile without being noticed. They hadn't spoken since they had left the hospital, each lost in her own thoughts.

"I'm glad you were there tonight," Jinx said finally.

E. J. shifted her gaze from Jinx's earlobe to the muscles of her jaw as she spoke. "Me, too," she said, still a little unfocused.

She pictured Jinx's face, the face now closed and contemplative, as it had been during the altercation with Pablo. It had been so intense, so many emotions passing over it—sincerity, concern, anger, pain, relief—all in such a short period of time. Regardless of what she had been feeling, despite whatever emotions and memories were being resurrected, she had been relentless. She had thought only of Pablo and how devastatingly his life could have been changed if he had walked out that door. She had fought for Pablo—and won. *At least for tonight.*

"I wish you hadn't seen me like that," Jinx said as though reading E. J.'s mind.

Startled out of her trance, E. J. straightened slightly. "Why?" she asked, confused.

"Because that isn't who I am anymore." Jinx remained focused on the early-morning traffic.

"It's a part of you, Jinx. Everything you've been through makes up who you are today. Everything you've been through makes up..." The words in her mind were *the woman I love*, but she caught herself before they came tumbling out. *Whoa.* She'd have to think about that one, later. Instead, she said, "...who you've become. And who you've been and who you are today came together to help Pablo, and I'm thrilled I was there to see it. It was the most amazing thing. I was so proud of you."

Jinx looked incredulous. "Really?"

"You kept him from making a bad decision that would have changed his life forever. It's admirable."

"It didn't scare you?"

E. J. recalled the instant when Jinx had stepped in front of Pablo to block his way. "A little, when it became physical. I didn't know if he'd hurt you."

Jinx turned to her, eyes wide. "You thought *he'd* hurt *me*?"

E. J. laughed and stroked Jinx's hand. "I know, silly me. I certainly know better, now." She tilted her head and gave Jinx a lascivious smile. "Is it okay that I thought it was kind of hot?"

Jinx grinned. "Absolutely. Anything you find hot, as long as it's to do with me, is more than okay."

As they pulled into the driveway, Jinx thumped her fist against the steering wheel. "Damn it! I didn't make anything for Kenny last night."

"I did," E. J. said, marginally self-satisfied. Did that make her a hero, too?

"You did?"

"Mm-hm. I threw together a couple of PB&Js and some fruit before I left to take Pete to Reggie and Sparkle. It wasn't lobster, but he didn't seem to mind."

Jinx leaned across the console and kissed her. "You are awesome."

E. J. smiled. "Thank you for noticing. I'm also exhausted. Can we sleep for a while?"

"You bet," Jinx said, climbing out of the car.

As E. J. crawled into bed, she reveled in its comfort. Had it always been this soft, or was it simply in contrast to the hard plastic chairs in the waiting room? She let out a deep sigh. "This feels so good. I'm so tired."

Jinx slipped in beside her and rested on an elbow. She gazed down at E. J. "We didn't get a chance to talk about what happened between us yesterday. Are you okay?"

E. J. looked into Jinx's eyes, touched that, with everything else that had happened since, she was thinking about their argument. "Yes," she said softly. "Between what you said to me about not dumping you every time I get scared and everything tonight with Pablo and Angelita, I realized I need to put things into perspective. I need to be honest about who I am." She swallowed against a tide of emotion. "I thought about Mandy when Angelita was in the ER, and what that would be like, and I realized, if something happened to her, or me, she wouldn't have even known her mother. Especially now." She traced the curve of Jinx's lower lip. "She wouldn't know anything about how happy I am."

Jinx kissed the tip of E. J.'s finger. "And Jacob?"

Fear lingered in E. J.'s heart, but she took strength from Jinx's proximity. "Jacob, too," she said. "I don't know when or how I'm going to do it, but I need to be honest with both of them. And I have to trust."

Jinx said nothing for a long moment. "Now, *I'm* proud of *you*." She kissed her gently on the lips.

"And," E. J. said, tearing her attention away from Jinx's mouth. "After *our* disagreement and watching you with Pablo, I don't think I want to fight with you anymore. You're too good. You'll always win. It would be bad for my self-esteem."

"Very wise decision."

E. J. considered the different side of Jinx she had seen. "Can I ask you something?"

"Anything."

"What were those things you were saying to Pablo? The wing ding?"

Jinx chuckled. "Ding wing," she said. "That's the psych ward."

"Psych ward?"

"In prison. It's slang for the psych ward. And brake fluid is psych meds. They stop you in your tracks."

"What about the dance on the blacktop?"

Jinx's expression clouded. "It means getting stabbed."

E. J. drew in a breath. "I'm sorry."

"It's okay, baby," Jinx said, trailing her fingers through E. J.'s hair. "That's all in the past. I'm here, now. With you."

"Yes, you are." E. J. pressed her palm to Jinx's chest. She felt her steady heartbeat. "And I'm here with you."

Jinx sighed. "That amazes me."

"Why?" E. J. smoothed the fabric of Jinx's shirt.

"Because of where here is." Jinx glanced around the room. She laughed. "I can't believe I brought you here that first time. I was just so excited to see you again, that's all I could think of."

E. J. smiled. "I love this place. I told you that."

"Because it reminds you of your grandparents' house."

"That's what I thought, at first." E. J. caressed the hollow of Jinx's throat. "But now I know it's you I feel here. Your warmth. Your..." She searched for the exact word. "Your authenticity. Your heart."

Jinx pursed her lips. "What I'm about to say seems so obvious, but I still need to say it." She paused. "E. J., I don't have anything."

E. J. fought back a swell of emotion. "Sweetie, you have everything I need."

"You know what I mean." Jinx rested her head on her arm, her lips close to E. J.'s ear.

"You mean money."

"Yes."

"I *have* money. Enough for both of us for a very long time."

"Oh," Jinx said, a smile in her voice. "So I get to be a kept woman?"

E. J. stared at the ceiling, enjoying the feather-light play of Jinx's breath on her neck. She laughed. "You won't get any argument out of me. I think that sounds fun. But somehow, I think you have way more to do in the world than sit around and wait for me. I think it's interesting that we both know both worlds, though."

"You mean because you grew up wealthy, but still shared your grandparents' life and home? And I spent most of my childhood living at the estate, but also have lived without much of anything?"

The hush of Jinx's voice, the warmth of her breath, soothed E. J. She turned her head, until her cheek pressed against Jinx's, and closed her eyes. "Mm-hm," she murmured. "So, wherever we are, we know we'll be happy."

"You're happy?" Jinx draped her arm across E. J.'s stomach and snuggled closer.

"Very," E. J. whispered. "And before yesterday, I thought I could be completely happy right here, just like this, forever. But now…"

Jinx raised her head and waited.

E. J. opened her eyes and stroked Jinx's cheek. "Now, I want it all. I want you. I want this." She kissed her tenderly. "*And* I want my kids. I want all of it, all of you, all together. And, yes, I do want my job and money."

"Then *all* of it you shall have." Jinx slid her that slow, easy smile.

E. J.'s arousal ignited. "Oh God. Don't do that. I'm too tired to make love." It was something she thought she would never say where Jinx was concerned, but her body had its limits.

"What?" Jinx asked with the best, wide-eyed innocent expression E. J. had ever seen.

"You know exactly what." E. J. turned onto her side in defense and pulled Jinx's arm around her. "You know what that smile does to me."

Jinx settled in behind her. "I don't know what you mean," she murmured in E. J.'s ear. Her warm breath fanned E. J.'s desire.

E. J. moaned softly as Jinx's hand ran down her side and slipped beneath her T-shirt to find bare skin, before it inched lower. Her touch was now so familiar, so knowing. E. J. parted her thighs as one finger slid between them. She moaned softly. Maybe there would never be a time when her body was too tired for Jinx.

CHAPTER SEVENTEEN

E. J. sipped her third cup of decaf for the evening as she stood in the doorway of her kitchen and examined the elegance of her living room, trying to imagine how Jinx would see it. The hardwood floors were polished to a high sheen, and finely stitched Persian rugs designated the sitting area that held a large, plush sectional sofa in front of an enormous fireplace, the rock facing of which stretched all the way to the fourteen-foot ceiling. A shiny, black baby grand piano sat on a raised platform in the corner. Delicately crafted, smoked glass lamps lit the room.

She had bought and decorated the place primarily with money out of her divorce settlement, which allowed her a large enough down payment that she was able to pay off the balance quickly with her ample salary from Bad Dog. Marcus had been extremely generous in their split—out of guilt for the affair, E. J. suspected, though she had assured him guilt was unnecessary—and between that and her steady climb up the corporate ladder, she was financially flush. She had never had cause, however, to wonder about her life through someone else's eyes, particularly someone as down-to-earth as Jinx. She had always felt somewhat uncomfortable in this space but viewed that as fine, given she mostly only slept there and, even that, only about half the time.

But now, she was nervous. Jinx was stepping into her life for the very first time.

In the weeks since the shooting, a lot had changed. E. J. had spent the weekends, and any additional time she had, with Jinx and

Pete. They seemed to be settling into an easy routine. Kenny had gone into the VA hospital with a severe bladder infection, and a sister who had been looking for him in the system, found him. He had accepted her invitation to come live with her in San Diego. Pablo, Mercedes, and Angelita had been staying with one of Mercedes's sisters across town, outside of the gang's territory, and were now officially moving in with her so Pablo could make a fresh start. He had begun art classes at a community center, and Reggie had given him a job in the kennels. He planned to enroll at the junior college for fall courses. Jinx, of course, was helping him with his GED.

E. J. had yet to face her moment of honesty with either of her children. She'd had the idea of getting together with Jacob and Mandy tomorrow for her birthday and having the conversation then, but she had learned both kids, along with Tiffany and Mandy's boyfriend, Russ, had plans to spend the weekend in New York. There had been no mention of her birthday, but she had no one but herself to blame for that, since she hadn't celebrated with them in years. With everyone out of town, she had decided to invite Jinx to Sacramento. But E. J. was tiring of all the sneaking around and of her heart jumping every time her phone displayed an incoming call from Jacob, always wondering if Tiffany had unintentionally—or intentionally, for that matter—let the proverbial cat out of the bag. She had to do it soon.

For now, though, she hadn't even told Taylor and Gwen that Jinx was coming. Yes, she was nervous, but she was also excited about having Jinx here with her in her space, maybe taking her to see the office, and perhaps an ice cream at Gunther's and a stroll along the river, something E. J. hadn't done in a long time. There would probably be a point during the weekend at which she would be comfortable inviting her friends to meet Jinx, and she could call them then, but she didn't want the pressure of it needing to be at a specific, prearranged time.

E. J. checked her watch.

Jinx should be there soon. She had called during Pete's last potty stop, about an hour out.

They had spent the night together on Tuesday, and it was only Friday, but E. J. felt as though she hadn't seen Jinx in weeks.

The doorbell rang.

E. J. jumped. A splash of coffee landed on the front of her sage-colored blouse, the heat seeping through to her skin. *Damn it!* She grabbed a dish towel and patted at it, then hurried to answer the bell. Her heartbeat quickened as she got closer, and she couldn't suppress a burgeoning smile. She opened the door.

Pete raced inside.

Jinx grinned at her. "I found you." The strap of a duffle hung over her shoulder, and she carried a Canine Complete tote in one hand and Pete's bed in the other. The light blue of the replacement Bad Dog shirt E. J. had gotten her deepened the color of Jinx's eyes, and E. J. fell in.

She grabbed the front of the shirt and pulled Jinx across the threshold.

As soon as the door closed, Jinx dropped everything, grasped E. J.'s hips, spun her around, and pressed her against it. Her lips found E. J.'s, and she took her, owned her.

E. J. expected the kiss to be hard, to be bruising. But it wasn't. As burning and demanding as it was, it was still gentle. It consumed E. J. in its tenderness. It stole her breath and the strength in her legs. She twisted her fingers into Jinx's hair and moaned as she felt Jinx's hands move upward, her thumbs caressing the sides of E. J.'s breasts.

"I missed you," Jinx murmured as she eased off and brushed her lips over E. J.'s, then along her jaw. She found E. J.'s earlobe and sucked it into her mouth, her teeth tugging on the small gold heart that adorned it, drawing another moan from E. J.

E. J. crushed Jinx to her and thrust her hips, desperate for purchase.

Jinx continued her trek down E. J.'s neck, gently but firmly nipping and licking her way to the hollow of her throat, then lower into the open collar of E. J.'s blouse. Her thumbs still maddeningly worked only the sides of E. J.'s breasts. "You spilled," Jinx said, an absent tenor to her voice.

E. J. laughed softly. "It's coffee."

"We need to get you out of this wet blouse," Jinx said without missing the next nibble. She undid the first closed button, then the next, and the next after that. Her mouth followed the path. She licked the swell of E. J.'s breast where the coffee had landed, then traced the edge of her bra with the tip of her tongue as she released the front clasp. The lace grazed E. J.'s stiffening nipples as Jinx eased the cups aside.

E. J. gasped and pulled Jinx's mouth to her breasts.

Jinx sucked the swell, licking the remnants of the coffee, then inched further to suck a throbbing nipple deep into her mouth.

E. J. cried out and closed her thighs around one of Jinx's.

"Unless you want me to take you right here," Jinx said, her breathing heavy, "show me your bedroom."

E. J. did want Jinx to take her right there, *and* in the bedroom—and on the couch, and in the kitchen, and on the dining room table, in the bathtub, the shower…She wanted Jinx everywhere. She wanted there not to be a single spot in the condo that didn't make her think of Jinx. She forced herself to ease Jinx away, whimpering at the release of Jinx's mouth, and took her hands. "Come with me."

In the bedroom, Jinx sat E. J. on the edge of the bed and knelt between her open thighs. She found E. J.'s nipple again and sucked it into her mouth as though no interruption had taken place. She palmed the other one to a harder point, then rolled it between her fingertips.

E. J. cried out and threw her head back. She leaned back on her hands, pressing harder into Jinx.

Jinx was merciless—slow, methodical, deliberate, and utterly ruthless. She touched nothing but E. J.'s nipples. She suckled and squeezed and pinched and nipped, then traded hand and mouth and began again.

E. J. gasped for air. She looked down at Jinx, at herself, her blouse half unbuttoned, her bra pushed aside. She felt wanton, a little slutty. Pure need pulsed between her spread thighs. She tried to close them, to gain some much-needed pressure, but Jinx's body blocked her. She tried to press against her but couldn't quite reach. "Jinx, please…"

Jinx groaned and dropped her hands to the waistband of E. J.'s slacks. She had them unfastened and off in seconds.

E. J. fell back on the bed.

Kneeling again at the edge, Jinx pulled E. J.'s legs over her shoulders and opened her, gently, almost reverently. She leaned in.

E. J. expected a touch, a stroke, a kiss, maybe to be taken. What she didn't expect was a delay, an excruciating moment of nothing. Her center ached. "Please," she whispered. Then she felt Jinx's breath, warm, light, *so* not enough. She groaned loudly and squirmed.

Jinx looped her arms around E. J.'s hips, opened her wider, and tightened her grip. Without warning, she drove her tongue into her.

E. J. screamed with pleasure. She clenched her fists into the duvet beneath her.

Jinx thrust into her in a steady rhythm.

E. J. tried to pump her hips to meet her, but Jinx held her still, relentless in her obvious mission to drive E. J. insane with need. She didn't let up.

E. J. came hard, screaming once again. She arched up off the bed, then flopped back. She tried again to pump her hips but could only lie there and take it, take Jinx's tongue still inside her, thrusting, licking—remarkably driving her toward another orgasm.

Jinx shifted her mouth slightly and sucked E. J.'s clitoris between her lips.

A new sensation overtook E. J., making her jerk and renewing her desire to squirm. "Oh God, Jinx," she cried out.

Once again, Jinx held her still and took her over the edge.

E. J.'s body thrummed with the release. She gulped for air.

Clearly, Jinx still wasn't finished. She moved her mouth more slowly over E. J.'s hot folds.

E. J. couldn't even attempt to move anymore. She lay back and relaxed into the pleasure. She twined her fingers into Jinx's hair and held her close.

Jinx nuzzled her head into E. J.'s grasp, the movement accentuating the caress of her mouth against E. J.'s center. She released E. J.'s hips, pressed her lips around her pulsing clitoris, and eased her fingers inside her.

E. J. came one last time, so deeply she thought she might implode.

Finally, Jinx stilled. Her mouth remained on E. J., her fingers lingered inside, but nothing moved.

They lay quietly, E. J. catching her breath, Jinx doing God knows what.

E. J. stroked Jinx's hair, the silken strands caressing the pads of her fingers. "What have you done to me?" she murmured.

"Hmm?" Jinx eased away and moved up beside her on the bed.

"I've never been like this."

Jinx combed her fingers through E. J.'s hair. "Maybe you've always been like this, and you just never got close enough to anyone to know it."

E. J. gazed up at her. "As I said, I've never been like this." She ran a hand over the front of Jinx's shirt. "You have too many clothes on," she said, surprised at the lust still in her voice. "Get naked."

"I have to use the bathroom," Jinx said, touching a kiss to E. J.'s lips.

E. J. pointed behind her to the archway at the end of the master suite.

While she waited, she stared into space, marveling at how different her life was now from a mere three months earlier. Before, most Friday nights were spent at a club with Taylor, perhaps picking up a woman for a night, or here at home, curled up with a book. She certainly wasn't lying half naked on her own bed after having had three orgasms in a row with a woman she was...maybe...in love with. There was that thought again. She remembered having it the morning after the shooting, in passing, and that she had intended to think about it further. But she hadn't. And now, it was no wonder she was thinking it—feeling it—after what Jinx had just done to her. How many times had women told her they thought they were falling in love with her after several orgasms?

The sound of water running in the bathtub drew E. J.'s attention. Curious, she rose, dispensed with her blouse and bra still hanging off of her, and padded to the bathroom.

Jinx stood beside the large Roman tub, holding a bottle of bubble bath. She lifted it and arched an eyebrow in question.

"Sure," E. J. said with a smile. "Can I join you?"

Jinx poured some of the liquid into the filling tub, then, without a word, pulled her T-shirt over her head and dropped it to the floor. She met E. J.'s eyes, unmistakable invitation in hers.

E. J. went to her. She spread her hands over Jinx's bare breasts and pressed her mouth to Jinx's. She trailed the tip of her tongue between Jinx's lips, reveling in how swollen they were from everything they had done to her, tasting her own arousal and release. She lowered her head and took one of Jinx's tight nipples into her mouth. "You're still way too overdressed," she whispered and sucked worshipfully while Jinx struggled out of her jeans.

When the tub had filled around them, E. J. turned off the water and stretched her body on top of Jinx's.

Jinx sighed as she tilted her head back against the edge. "This is an enormous bathtub."

"I had it custom made when I remodeled." E. J. spread bubbles across Jinx's shoulders. "I wanted it big enough I could stretch out in it. And big enough for two, if I ever wanted that. It has Jacuzzi jets, too. Do you want me to turn them on?"

"Mmm, no. This is nice." Jinx ran her hands up E. J.'s wet sides. "Do you like baths with other people?"

E. J. looked into Jinx's face and smiled. "So far. You're the first."

Jinx looked doubtful. "That can't be true. How long have you lived here?"

"Nine years," E. J. said, shifting to slip between Jinx's legs.

Jinx moaned softly and moved against her.

"But I've never had anyone over. Not like this." E. J.'s breasts rubbed against Jinx's stomach as she settled in. "I mean, Gwen and Taylor have been here, and the kids, of course, but no one else."

"Why not?"

"Because I don't do that." E. J. realized she could no longer say that. "I haven't done that until now," she said, correcting herself.

Jinx tightened her arms around E. J. "I like the way that sounds."

"I know," E. J. said, snuggling against her. "I like that I'm the only woman who's been in your bed."

"I do find it hard to believe, though. I mean you're…you're *you*. It's hard to believe you haven't been involved with anyone in all that time."

E. J. rested her head in the hollow of Jinx's shoulder. "I didn't get involved. I just got laid. Until you."

"Hey, you get laid with me," Jinx said with a smile.

E. J. laughed. "You think you have to remind me of that after what you just did to me?"

Jinx chuckled.

They settled into a comfortable silence, E. J. smoothing bubbles over Jinx's chest, Jinx trailing warm circles on the small of E. J.'s back.

"Can I ask you something?" E. J. said finally.

"Mm-hm."

E. J. tilted her head to look at Jinx. "How do you..." She wasn't sure how to word it. "How do you do all those amazingly, sexy, and arousing things to me and give me bone-melting orgasms without needing release, yourself?"

"You don't think I need release?"

E. J. smiled. "I know you do, because when you do get it, you're right there. It's just that you're not usually in a hurry. Like right now. If I was in your place tonight, there's no way we'd be lying here in a bath cuddling and talking, at least not before I got my turn."

Jinx stilled. She searched E. J.'s face. "I can answer that," she said slowly, "but I'd rather do it another time."

E. J. waited for her to continue.

"The answer involves another woman, and I don't want that between us tonight." Jinx's tone was serious. "I *do* want my turn tonight, and I want to just be able to focus on our pleasure."

E. J. considered her response. "Is it Val?"

Jinx gave a short nod.

E. J. settled against her again. Jinx had been so honest and up front about her life and so patient with E. J., she wanted to respect her need for timing on this. Besides, she liked the part about focusing on *their* pleasure tonight. She ran her hand down Jinx's body and between her legs. She parted her and dipped a finger inside. "Are you ready, now, then?"

Jinx moaned and lifted her hips. "Yes."

E. J. found Jinx's clitoris swollen and hard, her moisture slick, such a different consistency from the warm water. She slid her fingers along the length of Jinx's sex, up her shaft, over her tip.

Jinx held her tightly and moved against her. She cupped E. J.'s breast and kneaded it in the same rhythm. "I want to suck you," she murmured, her eyes closed.

E. J. shifted to straddle Jinx's thighs. She kept her fingers working Jinx's need. The air, cooler than the water, tightened her nipples just before Jinx's hot mouth and fingers found them again. They were still sensitive from the earlier attention, and E. J.'s own arousal built quickly.

Jinx groaned as she sucked and teased, thrusting upward into E. J.'s hand. She slipped her fingers into E. J.'s slick opening.

E. J. gasped. "Wait. I want to do you."

"Come with me, baby." Jinx moaned. "I love it when you come with me." She pumped into her as she found her clitoris with her thumb. "Tell me when you're ready." She sucked unyieldingly on E. J.'s nipple.

Even with three prior orgasms, it didn't take long. "Now," E. J. cried as her pleasure threatened to explode. She pressed harder into Jinx, rubbed her clitoris faster.

Jinx lifted into her, and they came together, breathing fast. They filled the bathtub two more times, and E. J. pleasured Jinx an equal number before she lay on top of her again, feeling the comfort and safety she always felt in her arms.

"I want to see the rest of your place," Jinx said finally. "So far, I've only seen your front door, literally a small portion of your bed that fits between your legs, and the bathroom."

E. J. laughed. "Those are the only important parts." She eased off Jinx and reached for a towel.

"We should see what Pete's been doing, too." Jinx ran her gaze over E. J.'s naked body as she dried herself. "You might not have a sofa anymore."

E. J. inhaled sharply. "He wouldn't do such a thing."

"He is a puppy." Jinx stood and stepped from the tub into the bath sheet E. J. held open for her.

Dressed again, they ventured out into the living room. It was quiet. E. J. dared a glance around for Pete. He lay curled in his bed where Jinx had dropped it by the door, his squeaky rabbit between his front paws and his Kong a few feet away. He slept peacefully.

"I guess he got tired of waiting for us," Jinx said.

Pete opened his eyes, looked up at E. J., and shook himself. Then he ran to her, tail wagging.

"I know. I'm sorry." E. J. picked him up and hugged him. "I didn't even say hello, did I? Your other mama distracted me."

Pete licked her face.

E. J. noticed Jinx walking around the living room, taking it all in. It reminded her of Jinx's exploration of the hotel suite that first morning.

She circled the sofa, stared down at the rug, looked out the panel window beside the fireplace at the lights of the city, and studied the Steve Hanks painting hanging above the dining table for a long time. "What's the name of that?" she asked as she examined the picture of a woman and a little girl sitting on a dock, each with her foot barely skimming the water.

"*Touching the Surface*," E. J. said, still snuggling with the puppy.

"I like it," Jinx said.

E. J. smiled. "I'm glad."

Jinx turned and cocked her head, seeming to notice the baby grand for the first time. "You play?" She walked toward it.

"No." E. J. cradled Pete in her arms and rubbed his tummy. "I wish I did."

"Why do you have it?"

E. J. felt herself blush. She didn't want to answer. "Because when I bought the place, my Realtor told me that that's what that platform was for."

Jinx looked at her as though trying to determine if that could possibly be true.

E. J. understood. She'd had the same thought, herself, a time or two.

"So you bought a piano?"

E. J. nodded.

"*This* piano?"

She nodded again.

"This is a really expensive piano."

Another nod.

Jinx crossed to her and slipped her arms around her waist. "You have way too much money. You know that, right?"

E. J. looked up at her. The words and tone had been playful, but there was the slightest edge to them. "Probably. Is that okay?"

Jinx took a moment to look around the room. She inhaled deeply, then sighed before returning her attention to E. J. "My experience with the world of money, as you know, is that it can be a not very nice place, so it makes me a little nervous." She shrugged. "I think that's why I don't mind where I live, now."

Once again, E. J. was touched by Jinx's honesty, her willingness to be vulnerable. She moved closer in the circle of Jinx's arms, snuggling Pete between them. "Maybe I can show you a different side of it, and we can find a happy medium."

Jinx's expression softened. "I'm open to that," she said quietly. Then humor sparked in her eyes. She dropped her gaze to Pete. "I mean, we have to make it work. We have a puppy together."

E. J. smiled. "Are you hungry?"

"Starving," Jinx said.

E. J. busied herself heating the manicotti she had picked up on her way home and tossing the salad, while Jinx took Pete outside and then fed him. They talked while they ate at the small breakfast table in the kitchen—E. J. had only used the dining room for a couple of dinner parties she had hosted for work. Jinx filled E. J. in on the gossip at Canine Complete, gave her an update on Reggie and Sparkle's upcoming anniversary party, and Trisha's new boyfriend, while E. J. shared her concerns about the ongoing sexual harassment suit and her hope that she was correct in her suspicion that Mandy and Russ might be thinking about moving in together. Somewhere in the course of the meal, she realized being with Jinx felt just as right here in her space as it did in Jinx's. She hoped Jinx felt the same way. "So, what do you think?" she asked.

"About what?"

"About being here, at my place? I mean, other than what you've already said about the money."

Jinx leaned across the table and took E. J.'s hand. "I like being wherever you are."

E. J. warmed at the thought. "Oh, the things you say." She bent forward and kissed her. "I'm serious, though. Do you like it?"

Jinx looked surprised. "It's great. Beautiful, and yes, I like it better because you're here with me." She paused. "But I don't feel you much in it."

"What do you mean?" E. J. asked, running her thumb over Jinx's knuckles.

"It's beautiful, but it's like it's for show, like no one actually lives here. Or, at least, not you. I didn't feel you at all in the living room, except for the one picture. A little bit in the bedroom and bathroom."

E. J. laughed. "After earlier, that will most likely change. I think I left half my soul in the bedroom and bathroom tonight. But I'll feel you in there with me from now on, too."

Jinx grinned and brought E. J.'s hand to her lips. "Maybe we can add some feeling to the rest of the place while I'm here," she said with a suggestive lilt. "Make it ours."

E. J. smiled. They could. And it would be fun. But deep down, she knew this wasn't their place, nor was Jinx's rental theirs. *Their* place was still in the making, as *they* were still in the making. The concept startled E. J. What was she thinking? Were she and Jinx becoming a *they*? A *we*? A couple? "I'd like that," was all she said.

As she loaded the dishwasher, she imagined Jinx moving through the condo, maybe hanging up some clothes for the weekend, putting some toiletries in the bathroom, getting Pete settled in his bed. If it had been anyone but Jinx, it would have felt invasive, even suffocating. Even she and Rhonda had spent what time they had shared in Rhonda's home, so E. J. could leave whenever she needed space. And yet, it felt so natural for Jinx to be there. E. J. knew, however, they weren't fully *there*.

There were still things in the way, the biggest of all being honest with her children. They were grown adults with lives of their own. They were in New York, seeing plays and staying in hotels. They had their own lovers. They wouldn't care if their mother was gay. Mandy probably never would have, and Jacob had Tiffany. He had overcome his emotional trauma enough to fall in love and be in a healthy and happy marriage. Surely, he could accept the same for her by now. The reasoning was sound.

What about the prison sentence, though? The bank robbery? The fact that the woman his mother wanted to be with was his wife's aunt, an aunt that his wife's mother had rejected long ago. But his wife's *mother* had rejected her, not his wife. E. J. squeezed her eyes shut. It was all so screwed up. She just needed to do it and—what had Jinx said—let everything be what it is and everyone be who they are.

There were still things of Jinx's standing between them as well, though—like Val. Yes, E. J. knew of her, but she didn't know much about her, about Jinx's relationship with her, the elements of it that made Jinx hesitant to discuss it.

Soft music invited E. J. out of her swirling thoughts. It was the tinkling of the higher register of a piano. It was familiar. What was it—the introduction to the theme from *Ice Castles?* At first, she thought Jinx had figured out the stereo system and was setting a romantic mood, which brought a smile to her lips, but then she heard the slightest hesitation in the music, as though the pianist forgot the next hand position for the briefest instant. *Jinx is playing the piano?*

She moved to the kitchen doorway and peered into the living room.

Jinx sat at the piano, her back to E. J., her hands moving carefully over the keys, as though she was remembering the positions. Those hands that made such sweet love to E. J., that were so gentle with Pete, were now making the loveliest music on a piano that had been played maybe twice by a hired musician at a catered dinner party.

E. J. leaned against the doorjamb and watched, mesmerized.

Soon, Jinx seemed lost in the music, not even looking at the keys. Her fingers appeared to glide as she played under the soft illumination of a single lamp.

E. J. closed her eyes and listened as the verse moved into the bridge. She had always loved that song, but hearing it now, knowing Jinx was playing it…How did she know how to play the piano? She listened as the song went on, and its slightly haunting quality drew her in. She let it pull her, coax her across the room to stand behind Jinx. She wanted to touch her but was afraid if she did, Jinx would stop. At length, she brushed her knuckles across the back of Jinx's neck, beneath her hair.

Jinx leaned into her caress but kept playing.

E. J. slipped onto the bench beside her, her heart swelling with the crescendo, her gaze fixed on Jinx's hands. She, too, was lost. She rested her head on Jinx's shoulder.

As the remnants of the final notes reverberated in the quiet all around them, they sat together in the stillness, neither one moving. Finally, Jinx lifted her fingers from the keys.

"That was beautiful," E. J. said, her tone hushed. "Where did you learn to play?"

Jinx rested a hand on E. J.'s thigh. "It's the one thing I can patently thank Nora for. She insisted both Andi and I take lessons.

I never let her know I liked them because if she knew, she probably would have made me stop."

E. J. smiled at the cleverness of the little girl Jinx had been. "And you've remembered all these years?"

"There was a piano in the facility where I served most of my sentence. They let me play it because I accompanied all the Christmas programs and talent shows and played for the different religious services every week. It was a good trade." Jinx traced the silk seam of E. J.'s pajama pants. "It probably saved my sanity quite a few times to be able to drift away with the music. It wasn't a piano like this, though." She touched the keyboard reverently with her other hand. "And they hardly ever tuned it."

E. J. found herself without words. She tried to imagine this gentle soul, sitting at a raggedy old piano, playing beautiful music in the midst of a prison. She tried to reconcile that image with the things Jinx had said to Pablo about what life in prison could be like and the change that had come over Jinx in that moment. She tried to integrate both with the woman she sat beside, now, the woman who touched her so deeply, the woman with whom—yes—she had fallen in love.

She sighed. "Take me to bed," she whispered. "I want to fall asleep in your arms."

CHAPTER EIGHTEEN

Jinx opened her eyes to the gray pre-dawn light through the huge plate glass window of E. J.'s bedroom. She still woke at that time out of habit, from so many years of being rousted from her bunk for showers and mess. On the inside, she'd caught the sunrise occasionally, depending on its timing and if she was on an early, outside work detail, but once she'd gotten out and she continued to wake up so early regularly, she made a point of watching the miracle of another beginning much more often. She especially liked the few times she and E. J. had shared the experience, because she couldn't help but feel that E. J. represented Jinx's own dawn, the opportunity to start fresh, to leave yesterday behind.

She rested her head in the crook of her arm and allowed the pinks, purples, and blues to wash over her, their fluid swirls bathing her, cleansing her of lingering mistakes and remaining guilt. With every sunrise, with every new day, came vast possibilities to experience things she never had before and to reclaim emotions she'd once thought gone forever. She'd let go of a lot over the years, forgiven herself for many things, but there was still Andrea. *What did I do?*

According to Tiffany, Andrea said Jinx wasn't welcome in the family because she was a criminal and had chosen prison, but whatever happened between them took place long before that. Jinx was learning family didn't have to be those she was related to by blood. Reggie and Sparkle were her family, Trisha, and now— maybe even—E. J. She could hope. And she also had Tiffany, but she couldn't let go of Andrea—of Andi. And even if Andrea never wanted anything with her again, if she just knew what she'd done and could forgive herself for that like she had so many other things, maybe she could move on. Although, maybe she could let it go anyway, with enough new chances. As the skyline began to glow with shades of golds, oranges, and yellows, she let herself hope this might be the day of her full redemption at long last. If not…Well, there was always tomorrow's dawn.

"I left the blinds open for you," E. J. murmured in her morning voice Jinx loved so much.

Jinx smiled and pulled her gaze from the window to study E. J. "Thank you." She kissed the tip of E. J.'s nose.

Pete squirmed between them, tucked in the curve of E. J.'s tummy beneath the covers. He wriggled his way up until his nose poked out from the blankets.

"Why is it when you're not with us, Pete sleeps in his bed all night, but when you're here, he finds his way into ours?" Jinx asked.

"I have no idea," E. J. said, petting Pete's head. "But I'll think about it while you take him out." She gave Jinx a sleepy but guilty grin.

When Jinx returned, she found E. J. sitting up in bed, sipping a cup of coffee. A glass of apple juice sat on the nightstand. Jinx eased onto the mattress beside her and rested her head on E. J.'s lap. She nuzzled her cheek into the softness of E. J.'s silk pajamas.

E. J. combed her fingers through Jinx's hair. "Everything go okay downstairs?" she asked lazily.

"Pete did great, but your doorman looked at us funny."

E. J. paused. "That's probably because you're barefoot and your shirt's on inside-out."

Jinx looked down at herself. "Oh. That could explain it."

E. J. chuckled.

In the comfortable quiet that followed, Jinx noticed a grouping of three small framed paintings arranged on the wall beside the bathroom doorway. She hadn't noticed them the night before. She hadn't noticed anything in E. J.'s bedroom the night before, except E. J. She took them in as she enjoyed E. J.'s gentle stroke of her nape. The largest was of a sleeping woman with the sun's rays spilling across her face and golden blond hair. Two smaller ones showed the same woman half draped in a sheet, sitting on the edge of a tub and seated at a dressing table in a robe, looking directly at the artist from her reflection in the mirror. "How do your kids not know you're gay?" Jinx asked, genuinely perplexed. "You have pictures of women all over your house."

E. J. laughed softly. "They hardly ever come here. When Mandy and I get together, we usually go out to eat or to a play or movie, and Jacob hasn't lived in Sacramento since he went off to college. I've almost always gone to see him wherever he's living." She went back to playing with Jinx's hair. "I don't think either one of them has ever been in this bedroom. Besides, you can get away with a lot in the name of art."

Jinx closed her eyes and felt herself slip away into E. J.'s touch. As much as she could lose herself in making love to E. J., she could just as easily stay right there forever under her nurturing caress.

"Jinx," E. J. said after a while. "I want to tell you something. I feel a little awkward doing it, though."

"Hmm?" Jinx tried to focus on E. J.'s words rather than her fingers.

"I want to tell you something." E. J. shifted slightly beneath Jinx's head. "Are you listening?"

Jinx opened her eyes and eased out of E. J.'s lap. She sat up. "Yes," she said with an effort to focus. "I'm listening." She made eye contact.

"Today's my birthday."

Jinx's eyes widened. "No way. Why didn't you tell me? I would have brought you a present."

E. J. smiled and brushed her fingertips across Jinx's cheek. "You're my present. You being here, in my bed, in my house. You playing the piano for me last night." She ran her thumb over Jinx's lower lip. "Maybe meeting my friends later?"

Jinx sucked the tip into her mouth. "Anything," she said when she'd released it. "It's your birthday. Sparkle says on your birthday, you get anything you want."

"Anything, huh?" E. J. pressed back into the pillows and let Pete plop into her lap. "I'll have to think about that."

"I wish you'd told me ahead of time, though, so I could have brought you a real present." Jinx climbed off the bed and retrieved her duffle from the walk-in closet.

"What are you doing?" E. J. asked.

"Well," Jinx said, unzipping the bag. "Sometimes, in my *vast* travels, I carry with me an extra birthday present." She pulled out the flat package she'd wrapped the day before. "You know, just in case one of the many people I visit is having a birthday." She held it out.

E. J.'s jaw went slack. "How did you know?"

"I didn't," Jinx said, feigning innocence. "I told you, it's just an extra. Something generic. Hopefully, you'll like it. I don't even remember what it is."

E. J. grinned at her and took the gift. "You're sneaky."

"No more than you, little Miss Don't-tell-me-it's-your-birthday-till-the-day-of." Jinx took a long swallow of the juice from the nightstand, then lay on the bed beside E. J. again. "Are you going to open it?"

Excitement flashed in E. J.'s eyes. "Yes." She looked at the present, twirled the twisty ribbon, and ran her hand over the bright purple Happy Birthday paper.

Jinx blew out an exaggerated sigh. "While it's still your birthday?"

E. J. laughed and tore into the present. As soon as its front was visible, she stilled and her expression went soft. "Oh, Jinx." She lifted out the framed sketch of herself, Jinx, and Pete that Jinx had asked Pablo for and examined it in the morning light. A slow smile made its way across her lips and lit her face. "It's amazing. And perfect. And so very sweet."

Jinx felt herself blush. "I guess it's really more from Pablo, since he's the one with the talent. He drew you from his draft sketches, the ones he did that first day you two met," she said, liking the joy in E. J.'s response. "But Pete and I had to sit for it, and I got the frame."

E. J. lowered the picture and took Jinx's face between her palms. "And you thought of it. And you brought it to me. And you always know just the perfect thing to say or do to make me smile." She kissed Jinx, slow and deep, urging her down onto the mattress.

❖

"So, how *did* you know it was my birthday?" E. J. asked Jinx as they walked along the sun-dappled jogging path beside the river.

"I *didn't* know," Jinx said. "I told you—"

E. J. cut her off with a playful, warning glance.

"Tiffany told me."

"Ah, I can tell I'm going to have to keep tabs on you two. Otherwise, all my mystery will be gone." E. J. paused. "Seriously, though, why'd you ask her and not me?"

"I didn't. She just mentioned it. Something about wanting to do something for your birthday, but she and Jacob already had plans." Jinx unhooked Pete from his leash and picked up a stick. "Watch this." She threw it. "We've been working on fetch," she added proudly.

Pete raced after it. He followed it, slowed, then dashed off into the woods behind the path.

"Hey, come back here," Jinx called. "Stay! Come! Stop!" She ran after him and disappeared among the trees.

E. J. laughed and waited. She wondered about Tiffany saying they had wanted to do something for her birthday, about whose idea it had been. She was touched but couldn't imagine a better day than the one she was having—and it was barely half over.

"E. J.?" someone called.

She turned to see Gwen and Taylor jogging around the curve in the path, Gwen looking fresh and bouncy, Taylor, winded and sweaty.

They trotted up to E. J.

"Since when do you jog?" E. J. asked Taylor.

"Since she broke up with her boyfriend and needed a *project*." Taylor hooked a thumb at Gwen, panting.

E. J. looked at Gwen. "So, what? Things didn't work out between you and Richard, so you thought you'd kill Taylor?"

Gwen shrugged. "I thought it'd be good for her. Build up her stamina before she gets too old."

"Hello," Taylor said, looking over E. J.'s shoulder. "Hot woman with cute puppy, twelve o'clock."

E. J. turned, knowing what she would find. "Very. On both counts."

Jinx trudged back onto the path with Pete, once again, on his leash.

Taylor flashed her a grin. "You ladies don't mind, do you?" she asked E. J. and Gwen.

"Not at all," E. J. said, feeling a little evil.

Gwen rolled her eyes. "You might want to check a mirror before you get too confident."

"No worries, Lady Gwen," Taylor said, her tone cocky. "Look, she's already coming over."

Jinx stepped up beside E. J., Pete in tow.

Taylor opened her mouth, the spark in her eyes indicating something flirty was on the way.

"This is Jinx," E. J. said quickly to save Taylor any real embarrassment.

Taylor snapped her mouth shut.

"Jinx, this is Taylor and Gwen." E. J. pointed to them respectively.

Gwen gave a surprised, "Oh!" She glanced at E. J., then back to Jinx. "It's so nice to finally meet you."

Taylor glared at E. J. before turning to smile at Jinx. "Uh, yeah," she said, managing only a partial recovery. "It's great to meet the woman who could—"

"And this is Pete." E. J. cut Taylor off, knowing whatever was about to come out of her mouth was revenge.

Gwen and Taylor oooed and aaahed over Pete a sufficient amount, then gave birthday wishes and hugs to E. J. There were the expected inquiries into how long Jinx was staying and what their plans were for the rest of the weekend.

"We haven't actually planned anything specific," E. J. said, wishing her friends could spend a little more time with Jinx. She wondered if Jinx would mind.

"Maybe you two could join us for dinner tonight," Jinx said, as though reading her thoughts. "We could all celebrate E. J.'s birthday?" She glanced at E. J.

"That would be perfect," E. J. said, taking Jinx's hand. "Are you guys free?"

"We were just going to spend the rest of the weekend cleaning Gwen's carpets, rearranging furniture, and generally clearing out the ex's bad joojoo. Oh, and more jogging, I'm sure," Taylor said with a grimace. "But celebrating your birthday sounds like a lot more fun."

"We'll be able to do it all." Gwen smiled. "We'll just take a break for dinner. Then maybe Gunther's?"

"Sounds wonderful," E. J. said.

"How about six?" Gwen said, continuing in admin assist mode. "We'll pick you two up."

As the pair started off down the path, Gwen spouting support and encouragement and Taylor groaning, Jinx smiled. "They seem nice."

E. J. watched her friends, and her heart warmed. "They're my Reggie and Sparkle," she said. "I don't know what I'd do without them."

Jinx put an arm around her and pulled her close. "It's important to have people you can count on."

E. J. nodded. She kept her attention on Taylor and Gwen as they disappeared around a bend. She thought of Jacob and Mandy, and now Tiffany, and what Jinx had said about letting them in, letting them love her. She thought of Reggie and Sparkle and what even Andrea had once been to Jinx. She thought of Val and wondered. She hesitated. "Was Val someone you could count on?"

Jinx's expression went distant as she stared out over the water. "Yes."

"Will you tell me about her?"

Jinx led her to a bench near the riverbank, and they sat, Pete on the grass at their feet. Jinx leaned forward, her elbows on her knees, and was silent for a while, seemingly collecting her thoughts.

E. J. waited. She could tell from Jinx's faraway look this was important to her—Val had been important to her.

"In order to understand my relationship with Val," Jinx said finally, "you have to know who I was when I met her." She toed the dirt at her feet. "I was a junkie, E. J. And not the clean, white-collar, functional kind. On the streets, I was strung out on heroin. Then when I was shot during the robbery and waiting for trial, I was in the infirmary and got addicted to pain pills. When I finally got sentenced and went to prison, I'd pretty much take anything. But once I was on the inside, it got harder. On the outside, I could steal to get drugs. And I did. I stole from people, from stores. I robbed. I did whatever

I had to do. On the inside, there were only other cons, most of them way tougher than I was. And there's a much higher price on drugs in prison."

"I didn't know you could get drugs in prison," E. J. said. "I mean, I've seen it on TV and in movies, but I thought that was just Hollywood."

"No. You can get almost anything you want in prison if you can, and are willing to, pay the price." Jinx paused, searching E. J.'s face. "Do you remember what I said to Pablo about not having anyone on the outside to put money on your books or send you things?"

E. J. nodded.

"That's all true. You can get anything you want, but you need to be able to pay for it. If you have people on the outside and money coming in, you're okay. Money on your books can be converted to commissary items, which can be traded. Stamps and cigarettes have high trade value, too. But if you don't have that, all you have are your wits, your skills, or your body. And when I first went in, I had a barely-contained addiction that took about two free fixes to get raging again and no way to pay for it. So, I started turning tricks. I'd done it on the outside, so it wasn't new. I'd let anybody use me for a hit." Jinx held E. J.'s gaze as if gauging her reaction.

E. J. made a point of not having one. In truth, her only reaction was anger—at Nora Tanner, at Andrea, even at Jinx's father, for not making arrangements for her in the event of his death—but she knew any reaction at all might be read as judgment or aversion, and she wouldn't risk that. She had hurt Jinx too much already. This time, she would listen, and she would *be with* her, as Sparkle had said.

Jinx looked down at her hands. "I lost track of what I did or who I was with or what they did to me. After a while, a few of the members of Val's gang decided they wanted me for themselves. They didn't want to share anymore." Jinx shrugged.

E. J. swallowed.

"So, it got a little easier, in a way. At least then, I didn't have to be with so many. But one of them was Val, and she was tough." Jinx's color had gone gray at some point and now edged on white.

E. J. stroked her forearm. "Sweetie, if this is too painful—"

"No, I want to tell you. The hardest part's almost over." Jinx took E. J.'s hand between her own. "Then Val decided I was hers." She stared out across the river, but she was clearly seeing into the past. "You know all the jokes about being someone's bitch in prison?"

E. J. knew she didn't need to answer.

"They're not jokes," Jinx said, her tone hollow, as though she had gone somewhere else. "You do whatever you're told, exactly when and how you're told to do it. And that's what I was. I was Val's bitch. I took care of her every need. She did whatever she wanted to me. But you know what? It was worth it, because for the first time in a lot of years, I was safe." Jinx's voice quavered. "She took care of me. No one else could do anything to me. I didn't have to worry about not having any money or special packages coming in. And she didn't tolerate drugs in her gang, so she got me clean." Jinx turned back to E. J. "And I stayed clean. Even after Val was gone." Jinx sat, silent in the warmth of the afternoon. "That's the gift she gave me," she said finally. "At least, one of them."

E. J. searched for something to say. "There were others?"

"Mm-hm." Jinx shifted, resting against the back of the bench. "Nobody could mess with me as long as I belonged to her. Even the guards gave her—us—a wide berth. She had a lot of clout, a lot of influence, in the general population and among the other gang leaders, whether through respect or fear. She could help keep things under control. In return, she got favors from the staff. Even the warden. She could make things happen. People she didn't like got transferred. People she did like, who did things for her, got what they wanted. *She* got pretty much anything she wanted. She even got us assigned as cell mates for a lot of the time we were together."

"How long was that?"

"Almost ten years.

Ten years? E. J. was stunned. She'd had no idea Jinx had been in a relationship that long, with anyone.

"She saved my life, E. J." Jinx searched her face. For acceptance? For rejection? "There were times I didn't care about that, but, now, I do. Now, I'm grateful to her."

"Did you love her?" E. J. asked.

"Yes. In a way a lot of people wouldn't understand, maybe. But, yes."

"Is she the one who was killed in that turf war?" E. J. asked hesitantly.

"One of them. There were three, but Val was the main target. They took her out first."

E. J. took a steadying breath. She had no concept of anything like that. She had to move forward. "What did you do when she… when she died?"

Another long pause as one more chapter of Jinx's past seemed to play out before her. "I almost died, too," she said. Her voice was barely above a whisper. She cleared her throat. "That's when I got stabbed. It was bad. They had to remove a kidney. There were complications. The recovery was long, and I almost gave up a few times. Looking back now, I think it was because I didn't think I could make it without her—literally. I missed her, but more than that, I didn't know who was going to protect me. They kept me in solitary for the last part of my recovery, and while I was there, I decided I didn't want to be someone's bitch again. I decided I'd rather die. And I really thought I would."

E. J. tensed. Anxiety and fear rose into her throat, the same that had overtaken her the first time she had heard about Jinx almost dying. *That's the past. She's here, now. With me.* She squeezed Jinx's hand. "What happened?"

Jinx inhaled deeply. "When I was put back in general, the new leader of our gang wanted me. When I told her no, I really expected to be taken out. And I was ready. But nothing happened. She told me later she'd honored what I'd said out of respect for my and Val's relationship. She and the rest of the gang kept an eye on me but gave me my distance. That's when I started working as a tutor and teacher for other inmates and got to know Trisha better…Sparkle's sister?" Jinx glanced at E. J. questioningly.

E. J. nodded, letting Jinx know she was following.

"Then I met Sparkle and Reggie, who started sending me money and things that made life easier, and from there, everything just sort of turned around. Reggie even helped me bring the service dog training program into the prison, and that's when I found out how much I love dogs. I'd never had one before." Jinx leaned down and rubbed the underside of Pete's chin.

He looked up at her and wagged his tail.

E. J. didn't know what to say, wasn't even sure what to think or feel. She didn't want to feel sorry for Jinx, because Jinx didn't need that. Yes, going into her past for Pablo had brought up emotions for her, but as she herself had said several times, she was a different person today. As E. J. watched her with Pete, Jinx already had the beginnings of a smile tugging at the corners of her mouth. She didn't need anyone's pity. She had come through it all and was standing tall and strong on the foundation of her past.

"With all that said—and now that we're not naked—I can answer your question from last night," Jinx said.

And just that easily, they returned to the present.

Jinx eased back and took E. J.'s hand again. "I have the control I have during sex because with Val, it was required. I was ordered to hold back for long periods of time, to put her first. I guess I was trained." Her cheeks pinkened. "With you, though..." She met and held E. J.'s gaze. "I like doing it. I want to focus entirely on your pleasure. On, hopefully, taking you places you've never been." She brought E. J.'s fingers to her lips.

"You've definitely done that." E. J. enjoyed the soft play of flesh.

"I like waiting while I bring you down slowly and holding you afterward." Jinx kissed E. J.'s fingertips, then sucked one into her mouth.

E. J.'s pulse quickened, turning to a throb of desire between her thighs.

"And I *love* prolonging the feeling of wanting you." She ran the tip of her tongue between E. J.'s fingers, then to another tip. "Of needing you."

E. J.'s breath caught, and she closed her eyes.

"It's quite a while before six o'clock," Jinx whispered. "Is there anything else you want to do, or can I take you home and do what I like doing?"

E. J. moaned quietly.

❖

At five fifteen, Jinx stepped from the shower and into a towel E. J. held for her. The afternoon had been long, luxurious, and decadent in its offerings. They'd picked up salads and bread sticks from a deli on the way back to E. J.'s, had a picnic on the living room balcony, spent the next few hours in bed, at the piano, on the couch, back in bed, and finally under a stream of soothing hot water.

Jinx couldn't remember a time in her life when she'd felt as free as she had for the past few weeks with E. J. Well, she could, but she had to go back a long way, back to those days with Andi in the gardens, in the tree house. As she had back then, she was beginning to think anything was possible, any dream might very well come true. That time had ended, though, had shattered for reasons Jinx had never figured out. Andi had simply turned away from her, left her behind. Would E. J. do the same?

Jinx looked into E. J.'s face, so open, her eyes so inviting. Her embrace felt so right, so safe. Could Jinx trust it? Or would E. J. leave, too? If she did, at least with her, Jinx would know why. Her kids still didn't know anything about their mother's new relationship, who it was with, or what it was. E. J. had said she couldn't leave Jinx, and she'd taken a stand with herself to prove it where Tiffany was concerned, but Tiffany wasn't one of *her* kids.

Jinx pushed the niggling doubt from her mind. There wasn't anything she could do about it, and she didn't want this weekend ruined. If their time together could possibly be cut short, she wanted to enjoy every second of it. She'd never believed, since that very first night, she could have E. J. forever, and even though her heart kept trying to convince her otherwise, she'd been able to remind herself of it when necessary. This weekend, however, could change that. Being here in E. J.'s world, seeing where she lived, meeting her friends, spending time in places E. J. enjoyed, all of those things made Jinx want to know more, want to know everything about her. And she realized there were still a lot of basic things she *didn't* know. She took the towel and began drying herself. She hadn't known until that day it was E. J.'s birthday. So, that made her a…

"You're a Leo?" Jinx asked as if the conversation in her head had actually been taking place between them.

"What?" E. J. spread the lotion she'd squirted into her hand between her palms, then up her arms to her shoulders.

"Today's your birthday. Doesn't that make your astrological sign Leo?" Jinx grabbed her underwear from the pile of clean clothes on the counter and stepped into them.

"Oh. Yes, it does." E. J. smiled at her in the mirror. "I'm glad that wasn't your pickup line in the bar that night. It's a little outdated."

"*My* pickup line? I didn't pick you up. You picked me up," Jinx said, pulling on her black jeans.

E. J.'s smile widened. "I distinctly remember you picking me up. You couldn't keep your eyes off me." Her tone was playful.

"Yup, definitely a Leo," Jinx said. "Egotistical." But E. J. was right. She hadn't been able to keep her eyes off her.

E. J. laughed. "Leo is the sign of the Sun. Everything *does* revolve around us." She began applying mascara. "When's *your* birthday?"

Jinx chuckled. "I'll tell you the day of."

"You'll get a better present if I know ahead of time," E. J. said teasingly.

"*You* didn't tell *me* ahead of time, and you still got a good present." Jinx slipped into her shirt and started buttoning it.

"Okay," E. J. said, sounding self-satisfied. "I'll just ask Sparkle. She'll tell me." She dropped her makeup case into a drawer and turned to Jinx. She ran her hands lightly over Jinx's breasts.

Jinx's nipples hardened. She pressed against E. J.'s palms. "Your friends are coming."

"And I'll bet she'd also tell me some of those embarrassing things only best friends know, like which middle-of-the-night infomercials you've been sucked into and your most humiliating bathroom story."

"Oooh, you play hardball."

E. J. giggled. "You know it, baby."

The doorbell rang.

"Uh-oh." E. J. jumped back. "They're early. Will you please let them in? I'll be right there."

Jinx finished buttoning her shirt and tucked in the tail, but E. J.'s last comment lingered. She remembered the Rejuvenation Barre she'd ordered late one night when she was living with Reggie and Sparkle. She hadn't been able to afford her bike yet, and wanted a way to exercise. It'd been *available for the amazingly low introductory price of $14.95*—she'd missed the ten additional monthly payments of $39.95—and promised to be *the secret to a toned, fit, and beautiful body*. She remembered thinking that because it was spelled b-a-r-r-e, not just b-a-r, it *must* be good. What had she known? She'd been out of prison for about three weeks, and it'd been three thirty in the morning. If E. J. was going to hear that story, though, Jinx wanted it to be from her. She didn't want her talking to Sparkle.

"May seventh," she said hurriedly as she zipped her jeans. "My birthday's May seventh. But thanks for the ideas of what best friends can tell." She headed out of the room.

"Gwen's my administrative assistant," E. J. called after her. "She's used to keeping things confidential. And Taylor has way too many things she's not going to want her next girlfriend to know to tell you anything." There was a hint of panic in her voice.

Jinx chuckled, then came back to the word *girlfriend*. Is that what she was? E. J.'s girlfriend? Is that how E. J. thought of her? The question made her grin.

The bell rang again.

Jinx turned the knob.

Before the door was completely open, a chorus of "Happy Birthday" began.

The next second, Jinx found herself staring into the smiling faces of two young couples—Tiffany and Jacob, and, she assumed, Mandy and Russ.

Jinx froze.

The quartet silenced, shocked expressions all around.

Pete jumped off the couch and ran to Tiffany. They'd become good friends during her and Jinx's visits. He whined excitedly and wiggled around her feet.

"We're sorry," Mandy said. "We're looking for our mother, E. J.?"

Jinx met Tiffany's wide eyes and looked away. "Yes." She faltered but recovered quickly. "She's here. Come in." She wasn't sure if that was the right thing to do, but she couldn't think of anything else. It wasn't as though she could pretend E. J. had moved and she was the new owner, especially since E. J. would be walking out of the bedroom any second. *Christ.* She had to warn her. "I'll get her."

"I'm sorry," Jacob said, looking from Jinx's damp hair to her bare feet. "I'm Jacob, E. J.'s son. And you are…?"

"I'm a friend of hers." Jinx extended her hand. She glanced at Tiffany.

Jacob studied her. "Aren't you…?" He turned to Tiffany, too. "Isn't she…?"

Tiffany inhaled a deep breath. "Jacob, this is my aunt Michelle. You met her at the wedding."

CHAPTER NINETEEN

E. J. quickly dressed and started down the hall. A small smile played on her lips as she replayed the banter over the birthdays. She couldn't remember ever being with anyone as much fun as Jinx. More interestingly, *she* was more fun with Jinx.

"But what are you doing here?" A voice drifted to E. J. from the living room just as she reached the doorway.

Jacob? She missed a step and gripped the corner. The room spun as she took in the scene.

Jinx stood near the sofa, Jacob in front of her. Mandy and Russ were off to the side. All three stared at Jinx, obviously waiting for an answer. Tiffany also watched Jinx, an apology in her eyes.

Jinx's gaze met and held E. J.'s, flashing the same shock and panic E. J. felt. The only thing that kept E. J.'s from transforming to terror was the clear question in Jinx's expression—*What do you want me to do?* Her evident distress snapped E. J. into action.

She steeled herself. "Jacob, Mandy," she said as she stepped into the room. "What are all of you doing here? I thought you were in New York." She hugged Mandy, who was closest.

"We were, but we came back today to surprise you for your birthday," Mandy said, returning E. J.'s quick embrace.

A surprise. Isn't that the truth. E. J.'s heart raced. She finished hugs all around, thanking everyone for their murmured happy birthdays, all the while trying to come up with a plan. It was clear, the time for the conversation had arrived, but what would be the best approach? Work mode? Yes, that might help her keep her emotions under control. She was grateful she had put on heels, even low ones. Heels always made her feel more powerful, more in charge. She took a moment to text Gwen to let her friends know the evening plans had changed, and they'd have to reschedule.

"Mom, what is Tiffany's aunt doing here?" Jacob asked, his tone brittle.

E. J. hesitated. She looked from Jacob to Mandy. Once she told them the truth, her relationship with each of them would be different—whether closer or destroyed remained to be seen. She took one last look at her children as the mother they knew, then stepped into the next moment. "Jacob, Mandy, I'm glad you're both here. There's something I want to talk to you about. Russ." She glanced to Mandy's boyfriend. "You're more than welcome to stay for this. Tiffany?" She gave Tiffany a half smile and a look of gratitude. At least she knew one person was already on their side.

Tiffany returned a knowing look.

"What's going on?" Jacob asked.

"Everyone, please, sit down." E. J. gestured to the half-circle sectional, then took a seat toward one of the ends. "Jinx, you, too." She patted the spot beside her. "Please?"

"Jinx?" Jacob said with a scoff. "What's that? Her prison name?"

"Jacob, please," E. J. said. "I'll explain everything you need to know." She could hear herself, how calm and at ease she sounded, but anxiety twisted her stomach. "Jinx?" She ran her hand over the cushion beside her.

Jinx faltered, then came and sat next to her.

When everyone was settled, E. J. took a deep breath. "Do you kids remember when your father and I were still married—"

"What does she have to do with your and Dad's marriage?" Jacob asked, glancing at Jinx. "She was locked up then."

"Jacob, please—"

"Let her talk, Jake," Mandy said, nudging her brother with her shoulder.

Jacob fell silent but kept a hard stare on Jinx.

"Do you remember how your father and I didn't have much to do with one another? We lived under the same roof and made social appearances together, but we didn't really have a marriage."

"I don't remember that." Jacob finally looked at E. J. "I thought you and Dad were happy."

"I remember it," Mandy said. "You both always seemed sad, unless you were in front of other people."

"That's not true." Jacob turned to Mandy. "What house were *you* living in? Dad was really happy the last couple of years before the divorce."

"Yes, he was," E. J. said, pulling his attention back to her. "Because he had fallen in love with Susan, and they were together."

"What?" Jacob jumped up. "Dad had an affair? He cheated on you?"

"No, it wasn't like that," E. J. said, trying to rein in the conversation. "Please, sit down."

"Look," Jacob said, his tone hardening. "I don't know what's going on here—"

"And none of us will, unless you sit down and shut up," Mandy said, her voice rising. She looked at Jinx, her own bewilderment evident in her expression. "Just let Mom talk."

Jacob flopped back onto the sofa with a huff. "Fine."

"Your father met Susan several years before we divorced. They started seeing each other. They fell in love. I knew about it. I mean, I didn't know Susan or any details, but I knew he was seeing someone, and I was fine with it. We lived under an unspoken agreement until both of you had graduated high school and were settled into college. Then we got the divorce."

"How could you be fine with your husband being in love with someone else?" Jacob asked, clearly still agitated.

"Because I wasn't in love with him. I wasn't happy and hadn't been for a long time. And it had nothing to do with him." E. J.'s mouth felt dry. She wished she had some water.

"What did it have to do with?" Mandy asked.

E. J. met her gaze. It was curious, but soft. "It was me," she said, accepting solace from Mandy's demeanor. "I wasn't happy with your father because…" She wavered. Her palms were sweating. Her heart was pounding. She could feel Jinx beside her, her energy, her strength. She wished she could touch her, hold her hand, absorb some of her courage, but that would be a step too far at the moment. "I wasn't happy with him because…" She looked away. "Because I'm attracted to women."

An awkward pause followed.

"Oh, Mom. I'm sorry," Mandy said finally. "Is that why, since the divorce, you've pulled away from us?"

Tears welled in E. J.'s eyes. She nodded.

"What?" Jacob asked. He turned to Mandy. "Why are *you* sorry?"

"I'm sorry that Mom was unhappy for so many years, and she's been afraid to tell us." Mandy's focus remained on E. J. "She's been afraid to tell us because she was afraid of…losing our love? Losing us?"

"Tell us what?" Jacob asked, his frustration evident. "Why would we stop loving *her* because Dad had an affair?"

Mandy rolled her eyes and turned to Jacob. "Jake, Mom's gay. She was gay when she was married to Dad, so she was unhappy. And she's been afraid to tell us because she was afraid we wouldn't love her anymore."

Jacob went still. He shifted his attention to E. J. "You're gay?"

E. J. nodded.

He stared at her for a long moment, then rose and walked slowly to the window.

E. J. watched him.

"Mom?" Mandy said gently.

E. J. returned her attention to her.

"This is the twenty-first century, the Age of Aquarius. Gay marriage is legal. There are openly gay politicians and clergy. But most importantly, you raised us to be good people, kind people, accepting people. How could you think you being gay could change how much we love you?"

E. J. looked again to Jacob, his back still to her. Her throat constricted. Could she do this next part? "I was afraid it would hurt Jacob."

He said nothing.

She went to him. "I was afraid it would rip open your old wounds from your childhood." She tentatively touched his shoulder. "I couldn't take the chance of hurting you again."

Jacob turned to her. "Mom, *you* didn't hurt me."

She squeezed her eyes shut, fighting back tears. "I should have—"

"No," Jacob said firmly. "*He* shouldn't have done it. That's all. Everything else is just the wreckage he left behind. And I couldn't have gotten through that without you."

"But you said you hated gays, that all gays were perverts, like him."

"I was fourteen when I thought that. And I was still messed up and angry." Jacob cupped her chin and lifted her face to his. "And you're the one who loved me through that. It was your strength I held on to." His voice broke slightly. "Nothing you do could ever make you the same as him."

E. J. began to cry.

He hugged her to his chest as she felt Mandy's arm encircle her shoulders.

"Mom, we've really missed you," Mandy whispered through her own tears.

"I've missed you both, too," E. J. said, feeling connected to her children for the first time in almost a decade.

As they loosened their embrace, she became aware again of the others in the room. There wasn't a dry eye among them. Even Russ swiped at his face.

Jacob chuckled. "Well, Russ, welcome to the family. I guess you know it all, now."

Russ waved dismissively.

Tiffany's smile lit her entire being.

Jinx's shining eyes held an emotion they'd have to talk about, soon.

As Jacob scanned the room, his grin faded when he came to Jinx. He narrowed his eyes, and realization moved across his face like a cloud. He returned his attention to E. J. "You...and *her*?"

E. J.'s short-lived celebration of feeling completely loved and accepted by her children came to a crashing halt. *Round two.* She dried her eyes. "Yes. Me and Jinx."

Jacob ran a hand through his hair and blew out a deep breath. "How did that even happen?" he asked incredulously. "You just met at the wedding, and now she's in your house and you're together?"

Well, two days before the wedding...in a bar...as a one-night stand...and yes. E. J. didn't think those particular details would help the situation. She wondered if Tiffany knew.

"Mom, she's a...a..."

"Felon," Jinx said quietly.

Everyone turned to her.

"The word you're looking for is felon," she said to Jacob.

He glared at her. "Okay, for starters. A felon."

"I know that," E. J. said. "I know she was in prison."

"Do you know what for? And for how long?"

"I do." E. J. kept her tone level.

Jacob paused. "Andrea said she was sentenced for twelve years, but she ended up serving twenty. God knows what else she did to get the additional eight."

"*I* know." E. J. passed a tender look to Jinx.

"Really? From her?" Jacob pointed at Jinx. "How do you know she's even telling you the truth?"

E. J. couldn't restrain a laugh. "Because only an idiot would make up the things she's told me. And she isn't an idiot."

"I don't trust her." Jacob thrust his hands into the pockets of his slacks.

"That's because you don't know her, and that's understandable," E. J. said.

"You don't know her either. You met her three months ago. She's probably running some kind of elaborate con to get your money. Andrea wouldn't talk to her when she came sniffing around *her* money, so she had to find something else. She shouldn't have even been at our wedding."

"Jacob, Jinx isn't—"

"It's okay, E. J." Jinx rose. "I can speak for myself." Her eyes were on Jacob. "I'm not after anything from your mother other than her company. I enjoy spending time with her, and she appears to like it, too. I haven't contacted Andrea for anything other than to try to heal our relationship. I've never asked her for anything. I have a life. It's just that my life's better since I met E. J."

"Yeah." Jacob snickered. "I'll bet it is." He turned back to E. J. "Look, Mom, it's one thing to be gay, but...a criminal? What kind of a son would I be if I was okay with my mother dating an ex-con? Male *or* female? I don't think I'm alone here." He looked to his sister. "Mandy?"

"The kind who listens," E. J. said before Mandy could answer.

Mandy looked from Jacob, to E. J., to Jinx.

"The kind who trusts my judgment." E. J. touched Jacob's arm. "The kind who wants me to be happy. The kind who doesn't judge other people."

He took her hand. "I do want you to be happy, Mom. And I do trust you. I just can't let you...You don't know the whole story. You can't. She robbed a bank." His voice rose. "She was high on drugs. An old woman almost died."

"That isn't who she is, now. Once you get to know her—"

"I don't intend to get to know her." His face reddened as he pulled away. "It's fine that you're gay. I get that. It's a little weird, but okay. But to be sleeping with...You're sleeping with her, right?"

E. J. stiffened.

"To be sleeping with someone like *her*." He gestured at Jinx angrily. "A criminal. My wife's aunt, who everyone in the family hates...Hell, Mom, couldn't you have picked...like...*any other woman on the planet?*"

"Not everyone," Tiffany said before E. J. could respond.

Jacob jerked around to her. "What?"

"Not everyone in my family hates her," Tiffany said. "I don't."

Jacob looked confused.

"After the wedding, I wanted to get to know Aunt Michelle. I always have. You know that. And since she came to the wedding, I knew she hadn't turned her back on us the way Mom said, so I contacted her. I've spent some time with her, Jacob. She really isn't what Mom says."

"You've been seeing her behind my back?"

"I was about to tell you." Tiffany spoke quietly, but her manner was unapologetic. "You were so upset that I invited her to the wedding, I wanted to see if we even liked each other before I told you. I thought—"

"You thought it'd be better for me to find out *this way?*"

Tiffany leveled her gaze on him. "I didn't know we were coming here. You and Mandy decided that this morning, barely in time for us to catch a flight. And it never occurred to me they'd be here."

Jacob's lips parted, and his eyes rounded slightly. "You knew about them?"

Tiffany's expression softened, but she held her ground. "It wasn't my place to tell you," she said, answering the unasked question.

He stared at her.

"I asked her not to," E. J. said, stepping in front of him. She touched his cheek and brought his attention to her. She couldn't let this cause a problem between them. "I asked her not to. She said you'd want to know, though, and I should be the one to tell you. I just needed some time to work through my fears. I was going to do it this weekend. That's why I asked what you were doing. But when you said you four already had plans to go away, I figured it could wait." She was rambling.

Jacob shifted his gaze between E. J. and Tiffany. "How could either of you keep all this from me?"

"Jacob," Jinx said softly.

He pointed at her. "You shut up. You're the reason both my wife and my mother feel the need to lie to me. What do you want? What the hell are you doing here? Get the hell out of this house," he yelled.

E. J. froze, remembering those same words from Andrea. Had Andrea tainted him so badly? She couldn't have. E. J. had to trust Mandy's words, that she had raised her children to be kind and accepting.

Jinx started to turn away.

E. J. couldn't bear the pain in her eyes. Jacob was upset. This was a lot. He just needed time to calm down. *She* needed time to calm him down. She knew she could, just like when he was a little boy. But Jinx…If Jinx left now, after those words, E. J. knew she'd never get her back. In that moment, she had to choose. "Jacob Ryan Bastien," she said, her voice hard. "This is *my* home, and Jinx is *my* guest. You will not order her out. And you will treat her politely and with respect." It had been a long time since she had played the mom card. It felt good.

Jacob looked stunned. "Mom, I—"

"I'm *not* finished." E. J. took a breath. "I have supported you in every decision you've ever made, whether or not I agreed with it. I backed you in high school when you wanted to start a rock band instead of focus on college applications. I stood up for you with your father when you blew off an entire semester of law school to try your hand at graphic novels. I've made an effort with *anyone* you brought home over the years. I didn't even like Tiffany when you first introduced her..." With a start, E. J. realized what she had said. She glanced over her shoulder, feeling her cheeks heat. "I'm sorry, Tiffany."

Tiffany shrugged. "That's okay. I didn't like you much either, until recently."

E. J. smiled. She definitely liked her, now. "But I always trusted you," she said to Jacob. "Trusted that if you saw something in someone, there must be something there. Now, I expect the same from you. Jinx is important to me, and I expect you to honor that."

Jacob glared at her but said nothing. He moved past her and grabbed his jacket from the arm of the couch. "I'm leaving," he said to Tiffany. "Are you coming?"

Tiffany sighed and picked up her jacket. She gave E. J. a kiss on the cheek, and Jinx a quick hug, before following Jacob.

E. J. looked at the floor and listened as the front door closed.

"Mom?" Mandy said after a moment. She took E. J.'s hand. "Are you all right?"

E. J. steadied herself and nodded.

"He'll come around." Mandy rested her head on E. J.'s shoulder. "You know he will. He just has to have some drama first."

E. J. gave a tentative laugh and squeezed Mandy's fingers.

"Is there anything I can do?" Jinx asked as she stepped closer.

E. J. looked into the depths of those blue eyes and emotion flooded her. "Thank you for staying," she said. "I know how hard it must have been to hear all that."

"Thank you for making it clear you wanted me to." Jinx's gaze held E. J.'s. "I'm here, baby. As long as you want me."

Mandy cleared her throat. "I guess we'll go ahead and take off." She hugged E. J. "Mom, now that all this is out in the open, can we, *please*, go to dinner?"

E. J. smiled through welling tears. "Yes," she said. "But you have to pay."

Mandy laughed. She took in Jinx. "I'm about to say some things that, given everything that happened tonight, are going to sound ridiculous, so just bear with me."

"Okay." Jinx looked wary.

"It's been very nice meeting you, Jinx. I hope I get to spend some time with you soon, so I can get to know you." Mandy's expression was sincere. "I really want to know the woman who's made my mom happy."

Jinx smiled. "It was nice meeting you, too. I hope we see each other again soon."

Mandy gave Jinx an awkward hug.

E. J. warmed at the sight, then winced with embarrassment as Russ strode up to the group. "I'm so sorry you had to witness all this, Russ. I hope you won't hold it against us." She tried to make light of it.

"No problem," Russ said with a wide grin. "I was nervous about Mandy meeting my family next month, but now…" He lifted a shoulder. "Pshhh."

When she and Jinx were alone, E. J. opened the sliding glass door and moved out onto the balcony. "I need some air." She stared out at the lights of the city that stretched into the distance. The night breeze cooled her skin. She closed her eyes. It was done. She sighed with relief. Now, it was time to—what had Jinx said? *Let everything be what it is, let everyone be who they are, and see what happens.* She cringed inwardly at the loss of control, but at least her kids now knew who she was.

Jinx leaned on the railing beside her. "What can I do?"

E. J. took her hand. She remembered the afternoon on Jinx's front steps when Jinx had so effortlessly made her feel better. "Make me laugh," she said, as she had that day.

Jinx chuckled. "That's easy." She paused. "Where does the king keep his armies?"

E. J. felt the beginnings of a smile. "Where?"

"Up his sleevies."

E. J. laughed, as she knew she would.

"An eight-year-old boy," Jinx went on without the slightest hesitation, "was failing math when his family moved to a new city and he began attending a Catholic school. On his first day, he came home, ran straight upstairs, and started on his homework. Later, he came down for dinner, but went straight back up afterward and did more homework. His mother didn't know what to make of it, but she didn't want to ask about it in fear of ruining it, so she said nothing. He did that for the entire first week. His mother was still puzzled but didn't say anything for fear of jinxing the whole thing. Finally, when his first report card came home and he had an A in math, his mother couldn't stand it any longer and had to ask, 'What made the difference?' 'Well,' the boy said. 'On the first day, when I walked into class and saw that guy nailed to the plus sign, I knew they didn't mess around.'"

E. J. giggled.

Jinx shifted onto one elbow and slipped a fingertip behind E. J.'s earlobe. "I love it when you giggle." She caressed the sensitive spot. "Did you hear the one about the pizza?"

"Mmm."

Jinx moved closer. "Never mind," she whispered. "It's too cheesy." Her soft breath warmed E. J.'s skin.

E. J.'s chuckle caught on a quiet groan, prompted partly by arousal, and partly by the bad joke.

"How much does it cost for a pirate to get his ears pierced?" Jinx sucked the lobe between her teeth. "A buccaneer," she murmured, not waiting for a response.

E. J. laughed then stepped into Jinx's arms. "Thank you." She molded against her.

Jinx was trembling. E. J. found her mouth and teased the corner with the tip of her tongue.

"I was scared tonight," Jinx said, her tone so unguarded and vulnerable, it clutched at E. J.'s heart. "I thought I was going to lose you for good."

E. J. pulled back only enough to meet Jinx's gaze. She took Jinx's face in her hands and stroked her cheeks. "I don't want you to ever have to be afraid of that again. I know I've given you a lot of reason to doubt, but from now on, I want you to know that I know who you've been, and I know who you are now. And I don't care what you've done or what anyone thinks about it. I don't care what they think of *me*. I choose you." Her voice broke, and tears spilled down her cheeks. "I love you, Jinx, and I choose you."

Jinx choked back a sob and crushed E. J. to her. She kissed her hard, their tears mingling until E. J. couldn't tell whose were whose.

Finally, Jinx broke the kiss. Her breathing was heavy. She gulped for air through her quieting sobs. "I love you, too, E. J. I've never loved anyone the way I love you." She tightened her hold again.

E. J. brought Jinx's head down to her shoulder and stroked her hair. She knew she could now be that safe place for Jinx that Jinx was for her. She wanted to give her that. She wanted to give her everything, every part of herself. In that moment, E. J. felt the last inklings of doubt or fear about letting herself be loved, about Jacob or Mandy, about her heart being wide open, dissolve into nothing.

CHAPTER TWENTY

Jinx padded groggily into the kitchen, Pete at her heels, and swiped her finger through the frosting of the one-year anniversary cake E. J. had surprised her with two nights earlier. She shivered slightly at the chill of the tile on her bare feet from the early spring morning and rubbed the sleep from her eyes, then stopped dead at the sight of E. J., her lover, her partner, her heart. She still couldn't figure out how it'd all happened. She couldn't have predicted it or planned it—or even imagined everything that'd happened since that first night she'd seen her in the bar. It was so far from the realm of what her life had been for so long, and yet, here she was.

E. J. was seated at the patio table outside the open French doors of the upscale track home she'd bought. It wasn't far from Jacob and Tiffany, and her three-month-old grandson, Ryan. She'd made the purchase, wanting Jinx to move in with her, and they'd compromised between what E. J. could truly afford, and something Jinx, while it stretched her comfort zone, could contribute to from her now full-groomer's salary. Jinx consoled herself with a fondly-remembered, yet somewhat annoying, piece of Namastacey's wisdom—*no one grows in her comfort zone*. In general, though, she didn't spend much time thinking about it. She loved living with E. J. They were happy together, and that's all that mattered.

Sunlight glinted off the gold highlights in E. J.'s hair, and her floor-length silk robe draped her supple body. One smooth leg crossed over the other and slipped through the opening, reminding Jinx of what lay beneath and making her ache. Jinx could stare at her for hours, make love to her for days, and knew she'd love her forever. She still marveled that E. J. was hers.

The doorbell rang, and E. J. lowered the newspaper and started to rise.

"I'll get it," Jinx said, lingering another moment.

"How long have you been standing there?" E. J. asked as she settled back in her chair.

"Long enough to think about getting you out of that robe," Jinx called over her shoulder.

E. J. laughed softly. "Get rid of whoever's at the door, and come make good on that."

Jinx was still smiling when she turned the knob and found Tiffany and Jacob on the front stoop. "Good morning," she said, surprised. They'd all be together that evening at Tiffany and Jacob's first-year anniversary celebration. She enjoyed a silent moan at the memory of their own private celebration before she paid attention to their unannounced guests. "What are you guys doing here?"

"I need to talk to you," Tiffany said, planting a kiss on Jinx's cheek as she swept past her.

"And I need to talk to Mom." Jacob kissed her other cheek and scanned the foyer. "Is she here?"

"Out back."

Mandy had been spot-on in her assessment of Jacob's flair for drama and her prediction that he'd come around. It'd taken a few conversations with Tiffany and her stand that she intended to keep Jinx in her life. Then came a couple more with E. J. and *her* declaration that Jacob could accept Jinx or not but E. J. was with her, regardless, and an argument with Mandy in which she'd called him a pompous ass. Finally, after some time with Jinx, he *had* come around. Since then, he'd even conceded that she was good for his mother.

As Jacob took off through the house, Jinx followed Tiffany into the living room. She liked this room. It held two of her favorite things—the baby grand piano from E. J.'s condo and the framed sketch of E. J., Pete, and her, hanging above the fireplace. "What's up?" She grew a little wary as she watched Tiffany settle onto the couch, her expression serious. Tiffany was hardly ever serious.

"Sit down," Tiffany said. "I'm supposed to give you something."
She sounded irritated.

"From who?" Jinx sat beside her.

"Mom."

Jinx blinked in disbelief.

Tiffany handed her an envelope.

She stared at it.

She'd all but given up on things ever being right with Andrea.
Since E. J.'s coming out and the news that she and Jinx were together,
combined with Tiffany's now close relationship with Jinx, Andrea
seemed even angrier than before, if that was possible. It was only
after Tiffany's threat that Andrea wouldn't be included in any social
events or family gatherings hosted by Tiffany and Jacob that she
settled into polite tolerance. The baby had helped some, too, at least
for the public encounters, but she still wouldn't stay in the same room
with Jinx if she could help it.

Cautiously, Jinx took the envelope.

It was business-sized, not the dimensions of a greeting card or an
invitation. What was she thinking? *Of course, it's nothing personal.*
She sighed at the realization she still held hope. But what business
did they have?

"Okay, you two, what's going on?" E. J. said brightly as she and
Jacob entered the room. "It's awfully quiet in here."

"Tiff brought me something from Andrea," Jinx said, turning the
envelope over in her hands.

"From Andrea?" E. J. was obviously as astonished as Jinx.
"What is it?"

"I haven't opened it." Jinx looked at Tiffany. "Do you know?"

Tiffany shook her head.

Jinx examined the backside.

"Do you want us to leave so you can have some privacy?"
Tiffany asked.

"Of course not." Jinx stalled a little longer, unsure of her
reluctance. What was she afraid of? It couldn't be anything that would
change her life in any significant way, anything that could threaten
what she'd built. She tore it open and took out a folded piece of paper.
Something else fluttered to the floor. She picked it up and stared.

"What is it?" Tiffany asked.

Jinx could barely speak. She cleared her throat. "It's a check… for four hundred thousand dollars."

"What?" E. J. leaned over to see, resting a hand on Jinx's shoulder. "For what?"

Jinx couldn't take her eyes off Andrea's sculpted signature. "I don't know."

"Is that a letter?" Tiffany asked, pointing to the folded sheet.

Jinx couldn't respond. She handed it to E. J.

E. J. opened it and frowned.

"Is it a letter?" Tiffany asked again.

"More like a note," E. J. said with evident disapproval.

"What's it say?" Jinx asked.

E. J. glanced at her, then lowered herself onto the couch beside her. She hesitated, then read it out loud.

"Michelle. When I received my inheritance from our father at the age of twenty-five, there were instructions that a portion in the amount of $250,000 was to go to you. I have remained conservator of these funds until now due to your circumstances. I have included an additional $150,000 to allow for two percent interest over the past twenty years. Our dealings are now complete."

Despite the astonishing information, the temperature in the room seemed to drop with the frigidity of the tone.

"She can't do that, can she?" Tiffany looked at Jacob.

"It depends on what the actual instructions said. But you certainly have the right to demand to see them," he said to Jinx.

"You could have had this money all along, Aunt Michelle."

Jinx took the note from E. J. and reread it. Michelle, not Chelle. Our father, not Daddy as Andrea used to call him, or even Dad. *Our dealings are complete? What does that even mean?* They were sisters and always would be. Andi had promised her that.

"Jinx?" E. J. touched her arm.

"It's okay." Jinx couldn't quite clear her head. "I'm okay. Just a little stunned." She looked at the check again.

E. J. slipped her hand over Jinx's.

"She can't get away with this," Tiffany said with a bite. "She should have given you this a long time ago."

Jinx merely listened and thought.

"Sweetie?" E. J. caressed her fingers. "Do you want to do something about that?"

Jinx turned to her. She still couldn't speak. She knew what she wanted to say, but the words wouldn't come. She met E. J.'s searching gaze. "No," she managed finally.

"Aunt Michelle, that money could have made a huge difference in your life. You could have gotten a better lawyer and maybe not gone to prison. And *she* withheld it from you."

Jinx chuckled, thankful for another thought to focus on for a minute. "Tiff, I walked into a bank, high on drugs, in broad daylight, waving a gun around, and the security cameras got it all. The quality of my defense wasn't the problem. Besides, my trial was way over by the time your mom and I turned twenty-five."

"I'm just saying," Tiffany said.

"I appreciate your indignation, but it's all okay," Jinx said. But it wasn't. She couldn't get the note, the wording, the curtness, the finality of it, out of her mind. She felt E. J. watching her.

"Jacob," E. J. said, "didn't you say you needed to be home when your dad and Susan dropped off Ryan?"

"Oh, yeah. Thanks, Mom." He coaxed Tiffany off the couch. "Come on, honey, we have to go."

"Think about it, Aunt Michelle," Tiffany said as he pulled her from the room. "I just want her to think about it," she said to Jacob.

"And I'm sure she will." Jacob's voice faded into the entryway. "But *you* need to make sure you're not just trying to cause trouble with your mom."

The front door closed on the conversation.

E. J. reclined into the corner of the sofa and guided Jinx down against her. "Tiffany's right, in a way," she said, stroking Jinx's back. "That money would have made a difference to you in prison. You could have paid for the things you needed. You wouldn't have had to…you know."

Jinx considered the idea. "Maybe," she said slowly, enjoying E. J.'s closeness. "But you know what?"

"What?"

"If I could have bought what I needed—mainly, drugs and protection—I wouldn't have hooked up with Val, wouldn't have belonged to her. And if I hadn't belonged to Val, I wouldn't have been in that fight. And if I hadn't been in the fight, I wouldn't have been stabbed and been in the infirmary when they brought Trisha in, which means I would never have met Sparkle and Reggie. And that means I wouldn't have still been at the shop to take Reggie her phone that night you were at that bar, which means I wouldn't have met you and we wouldn't have fallen in love and we wouldn't have had that fight, so you never would have gotten me Pete." Jinx rose onto an elbow and looked into E. J.'s eyes. "And I can't imagine my life without Pete."

"Ah, you went too far." E. J. smiled and tilted her head.

Jinx grinned, then grew serious. "I can't imagine my life without *you*, baby, and what we have. I wouldn't go back and change a thing." She leaned in and kissed E. J.'s neck.

"Mmm, much better." E. J. slid her fingers under Jinx's T-shirt and trailed them along the bare skin at the waistband of her jeans. "Are you going to keep it?"

"The money? Heck, yeah." Jinx sat up. The money wasn't what gave her pause. It was the damned note. "My dad wanted me to have it. He left it for me." She looked at the check again and a lump rose in her throat. "I thought he forgot about me."

E. J. moved up beside her and took Jinx in her arms. "No one could ever forget about you."

Jinx kissed her, but her thoughts had already raced on. "I even know what I'm going to do with it."

"What?"

"Part of it's going toward the house—toward *our* house—and then I'm going to invest in Canine Complete, to go with the money Reggie and Sparkle have saved for the emergency vet clinic."

"That's a great idea. Sparkle and Reggie will be touched." E. J.'s own emotion shone in her eyes.

"And a new car, I think." Jinx smiled. "Yeah. A new car." She eased E. J. back down onto the couch and settled on top of her. She grinned as she combed her fingers through E. J.'s short hair. "Our life just keeps getting better and better."

E. J. looped her arms around Jinx's neck. "I guess you'd better stay with me, then."

"Oh, baby. There's no doubt about whether or not I'm staying with you." Jinx kissed her gently but deeply.

E. J. pulled her in more tightly. When they broke the kiss, she was breathing hard. "God, will I ever get enough of you?"

Jinx pressed her thigh between E. J.'s. Her own breath came fast. "I hope not."

E. J. lifted her hips. "Get me out of this robe?"

❖

Jinx filled a plate with an assortment of gourmet finger foods from the buffet while she and Tiffany listened to Mandy's story of the time she and E. J. had gotten stuck in an elevator during one of their biggest fights of Mandy's adolescent-angst-years.

"I'm not sure we ever would have made up if we hadn't been trapped together," Mandy said with genuine amusement. "Mom's always said it was Divine Intervention."

Jinx laughed as she slipped a couple of crab cakes onto the plate amongst the canapés and a few caviar puff pastries. She loved hearing the stories about E. J. from Mandy and Jacob that E. J. would never share, although she'd certainly heard plenty from E. J. as well. As she turned to take the plate to E. J., she caught a glimpse of Andrea disappearing through the kitchen doorway. She'd been trying not to watch her throughout the evening.

Andrea's note had nagged at her all morning, niggling in the back of her mind. The more she tried to forget about it and simply let everything be, the more annoyed with the tone and the superiority of it she became, until finally, she had to admit she was just pissed. Who was Andrea to say things were *complete* between them? There were *two* of them. Andrea didn't get to make a unilateral decision about their relationship. And yet, Jinx realized, she had been letting her do so since they were thirteen years old. But did she have the right to force the issue?

As she handed E. J. the plate, Jinx noticed Andrea return to the party and greet one of her husband's business partners, one of Jacob's bosses, with that practiced smile that never reached her eyes. Who *was* this person? And where had Andi vanished to? Jinx might never know. Should she, at least, say thank you to Andrea for giving her the money before everything that'd once been between them completely slipped away as well?

When Andrea returned to the kitchen, Jinx followed.

She waited until Andrea finished with the head of the catering staff. "Andrea?" she said from behind her.

Andrea turned, her expression hardening at the sight of Jinx.

"I wanted to—"

"We have nothing to say to one another. I thought I made that clear in my letter." Andrea tried to move past her.

"Letter?" Jinx had to laugh. "You call that a letter?"

"I'm not going to argue semantics," Andrea said. "It said everything I have to say."

Jinx tensed. "Well, maybe *I* have some things to say."

"I don't want to hear them."

Jinx sighed. "I just want—"

"I promised Tiffany I would be civil to you," Andrea said, cutting her off. "I was forced to, in order to continue to see my daughter. You've insinuated yourself into my family by conning her, and somehow managing to seduce her husband's mother, for God's sake. But it's only a matter of time before they see you for who you really are." She kept her voice low, but its tenor held a rage that, if unleashed, could have brought down the house.

The words sparked Jinx's own long-pent-up hurt, confusion, and anger. "I didn't insinuate myself into your family," she said, her jaw clenched. "I *am* your family." It felt good to say it, to claim it after all this time. "Whether you like it or not."

Several members of the catering staff looked their way.

They'd both been careful to hold their volume in check, but the energy between them apparently couldn't be contained. They inched away from one another.

The last thing Jinx wanted was to cause a scene at this celebration. All she'd intended was to thank Andrea and maybe leave the door open for something more at a later date.

"I'm finished with this conversation," Andrea said. She grabbed a key from a hook above a built-in desk and turned away. "I promised Tiffany I would oversee the details tonight, and we need more wine from the cellar." She stalked across the kitchen and through a side door.

Jinx glared after her.

"Aunt Michelle?" Tiffany said, coming up beside her. "Is everything okay?"

"I don't know how you came from that woman," Jinx said. She released a breath in exasperation.

"Awww, that's the nicest thing anyone's ever said to me." Tiffany looped her arm through Jinx's. "Come back to the party. Mandy remembered another story she said we'd like. Something about Jacob, a brand new pair of E. J.'s Manolos, and a fish pond."

Jinx laughed. "That has to be good." She glanced at the door Andrea had disappeared through. She frowned. "I wish I could either get your mom to listen to me, or forget all about making things right with her." She thought of Mandy and E. J. needing to be trapped together to work through their argument. "Where's an elevator when you need one?"

Tiffany followed Jinx's line of sight. "Why don't you try one more time?"

"I just did," Jinx said with resignation. "Besides, I don't want to upset your party."

Tiffany shrugged. "She went to the wine cellar. Talk to her down there. She can yell all she wants. No one will hear her up here."

Jinx pondered it.

"It's important to you," Tiffany said. "One more try. I'll go with you."

As Jinx stepped into the wine cellar, she saw Andrea toward the back, examining the label on a bottle.

Tiffany held back.

"I'm almost done," Andrea said. "I just want to make sure your guests…" Her gaze swept over Tiffany, then landed on Jinx. "I told you, I'm finished."

"You owe her an explanation, Mom," Tiffany said before Jinx could speak.

"What I owed her, you gave her this morning." Andrea fitted the bottle she held into a crate on the table in the center of the room.

"Then you need to listen to what *she* has to say. Here's your elevator," Tiffany said to Jinx. She stepped back and slammed the door.

Jinx heard a scrape on the other side, then a thump. "Tiff?" she called through the panel. She tried the handle and pushed. Nothing happened. "Tiffany?"

In an instant, Andrea was beside her. She pounded on the door. "Tiffany, you open this door this minute."

"You two need to talk." Tiffany's voice was muffled from the outside.

"Tiffany Nora Stanton," Andrea yelled and slapped her hand against the door.

Jinx jerked her head around to stare at Andrea. "Are you kidding me? You named her after *Nora*?"

"My last name's Bastien, now, Mother," Tiffany said sweetly. "I'll check back with you two in a bit to see how things are going."

"Tiffany, don't you dare leave." Andrea's pitch was frantic.

No answer.

Jinx still stared at her. "*Nora*? Really?"

Andrea whirled to face her. "What I named my child is none of your business."

"But seriously. *Nora*?"

"This is your fault. You put her up to this."

"I did not. I was just trying to talk to you."

"We have *nothing* to talk about. How many times do I have to say that?" Andrea rattled the handle.

Jinx leaned against the door. She took in a deep breath. "Maybe until it makes sense." She looked around the wine cellar.

Andrea slammed her fist on the door again. "How did she even do this? This doesn't lock from the outside."

"A chair," Jinx said simply.

"What?"

"She wedged a chair under the handle." Jinx felt a smile tug at the corners of her mouth. "Don't you remember when we locked Nora in her wardrobe closet?" She chuckled.

Andrea glanced at her, her expression still stony. "She beat you until you could barely walk. You missed two weeks of school while the bruises healed." She spun around and slumped beside Jinx, her arms folded across her middle. "It wasn't funny."

"It was so worth it." Jinx grinned. "The sound of her bellowing for Emmy."

Neither one spoke for a long moment.

Andrea pushed off and strode across the small room. "I'm not going to do this with you."

"Do what?"

Andrea glared at her. "Walk down memory lane. Wax nostalgic. Visit the past. Whatever it is you're trying to do."

Jinx looked at the ceiling. "Why are you so mad at me?"

Andrea laughed sardonically. "I'm *not* doing this."

Jinx walked toward her. "C'mon, you don't have to tell anyone else. We're locked in here. It's just you and me. What did I do, all those years ago, that was so bad you still hate me today?"

When Jinx reached her, Andrea turned away. Her shoulders trembled.

Jinx softened. "What did I do, Andrea?"

Andrea didn't answer.

"Andi?"

"Don't call me that." Her attempt at defiance was evident, but there was a tremor in her voice.

Jinx brushed her fingertips over Andrea's shoulder.

Andrea whirled around and slapped her hand away. "Don't touch me." Her voice rose, cold and sharp again.

Jinx didn't flinch. "What did I do?"

"You know what you did," Andrea yelled.

"Say it." Jinx fixed a hard stare on her. She *didn't* know. "I want to hear it."

"Fine." Andrea straightened. "You started messing with drugs, and you ran away. I didn't know where you were. I didn't know how to find you. Then you robbed a bank. You got shot. You went to prison, and you were just gone." Tears filled her eyes. "You left me." She balled her fists and swung at Jinx.

Jinx caught her wrists.

"You left me with *her*." Andrea began to cry. "We were supposed to be there for each other, and you left me alone." She choked on a sob.

Jinx pulled her in.

Andrea tried to fight, but Jinx hugged her tightly, pinning her arms to her sides. "Shhh," she breathed in her ear. "I'm here, now. I'm right here."

Andrea broke free and shoved her away. "I don't need you, now. I needed you then, and you left." She retreated to the other side of the table.

Jinx stared at her, confused. "Andi, *you* left way before that."

Andrea clenched her eyes shut. "*Stop calling me that*," she screamed.

"Okay," Jinx shouted above Andrea's rage. "Andrea! But you did. *You* left when we were thirteen—not physically, but just as completely as if it had been—and I couldn't get you back. I tried to talk to you, but you wouldn't tell me anything. You wouldn't have anything to do with me. And when Dad died, I didn't have anybody."

Andrea buried her face in her hands. "Stop it!" She backed away until she was pressed against the far wall. She was crying again. "Stop it." She slid to the floor. "I'm sorry."

Jinx blinked. Had she heard correctly? Andrea was sorry? She waited.

"I'm sorry," Andrea said again, crying into her hands.

Jinx crossed to her and sat beside her on the floor.

They were close but didn't touch.

Andrea cried for a long time.

Jinx leaned her head against the wall. This was it, the moment she'd wanted with Andrea for so long, and yet, she didn't know what to say. Maybe there was nothing to say. Or, maybe what there was to say, wasn't hers. She'd always thought she needed to explain how she'd ended up in prison, what'd made her walk into that bank that day. But what explanation was there—really? Andrea had said she was sorry. *Sorry for what?*

Finally, Andrea lifted her head. She stared at the opposite wall. "My mother *hated* that I spent all my time with you, that you were my best friend. She said she expected better of me. She said if I was going to spend all my time with…Well, you know what she called you…"

Jinx nodded.

"She said she'd treat me the way she treated you." Andrea sniffed. "I knew I couldn't take that. I wasn't as strong as you. I was afraid of her. And then when I started hanging out with other girls at school and they started coming over, I was so ashamed. I couldn't face you." Tears spilled down her cheeks again. "I couldn't stand the sadness in your eyes, so I just stayed away from you. And it was easier, but I missed you so much. I always thought if we could just make it through high school, and we could graduate, maybe we could move out, get an apartment or something—just get away from her, so she didn't control *everything*. But then one day, you were just gone." Andrea's voice broke, and sobs overtook her again.

Jinx shifted and enfolded her in an embrace.

Andrea fell against her.

"Why didn't you tell me?" Jinx whispered.

Andrea gripped the lapel of Jinx's blazer. "I felt so guilty for not choosing you, for not standing up for you. I couldn't even look at you. How could I tell you what I'd done?"

Jinx hugged her more tightly.

"Then, once you were gone and I found out what had happened to you, that you'd been shot and were arrested, and then you went to prison…" New sobs racked her body. "The guilt consumed me. And when you showed up at the door when you came home…I don't know…I think I dumped all my anger, all my self-loathing, on you. I'm so sorry, Chelle."

The name washed Jinx's soul like the moonlit tide caresses the seashore. The sound of it coming from Andrea, the name from her childhood used only by those who'd truly cared about her and loved her, healed ancient wounds. "It's okay, Andi," she murmured. "It'll be okay."

They sat there on the floor, holding onto each other until Andrea had calmed, and Jinx wondered if this was only a moment in the elevator, so to speak, or if they could carry it out into the world. Before she could broach the subject, she heard a scraping sound from outside the door and the rattle of the handle.

Andrea straightened abruptly and scrambled to her feet.

"Is everything okay in here?" Tiffany asked tentatively as she entered the cellar.

Andrea scrubbed her face. "Of course. We can be civilized, but I don't appreciate your stunt, young lady." Andi was gone.

Tiffany stared, wide-eyed, at her mother's tear streaked mascara. "Are you all right, Mom?"

"I'm perfectly fine," Andrea said, adjusting her dress. "If you'll excuse me, I'd like to freshen up." Without so much as a glance at Jinx, she left the room.

"Wow, what happened? I've never seen Mom like that." Tiffany looked to Jinx with a hopeful expression. "Did she hear you out?"

"We talked," Jinx said, getting to her feet.

"Are things better?"

"We'll have to see." Jinx wrapped an arm around Tiffany as they headed back to the party. "However it turns out, though, thank you for giving me that opportunity. You're amazing."

Back upstairs, many of the guests had gone, leaving mostly family still lingering in conversations. After downing an entire glass of juice, Jinx came across Jacob trying to manage Ryan, a bottle, and a dignified good-bye to one of the senior partners of his firm. She liberated him from the baby and relaxed into a chair in the corner of the living room. She eased back and began feeding Ryan. Her eyes met E. J.'s, who sat outside at a table with Marcus, Susan, and Andrea's husband, David.

E. J. lifted an eyebrow.

Jinx was sure Tiffany had filled her in on where she'd been. She offered a reassuring smile.

Tiffany stood in the archway between the living room and the family room, talking with her cousin, Harold—the paste eater—and his wife Sylvia, and Russ picked over the remnants of the buffet table. Mandy sat on the couch with Jacob, where he'd flopped down after his farewell to his boss. They were using rock, paper, scissors to determine the outcome of some important sibling decision. Andrea was nowhere to be seen.

All of them were part of Jinx's family now, all of whom she hadn't even known a year ago, with the single exception of Andrea.

She looked down at Ryan and made a mental note to talk to E. J. about throwing their own party and adding Reggie and Sparkle, Trisha, Pablo and his family, and Taylor and Gwen to the guest list. She winked at Ryan. "That gives us a pretty darn good family, don't you think?" She smiled.

"Are you about ready to go, sweetie?" E. J. eased onto the arm of Jinx's chair and kissed the top of her head.

"Yup. My great-nephew," Jinx said proudly, "just finished his late night snack and is due for a diaper change, so it's the perfect time to hand him off to Aunt Mandy."

E. J. laughed and took the baby. She pressed her cheek to his and held him close. "Come see us soon, okay," she said softly.

They made their way through all the good-byes and were in the foyer hugging Jacob and Tiffany when Jinx noticed Andrea off to the side.

Her expression was hard to read.

Jinx gave her a hesitant smile.

She didn't respond at first. Then the corners of her mouth lifted ever so slightly. "See you later, alligator," she said quietly.

A rush of emotion flooded Jinx. Suddenly, she was back in the tree house, in the gardens, in a world where all things are possible. Her eyes filled with tears. "After while, crocodile."

CHAPTER TWENTY-ONE

Jinx woke in the pre-dawn hours to find herself alone in bed. She knew she'd find both E. J. and Pete in the kitchen. Party snacks, no matter how rich and elegant, never stayed with E. J. long, and Pete could always be found where there was food. After they'd left Tiffany and Jacob's place, Jinx had shared her conversation with Andrea in the wine cellar with E. J., as well as their quiet good-bye that simultaneously held the depth of their connection from the past and the promise of its return for the future. She smiled to herself and blinked back a fresh batch of tears as she replayed it one more time in her mind before dragging the comforter off the bed. She wrapped it around her and headed downstairs.

"You're just in time," E. J. said the instant Jinx walked through the doorway.

"For what?"

Pete looked at Jinx from where he sat attentively beside E. J. at the counter.

She moved up behind E. J. and pressed her naked body against her thinly robed backside, then enfolded her in the warmth of the blanket.

E. J. shimmied against her and sighed. She held up a slice of bread covered with peanut butter.

Jinx smiled and touched her fingertips to her lips, kissed them, then pressed them into it. She'd revealed her secret ingredient as part of E. J.'s Christmas present.

E. J. had beamed, just as she did, now. "As corny as it is," she said, "it really does turn it into the best PB&J ever."

Jinx grinned. "That's what love does." She held her fingers to E. J.'s lips and let out a soft moan as E. J. sucked them clean. "It makes everything the best."

They settled onto the double lounge chair on the patio with the sandwich and a glass of milk and shared the snack in a comfortable silence.

"The sun's coming up," E. J. said, snuggling against Jinx beneath the blanket after setting the dishes aside. "I love watching the sunrise with you."

Jinx looked to the horizon and took in the first shimmer of pink announcing the new day. She thought of all the dawns she'd watched over the years, including those in prison when sometimes she'd wondered if she'd see another, then, as time passed, if she'd ever see one where the sun wasn't coming up over a stone wall or barbed-wire. She remembered the first morning she'd been free and had watched it rise while walking through the training field at Canine Complete, and the exhilaration of witnessing the sky turn from pink, to mauve, then purple, from the back porch of her little rental, or while riding along the bike path. Now, there was the memory of pure joy while holding E. J. in her arms, tasting her skin, pleasuring her beautiful body, that first time—and so many since—they'd shared this very moment of the day. She remembered feeling as though meeting E. J. represented her own private dawn, the opportunity to start fresh, to leave yesterday behind. "You're my sunrise," she whispered into E. J.'s ear.

E. J.'s lips curved into a smile against the hollow of Jinx's shoulder. She tightened her arms around Jinx's waist.

"The dawn is a promise of another day, another chance," Jinx said, watching the pink expand into the sky. "Another opportunity to be happy. And every day, I think I couldn't possibly be happier." She crooked a finger beneath E. J.'s chin and tipped her face to hers. "And then, I wake up and see you." She kissed her.

E. J. moaned into Jinx's mouth and pressed against her.

"And this morning..." Jinx looked back to the colors moving through the sky, tinging the clouds with their soft shades. "It all feels so perfect. I have you. I have Pete. I have my family, and that includes yours, too. My friends. I think I might even finally have Andi back. I can't imagine how I could be happier."

E. J. squeezed her, then trailed her fingers across her stomach and abdomen. "How about this?"

At the simmer of her arousal, Jinx closed her eyes.

"No, no. Keep them open," E. J. whispered.

Jinx complied, then parted her thighs as E. J.'s hand slipped between them. She watched the colors swirl and blend with one another as E. J.'s touch fully ignited her desire. She lifted her hips to meet her strokes.

E. J. pushed deeper as she worked Jinx's clitoris with the heel of her hand. She held the pace slow and steady.

As the sky gradually brightened, Jinx's orgasm grew closer. She tightened around E. J.'s fingers.

"Don't hold back," E. J. murmured. "Come for me."

As the sun crested, Jinx did.

And E. J. drew it out, with long, languid thrusts.

Finally, Jinx lay back and sighed. She held E. J., wanting that moment to never end, yet looking forward to every one that followed. "Knock, knock," she said quietly.

E. J. laughed. "Are you kidding?"

"No. You'll like this one. I promise. It's a good one."

E. J. cuddled closer. "All right. Who's there?"

"Olive," Jinx said.

"Olive who?" E. J. smiled, her cheek against Jinx's chest.

Jinx tightened her arms around E. J. "Olive you, forever and always."

"Oooh, you're right. That *is* a good knock-knock joke." E. J. nestled against her. "And I'll love *you* forever and always," she said softly.

They lay quietly in each other's arms, all yesterdays behind them, embracing a new dawn.

About the Author

Jeannie grew up in Tehachapi, CA, a small town in the southern foothills of the Sierra Nevada mountains, the kind of town where everyone knew everyone and lived with unlocked doors. Raised by an English teacher, Jeannie has always been surrounded by literature and novels and learned to love reading at an early age. She tried her hand at writing fiction for the first time under the loving encouragement of her eighth grade English teacher. She graduated from college with a bachelor's degree in English.

Jeannie's loves include her beautiful family, an amazing circle of friends, and her four-legged best friend, Dexter. She enjoys many genres of novels, movies, and theater; is a cliché as a George R. R. Martin fan in her grumblings about the wait between *Song of Ice and Fire* books; and is deeply committed to her spiritual path.

Jeannie's debut novel, *Threads of the Heart*, was a finalist in the 2015 Rainbow Awards, and she is currently working on her third novel, *Into Thin Air*, scheduled for release from Bold Strokes Books in January of 2017.

Visit Jeannie's website at www.JeannieLevig.com or email her at Jeannie@jeannielevig.com.

Books Available from Bold Strokes Books

A Reluctant Enterprise by Gun Brooke. When two women grow up learning nothing but distrust, unworthiness, and abandonment, it's no wonder they are apprehensive and fearful when an overwhelming love just won't be denied. (978-1-62639-500-8)

Above the Law by Carsen Taite. Love is the last thing on Agent Dale Nelson's mind, but reporter Lindsey Ryan's investigation could change the way she sees everything—her career, her past, and her future. (978-1-62639-558-9)

Actual Stop by Kara A. McLeod. When Special Agent Ryan O'Connor's present collides abruptly with her past, shots are fired, and the course of her life is irrevocably altered. (978-1-62639-675-3)

Embracing the Dawn by Jeannie Levig. When ex-con Jinx Tanner and business executive E. J. Bastien awaken after a one-night stand to find their lives inextricably entangled, love has its work cut out for it. (978-1-62639-576-3)

Jane's World: The Case of the Mail Order Bride by Paige Braddock. Jane's PayBuddy account gets hacked and she inadvertently purchases a mail order bride from the Eastern Block. (978-1-62639-494-0)

Love's Redemption by Donna K. Ford. For ex-convict Rhea Daniels and ex-priest Morgan Scott, redemption lies in the thin line between right and wrong. (978-1-62639-673-9)

The Shewstone by Jane Fletcher. The prophetic Shewstone is in Eawynn's care, but unfortunately for her, Matt is coming to steal it. (978-1-62639-554-1)

A Touch of Temptation by Julie Blair. Recent law school graduate Kate Dawson's ordained path to the perfect life gets thrown off course when handsome butch top Chris Brent initiates her to sexual pleasure. (978-1-62639-488-9)

Beneath the Waves by Ali Vali. Kai Merlin and Vivien Palmer love the water and the secrets trapped in the depths, but if Kai gives in to her feelings, it might come at a cost to her entire realm. (978-1-62639-609-8)

Girls on Campus edited by Sandy Lowe and Stacia Seaman. College: four years when rules are made to be broken. This collection is required reading for anyone looking to earn an A in sex ed. (978-1-62639-733-0)

Heart of the Pack by Jenny Frame. Human Selena Miller falls for the domineering Caden Wolfgang, but will their love survive Selena learning the Wolfgangs are werewolves? (978-1-62639-566-4)

Miss Match by Fiona Riley. Matchmaker Samantha Monteiro makes the impossible possible for everyone but herself. Is mysterious dancer Lucinda Moss her own perfect match? (978-1-62639-574-9)

Paladins of the Storm Lord by Barbara Ann Wright. Lieutenant Cordelia Ross must choose between duty and honor when a man with godlike powers forces her soldiers to provoke an alien threat. (978-1-62639-604-3)

Taking a Gamble by P.J. Trebelhorn. Storage auction buyer Cassidy Holmes and postal worker Erica Jacobs want different things out of life, but taking a gamble on love might prove lucky for them both. (978-1-62639-542-8)

The Copper Egg by Catherine Friend. Archeologist Claire Adams wants to find the buried treasure in Peru. Her ex, Sochi Castillo, wants to steal it. The last thing either of them wants is to still be in love. (978-1-62639-613-5)

The Iron Phoenix by Rebecca Harwell. Seventeen-year-old Nadya must master her unusual powers to stop a killer, prevent civil war, and rescue the girl she loves, while storms ravage her island city. (978-1-62639-744-6)

A Reunion to Remember by TJ Thomas. Reunited after a decade, Jo Adams and Rhonda Black must navigate a significant age difference, family dynamics, and their own desires and fears to explore an opportunity for love. (978-1-62639-534-3)

Built to Last by Aurora Rey. When Professor Olivia Bennett hires contractor Joss Bauer to restore her dilapidated farmhouse, she learns her heart, as much as her house, is in need of a renovation. (978-1-62639-552-7)

Capsized by Julie Cannon. What happens when a woman turns your life completely upside down? (978-1-62639-479-7)

Girls With Guns by Ali Vali, Carsen Taite, and Michelle Grubb. Three stories by three talented crime writers—Carsen Taite, Ali Vali, and Michelle Grubb—each packing her own special brand of heat. (978-1-62639-585-5)

Heartscapes by MJ Williamz. Will Odette ever recover her memory or is Jesse condemned to remember their love alone? (978-1-62639-532-9)

Murder on the Rocks by Clara Nipper. Detective Jill Rogers lives with two things on her mind: sex and murder. While an ice storm cripples Tulsa, two things stand in Jill's way: her lover and the DA. (978-1-62639-600-5)

Necromantia by Sheri Lewis Wohl. When seeing dead people is more than a movie tagline. (978-1-62639-611-1)

Salvation by I. Beacham. Claire's long-term partner now hates her, for all the wrong reasons, and she sees no future until she meets Regan, who challenges her to face the truth and find love. (978-1-62639-548-0)

Trigger by Jessica Webb. Dr. Kate Morrison races to discover how to defuse human bombs while learning to trust her increasingly strong feelings for the lead investigator, Sergeant Andy Wyles. (978-1-62639-669-2)

24/7 by Yolanda Wallace. When the trip of a lifetime becomes a pitched battle between life and death, will anyone survive? (978-1-62639-619-7)

A Return to Arms by Sheree Greer. When a police shooting makes national headlines, activists Folami and Toya struggle to balance their relationship and political allegiances, a struggle intensified after a fiery young artist enters their lives. (978-1-62639-681-4)

After the Fire by Emily Smith. Paramedic Connor Haus is convinced her time for love has come and gone, but when firefighter Logan Curtis comes into town, she learns it may not be too late after all. (978-1-62639-652-4)

Dian's Ghost by Justine Saracen. The road to genocide is paved with good intentions. (978-1-62639-594-7)

Fortunate Sum by M. Ullrich. Financial advisor Catherine Carter lives a calculated life, but after a collision with spunky Imogene Harris (her latest client) and unsolicited predictions, Catherine finds herself facing an unexpected variable: Love. (978-1-62639-530-5)

Soul to Keep by Rebekah Weatherspoon. What *won't* a vampire do for love... (978-1-62639-616-6)